RUN ME A RIVER

Books by Janice Holt Giles

JANICE HOLT GILES

RUN ME A RIVER

HOUGHTON MIFFLIN COMPANY · BOSTON

The Riverside Press · Cambridge

1964

First printing

To
All the generations
of
Green River people

FOREWORD

EVEN within the state of Kentucky it is not generally known that there was steamboat navigation on Green River for one hundred and four years. The first small steamboat pushed its way upriver as far as Bowling Green in 1828, and the river trade did not end until 1932.

The Green is a fascinating river, lying wholly within the boundaries of the state of Kentucky. It is a little over four hundred miles in length, with a general east to west course. It is one of the oldest rivers in the United States and its drainage is responsible for the great caves, including Mammoth Cave, which lie along its gorge. It is the deepest river, for its length and width, in the United States, having a depth in its lower reaches of as much as two hundred feet. Unless in flood, its color is a beautiful deep green which is caused by the mineral contents.

My husband's people have lived on the upper reaches of the Green since 1803 and our own home lies on it. Although steamboats could never come this far upriver, we feel a kinship with those engaged in the trade and think of ourselves as Green River people.

For those who like to distinguish fact from fiction I should say that except for the known historical figures, who are only mentioned in this book, all characters are fictional. So far as I know there was never a steamboat named *Rambler,* nor one that looked or operated like the *Rambler.*

It is true that Bowling Green was occupied by General Simon Bolivar Buckner on September 18, 1861. It is true that he marched on Rochester the following day with the intention of dynamiting Lock #3. It is true that he was persuaded to jam the lock with logs instead. I ask forgiveness for giving credit for the idea to Bo Cartwright.

There are no facts to back up the supposition that Federal gunboats were on the river at the same time. There is, however, a strong oral legend. People living today tell the story as heard from their parents and grandparents who saw them. I have chosen to believe the legend.

I have taken liberties with two dates for purposes of rounding out my plot. General Don Carlos Buell did not relieve General W. T. Sherman as commanding officer of the Federal troops at Louisville until January of 1862; therefore the order requiring steamboats to have special permits and to operate within certain restrictions was not issued until that time.

The fleet of Federal ironclads was not refitted at the New Albany works until April of 1862.

I was helped by many people while doing research for this book. I cannot begin to list them all, but I am particularly grateful to the following: Captain J. Frank Thomas, last master of the *Evansville* which burned at the wharf at Bowling Green on July 25, 1931, and for all practical purposes ended the river trade; Mrs. Beulah Thomas, his wife, who gave me a woman's point of view of life on the river. I had three long interviews with Captain and Mrs. Thomas, whose patience extended beyond courtesy.

Captain Jim Wallace, retired towboat pilot and Mrs. Thomas' father, also granted me an interview. It was he, now past ninety, who "wrote the river" for me and whose river tongue gave me much of the language.

Through our good friend, Joe Covington, of Bowling Green, I met Warren Hines, a vice-president of the Hines Marine Towing Company, who interrupted a busy schedule to see me several times, loaned me the company Scrapbooks (which were invaluable since the family has been in the river trade for four generations) and who finally did me the inestimable service of arranging a towboat trip downriver.

To no one else, however, am I more grateful than to Jim Nasbitt, owner of the towboat *Maple,* on which I made the downriver trip, and his son Buddy Nasbitt, pilot of the *Maple.* They were gracious, hospitable and helpful. Without their help I could not possibly have learned as much as I did about the river and they gave it so cheerfully and willingly.

Miss Elizabeth Coombs, librarian of the Kentucky Building Library, Bowling Green, is an old friend and valued assistant in research. She is invariably interested, and wholly tireless in her efforts. She found the old river map which is reproduced on the end papers in this book, as well as many old newspaper clippings, journals, histories and other useful documents.

None of these people are, however, responsible for my interpretation of the facts or for any errors in judgment. The responsibility is wholly mine.

JANICE HOLT GILES

Spout Springs, Kentucky
August 6, 1963

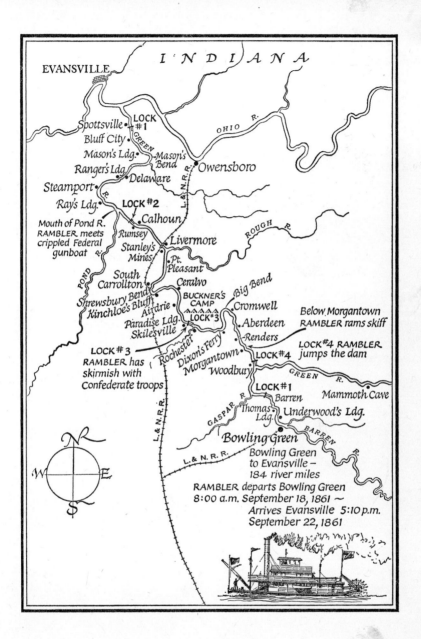

INDIANA

EVANSVILLE

OHIO R.

Spottsville
Bluff City
Mason's Ldg.
Ranger's Ldg.
Steamport
Ray's Ldg.

LOCK #1

Mason's Bend
Delaware

Owensboro

LOCK #2
Calhoun

Mouth of Pond R.
RAMBLER meets
crippled Federal
gunboat

Rumsey
Stanley's Mines
Livermore

Pt. Pleasant

ROUGH R.

South Carrollton
Shrewsbury Bend
Kinchloe's Bluff
Paradise Ldg.
Skilesville

Ceralvo

Airdrie

BUCKNER'S CAMP
LOCK #3

Big Bend

Cromwell
Aberdeen
Renders

Below Morgantown
RAMBLER rams skiff

LOCK #3
RAMBLER has
skirmish with
Confederate troops

Rochester
Dixon's Ferry
Morgantown
Woodbury

LOCK #4

LOCK #4 RAMBLER
jumps the dam

GREEN R.

Mammoth Cave

LOCK #1
Barren
Thomas Ldg.
Underwood's Ldg.

GASPAR R.

L. & N.R.R.

Bowling Green

BARREN R.

Bowling Green
to Evansville –
184 river miles

RAMBLER departs Bowling Green
8:00 a.m. September 18, 1861 ~
Arrives Evansville 5:10 p.m.
September 22, 1861

N
W   E
S

RUN ME A RIVER

CHAPTER 1

THE river was running full but making no boast of it. It was sliding along under the fog minding its own business as quiet and slick as if the banks had been greased. There came along now and then a patch of foam, sometimes a big patch, sometimes a little patch, looking like pieces of torn tan lace. Once in a while a tree slid down the middle of the current rolling along high and jaunty with a kind of young, wet look of surprise when it bobbled, as if it had committed a gaucherie.

Sometimes a little piece of drift nudged up against the boat and felt of it, rubbed shoulders a minute or two, then having made a long enough acquaintance ducked and passed on by.

There wasn't a thing on the river worried about the high water except maybe a piece of bank that now and then gave up and slid loose with hardly any commotion at all. Maybe the smallest willow trees were a little troubled for once in a while one of them gave up, too . . . just leaned over and let the river have it, with hardly a sigh for a leavetaking.

The big willow the boat was tied up to wasn't likely to pay the river any mind. It stood too far back for a cave-in and it was too old and used to the river to do anything more than dip its lowest branches into the water and let them trail out and see for themselves no harm was going to come of it.

Where the boat was tied a little creek ran in. Usually you could cross it on three steppingstones but this morning it was all puffed up with a pride of water. It didn't have any better manners than to rush at the river and try to push it over to make room. But rushing at all the water in the river was like rushing at a stone wall and the creek got piled back on itself roughly and had to make do with some bank room along the side of the river. It made a fuss around the boat, trying to agitate it a little, but the *Rambler* was hard to agitate. She rode low and light and it was as if she yawned in the little creek's face, lifting easy when she pleased and swinging on her line to suit herself.

The two men on the head of the boat were studying the river. This was the Barren, head of navigation on the Evansville-Bowling Green run. Thirty-four miles downstream the Barren flowed into the Green. It was another hundred and fifty miles down the Green to the Ohio and the end of the run, Evansville, Indiana. To steamboat men it was all the same river. You ran on the Green. The big man, named Cartwright, said, "Still bulging in the middle, Foss."

He was all easy built, with bones that were young and bendable and had sliding, fluid muscles to cover them. Lazy-draped over the capstan he was all curve and bend and the only thickness he had was in his shoulders and upper arms. The forearms were crossed and supported his weight on the capstan and his wrists dangled loose and free. His hands were big and brown and flat and quiet.

He hadn't ever tried to raise a beard and his face was oily from engine grease and dirty from wood ashes and smoke and the fog damped it and made the places where the brown skin showed through shine. The fog was like frost in his hair, each drop a whole and perfect sphere, as though the hair itself had sweated out the bead. The eyes fixed on the river were blue and at first notice they struck you as oddly out of place with the brown skin. You would expect eyes to match. Then you noticed they were a deep blue, like swimming water, and then they didn't seem peculiar any more. If you were a woman, and had got used to them, you wished they had been given to you instead. You felt a sort of waste they'd been given to a man, whose only need of eyes was to see with, not be pretty with.

The other man on the head of the boat would have been called big too if he hadn't been standing beside Bohannon Cartwright. He spirted spit in the water. "Pretty much of a tide," he said, "but likely it'll crest soon. Didn't rise but two inches last night."

Where the younger man was thick only through the shoulders, Foss was thick all over, chest, belly, thighs, arms, hands, and you'd guess that his legs would be like tree trunks. He was a little lighter skinned than the big man but there was a heaviness of texture as if he had been dipped in a tanning vat and left too long. It gave his face a thick cured look and left it with no expression save that of innocence. You could say he went clean-shaven although since he only shaved on Sundays he carried a graze of stubble on his jowls most of the time.

On the river they said he was baldheaded and that was why he always wore a cap. Bo Cartwright knew better but he agreed with Foss that it might be just as well to keep between themselves what the Lord had furnished him in the way of hair. Foss felt no bitterness about it. "He was running short when he finished me off," he said.

So, not to shame the Lord, to say nothing of himself, Foss kept his head covered. He tested his beard, now, with a thick thumb and eyed the sheet of water sliding by. Then he repeated himself. "Just riz two inches, Bo."

Bo cooped a knee around the capstan bar. " 'Bout dreened off upriver, I'd say."

Upriver was two hundred miles of bending water and if you knew it from rafting logs and flatboating down it, you knew all the slides and bends and shoals and bars and snags, and you knew Bluff Boom and Greensburg and the Mammoth Cave and Munfordville, and you knew all the creeks and brooks and licks and runs and branches and sloughs, and it was a good thing to know it all; for if you only knew the hundred and eighty miles of river you could steamboat on, you didn't know what made the river at all.

You didn't know it headed up under a cliff on a mountainside and ran a trickle down a hollow and then took in other trickles until it could call itself a creek, and then took in other creeks until it could spread itself into a river. There was a place not more than five miles upstream from his home at Cartwright's Mill where he knew, just by looking at the water, that this was where it happened . . . right there, and almost suddenly, the Green was a full-sized river.

Once when he was a little fellow his father had put him on a horse and had ridden him thirty-five miles upriver to the spring that started it all. Bo had drunk from the spring and then his father had pointed to the trickle and said, "Jump." When Bo jumped his father had laughed and said, "Now you can say you've jumped across Green River."

It made a difference when you went to steamboating for you never forgot what made the river all the way down.

Foss stumped away to douse the lanterns on the stern, observing cheerfully, "Sun'll be up soon."

Bo grunted, which was enough to let Foss know he'd heard.

The fog was sleaving up from the river now, drifting and smoking around the trees and dripping with little slow drops like rain onto the leaves underneath. Bo drew it into his nose with a long breath and it was musty with the dank of wet leaves and sycamore balls and walnut hulls and fish and mud and river water and rotted logs and sweetgum wax. He licked his lips and tasted the fog and all the river smells on his tongue and in his throat and he let the breath out and smelled the smells sharp and acid in the roof of his mouth and at the back of his nose and out his nose.

The patch of sky above the river was reddening and the old gladness in sunup rose in him as it always did. There was never a morning he didn't feel it, nor ever had been all his life. He didn't wonder about it. It was for him the best time of day, that was all. He felt the best . . . felt too big for himself. His feet could cover twice the ground and leave it spurned behind. His lungs could burst with his breathing and he felt like shouting and often did, careless of who heard. "Bo!" his father would yell, "quit that bellering!"

In those days, and yet, he felt sorry for a man getting old, who couldn't any longer jump a rail fence from standing, or walk ten miles every night for a week following the hounds, or climb their one real mountain, old Lo and Behold, without tightening his chest. He felt sorry for it, but sorrier for losing the wish to do such things. That was the real pity—to have time dry up your well of pleasures.

Now, this morning, with as little sleep as he'd had last night and with his load of weariness, the brightening sky lifted his spirits and eased his tiredness. He shoved up away from the capstan and straightened and stood looking and sniffing.

A limb shook above him and rained off its fog. There was a whiffling of wings and a crow flew away, without cawing. Bo watched it thrust across the river and circle and settle in another tree, no different, no better, maybe not even chosen, just suiting the crow as well. From some place far off a rooster crowed. There was a silence and wait, but no answer. The rooster tried again, and waited. Then he tried once more. He sounded fainthearted the third time and not very hopeful and he let his clarion die away only half finished.

Bo grinned. He spraddled his legs and flapped his elbows and stretched his neck and did a thing he had used to do at home. He sent forth a long hoarse challenge which split the air and volleyed and roared and came bouncing back from the cliffs downstream.

When the last echo had died away the cock ashore replied joyously. Bo gave him the proper interval then sent him another blast. He exchanged two more with the cock, then gave him the downdropping sign-off signal that said, we've taken care of the sun so let's get on with the rest of the day.

Foss trod onto the head softly. "Ain't you ever gonna grow up, Bo? Standin' there crowin' at a fool rooster!"

Dropping his elbows but not feeling too much of a fool, Bo laughed. "Wouldn't no other answer him. He was giving out of hope. You hear how glad he was to find there was one more rooster in the world knew what he had to do when the sun come up?"

"I heard," Foss said. "You're both a mite late. I'd say he's a lazy bird and deserved no better'n he got. Other roosters got their crowin' over at daybreak."

"He must of overslept."

Foss started to speak but a round belch rumbled out and he stopped, surprised. He studied the third button of his shirt profoundly and then, arriving at a conclusion, announced, "That comes of a empty stummick this late in the mornin'. Nothin' but air in that belly and it's backin' up on me. I aim to remedy that right now." He started off. "You comin'?"

"Right away."

Bo put his hand on the rope that made the boat fast to the willow and rubbed it up and down some frays. "Wish we had some new lines."

Foss caught his step on one heel and half turned on it. "New lines is not all we need. We need everything new but a hull. And the only reason we got a new hull is on account the old'n wouldn't float no more. That machinery . . ." He hauled up and looked directly at Bo.

Bo slapped the line and joined him, his heels clicking as light as a dog's nails on the decking. "Nothing wrong with that machinery you can't fix, Foss." He grinned broadly at the thickset man. "Never was a good steamboat engine ever wore out. You know that."

"Not a *good* 'un," Foss admitted, "but this'n . . ."

"You can *sink* 'em," Bo went on, "you can *burn* 'em, you can leave 'em *lay* and rust, but they're not made to quit and you can raise 'em up and clean 'em up and set 'em proper and they'll chug right along. Now, won't they? Nothing wrong with that engine except I'm not able to buy new parts like I wish I could."

Foss remained stubborn. "Ain't no few new parts gonna change what's mainly wrong with that machinery, Bo. It'd take enough new parts to make a new engine. She's just plumb wore out."

Bo made a rough sound in his throat then leapfrogged over some hogsheads lined in a single row. "Don't harp at me about no old machinery, Foss. I got me a steamboat. You know how bad I wanted her, and I *got* her. I had to go to the boneyard to get her and to most she's not much maybe. But I'm not the most. I'm me, Bohannon Cartwright, and to me she's fine because she's mine. Don't keep on at me about the machinery. I'm just proud we got an engine at all."

"Well," Foss hedged, "so'm I, but I got worries, Bo. You can't git up no . . ."

"What we need to get up we can't get up? Tell me that. On the Green. Now, tell me. We ain't aiming to run no races. Ain't needing a lot of speed. We're needing just what we got. Something that'll get up steam and chug along and leave us pick up our freight."

Foss plodded around the row of hogsheads and Bo watched him with good humor welling up inside him. Foss looked a little like a hogshead himself and it was best he hadn't tried to handstand over. He never thought whether he liked Foss or not. They had been such a long time together they knew each other as if they lived inside the same skin. You could always depend on Foss. He would always grumble some, for it was his nature; but his grumbling didn't mean he'd turn away and leave you flat. Turning away wasn't his nature either. He'd grumble and then he'd use that magic he had with all kinds of machinery and work a new miracle.

He watched the thickset older man pause at the guard and thrust a floating limb away from the boat with the toe of his boot. He watched the brown water swirl around it. "Now, ain't I right?"

Foss looked across the river where a stork-legged crane took fright at something and lifted himself cumbersomely off a snag and then, airborne, became a thing of graceful flight. Mostly he agreed with Bo. Bo was bold but he wasn't any fool. He calculated his risks with this old machinery mighty close. Trouble was, Bo wasn't an engineer. He couldn't know how it was when there was a knock or a vibration you couldn't pin down; or when things didn't gear together perfectly, how it could trouble you. He guessed the difference was that Bo had the whole boat to think about and he thought of little but the machinery. "Well," he said, "we got that piston reseated about as good as we could, I reckon. May come unsettled on us first hour we're running, though."

"May," Bo admitted, "may not, either. How much longer you need?"

"Gimme till noon? I got to tighten her in."

They had been a half hour downbound—Bowling Green to Evansville—when the piston had begun to rock. They had tied up and fiddled with it, then seeing it was going to take longer than a few hours Bo had let the roustabouts scatter for a night in town while the two of them got to work. They hadn't come to the end of it yet, but the end was in sight. "Believe I'll wake Luke and send him in to round up the hands," Bo said.

"Might as well. It'll likely take him till noon."

Bo went up the companionway and Foss went into the galley.

He didn't really worry about the boy for there wasn't any use worrying. For as long as they had been on the river together Bo was the one who said what they were to do. Sometimes he would grumble a little, for that was his way, and it might sometimes provoke Bo a little, but in the end he always did what Bo wanted. He always had and he knew he always would, for his world held only two things, Bohannon Cartwright and machinery, and it was Bo who had opened the door to admit the machinery. He didn't know any other way to do but the way Bo said, nor want it any different.

They had started out when Bo was only sixteen. He was ten years older, but from the beginning Bo was the one who thought ahead for them. Bo was used to thinking and he'd had the schooling and to Foss it had seemed right for Bo to be the leader. Bo had said, first, they were going to raft logs down to Bluff Boom and they did. They'd rafted logs almost a year till Bo had said now they were going to flatboat, and they did that, too. They had flatboated for a couple of years. In those days he'd been scared of the Ohio and the Mississippi, but Bo hadn't been. He'd used them as if they were the Green. He didn't scare easy, Bo Cartwright.

They'd taken their flats plumb to New Orleans, not loading them off the easy way at Evansville. Then they'd sold them for lumber and come back upriver on the steamboats.

They'd ridden some mighty fine boats and he guessed that riding on those fine boats was what had put it in Bo's head they had to go to steamboating. And they'd done that, too.

They'd gone on the *Fanny Bullitt* in the Ohio trade, Lightning Line, and when they'd got their two years on the decks behind them, Bo had gone as a cub pilot and he'd gone as a striker and they'd got their licenses. He had thought, then, with Bo a real pilot and him an engineer, they had got where Bo wanted them to be, but it was just the beginning. For what Bo wanted was his own boat.

Next thing Foss knew Bo had found the *North Star* in the boneyard and wanted to know what Foss thought of her and Foss had told him straight out he didn't think much. She was built a little boat and never would be anything but a little boat and her hull was rotted and most of the buckets on her wheel were rotted and her machinery was rusted and some of it missing and he wouldn't have her as a precious gift. That was exactly what Foss had thought of a little single-engine sternwheeler and that's what he'd said.

All Bo did was laugh and say he'd just bought her and they were going to take her up to Evansville and refit her and put her in the Green River trade. Foss remembered what a big sigh that had fetched from him. "I'm going to call her the *Rambler*," Bo had said.

Foss couldn't see much use quitting good jobs with the Lightning Line, with regular pay and somebody else to do the fretting, and he'd felt called on to say so. "I don't mean for us to work for no company the rest of our lives," Bo had said. "I aim for us to be our *own* company."

As cheap as Bo had got the *North Star* it had taken a power of money to refit her, in Foss's eyes. Bo had saved for it and had about half of it. His father, though he didn't hold with Bo being on the river, had loaned him some—against the land that would someday come to Bo—and Foss had scraped up a hundred dollars to put in. The rest, about five hundred dollars, Bo had borrowed from a man in Evansville, giving a mortgage on the boat to secure it. He had paid it down to around two hundred dollars by doing just what he was doing now. Risking here and risking there and minching along. They needed a new piston rod and Foss knew if the mortgage on the *Rambler* had been paid off, Bo would be the first to see to it. He wouldn't be easy until his boat was clear, though, and every dollar he could spare went to that end.

Been him, Foss would've waited till he had the money to build a good boat. Bo said it would take a lifetime and he was twenty-four years old and didn't have any time to lose. As if the river would dry up or go away before he could run his own boat on it; but what Bo wanted he wanted and he knew if Bo never did get a better engine he would go right on nursing all his old engines for him the rest of his life. That's the way it was and no use troubling about it.

Foss's thick hands had built a fire and set coffee on the stove caps and mixed up bread and put meat to frying. Foss's thinking never followed a straight line but it never got in the way of using his hands, either.

Bo came in and sidled around back of the table to get out of the way. Foss took his eyes off the skillet long enough to look at him and saw that he had washed his face. Almost got it clean, too. "Get him up?" he asked.

"He's on his way. Said he'd eat in town. Told him to scour the Row."

"He'll need to. We got eggs this morning."

"I'll have four."

A newspaper folded into a square was on the table. Bo spread it out. "Where'd this Louisville *Journal* come from?"

"Feller at the wharf give it to me."

Bo read off the date. "September 6, 1861. What's today?"

"The eighteenth."

"Nearly two weeks old. No wonder he was willing to give it away. You looked at it?"

Foss speared a piece of meat and turned it. "Nothin' in it but war news."

Bo scanned the headlines rapidly. Federal troops under General U. S. Grant had occupied Paducah, Kentucky. Confederate troops were in Columbus, Kentucky. He folded the paper and laid it aside. He didn't like to think about this war. It didn't make sense to him and what didn't make sense was just a fog to try to work your way through. "Hope Luke don't lose none of the boys. Bad enough we lost Lige the other day. Told Luke to see if he could find somebody to cook—this downbound run, anyway."

Foss grinned. "You don't like mine and Tobe's cooking?"

"I've eat better." Bo grinned back.

"So've I," Foss agreed. "You can't get a new cook soon enough to suit me." He lifted the meat onto a cracked platter and began breaking eggs into the grease, four for Bo and four for himself. He broke the shells carefully and slid the eggs out gingerly. It would be hard to know how old they were. He had found the nest near the woodpile yesterday. Some old hen had hid it out but they didn't look too old and if they didn't have a chicken in them or stink too bad they'd be a saving. Foss studied them thoughtfully. The war was making food prices rise, adding one more thing to their difficulties, for if there was one thing you had to do on the river it was feed good. If he could get these ripe eggs past Bo, it would save the good ones for the hands.

He served up the food and slid his bulk into a chair. A gusty sigh blew out as he compressed his paunch between the chair and table. Foss sighed a lot and Bo sometimes thought it was a kind of consolation to him for all the things he thought were forever going wrong with his world. Half an egg stopped the sigh and when he had swallowed, Foss said, "Studied any more 'bout where you're gonna get a new cook? Permanent, that is."

Bo looked at the four yellow suns shining up at him from his plate. They looked flat and limp and funny-colored. "I've studied," he said, "but I don't know as it's done any good. Finding a good one that'll stick is hard to do."

A black cook was best for a boat like the *Rambler*, but a black cook you could lose without blinking an eye. They'd get cut up in a razor fight, or go on a big drunk and disappear, or with gambling money in their pockets get notional and quit. Bo fiddled with his knife. "Seems like we've had 'em all."

"Been nice, wouldn't it," Foss said, "if your pa was gonna

give you the loan of a nigger when you left home it could of been a house nigger instead of a field hand. Wouldn't've had no worries 'bout a cook, leastways."

"Had plenty about a good deckhand," Bo said. "I'd rather fret about a cook than do without Tobe on the deck." He sprinkled pepper liberally on the eggs. "We'll make out." He wrinkled his nose and sniffed. "Something don't smell good in here. We got rats?"

"Not any dead 'uns, we ain't."

"Smells like one. Better get Tobe to look around good." He put sugar in his coffee.

Foss sopped a bannock in the soup of his eggs. "Even a cook's got a pride in the kind of boat he works on, Bo. There's some sweet boats on the Green. Rousters and cooks, any kind of riverman, they like to brag about the boats they work on." He took the coffee in his cup halfway down and blinked at Bo over the rim. "Ain't much brag to the *Rambler*."

Bo studied the bent tines of his bone-handled fork. He loved the *Rambler* fiercely but he didn't look at her through the dazzle of illusion.

They had laid down a sixty-foot keel, planked it, built a roof that would pass for an upper deck, stuck a cabin and a pilothouse on it, set the *North Star*'s machinery and her paddle wheel, and had themselves a steamboat of sorts.

She only grossed ninety tons and couldn't accommodate first-class passengers at all. He hadn't meant her to. Deck passengers he could haul, short trippers, but first-class passengers were gilt and gingerbread and right now he couldn't afford them. You made money carrying freight, not passengers, and he'd left every inch of deck he could to carry freight. Not that he didn't expect to have the gilt and gingerbread, too,—but later, not now.

He'd kept the *Rambler* under a hundred tons not only because he couldn't afford a bigger boat but because under a hundred tons the law said he could serve as pilot and master too. He liked it that way, besides. Owning his own boat, running it his own way, answerable to nobody but himself, he didn't have to carry a full crew. Foss was the engineer and black Tobe made a good second. Both could also relieve at the wheel in good water. Nor did he carry a mate. He or Foss or Tobe or all three working together stowed the cargo. That way he never found his head riding high and his stern dragging, or his head plowing and his wheel kiting.

He made do with one clerk and he did his own bookwork. He didn't have to answer to a company and he could do it his own way and when he got around to it. Right now his clerk was an eighteen-year-old boy from home named Luke Pierce. He was doing a fair job and would do better with more experience. He was husky and in prime health and he'd had enough schooling to cipher without making mistakes. He took pride in doing it right and he took pride in being dependable but he wasn't too proud to turn to whatever work he was needed to do. Best of all he liked being on the river and Bo thought he was going to make a riverman. Bo hoped that by the time Luke needed to move on up the ladder he would have the fine boat he wanted and Luke could move up with him.

They didn't stand on ceremony on the *Rambler*. When running, everybody worked. Mostly they tied up at night and all hands slept except one watchman. When they had some freight a shipper wanted hurried they parceled out the work as best they could and Bo stayed at the wheel, making do with catnaps on good water when Foss or Tobe could take it. Everybody had to double for another man's job and sometimes two or three other jobs and it looked like no way to run a steamboat. But it worked out better than you'd think. He had a good crew in Foss and Tobe and Luke—all from Cartwright's Mill they had a way of tacking into things alike. You couldn't ever say you knew another man's mind for sure, but as nearly as possible it could be done if he'd grown up in the same place and ways you had. At least there'd be no strange and surprising kinks in him.

Getting roustabouts didn't give him too much worry either. Even though they were the braggiest bunch on the river he had worked up some liking and good will among them and there were many that let brag go and said plain out they liked to work for Capt'n Bo. He knew what they said about him. "He wuk you ha'd. Wuk de laigs off you. But he know how to git along wid you."

"Sho', he do. Ain't he been raise up wid niggahs?"

"He know whut us needs."

And Bo knew that he did know, although he hadn't given it much thought. His father owned enough to work the place and raised with them as he'd been he'd absorbed, without thinking about it, his father's way with them. Portion out the work and see it was done. Allow a little tomfoolery but not too much. Punish infractions justly but never cruelly. Reflecting on it now, it surprised Bo to think his father had treated the blacks about as he had his own children—riding them with a firm hand but a not unkind one, saying do this and do that, putting up with no lallygagging, carrying them, as a responsible man does his family, on shoulders used to the load in a world he himself made safe and secure for them.

On the *Rambler* it meant hustling them when there was need to hustle, leaving them alone between times to sleep or shoot craps, and giving them plenty of what they liked best to eat and thrived on. It meant never taking advantage of them, but it also meant never allowing them to take advantage of him.

"The *Rambler*," he agreed with Foss finally, "is as plain as a plain-faced woman. But we'll make out. It's not to worry."

He sliced into his eggs, appeared for a moment to hang paralyzed over them as the heavy, offensive odor swam up into his face. Then he pulled his head back out of the waft and clanged his knife and fork down. "These eggs are old! They're high as a polecat. Where'd you buy 'em?"

Speech and food mixed rendered Foss almost inarticulate but Bo was accustomed to interpreting. He understood that they hadn't been bought. They'd been found.

Foss kept busy hunting down the last speck of food on his plate but he did take one quick look to see if a storm was breeding. Bo could raise a right smart rumpus when riled up. You could tell when he was weathering for it if his mouth got thin. And it was thin. Foss sighed.

Bo shoved his chair back from the table and carried his plate away. "Foss, I've told you so many times I've lost count that I'm not having anything to eat on this boat but what's fit. And rotten eggs ain't fit! I've thrown out maggoty bacon and spoiled catfish and I've even thrown out a skinned skunk you tried to pass off for coon. When are you going to learn that what comes free usually ain't worth nothing?"

Foss reflected slowly, "Ain't much to buy with, Bo."

"I know there ain't much to buy with. Know it as good as you do. But long as there's a dollar in my pants it'll buy something fit to eat. And when there's no dollars left, I still got credit."

"Been usin' that a right smart lately." Foss's voice was mildly chiding.

"Well, I've not used it up yet. Any good eggs?"

Reluctantly Foss admitted there were. "In that basket on the shelf."

It didn't make sense to him to waste anything, especially when they were needing so bad. But Bo had this notion of what was fit and what wasn't. Didn't seem to him deckhands were all that finicky. He thought it must be because Bo'd never had to scrabble the way his folks had done. You stayed as hungry as he'd been most of his life, till Bo took him with him, and there wasn't anything didn't taste pretty good.

In the home he grew up in you didn't think about what kind of meat you had. There wasn't any smokehouse full of hams and bacon. If there were a few cartridges you went out and killed what you could find and counted it good luck to find anything. Or you bought, if you had a little cash money, some rancid fatback because it was cheaper and you got more of it. If you'd eaten as many soup beans as he had with nothing but salt for seasoning, and if you'd eaten as much water gravy because there wasn't any milk, and if you'd gone for months without an egg because the hens couldn't lay without you had something to feed them, you didn't quarrel with anything that came your way. If it filled the emptiness inside you, it tasted good. "These ain't but a little ripe, Bo," he said apologetically.

"That's riper than I want 'em," Bo said. He pumped river water into the little sink and washed his plate. He slid the skillet forward and cracked four more eggs into it. "And you throw the rest of 'em out, you hear. Don't save 'em for yourself. Tobe'll be having to cook this trip and he won't know the difference."

Obediently Foss got up and heaved the offending eggs overboard. He pondered them with surprise when they floated. Bo's laugh was short. "Ain't but a *little* ripe, huh? Been any riper they'd been ready to pip."

Ruefully Foss said, "Some older'n I reckoned, looks like." He slid his hand back and forth across his paunch and ruminated, then said cheerfully, "Least they *set* light."

Bo snorted. He dished up the fresh eggs and ate quickly. "Been thinking some," he said, "of seeing if Pa'd let me bring Tobe's mammy to cook. Last letter I had Pa said she wasn't much use to him any more. Said all she did was pine away for Tobe. Tobe's her least one, and her favorite, I reckon. Might be Pa'd be willing to let her come."

Foss chucked his own plate into the sink and pumped water over it. He poured each of them more coffee and stayed standing to swallow his. "He could easy spare you half a dozen blacks off the place. Be good if you could run the *Rambler* with your own hands and save payin' for rousters."

Bo lifted his shoulders. "They're his and he don't hold with me being on the river. Don't want to be beholding to him, anyway."

Foss set his cup down. "Count it lucky, I reckon, he give you Tobe." He scrubbed his mouth and hitched up his pants. A thought set him grinning. "You see him dressed up to go into town last night?"

"I saw him." Bo mopped up the last of his eggs with a piece of bread and washed it down. "Couldn't have missed him. Looked real elegant, didn't he? Where'd he get that green silk shirt?"

"Off'n Sportin' Sam. Last trip."

"Hummph. Tobe's luck with them dice is going to change one of these days and he's going to be the one left without a shirt."

"Which wouldn't worry him one par*tick*le bit," Foss said, "long as he didn't lose none of his wimmin."

Bo drifted to the door. "And if he don't quit that somebody's going to cut him with a razor."

"He does prolificate around a right smart," Foss admitted.

Bo chuckled. "Reckon how many younguns he's planted up and down this river?"

"Enough," Foss said, "to furnish several steamboats with rousters when they git their growth." He did a little ordering of dishes and stores and called the galley clean.

The sun was bright on the river now and all the fog had burned away. The tan water looked hard enough to walk on. It was running so deep it made hardly a riffle and it looked solid and heavy. Bo watched it. You spent any time at all on the river, got used to it, you never really quit watching it. The look of the water was all you ever saw. It might always look the same to a dry-lander but a riverman saw it different all the time. Little things, little ways, like now the bulge in the middle wasn't as big and you knew the crest was passing and soon the middle would be troughing.

There was this drag of impatience inside, though, because this lay-up had made you have to let the hands scatter and only the Lord knew whether you could round them all up. Rousters had to do something on a lay-up, however. You couldn't keep them hanging around the boat. Nothing to do but get in fights and gamble. They'd do both in town, too, but they might not whittle on each other. They might take it out on town Negroes.

He ran his hand down the wall. The *Rambler* wasn't such an old tramp. In a year they had learned most of her crankiness and she wasn't all cranky. She wasn't a bad old workhorse. She was wheezy in her machinery but nothing had happened so far Foss couldn't fix. She plowed a little deep and she didn't have much grace; but she wasn't built for grace and swiftness. She was built to work.

Foss joined him on the fantail and wandered over to the guard. He looked down the deck. They had a pretty good cargo this time. Not a full one—they hadn't ever had that—but a better one than usual. Bo was little by little getting more business and if this war didn't put too big a crimp in shipping they'd see that deck stacked to the guards some day. Absently, he said, "Ain't it lucky we hadn't took on no hawgs or chickens or cows to be pestered with this lay-up?"

Bo exploded on him. "You can think of the damndest things to feel lucky about! I'd rather to been pestered. And collect for 'em."

Foss rubbed his nose. He hadn't meant anything. "Well," he said, "I got work to do." Starting away he added, "River's crested."

And he could have saved his breath. Bo knew the river had crested. You didn't ever have to tell Bo anything about the river, any time. He was the most noticing riverman Foss had ever known. He sighed. He didn't know as he was trying to show off, but it went a little like it. Times, he thought, he just talked too much.

Bo watched Foss with his wrench. He ought to have hog-tied Tobe last night and made him stay aboard to help Foss this morning. Trouble was, hog-tying Tobe was a little hard to do with a town as full of pleasure as Bowling Green handy. He wished, though, he hadn't been short with Foss. The poorest paying thing he could ever do was be short with Foss.

Might as well, he thought, do some of the rousters' work and get some wood stacked up. He filled his arms and Foss looked around and grinned at the clatter and Bo felt better. Foss and him . . . they were all right.

Foss set up a whistling and Bo joined in. He sometimes thought he and Foss could run the *Rambler* with nobody but themselves.

Two hours had gone by perhaps and Bo was frapping some frayed lines when Foss yelled at him. "There's Luke!"

Bo looked up. Luke had hired a wagon and driver to bring them out and as they clambered over the wheels he counted. He began to laugh. "By george, Foss, he's got 'em all. I just counted." His laughter rose. "Look at him, Foss. Look at that boy. Herding them wrecks in front of him like they was cows! Ain't a one missing. How about that, huh? How about that! Sent a boy to do a man's job and he's done it. That Luke is going to make a real riverman!"

Foss drifted up alongside. "Ain't got no new cook, though."

"We can make out with Tobe this trip."

"Where all you reckon he's had to go to round up that trash?"

"It's untelling. Highly untelling."

The boy trudged sturdily behind the ragtag crew of rousters so totteringly unrecovered from their night of high living. Bo nudged Foss. "Tobe's lost his shirt. See him?"

Foss said serenely, "He ain't gonna need it. Way I'm aimin' to work him when we get to runnin' he'll be hot enough without." He trudged back to his machinery.

Bo waited for Luke, who came aboard hustling the hands ahead of him. His young face was trying to look stern. Instead it looked very concerned.

"See you got 'em all," Bo said, showing his pleasure. "Good job, Luke. Don't know how you did it, but . . ."

"Bo," Luke interrupted, "this here war is getting close to home. The Confederates have took Bowling Green."

Bo took a moment, racked back by the stunning news. "Who says so?"

"I seen 'em myself, Bo. Right smack in the middle. General Buckner marched in this morning with fifteen hundred troops. I seen 'em myself! Things are in the biggest state. Don't nobody know what's gonna happen next. Most is afraid of a battle. There's talk General Johnston is going to make Bowling Green his headquarters. They're already digging up on the hill. Say they're entrenching." In his excitement the boy was stumbling over his words. "Gonna fortify the town. Claim they've got several thousand more troops on the way. Folks is scared. Say when the Federals hear about it they'll come down on the town like a duck on a bug. Some folks are already moving out."

Bo swung around. "Foss! Tobe! Get up steam, fast!"

Foss faced him slowly. "I ain't done yet, Bo . . ."

"Get done. Quick. Get done while Tobe and the boys fire up. The Confederates have taken over Bowling Green. We got to get on downriver fast. I'm not aiming to be caught here in a trap! Get moving, hear!"

Foss stuck his chin down on his chest and got moving.

CHAPTER 2

Foss caught him later as he started up the companionway. "She's still loose, Bo, but she's fixed as good as could be expected. Don't put no strain on her, though."

Bo clapped him on the shoulder. "Don't mean to if I can help it. When did I ever? The *Rambler* don't run if the machinery don't run."

Foss rubbed his hands on an oily rag, which did little to clean them. It was a habit. "What you mostly skeered of? He ain't likely to close the wharf, is he?"

"No, but he's likely to take my boat. Stands to reason if this is going to be their headquarters they'll be needing boats —ship up supplies—maybe troops. I don't want my boat confiscated."

Foss shifted the rag and rubbed the rail with it. "Aimin' to make your stops?"

"Sure I'm aiming to make 'em. I ain't that scared. We got cargo to load off and we'll have cargo to load on. I just want to get some distance between me and Bowling Green. You ready?"

Foss nodded. "You got your steam."

Though they didn't stand on ceremony on the *Rambler* there were some things Bo Cartwright took pride in and did by the book. He liked a smart departure, for instance, and today made no difference.

Tobe, tough, runty, black as a tar bucket and as shiny— who swaggered even when he stood still and full drunk could walk a staging plank steady—stood beside the willow tree ready to cast off. Without sadness or regret he'd covered his naked back with his old ragged shirt. He had worn Sportin' Sam's elegant green silk shirt with pleasure but he'd lost it having a fine time. It wasn't to worry about. If he wanted it back, or any other he took a fancy to, he had full confidence in his powers to win. But what you got free you could let go of easy.

Some things belonged to you always, like your black skin and your mam and the cabin on the Cartwright place. Some things you didn't have such a strong hold on but would go deep if you lost them, like the *Rambler* and Capt'n Bo and the river. But there were some things that didn't count for much. Too frail to fret over. Good if you had them, not mourned if you didn't. He didn't waste a minute grieving over a green silk shirt. With his hand on the line he waited for Capt'n Bo's signal.

Down by the engine, Foss was waiting. He had his eye on the gauge but he had his hand on the gong. Two rousters were firing for Foss and two stood ready to raise the stage. The others loafed and watched. Luke Pierce was up in the cabin, shuffling through cargo bills.

Up in the pilothouse Tobe saw Capt'n Bo square up to the wheel and he knew he'd felt with his feet and shuffled for his best balance. And then Tobe saw him lay his hands on the wheel and turn it a little and test it. Then Capt'n Bo looked around good, back of him and on all sides. Wasn't a thing on the river but them and the fat water hissing along, but might be a little skiff come nosing round just as Capt'n Bo give Foss his backing bells.

Capt'n Bo raised his arm to the whistle cord and Tobe, the knot already loose, stooped so he could free it fast and send it looping. Capt'n Bo didn't want a second of waste. Smart was what he wanted. Real smart.

The arm jerked down and the *Rambler*'s hoarse, un-chimed whistle blew out like a bull roaring. The sound sent a spasm of pure prickling joy through Tobe's head and down his back, but it didn't stop him from jerking his line free and heaving it, romping across the stage and yelping loud at the rousters, "Heave away!"

The stage went up smooth and was made fast. The two rousters circled their signals and whooped proudly. In an excess of zeal Tobe cut a buck and wing.

Up in the pilothouse, Bo grinned. If *he* took pride in the *Rambler*, it was nothing compared to the blown pride Tobe took. To Tobe the *Rambler* was the finest steamboat on the river. "Shoo," he said, "whut de *Lucy Wing* got we ain't got? We got a engine, ain't we? We got a paddle wheel, ain't we? We pushes up an' down de river, don't we?"

"Ain't got no boiler deck," he was reminded.

"Ain't needin' no boiler deck. Got us a main deck. Got us a hurricane roof. *Rambler* ain't needin' nothin' more. *Rambler*, she ramble. Dat's all me'n Capt'n Bo needs."

Tobe hadn't been a real troublemaker at home, but as a field hand he had been bothersome. "Lazy," Bo's father had summed him up, "just pure lazy."

On the river he still liked his lazy times, and was due them. But they never came when Bo needed him. On the river he had come into something proud, something he could brag and swagger about, something he didn't mind putting his back into, something, he told Bo, that made him swell up inside with a good feeling. "Doan know," he said, "whut for, but I ain't never lak wukkin' in de cawn an' de terbacker. Same evah day. Jist up an' down dem rows. Ain't no sight to lift yo' eyes. Ain't no proud to lift yo' sperrit."

Bo knew exactly what he was talking about. Cartwrights were land-tending people and had been since his grandfather, proud old Cassius Cartwright, had settled a whole valley, peopled a village, and got land rich. Every Cartwright man since had been just as land proud, had hoarded land, got more, and tended well. There wasn't anybody in the whole family or its vast connections that had the least understanding of why Bo didn't have the same values they did, didn't think husbanding land the best life, in fact the only life, for a Cartwright. He didn't know why he didn't, either. There had to be people who loved land and worked it and raised corn and tobacco and wheat and hemp and oats and barley. And there had to be people that liked to tend cows and hogs and chickens. All he knew was it would have bent his head to the ground to be one of them. Tobe had said it, he guessed. Nothing to lift your eyes. No proud to lift your spirit. Not for him, anyhow.

Bo flipped a hand at the rousters. He gave Foss three gongs and got them back promptly. Then he gave him two bells and as they rang back to him the *Rambler* backed out, slowly, the tan river water threshing and boiling as the wheel's buckets grabbed and bit and shoved.

Watching his stern, squinting against the bright glint of the sun, Bo felt of his spokes, cramped the wheel a little, let the *Rambler* slip down easy, easy. He rang for stopping and then to ship up. They moved upstream sweetly and smoothly. Lord, he thought, Foss is good. A slow engineer could drive you out of your mind but you never had to wait on Foss. He came back to you and gave what you wanted smart and fast.

Bo backed the boat up the swollen little creek, then shipped up again and they were on their way. It made him feel good, the way they nearly always got away clean and smart. It didn't matter whether anybody saw them or not. It didn't matter whether a living soul was watching and judging and commenting and comparing. It wasn't to show off. He and Tobe and Foss, they all liked to steamboat and there wasn't any excuse for sloppiness in real steamboating. The *Rambler* might be as plain as a plain-faced woman but that didn't keep you from working her smart and sharp and right.

They went scooting down behind the tide. Bo liked the room the tide gave him. It made him feel comfortable. Up here on the Barren it wasn't a real big crest—the water wasn't all over the bottoms—but the current kited along just right and the depth was welcome.

The weak piston made a shadow on perfect pleasure, but even so there was an exactness today Bo relished. No risk that was foolish, but not fearing a risk that had to be taken. He had learned a long time ago, maybe been born with the knowledge that if you made a bold decision and followed it with bold action more often than not you could make it work for you. Maybe that was the way his grandpa, old Cass Cartwright, had got all his land and all his blacks and a place in Kentucky history for the Cartwright name. Maybe.

More than any place in the world, though, the river was where you had to be bold. The pilot he'd been cub to had been fond of saying, "There's no place on the river for a timid man. He'll waver." It was a saying Bo agreed with.

At the wheel of a boat you had to size up a situation quick, decide quick, then act quick. You didn't have time for wavering. If you did, you stood a good chance to lose your boat and maybe your life.

They bent around the Big Eddy and he clipped close inside. One good thing about a little water in the Barren was you could steamboat with a little leeway. The Ohio pilots had all thought he'd lost his mind when he'd said he meant to run on the Green. "You ever seen the upper end of that run?" his old pilot had asked him. "Ever been up the Barren?"

"Plenty of times," Bo had said.

"Ever steamboated on it?"

"No. But what any other Green River pilot can do, I can do."

Mr. Gann had shaken his head. "Can't make you out. The Green's not much more'n a creek but a creek is *all* the Barren is and you got thirty-four miles of the Barren that loops back on itself like a snake and as narrow as your boat in places." He had scratched his beard. "Most of the time you got pretty good water in the Green but there's times when there ain't but five foot of water in the Barren and you can't steamboat in five foot of water and you know it. What you want to box yourself in up there for? Why don't you stay on a *river?*"

Bo had shaken his own head. "I just got to. The Green's my river and if I got thirty-four miles of the Barren to run at the upper end I got it to run and that's all."

He hadn't known any other way to put it. He just *cared* about the Green. And it was more than knowing it from its source to its mouth. He knew the Ohio, too, and the Mississippi well enough. He had run them enough to know them and when he took his license he'd had to write them both, every towhead and island and bend and landing and bar and shoal.

The way he felt about the Green was personal, as though it belonged to him, as though he'd made good friends with it and the river cared, too. He didn't go so far as to believe the Green was going to accommodate him any better than other men, but if you knew a river from its source to its mouth, in all seasons and tides, and if you loved it in all seasons and tides, you could do a pretty good job of *making* it accommodate you.

Sometimes what he felt for the river was a yearning over it, a tenderness for it, and a compassion as well as a passion. It had a quiet on it like no other quiet in the world, and it had a loneliness like no other loneliness, a kind of hurting loneliness that was at the same time an easing balm.

It was as if the river guarded its quiet and loneliness and sort of held them, like its water, between its banks. Not that it was a dead quiet the river had. There was life on it and there was life in it . . . a fish jumping, a crane lifting from a snag, beaver working their slides, deer coming down to drink, but they were all quiet and lonely things. Even the people that fished from their skiffs were quiet and lonely, for of all things men ever loved to do, fishing was one of the quietest and loneliest.

There were times when, sliding down the river, or pushing up it, he felt such a love for it that it filled him so full he thought he'd never need anything else as long as he lived. Just the river, and him on it. But that was something you kept quiet as the river about. It was something too terrible and too personal to talk about.

They passed Stephen's Bar and he watched his wash trouble the young willows.

Some pilots, ones that hadn't been raised near the river,

grumbled about this Barren River end of the run. "Why'd they put head of navigation at Bowling Green?"

He didn't like or dislike it. He didn't feel any way about it except that it was necessary. There wouldn't be steam-boats on the Green without it. It was mostly a bunch of Bowling Green men that had got the legislation through to build the locks and dams up and down the river. His father had been in the legislature then and he had heard him talk about it. His father had voted for the legislation.

And you couldn't blame Bowling Green men for want-ing the head of navigation at Bowling Green. They had paid out of their own pockets to get the legislation and they had worked like billy-be-damned to get it and if they ex-pected to get some of their own back by opening up the Bar-ren with a lock, too, they had a right to, far as he was con-cerned.

There had been steamboats on the Green, and up the Bar-ren to Bowling Green, before the locks and dams had been built but not regularly. They had always had to wait for a rise on the river before they could come up. Bo thought pretty highly of those men who had dreamed of slackwater navigation clear up to Bowling Green and hadn't quit till they made it come true. A hundred and eighty miles of the river was navigable now and that bunch of Bowling Green men, and men from the area, could be thanked for it.

Besides, Bowling Green was the biggest town on the up-per end. You could even call Bowling Green a city. There wasn't another town near its size on the river; you couldn't have head of navigation off in the wilderness. He thought about Buckner occupying the place now and uneasiness prickled at him. Why couldn't both sides stay out of Ken-tucky, the way the governor had asked them? Why'd they have to bring the war here?

He slid the boat into the bend around Sibert Island and took note that a towhead had been cut loose by the river. Next run there'd be a little new island in that place.

Luke Pierce came up onto the bridge and into the pilothouse. Without taking his eyes off the river and cramping the wheel right on round, Bo looked aslant at him. Luke'd been having Mr. Rand's corn pulled out, he guessed, and his new plow and the barrel of molasses and the flour and candles and sewing thread Miss Evie had ordered—getting ready to set them off at Underwood's Landing.

The *Rambler* didn't only haul freight, they did a terrible amount of shopping for their customers. Nearly every stop they made, somebody, man or woman, handed them a list, and it could have anything on it from a length of calico to a coffin. Mostly Luke saw to filling the orders, the merchants in Bowling Green or Evansville crediting the boat till the pay was in. It made double bookkeeping but it accommodated the customers and there weren't too many captains on the river who liked to piddle with such things.

Bo had done that kind of thing since he went to flatboating. He had brought back silks and shawls and spices and whatever nice things people couldn't get inland from New Orleans. He didn't mind anyhow, but he knew if you took pains with Miss Evie's sewing thread and Miss Sallie's muslin and Judge Wescott's newspapers and magazines, it was likely that Miss Evie's husband would ship more of his tobacco and cattle and hogs and corn, and Miss Sallie's husband would do the same and Judge Wescott would do the same. If you meant to earn your living off people, serving them in little ways as well as big ones was nothing more than you owed, Bo believed.

Luke had been a little uneasy when he began to fill the orders. As troubled as Bo had ever seen him he had come one day, a list in his hand. "Bo," he said, "how much is a length of calico?"

"Enough for a dress."

"How much is that?"

"No need worrying about that, Luke. Just tell Mr. Shepherd at Shepherd and Redding's you want a length of calico."

When he was thinking, Luke had a way of squinching his eyes a little, which shut down on their natural brightness. You could always tell when he'd got a thing straight in his head because he blinked a couple of times then opened his eyes wide again. But that wasn't all he needed to know this time. "How do I know what color to get?"

"Who's it for?"

"Miss Sallie . . . Hightower Landing."

"Well, when a woman gives you an order, Luke, if she don't put down the color, like, say, black and white print, or bright print, or a kind of light print, if I was you I'd just take a real good look at *her*. Look what she's got on. Chances are something close to what she's wearing is what she's wanting. Now, Miss Sallie likes something bright, but not too bright. She'll be wanting a serviceable black ground with a little fine print of red or blue scattered over."

Luke studied some more. "Sometimes it ain't the woman gives the order and you can't study her. She's got it wrote down but her man hands it over."

"Stick to the meagerest print on the shelf, then. Keep to a plain black and white. Safest that way. There is some," he warned, "that if you was to get something real bright for would be insulted. They'd think you was treating 'em like a high-yaller."

Luke studied Bo, then. "You wouldn't think," he said after a while, "that you got to be noticing of women to steamboat, would you?"

"I ain't ever found it a chore," Bo said, grinning. Then he added, seriously, "Just like you got to know the river, Luke, every bend and slide and snag, you got to know the folks on it. You got to get in your head and keep it straight where they live and how they live, what they like and what they don't like, if they're tempery or if they're not. And they look for you to remember. There's nobody but them, far as they're concerned, on the river. They aren't gonna be taking into account you got twenty or thirty other orders to keep in mind. Theirs is the only order that counts. And half the time they won't even write it down for you. Just yell at you and say, 'Bring me a keg of tenpenny nails,' and if you bring twenty-penny instead, they won't allow for you mishearing 'em or forgetting. They'll say, 'Bring Sallie enough muslin for curtains for her best room.' You've not ever seen Miss Sallie's best room, but no difference. Just figure out the best you can how much muslin it's going to take. And don't ever take Judge Wescott the *Harper's* instead of the *Atlantic*, or the *Courier* instead of the *Journal*. He'll shout till you can hear him to the lock!"

Luke went away shaking his head over what a steamboatman had to learn and keep in his head; but Bo knew he had set himself to learning.

This morning he stood in the sun, his hands in his pockets. He shivered a little. "Coming on cooler every day, ain't it? Won't be long till the leaves commence to turn. And winter'll be right behind."

"Not much warmth in the sun today," Bo admitted.

"It's a thin sun, too. Likely to mizzle again 'fore noon."

Bo held the wheel down and stepped up on it using his weight to keep the *Rambler* nosed in, sliding her round the last sharp swing of the bend. Easing off then, he said,

"Wouldn't surprise me. But I got a good sweat worked up already."

Luke had a pleasant laugh, deeper than you'd think for his age and size, a man's laugh already. "I've heard you say it," he said, "that you got to have heat in your blood, an awful good fire, or a bendy river to keep you working, if you can take the weather in a pilothouse. Looks to me you could see good enough through glass to have the front glassed in, too. That apron keeps out some of the rain but it don't do a living thing against wind and cold."

"Glass is flawed," Bo said. "You got to see clear and plain. Till the day they learn to make glass without flaws the front of the pilothouse has got to be open and a pilot's got to take the weather." He chuckled. "If it don't kill you it'll make you tough as cowhide. Pilots either die young or live forever, Luke."

Luke watched the big man handle the wheel. Luke had seen him grip the spokes hard. He'd seen him walk the wheel to cramp the *Rambler* round. Mostly, though, he handled it as if it only took a feather's touch, as if his fingers told him through their skin and nerves the play of the rudder.

Luke still stood in awe of the wheel and of the man who held it. He thought any river pilot stood just about as high as a man could go, but Bo stood higher than that. Whenever Bo let him take the wheel it made him shake in his legs and it made his stomach rise in him and, good water though he always knew it to be, he broke out in a sweat every time. He strained to watch ahead for snags and slides and wind ripples and small boats. It was at the same time the purest excitement he had ever felt, better than following the hounds on a coon trail up the hollow, or listening to them bell out for a fox, or finding a mink in his trap. There wasn't anything he'd ever done that mounted him up and up so far and gave him such a feeling of power and pleasure and plain biggety bigness inside.

He never would get through being grateful to Bohannon Cartwright for sending for him and giving him the chance to go on the river. He never would. He would make him the best clerk he could for as long as he wanted him, but maybe some day Bo would take him as his cub. Some day when Bo had his big fine steamboat, or maybe two or three big fine steamboats. Then when he got his license maybe Bo would just walk the bridge and let him walk the wheel. It would be the proudest day of his life, that one. He said, "Wonder if the locks can operate in this tide?"

"Brown's can," Bo said. "Not such a crest up here. Don't know about when we get on the Green. She'll be fuller. Bound to."

"What would you aim to do?"

"Not but two things you can do, Luke. If there's enough water, jump the dam. Lay up if there's not. I'd hope for enough water."

Luke's eyes lit with his own hope. "You've not jumped a dam since I been on the *Rambler*. I'd like to see you do it."

"Not overly fond of doing it," Bo said. "Can't take a boat kiting over a dam without creening it some, nor without jolting the machinery. You know the state our machinery's in. I wouldn't look forward to putting no strain on it. But I'd rather to than lay up. I want to get some distance between me and General Buckner."

"Reckon he would take the *Rambler*?"

"Don't know. But I don't aim to find out if he would or wouldn't. I mean to run the *Rambler* myself—not have her confiscated by either side."

"It's kind of scaresome, ain't it," the boy said, "way both are closing in on Kentucky?"

Bo nodded, his mouth tight. "Beginning to squeeze, all right." His arm went up and the hoarse, coarse-toned whistle blared out.

Luke came to with a start. "Jehosaphat, Bo," he said, a rueful twist on his grin, "what I come up for was to tell you we had some things to put off at Underwood's."

Bo kept in his own mind every barrel and hogshead, every sack, every bundle and parcel and box, but he didn't say so. Luke had to learn to be dependable. He let him off easy, however. "Time enough," he said. He rang for slow and the engine changed its sound and an exhaust of steam blew out. He slid the *Rambler,* by almost imperceptible degrees, in toward the bank.

The landing was nothing but a clearing in the woods, the bank cut to an easy slope. It looked slick and greasy from the recent rains. Bo began inching the *Rambler* up, the engine panting now in slow, deep breaths. "Well," he said, chuckling, "looks like you'll earn your name today. You boys ain't called mud clerks for nothing."

Luke shot a quick look at his feet. They'd be clogged to the knees by the time the rousters got through churning the muck. But he wasn't notional about his feet. He laughed. "Be enough to give poor jade the bots, won't it. There's Mr. Rand waving us down." He ducked out and down the steps in a hurry.

Bo brought the *Rambler* nosing in, set her just right and held her. Luke yelled, "Lower away!" and the stage went down slow and easy. It gave a thick squeezing sound in the mud and slowly made a bed in it.

The engine idled, its low, slow breathing like that of some great prehistoric animal swamped in the water, its giant tired lungs deeply respiring in heavy, rhythmic draughts. Bo made his wheel fast and went to the door. "Howdy, Mr. Rand."

The man on the bank was rotund and ruddy-faced, with the stub of a cigar stuck in his mouth. He lived back from the river and was a man of considerable property. He enjoyed a good life and was considered prosperous. He tilted his hat back and lifted a hand to Bo. "Get my stuff?"

"Every bit of it. Lucky, this trip. The boys'll set it off."

"Good. Evie'd been misput you hadn't. But things keep getting scarcer. Wouldn't have surprised me you hadn't filled the order." He shifted his cigar. "Got about fifty head of sheep I'd like you to take down to Evansville for me, Bo."

A charge of excitement shot through Bo. Mr. Rand hadn't ever shipped any livestock with him before, or given any evidence he ever meant to. Just hard goods that couldn't come to damage had been entrusted to him and small piddling orders. It just went to show. Look smart to the little things and the big ones'll take care of themselves. If Mr. Rand was going to start shipping with him . . . all his livestock, hogs, horses, sheep, cattle . . . others would hear. Might start something right lively for him. But they'd have to take pains with this first shipment. Mr. Rand didn't have to caution him. If this first shipment caused any doubts, he'd keep his big business with another boat. Bo answered him confidently. "Be proud to handle 'em for you, sir."

"Got 'em penned back in the woods a way," Mr. Rand said.

"The boys'll get 'em, Mr. Rand."

Before he got down the companionway the rousters had set the small order from Bowling Green ashore and Luke was driving them up the path into the woods. An affectionate amusement rippled through Bo. It was a good thing Luke had a deep voice already. It barked out like a soldier's and sounded proud. "Look sharp there, now, boys. Git a move on! Ain't no time for lagging, now. Keep a moving. Look sharp. Git a move on!"

The rousters romped up the path ahead of him. Bo waded out onto the bank, sinking to his ankles in the mud. He nodded pleasantly to Mr. Rand. "Hope Miss Evie don't find the sewing thread too coarse. It was all they had. Mr. Shepherd said they hadn't got any fine thread for a good while. Reckon the war is making things short all around. I can see about some in Evansville for her, if she'd like."

"Don't greatly matter, I'd think," Mr. Rand said around his cigar. "Best of my knowledge she wanted it for quilting. I'd like them sheep got downriver quick as you can, Bo. Wouldn't wish 'em to lose no weight. This high water make you have to lay up, you think?"

"No, sir," Bo grinned. "Don't aim to lay up. I'll get 'em there quick, Mr. Rand."

Mr. Rand took the cigar out of his mouth and grinned back. "Aiming to jump the dams, huh?" He put the cigar back and grunted. "Always had a liking for a man had daring."

"Yes, sir." Bo picked up a stout stick and turned and hefted it in his big hands. There was a sudden stirring in the woods and a great crashing about and a lot of high shouting and yelling and hipping, then the strident, earsplitting blatting of frightened sheep. Mr. Rand looked up the path. "Make a commotion, don't they? Them boys'll take care, I reckon."

It wasn't a question. Mr. Rand knew Bo's boys would take care. Privy to all the scuttlebutt on the river they knew, just as he knew and Bo knew, this was a shift of his habits and a favorance of Capt'n Bo. They would take good care. They'd do more than that. What boosted Bo's pride boosted theirs. They'd take it to themselves and they'd brag and boast downriver. "Cap'n Bo," they'd say, "done took Mr. Rand's business way fum Capt'n Drew. Capt'n Bo comin' up on de river. He smart. He don' wear no blinders."

There was a noisy wait and the two men looked at the river and talked about it, what stage it was upriver this morning, what it was likely to be downriver, how it would be if it rained any more, or if it didn't. River talk and weather talk were always mixed together.

Then Tobe raised a high yelp and came in sight, leading down the path. Close behind followed a ragged roustabout, another behind him and then another until they filled the path in a weaving single file. They looked like faded calico quilt pieces, any shirt, any pants that would hold together and cover their nakedness decking them out, frayed at the elbows, patched scrimble-scramble, or not patched and holey, rope ends mostly holding them together. Any old ragbag clothes did for rousting. They saved their best for flashing around in town.

Each rouster had a sheep slung across his shoulders, the legs fitted in a close hug around his neck. Tobe was leaning exaggeratedly under his load. Coming along he shot a sly-eyed look at Bo and glinted his teeth. Capt'n Bo had got his stick handy. Old river way to have a stick for rousters. Capt'n Bo didn't never use one. Just kept one by, old river way. Nudge a little, maybe, no more.

Tobe slouched a little more, loosened his hips and began crossing his feet in a bent-kneed shuffle. Bo's mouth quirked. Tobe was getting ready to put on a real good show for Mr. Rand.

The black hunched his shoulder and lowered his chin and commenced stepping his feet high, sucking them out of the mud, crossing them over, weaving his loose hips and knees, and then he raised up a song.

> Had me a shirt, green as de river;
> Yeah, Lawd. Yeah, Lawd.

> Roll dem dice, los' my shirt.
> Be quiet, sheep.
> Done got you.

The rousters cackled and whooped and rolled their eyes. They loosened their own hips and knees and began cross-stepping and shuffling. They came weaving down the path like a jointed snake, hips and knees and shoulders swinging along together, feet crossing and shuffling, cadenced perfectly to the beat of Tobe's song. The old coonjine roused them and sent them stepping on down.

Tobe's voice led out again:

> Roll dem dice an' whut come up;
> Yeah, Lawd. Yeah, Lawd.
> Craps come up, dat's whut come up.
> Be quiet, sheep.
> Done got you.

Bo grinned as they began to pass him. Rousters always coonjined loading a big load on or off, but Tobe had given them a special song. He'd given them himself to be the butt of their foolery and Tobe's own grin split his face as he went by. A high tenor took up the song:

> Tobe had a shirt, green as de river;
> Yeah, Lawd. Yeah, Lawd.
> Done crap out an' los' his shirt.
> Be quiet, sheep.
> Done got you.

Bo kept his stick moving, swinging it slowly, poking a man with it now and then, adding his voice. "Step lively, there. Keep a moving. You, Mose, don't you lag on me!"

A cracked laugh yelped out. "Ain't laggin', Capt'n Bo. Ain't ever lag on Capt'n Bo."

Another voice introduced a new theme:

> Tobe got a gal, Bowlin'Green town;
> Yeah, Lawd. Yeah, Lawd.
> Gal got a man. Tobe got trouble.
> Be quiet, sheep.
> Done got you.

Bo's grin stretched wider. Now they really had themselves a coonjine going. Anything could furnish a theme for a coonjine—the weather, an incident among them, trouble or grief, joy or happiness, or they could pluck one from thin air. They could enrich and embroider the weather till you'd believe in snowstorms in July. But what they liked most was a josh upon ageless ribald embarrassments—with the dice, with cards, with a woman, with a razor fracas, with pinning horns on some gal's man, with getting caught at it, with having a mean woman at home who took all your pay, or one whose bed opened to another man behind your back, or with that most irrevocable fact, having a black skin. Broad and coarse and having maybe only a nubbin of truth against the man they picked for their butt, but that a universal one they wholly enjoyed, they built it up and up until it threatened to topple of its own superstructure, but never quite did.

Bo had often thought it was a good thing they mouthed and drawled the words of a coonjine till you couldn't understand them unless you were used to them. The fine ladies who rode the big boats and always hung over the railing to watch the rousters load and thought the coonjine so fascinating might be more offended than fascinated if they knew what was being sung. All they saw was a line of black men, singing and doing a shuffling, loose-kneed step to their own singing. "How happy they are," he had often heard them say.

Maybe. But a nigger worked best when he sang. He guessed the first coonjine song began when the first nigger in black Africa hefted a load to his back. If he had to bend, it was easier and quicker to do it with a song.

Tobe reached the staging plank and it gave under him. It bounced up and the next man in line caught it perfectly, true with the give again. He'd better. You get out of step and hit the plank on the rebound and you'd pick yourself up out of the river.

> Man come home, what he fin'?
> Yeah, Lawd. Yeah, Lawd.
> Fin' ole Tobe warmin' his bed.
> Be quiet, sheep.
> Done got you.

Mr. Rand laughed. "Got a bunch of right cheerful boys this trip, ain't you?"

"Yes, sir. Right good boys."

"Tobe got in a little trouble in town, did he?"

"Tobe," Bo said, "gets in trouble any time, any town."

Mr. Rand's belly shook. "Probably makes you a good hand, though, don't he? Heard he belonged to you. Ever want to sell him, let me know."

"He ain't that much mine, Mr. Rand. Pa's still got his papers. Don't believe he's ever sold a black."

"Might be a good idea to." Mr. Rand shifted his feet in the muck. "But it ain't good business to buy 'em right now. Ain't no telling which way this war's gonna go."

"No, sir."

The line was double now, one file coming back down the other plank as the first one stepped on up. The time, the step, the shuffle and cross were the same for both lines. The suck and squeeze of the mud made a slap like a brushed drum, and the rousters timed it precisely.

> Tobe done caught, whut he do?
> Yeah, Lawd. Yeah, Lawd.
> Grab he pants an' shoo, fly, shoo.
> Be quiet, sheep.
> Done got you.

The song and shuffle were strangely calming to the sheep. One blatted now and then but for the most part they rode their perches quietly.

> Grab he pants, whut he do?
> Yeah, Lawd. Yeah, Lawd.
> Bust de window flyin' thoo.
> Be quiet, sheep.
> Done got you.

A white man couldn't have carried the tune. It was full of wavers and slides and odd, queer minor notes and quavering high tones and sliding low ones. Following down, following up, the lines kept on, the song working up and up to more and more richness:

> Bus' de window flyin' thoo;
> Yeah, Lawd. Yeah, Lawd.
> Bus' his haid on de hard groun', too.
> Be quiet, sheep.
> Done got you.

Window done cut him, man grab a gun;
Yeah, Lawd. Yeah, Lawd.
Gun got buckshot loaded down.
Be quiet, sheep.
Done got you.

Gun go off right down de line;
Yeah, Lawd. Yeah, Lawd.
Tobe pickin' buckshot fum his behime.
Be quiet, sheep.
Done got you.

From there the coonjine spiraled into such imaginative
bawdiness concerning Tobe's impairment, both in bed and
out of it, that Mr. Rand whooped and bellowed and wheezed
until he had to wipe tears from his eyes. "They don't get
done loading pretty soon," he sighed finally, "I'm gonna
bust a gut."

"Done right now, sir," Bo said.

He'd seen Luke coming behind the last rouster, checking
a tally slip as he slogged along down the path.

The last rouster, the tail of the line, was as tall as a bed-
post and thin as a slat. He loose-hipped past and pranced up
the stage. At the top he hoisted his sheep high and shouted,
"De las' sheep!" It was the privilege of the line's tail to make
an imposing announcement and the black did it lustily. He
held his pose a moment, as immobile as an ebony statue, then
romped his freight on back to Foss's pen. The whole crew
was howling and yelping and whooping. It had been a good
loading, fast and full of foolery and fun, not much toil and
easy on the back.

Luke, satisfaction written over his face, came up to Bo and

handed over the tally. "That's the lot." He added, a little diffidently, to Mr. Rand, "Mighty fine pen of sheep, sir."

"They're a fair lot," Mr. Rand said. "But you tell Jarvis they're worth his top price."

"I'll tell him," Bo promised.

Mr. Rand took his cigar out of his mouth and spat. "Any war news in Bowling Green?"

"You've not heard that Buckner has occupied the town?"

Mr. Rand's eyes shot open wide. "Bowling Green? The Confederates? When?"

"Early this morning. Marched fifteen hundred troops in and commenced fortifying right off. Talk is General Johnston aims to make the town his headquarters."

"Good. Good." Mr. Rand puffed fast on his cigar. "Glad to see 'em moving finally. I don't hold with this neutrality business the governor was so set on. Man can't be neutral. Got to pick your side. I've picked mine. Wish you was upbound, Bo. I'd go up and see Simon. Known him a long time." He stood bemused a moment. "Believe I'll hitch up and ride over."

"Yes, sir. Anything else, Mr. Rand?"

"No. No. You treat them sheep right now, hear?"

"We'll treat 'em right."

Mr. Rand trudged away up the bank without looking back. Bo watched him out of sight, then he sucked his own feet out of the mud. "C'mon, Luke. Let's get downriver."

Passing Tobe at the head of the stage he said, "You watch them sheep like they were your own personal property, hear? See they don't get jostled around and see they're watered plenty."

Tobe ducked his head. "I'll cosset dem sheep lak dey was chillun, Capt'n Bo."

"See you do. Say your prayers over 'em!" Bo took the steps up to the bridge two at a leap.

Tobe watched him affectionately. The *Rambler* hadn't had such a piece of luck in a long time and Capt'n Bo was sure spirited up about it. Only to himself would Tobe admit the *Rambler* needed the luck.

CHAPTER 3

FOUR miles by land, cutting across the snaking loops, they could have reached Thomas's Landing. It wasn't the first time Bo had wished steamboats could run on land, too, for they had to make eight miles around Boat Island and Buckner's Island, turning almost back upon themselves by water. He didn't often feel impatience with this winding, looping stretch of river but this morning he was anxious to get on down, get the loops and bends behind him, get into the Green.

They had a load of sawed poplar to put off for William Stern at Thomas's and Mr. Stern rose up tall from a stump he'd been sitting on when the *Rambler* tooted for the landing. It was on the left bank and like Underwood's was nothing but a clearing. Up above, at the top of the bank, Bo saw a wagon and team and two of Mr. Stern's boys waiting with them. He had come ready to haul the poplar home.

The rousters took care of the unloading quickly but they didn't bother with raising up a song. Wouldn't much more than have got into a song before the job was finished, but they stepped smartly without one.

Bo watched them a while, then seeing Mr. Stern picking his way to the river edge he went down to the main deck and over to the side to speak to him. Mr. Stern wasn't a very prosperous farmer. He had a big family and a hard time. He wouldn't ever be likely to be a big shipper. Bo was having a hard enough time himself to feel a sympathy for anybody else in the same fix. Besides he had an instinct for courtesy toward everybody. Big shippers or little, he treated them all politely and he served them all well whether he cleared a dime or a dixie. "Looks like you're aiming to fix up your barn, Mr. Stern," he said.

"The shed has fell in," Mr. Stern said. He kept his eye on the lumber. "Appears to be a middling good grade of poplar you got me."

"Not as good as I'd have wished," Bo said. "But you said rough-sawed and it was good as we could do for you."

"Yes. Well, I wouldn't have no use for the best. Couldn't run to such a price. I'm pleased with it."

He spoke patiently. He was a little taller than middle height, not yet an old man but past his first youth, and his face was roughly eroded by weather, the way all farmer's faces are. If your hands have fitted a plow handle most of your life and your feet have followed a furrow, your face takes a lot of wind and frost and rain and sun. It changes. And your lips get a bleached, tough look. The elements, over a given time, hammer a mouth out of shape and reshape it to serve you better than nature's original gift. They don't do a handsome job, but they do a useful one. A thickened lip-skin doesn't chap so easily, or crack so easily, or bleed so willingly. The elements turn a man's face-skin and lip-skin into an animal's hide and while it isn't pretty it is best that way.

Mr. Stern paid his bill, as he always did, with cash. One reason Mr. Stern had such a hard time of it was that he didn't hold with owing. He did without until he had money in hand to pay. Mr. Rand, on the other hand, used his credit extensively. He paid, but he paid when it suited him. You had to carry him sometimes for several months. Wryly Bo remembered that his own father did the same. It was the habit of men accustomed to plenty. They couldn't conceive of its lack. He wished, however, it had suited Mr. Rand to pay today. He could have put the money to good use.

He pocketed Mr. Stern's money. The boys had finished unloading and Bo was itchy to get away, but Mr. Stern was studying the ground, making no move to leave. Bo contained his impatience.

The lean tall man kicked a chunk of mud into the water and watched its ripple. Without looking up he said, then, very quietly, "Reckon you didn't hear no war news in Bowling Green."

Bo told him the news.

"Yes. Well, I just thought you might know."

He lifted one hand and looked at it as if something might have gone wrong with it since the last time he'd used it. " I got a brother went down to Camp Boone in Tennessee not long ago. Joined up with the Confederates. Reckon it's likely he's with Buckner's troops?"

Bo hesitated. "I wouldn't know, Mr. Stern. I'd say it was right likely, though. Buckner's come from Tennessee. Course, your brother might still be at Boone. Talk is Albert Sidney Johnston has taken over for the Confederates in Tennessee and is aiming to make his headquarters at Bowling Green. If your brother's not with Buckner's boys, he'll likely be on up this way with the main army."

Mr. Stern cleared his throat. "I've not got any leanings, myself, you understand, but Thomas, he got het up a right smart and nothin' to do but join up. He's not but eighteen. Youngest one of us. Went foolish to me but nothin' would do but march off and enlist."

"Yes, sir."

"Not heard from him since. Our old mam is poorly and it would help to have word of him." He cleared his throat again.

"Well," Bo said, feeling helpless and sorry, "it was Luke brought the word from town this morning. He went in to round up the boys. We'd been laid to tightening a piston. Luke run right into 'em but he didn't get the names of any regiments."

Mr. Stern brought one hand around and wiped it across his nose, sweeping away a drop of moisture that had been hanging there. "Wouldn't hurt none, I reckon, if a body went up to Bowling Green. Might find out."

"Best way, I'd say," Bo said.

"Well." The man pondered some more, than seemed to reach a decision. "Guess that's what I'll do. Satisfy Mam, if I would. Didn't disfurnish you none, did it? Buckner taking over?"

"Not yet," Bo said grimly.

"Well," the man said, hesitant again, "I'm keeping you. You get on. I'm obliged for your keer about the lumber." He turned away and plunged jerkily up the bank, as if, Bo thought, his joints hurt. He guessed more than Mr. Stern's joints hurt, though.

The helpless anger which the war, when he had to think about it or talk about it, always brought settled over Bo. Kentucky hadn't wanted this war and in his opinion Kentucky had a right not to be forced into it. If it had been the Union standing against some foreign nation, Kentuckians would have been as quick to answer the call for troops as any other men. But for a country to tear itself in two and for the two halves to take up arms against each other was senseless to him. He couldn't believe it could not have been avoided. It made him feel helpless and angry and as if something he had believed in all his life had suddenly become worthless.

If the North had its right, and if the South had its right, this middle ground had its right, which neither side was respecting. Between them they were raiding it and occupying it and they were riving the state itself in two and Kentucky was coming to have its own secession movement.

He shook off his gloom and went up the companionway.

They had barely slid around Slim Island ten minutes later when Foss brought Bo's dinner up to him. Dinner was usually at eleven o'clock on the *Rambler*. When his old pocket watch showed a bare ten, Bo looked a question at Foss. "Figured we'd best get dinner out of the way," Foss said, "so's I'd have Tobe handy at the lock."

Foss was the one who had thought ahead. He had let himself get stirred up again, and it wouldn't do. He took the plate and gave over the wheel.

Foss felt the spokes and settled himself. "Lost a pretty piece of time back there."

"Seemed to me the boys unloaded uncommonly quick," Bo said, hitching up a stool. "Don't know as they could have done it quicker."

Foss shot him a glance. "That," he said, "ain't what I was meaning."

"He wanted to talk," Bo said, surrendering. "Got a brother with the Confederates."

Foss grunted.

Bo said: "Where'd Tobe find these wild greens? Don't run across 'em in the fall much."

"Tobe didn't," Foss said. "I found 'em yestiddy. Same place I found them hen eggs you didn't value."

"Greens and rotten eggs are different things."

Foss's shoulders twitched. It had pleased him to find the little clumps of new poke shoots and the wild mustard. Bo liked them best of all wild greens. Foss didn't relish them much himself but he didn't turn down anything that could be put in the stomach.

Bo shoveled them down padded with fried bread and catfish. "Catch the fish, too?"

"I could of, but I never. Was a boy come by the boat 'fore you roused this morning. Bought 'em offen him."

"Must have just run his lines. They're tasty."

There was a long quiet while Bo ate and Foss trotted the *Rambler* along. Then a fork clattered and Bo stood up. "Good dinner," he said.

He came up beside Foss but he didn't take the wheel yet, just stood looking ahead. Foss flicked a look at him and saw a frown line between his eyes. He waited and wasn't surprised when Bo finally spoke he went back to the war.

"There are some things, Foss," he said, "that I know as well as any man and don't need straightened out for me. I know steamboats and I know rivers and I know what I want and I've always thought I knew right from wrong. I've got no uncertainties about such things."

"Wouldn't have as much sense as I give you credit for if you did," Foss said.

"But there's some things," Bo went on, "I've got nothing *but* uncertainties about and this war is one of 'em."

"It's nothin' to do with you," Foss said.

"That's what Governor Magoffin said. It's nothing to do with Kentucky and look at Kentucky. I don't know as any state's going to be hurt worse. It'll take years to mend the sores, if they can ever be mended at all."

"Whyn't they leave us alone like the governor asked 'em to?"

"That's something," Bo said slowly, "I've not got straightened out yet. And something they don't tell you. Both sides say they're trying to protect us. What we need is protection from them. Of course," he added, "we've got a lot of hotheads ourselves—spoiling for a fight—wouldn't quit till they got a hornet's nest stirred up. But the best I can figure it, both sides needed something here. Mostly stores and grain and food for the South. Mostly the Ohio for the North. You could say, and not be far wrong, the river's turned into a road for Federal troops. Without you do what that general in Louisville says, you don't run on it any more."

Foss kept quiet. Bo was just trying to sort his thinking out and he didn't need any confusement from him.

"Far as taking sides here in Kentucky is concerned," Bo went on, "it's about as poor paying as trying to sort out the water of this river, saying this piece is Barren water and this piece is Nolin water and this piece is Rough. There's plenty that think the country'll be ruined if the North don't win, and just as many that think it'll be ruined if it does. All I know for sure is that between 'em they're doing a good job of ruining it right this minute. What comes after, which side wins, *couldn't* be no worse.

"Worst is," he went on reflectively, "you take somebody doing the best he can, doing the best he can by his lights—somebody not used to going off half-cocked—got to have a reason for things—he's in a poor way. It's like having the wheel of a boat without no rudder. The helplessest feeling you could have. You'd like to knock their heads together and make 'em come to their senses. But one man can't stage a war all by himself."

"No," Foss said, "I wouldn't think it'd pay him."

Bo drew in his breath and let it out in one of Foss's own

long sighs. "I reckon all wars are bad, but this kind of war must be the worst kind there is. There's no real enemy. There's just your own kind, and maybe sometimes your own kin, to shoot at."

Foss moved his shoulders. "I ain't got to. Not unless they commence fighting on the Green, I ain't got to."

"If they commence that," Bo said grimly, "I just may have me a small war of my own—with whichever side starts it."

"Well, right now," Foss said, "the war ain't keeping this river from running, and it ain't changed nothing about that loose piston and it ain't keeping us from having to lock through Brown's pretty soon. It ain't but a mile to the lock and you best take this wheel and let me git down where I belong."

Bo laughed. "That's the beautiful truth. Get along."

Shortly he came into the straight piece of water up from the lock and he blew, one long, one short, and chugged the *Rambler* on down, easing her to the right bank. Through the glass he saw the lockmaster come out and signal. The gates were open. Bo cut out of the current a little and rang Foss for slow and heard the clunk of the loose piston and then the chuff of the slowing engine. They idled along, slower and slower, Bo handling the wheel delicately, feeling the slowness, inching along.

It was done, finally, and he nosed the *Rambler* into the crib. Gave Foss the stopping bell and they came to rest. The lockmaster and the tender went to work closing the upper gates behind them. A windlass on each wall propelled the two halves separately and it took time to do it. Luke and a couple of rousters jumped onto the wall and went to help. The lockmaster gave over to them and came alongside. "Woodbury ain't operating," he yelled at Bo. "Stage too high."

"Figured it might be," Bo yelled back. "High enough to jump?"

"Be risky."

Bo nodded. He wouldn't know until he got there.

The upper gates were closed now and the lower gates had to be opened. The boys ran to the other end of the lock and began the winding process all over. Slowly the gates inched open and as the water flooded out the *Rambler* sank and sank in the chamber until the pilothouse itself was almost level with the crib wall. Luke and the boys clambered down the ladders to the deck and Bo gave Foss slow ahead and the *Rambler* slid out of the chamber, free and loose and in the river again. Bo brought her into the current and looked at his watch. Thirty minutes to lock through. It wasn't good but it wasn't bad, either. They had to trot on down. They had a stop to make at Hightower Landing, another at Clark's, they had to get through the Narrows, and the morning was passing fast.

Even the soles of his feet itched to get out of the Barren and into the Green.

CHAPTER 4

WHEN they slid out of the Barren into the Green Luke was riding in the pilothouse for company. He eyed the water with astonishment and excitement and let out a long, low whistle. "Jehosaphat, Bo, she's *real* high! I never thought—look at that old river, Bo! Clean out of her banks! Spreading all over the bottoms."

"Pretty good stage," Bo admitted.

"Aw, you ain't got to worry about no dam. Not on *this* river. You can steamboat any place you like."

Bo gave him no more time. Woodbury Lock was built in a slow bend less than half a mile from the mouth of the Barren. They had a short piece of water, then, in which he could judge and decide. He blew, and caught the lockmaster's signal—no good. So.

He watched the race of the river, studying and judging it. It was glassy smooth and silky looking but running fast. He took up the glass to see how it looked beyond the dam and there it was a witch's cauldron of white water, crests building and tumbling and falling back, spume rising and boiling. He put down the glass.

It was about as he had expected. All down the Barren there hadn't been the stage he'd hoped for. If he jumped the dam he was going to have to jolt the *Rambler* considerably. He had a split second to make up his mind and he did it. The stage was too good to waste—too good to lay up. He would risk taking the *Rambler* over.

He was well in the slight concavity caused on the lens of the river by the slow-falling tide and he was now beginning to be caught up in the swiftening race. Might as well, he now decided, all things considered and known, take it tilting. He'd either rip the guts out of the boat or do the least possible damage.

He rang for full ahead, his mouth twisting into a grin. Foss wouldn't like that. Foss gave it to him, however, and the *Rambler*, seized by the change of speed, plowed her nose for a moment, sprayed white water, then lifted her head like a proud swan, shook of the drip and went skimming and sailing down the long, rapid race.

The roustabouts were shouting and yelling, urging the *Rambler* on, surged by excitement and the headiness of danger into yelps of laughter and cackling whoops of encouragement. "Take her on down, Capt'n Bo, take her on down!"

"Roll wid dis river, Capt'n Bo. Roll wid her!"

"Capt'n Bo, he ain't skeered dis ole river!"

"Man, look at dis ole *Rambler* git up an' ramble! Ain't she a ramblin' ole boat!"

"Ramblin'est boat on de river, dat's whut! Ain't no boat ramble lak de *Rambler*!"

The rousters were yelling, the machinery was clanking, and finally the sheep began bleating. It sounded, Bo thought, like bedlam. And the *Rambler* was committed now. There wasn't strength enough in two men to cramp her out of the flooding race. She was hell bent for election and all he could do was ride her on down, just ride her on down. Ride her, Bo thought exultantly, like you had the Ohio under you, or the sea.

Coming down full tilt, he caught a glimpse of the lockmaster and the tenders standing on the wall. He gave them a blast from the whistle, an impudent swaggering roar. Then he spread his legs and got a good stance and gripped the wheel. The tide was so swift he felt as if the *Rambler* had spread wings and his exultation rose to spread wings in his chest. This, he had time to think, is the moment a man lives for—this full, highest power he can reach, when every sense is sharpened painfully, when a sound hurt his ears and sight hurt his eyes and nerves hurt under every inch of skin, and he knows he was made in the image of God and for a few seconds is given his stature. He felt like shouting and what he wanted to shout was, *I'm a riverman! I'm a riverman!* It was the best there was to be.

He was conscious of silence below, now. It was an absolute stillness except for the noise of the machinery, as if rousters and sheep both sensed that even a sound might overbalance the *Rambler,* as though a breath expelled might weigh the outcome.

Now was the moment. The *Rambler* was suddenly tilted over the dam and down, sliding smooth and flying. She hit the trough and shuddered, racked by the jolt through every rib and her head went down and down and down as if it were nosing the bottom and never meant to come back up. The deck was flooded half to the stern and Bo heard the rush of feet to lend weight to the paddle wheel. There was a rending clank of metal and despair made even his hands feel heavy. He'd been the death of the machinery, sure.

The head came up slowly, slowly, shaking off water like a dog that's swum a river, the spray flying over the sides. Risen, she rode light and Bo cramped the wheel and swung her hard to starboard. Foss, right on the job, gave him everything he had. The buckets of the wheel bit as if they were chewing meat, got hold and gripped, flung water recklessly, then shoved and pushed.

The rousters raised a triumphant shout, which set off the sheep again. Amid whoops and fantastic bleating the *Rambler* slid out of the trough, rudder answering and paddle pushing grandly. Bo let her rack on down a piece, then he rang for half ahead, then slow, until finally he moved her into easy water and gave Foss the stopping bell.

"Take her," Bo told Luke. He went down the steps two at a time.

Foss was almost hidden in the machinery, poking around, testing bolts and nuts and screws. "What harm?" Bo asked tightly.

"Not as much as I expected," Foss admitted. "She held. Clanked once loud as a thunderclap. I made sure she was cracked wide open, but she held. If there ain't nothin' creened out of true . . . some screws got to be tightened . . ." Foss was peering and testing and trying as he talked.

"I heard that thunderclap. Made certain the piston had stove clean through."

Foss nodded. "Looked for it. Scared the hell out of me." He came wiping his hands on an oily rag. "No great harm. Rudder all right?"

"Answered good."

"Didn't take no creen, then. You was ridin' lucky, Bo." He cocked an ear to the slow chuff of the engine. "Ridin' on luck. How far you aimin' to ride this tide, Bo?"

"Depends. Far as I can."

"Be a better stage at Rochester, likely."

"Likely."

"But then it'll be dark."

"Yep. It'll be dark."

"Kind of unhealthy to jump that one in the dark."

"Might be. Depends."

Foss threw his rag down and swiped his hands for good measure against his pants. "Well. We'll find out, I reckon."

They came out on the stern and Bo looked up at the sky. The rain had begun again, slow and mizzly and gray. "If it was going to rain," he said, "I wish it would be a real goose-drownder. Maybe open up a few chutes so's I could make some time."

"I a little doubt it's aimin' to," Foss said dryly. "More'n likely you're gonna get fog."

"Don't be so cheerful about it," Bo said shortly. "You got wood to do to Highview?"

"Nope. If Bates ain't got sense to know his woodyard'll be under water and load us some to Morgantown, I'll have to hoist a sail."

Bo grunted. "Using a fishnet, maybe?" He turned away. "Well, if Bates hasn't brought some down, maybe the *Southern Belle*'s woodyard can spare some."

"Aw, I'll make out," Foss said, "I ain't ever run out of steam for you yet, have I? It ain't to worry."

Tobe came up, his face lit like a candle with pride. "Sho' jump dat dam, Capt'n Bo. Sho' did. Never see nothin' lak it. Ole *Rambler* jus' stick her nose down an' plow water an' nen shake lak a dawg. Sho' a fine boat, Capt'n Bo. Sho' is. Ain't *no* boat good as de *Rambler*."

"How're them sheep?" Bo asked.

"Jostle 'em some. Flang a few down. Done got 'em back up an' pacified. Dem sheep's fine, Capt'n Bo."

"Good. You help Foss here, now. We're moving on down."

"Yassuh."

He mounted to the bridge and stood a moment looking down the river in the mist. The day had sure turned whimsy on them, and it didn't look as if it was going to better itself any. He shrugged. Well, weather was one thing you could do nothing about. All you could do was read the signs as best you could and steamboat accordingly. As long as they didn't run into fog, they would trot on down.

Luke gave him an anxious look when he went into the pilothouse. He shook his head. "Still all in one piece." He took the wheel, signaled Foss and they got under way. Luke stood away, watching. Mid-channel again and chugging, Bo said, "We got anything to set off at Cook's?"

"No," Luke said. "Unless we get signaled down next stop is Morgantown."

"I'm going to let you take the wheel, then. I'm going to catch a little sleep while I can."

"Reckon I ought? All this water?"

"Wouldn't let you if I didn't think so. Just stay in the channel and ease her along. You've run this piece of water many a time."

Luke took a nervous hold on the wheel. He didn't know which he felt most, pride he was being trusted or fear he wouldn't measure up. He had run this stretch before, often, as Bo said, but he hadn't ever run it with a tide on before.

Bo watched him for a little while. "Luke—*you* run the boat, don't let her run you."

Luke braced back and settled his feet, made his hands steadier on the wheel and made his voice steady too. "Yes, sir."

Bo cast his eyes around and said reflectively, "Might be a

patch of fog now and then. Nothing to worry about, likely. Time of sundown is the worst for fog. But I'll be up if it thickens."

He went down to the engine room and fiddled around. Foss watched him eying the woodpile and followed him. "Gonna chute the Big Bend, Bo?"

Bo flicked a look at him and grinned. "Would if I could. I sure would if I could."

Foss's big shoulders lifted and twisted. "She's your boat if you want to risk her. I don't reckon you've forgot the time Dick January went kiting acrost a chute or what happened to him."

"I've not forgot."

Foss bored on with his story. "Misjudged the depth. Got stuck in a cornfield. The *Scotland Lass* stayed stuck in that cornfield for six months and cost the company five thousand dollars to warp her back into the river again. A sight to behold . . . steamboat settin' high and dry in a cornfield. Farmer had to plant around it. Dick January got laughed off the river."

Bo laughed, remembering. "And ought. But I'm not Dick January. He was always a fool pilot. I wouldn't have trusted Dick January with a skiff, been me. Poorest eye for water ever held a wheel."

"Got a high opinion of yours, I reckon."

"High enough. I'll know whether to take the *Rambler* across."

"So's you do," Foss said.

"I'm gonna catch a little sleep," Bo said. "No more'n an hour, though. You wake me."

"Sweet dreams," Foss said lightly; but he watched Bo walk away broodingly, with softened, concerned eyes. The boy walked light and quick, like he was walking on moss. He was feeling springy with good luck. And feeling springy, you'd have to give him that, for good handling of his boat. A sweet pilot the boy was, just about as sweet as they came. If he had the money, he'd ask nothing better to do with it than to see the boy had a sweet boat to match him.

He snorted. You'd think he was old enough to be Bo's father the way he was always thinking of him as a boy and wanting to ease things for him, see him get what he wanted, help him get it. The last thing Bo needed was somebody easing things for him. He was able. And the best way he could help him was to nurse the *Rambler*'s old machinery for him. Nevertheless, he hoped the boy got his full hour of sleep . . . hoped nobody hailed them down at a landing . . . hoped the river didn't fog up.

Luke trotted the *Rambler* steadily along. She went like an amiable old mare, chuffing and chugging, the slow deeps not hurrying her too much. This was a pool of nice water and about as straight a stretch as you'd find, except that long piece between Steamport and Mason's Bend on the lower river. Just a few wide, easy bends. It was even a little dull, but Luke was glad for that. He didn't want any trouble while he was at the wheel. It made him feel tight enough to be alone, nobody but him, in the pilothouse.

He steered carefully, watched ahead warily, worried when the mist thickened once and felt relief when it thinned again. He had only one bad scare, toward the last, when he cut a little close inshore on a slow bend. It startled the breath out of him to see willow tops dead ahead, but he had time to swing wide.

Foss came up afterwards. "Aimin' to commence clippin' bushes, Luke?"

Luke still felt shaky and he grinned sickly. "Appears so, don't it?"

"Just thought mebbe we'd better put a blade on the prow if you was. Be more handy."

"I oughtn't to done that," Luke admitted. "Bo'd cuss me out if he'd seen it."

"Seen him do worse," Foss said. "Seen him get flung crosswise in a tide once, up on the Barren, and lose his power and go skyhootin' for two mile downriver 'fore he grounded the *Rambler*. He mortally did clip a bunch of willows that time. Never missed many."

"Bo?" Luke was incredulous. "Bo did that?"

"Well," Foss admitted, "wasn't all his fault. I wasn't where I could give him what he needed and Tobe didn't, so he had a excuse. But there ain't nobody perfect. And no pilot but's had his scares."

"How'd he ground the boat?"

"He didn't. Current did. Plowed him into a bank." Passing out the door Foss added, "The jolt flung Tobe ag'in the machinery and stove in three ribs for him. Hampered him in *all* his duties for quite a spell. He felt right misput with Bo for some time."

Luke was still chuckling over the story when Bo came up. His face had a flush on the cheeks and a look of rest and warmth. He brought a cup of coffee with him and sipped as he listened to Luke's account of the incidentless run, except—and the boy told, painfully honest, his own small indiscretion.

"Learned you something, did it?"

"It learned me them willows on that bend overhang awful low," Luke said strongly.

"Might on any bend in a tide. Makes a difference."

They made their Morgantown stop and Bo was pleased to see that Bates had been enterprising and had brought them a full load of wood to the landing. If he couldn't run the neck of the Big Bend, if they had to make that long slow loop, at least they'd have wood enough.

It was a good enough piece of water, but there had been times before when he'd wished it didn't double back on itself so far. Twenty miles was a long way out of the way to go. He didn't know how far it was across the Bend by land but it couldn't have been, at any place down the long ten-mile arms, more than five miles. But the river never would cut a channel across. It flowed too straight and too deep and too slow. There wasn't anything for it to rage against and eat away. He often wished the state would cut a canal across but he knew it never would. The state had been grumbling for years that the locks didn't pay their way. They weren't likely to spend any more money on the Green.

Bo had never run this chute. Not many had. It took a lot of water. But it could be done and it had been done and he'd heard all the tales and stored them away. He sorted them over in his mind, now. However the stories differed in some respects, in one thing they all agreed. If there was water enough to run the Bend it was best to do it at the neck, before you got down into the arm, so as to catch the river again in the Little Bend. They all said that several miles below Morgantown you had some wide-spaced trees and a low bank and you could poke your nose through. Then you angled across a wide flat, usually planted to corn, and came into the river at Dixon's Landing near Mining City. It was just a short run then to Rochester and you'd saved yourself more than twenty river miles. Bo had always wished, more than a little, for a chance to try it.

They chugged along quietly and Bo studied the flooded bottoms, marking the stage on the trees, remembering his landmarks and comparing. It was a good stage all right, but just before reaching the place he decided regretfully it wasn't good enough. "There's a high place," he'd been told. "You got to have more than a plenty of water."

The time and the weather bothered him some, too. There was a saying on the river, don't run a chute upstream on a falling tide. He wasn't, but it was still to think about. The whimsy day was also bothersome. If there had been sun you could have counted on daylight till seven o'clock. The way it was there'd be what amounted to a long twilight with a chance of fog much earlier. He would risk his boat when the chances were even. When he had finished balancing it all out, he thought he didn't have that even chance. He grinned, thinking of Dick January up on the Kanawha. This tide was falling fast and he didn't mean to pull a Dick January stunt.

Tobe came up to bring him coffee. "Go tell Foss," Bo said, "he won't be needing his sail."

"Yassuh. No suh. Which, suh?"

"Just a little joke. Tell Foss he won't be needing his sail."

Tobe went away muttering. If Mr. Foss was aiming to put up a sail on the *Rambler,* he was plumb outen his mind!

Bo laughed and called after him, "And tell Luke if he'll bring his cargo slips up I'll work on 'em a little while he steers."

"Yassuh."

Bo thought of the long, slow-winding pool ahead of him —Aberdeen, Turkey Rock, Flowers Rock, Wilson's Rock, Ennis Ferry—and he sighed for his lost chance to pass them by. It just wouldn't have done and he knew it. Sometimes boldness lay in playing it safe.

CHAPTER 5

A N HOUR went by in silence. Bo was deep in his book-work. Unless they were signaled down they didn't have a stop until they got to Rochester. This piece of water was nice and easy and Luke could handle it fine.

A quiver and a slight roll of the boat made him look up quickly. "Wind getting up?"

"You better take her, Bo," Luke said uneasily, "that dark cloud's been shaping up last ten minutes. It ain't pretty."

"It's sure not pretty," Bo admitted. "All right, she's mine."

The overcast had been darker in the southwest for some time. He had seen it, taken note of it, but this time of year, this kind of day, you often got a dark southwest sky. Now, however, a greasy cloud had formed over the bank and it was so full of wind it was roiling and boiling and its edges were rifted and frazzled all around.

"I sure don't like the looks of that," Bo said. He kept studying it. They were a little below Aberdeen and coming up to Turkey Rock. No real good place to tie up. "Fog," he said, "wouldn't have surprised me—or even a heavy rain. But a wind squall on a day like this one wasn't to be expected. You don't get 'em on a misty, mizzly day."

"Appears we got one."

"And coming like a locomotive!"

"What you gonna do?"

"Plow into it. Ain't time to do nothing else!"

He heard Foss shout for Tobe and knew he had seen the cloud, too. And then he had his hands full for the squall hit with a fury that rocked the *Rambler* back on her heels and shivered her in every beam. He had to fight the wheel to keep her headed up. "Gimme a hand!" he yelled at Luke, "cramp them spokes down, boy!"

Luke sprang to the wheel.

The lightning was blue and keen and the thunder rolled like cannon fire. The wind whipped up the long flat water and rolled it and stirred it and made it a crosshatch of a thousand quarreling currents dragging at the hull. The rain blew in, a glassy wall as white as fog, and the apron was no more use than a woman's calico kitchen apron would have been. Both men were soaked in minutes and fighting to see. "I can't see nothing, Bo," Luke screamed above the uproar.

Bo yelled at him that he didn't need to see—just hang on.

The fury lasted less than ten minutes. It was only a squall, blown up quickly, blown on quickly, but there were times when it had felt as if the *Rambler* was being spun like a top —frightening times because of the rocks on the sheer bank. Wind—the deadliest enemy nature held for a steamboatman. Caught broadside by a hard gust, the *Rambler* would have been crushed against the rocks like an eggshell. Bo fought with as much fury as the wind to keep his boat mid-channel and when the squall passed on finally his arms felt knotted and they ached like a bad tooth.

He motioned to Luke, who turned loose of the wheel and stumbled away, his hands hanging limp at his sides like dead fish. The boy was as wet as if he'd been swimming. "Go change your clothes," Bo told him, "and get yourself a cup of coffee. See if we come to any harm."

"I'll bring you some coffee," Luke promised, "and I won't be long."

The rain kept on, though the wind had passed, and it was as bad as fog, heavy and thick and ropy. It was troublesome to keep your bearings with the water and the sky and the rain all the same gunmetal color and the edges of the timber almost blurred out. This was one of the times, Bo thought, not liking it but having to put up with it, when you had to steamboat by guess and by God and do it with considerable caution at that. He was going to have to feel his way in to the bank and tie up and wait it out. It was the only sensible thing to do.

Luke brought the coffee and set it on the chart table. "Foss said she was making a little more water than common," the boy said, "but he's got some of the boys on the pump."

"That blow creened her some and opened the seams," Bo said. "I figured it would."

Luke laughed. "I was scared to death. I figured we'd sink." He leaned out to peer ahead. "Lord, it's thick. How you know where you are?"

"Well, I'm in the river, boy, trying to find the bank."

"Can't see more'n fifty foot, can you?"

"Not much more."

He took his eye off the water for one second to find his coffee and reach for it, then he froze for perhaps five seconds before the cup crashed to the deck. "Goddlemighty!" he bellowed, doing a frantic dance to spin the wheel, reach for the whistle, the bell, all at the same time. When he found the whistle he yanked it down long and loud, full roar and long-blast. "Give Foss the stopping bell!" he shouted at Luke.

Bo walked the wheel to bring the *Rambler* around. He heard all the sounds that meant Foss was doing his best to stop her . . . the paddle churning, the machinery clanking, but he knew nothing could stop the boat in time. He kept pulling and cramping, waiting what felt to him like an eternity for a thud and a bump . . . and maybe human screams.

When it came it was easy and gentle, barely a felt little nudge. Slowly, slowly, the *Rambler* churned to a stop. "Take her!" Bo flung at Luke. "Just hold her like she is. We just run down a skiff!"

"Oh, my Lord God!"

Bo went pounding down the companionway yelling for Tobe. "That was a skiff we just run down. Launch the small boat, Tobe! Get a move on! We may have cut her in two!"

Tobe shouted for help. "Jonah! Boone! Catfish!"

There was an excited milling around on the deck, all the rousters shouting and crowding. "I seen her, Capt'n Bo! Jus' got a glimpse of her 'fore we hit. Off de sta'bbord!"

"Done slice her in two, likely!"

"How many ob 'em was dey?"

"Not time to see. Jus' see de boat."

"Whur she at?"

"Done gone down!"

"No, she ain't! Capt'n never hit her dat hard!"

Foss appeared at Bo's side. "Well, we done it now. Just cracked that piston a good foot. You can't wrack a engine like that . . ."

Bo glared at him. "Didn't you hear me? We just run down a skiff. There was people in it! I'll worry about the piston when I can quit worrying about them people. Tobe! What's taking you so long? God, they may be out there in the water . . . You see anything, Foss? Damn this rain. It's like having cobwebs in your eyes. Lord, I hope we didn't cut her in two and kill somebody!"

"I a little doubt it," Foss said comfortingly. "You nudged her easy." He wiped the rain out of his eyes and peered. "There she is, Bo. She's still afloat."

"Where?" Bo swung around to follow Foss's hand, pointing. They had left it farther behind than he'd reckoned. He blew out his breath. "She's stove in, likely, but maybe nobody was hurt."

He hailed the skiff. A strong voice answered him. "Ahoy, the steamboat!"

"How much are you damaged?" Bo shouted. "Can you stay afloat? Can you bring her around? We're launching a boat for you but if you can bring her alongside it'll be quicker!"

The man's voice was full, deep and rich and it came booming out of the rain. "All thy waves and storms have gone over me, sir, but I am not content with my harm. We are stove in the midriff, sir, and the tale of this tub is told!"

"Are you sinking?" Bo blinked against the rain and tried to pierce its curtain. They couldn't keep the boat in sight. They would get a short glimpse of it and then it would disappear.

"He ain't sinkin'," Foss muttered. "I just seen him. He's well up and somebody's rowin'."

The full orotund tones drifted over to them again. "We float, sir, we float, upon this watery bier, though we are in a

parlous state. Bail, Phoebe, bail, or this thundering misbegotten rotten hulk will sink under us!"

Foss sighed. "Either he's a loony or you stove him in the
head. He don't make a grain of sense."

Bo hunched his shoulders and tried again. "Shall we put
out a boat for you, sir?"

"You have put out one too many already," came back
sharply. "Why don't you watch where you're going, sir?"

Bo snapped back at him, "I want to know, sir, shall we put
out our boat for you or can you make it?"

"This barge," the man intoned, "is not like Cleopatra's,
sir. It is not a burnished throne nor is the poop of beaten
gold. It has, in truth, no poop. But we shall beat the water
with these splintered oars, sir. Alas, we have no tune of flutes
to keep the stroke." The voice roared again, "Bail, Phoebe,
bail! She's down by the helm!"

"I think he's drunk," Foss said.

"I think he's trying to tell us he can make it," Bo said. He
shouted for Tobe to hold up the small boat. Some of the
noise on the deck ceased. "Who's Phoebe, wonder?" he said
to Foss.

Foss grunted and sheltered his eyes against the rain, straining to see the figures in the slow-inching skiff. "There's two
of 'em, I make it. Him and another." He studied a moment
longer then dropped his hands. "Phoebe," he said lugubri-
ously, "is a woman. She's settin' in the bow a bailin'."

"Oh, God's britches!"

Foss chuckled. When Bo used the oath that was the
private property of the Cartwrights, that had begun Bo had
told him with his hot-tempered little grandmother, it was a
sign he was badly put out. He made do with ordinary cussing usually. When he hauled out Tattie Cartwright's special
swear words, he was feeling uncommonly boxed in.

Bo strode to the stern and again made a megaphone of his hands. "We make two of you, sir. Is that all? Has anyone been lost overboard?"

"Hark to this Triton of the minnows, Phoebe!" came the reply. "Sir! Had we lost so much as a suckling pig I should even now be weltering in this flooding foam to save it! I have been young and am now old but my age is as a lusty winter—frosty, but kindly, sir!"

"He goes the foolishest," Foss complained. "Who said anything about sucklin' pigs? And what's a triton of the minnows?"

"How the hell would I know? But I guess he's saying they've not lost anybody. He's taking an all-fired long time to come alongside, seems to me."

"And I can tell you why," Foss said. "That old gent goes as fur away from us on his off stroke as he comes nigh on his near one. Keeps on he'll bear up on the port, for it appears he's aimin' to circle us."

Suddenly the woman in the skiff spoke. Her voice was too soft or too low for them to hear her distinctly. They made out a few words, however, and Bo said, "She's asking him to let her row a while."

"Silence, wench!" the old man roared, "and attend to your bucket! leave me to my labors. I'll cross this vasty sea, though it blast me."

The girl laughed, and it was a nice sound, as low and soft as her voice. It was a real laugh, cheerful and amused. They heard her say, plainly now, "There was no vasty sea in *Hamlet*, Grandfather."

"I have just put one there," the old man said. "How far is it to that blasted seacook of a steamboat?"

A great, blowing sigh passed from Foss. "I could overlook one of 'em in that skiff bein' foolish in the head but it's

goin' to tax me to be housed up with two. The girl is as simple as the old man."

"Oh, shut up," Bo said. The girl's voice teased him for a
comparison. It was soft and slow, but not silky or smooth. It
had a little roughness in it; at the same time it was rich.
Fur, he thought suddenly, getting it to suit him. If a voice
could sound the way a prime pelt felt in the hands, say a
mink, that was what her voice sounded like—well-bodied,
dark, soft, plushy and textured. He had never heard a woman's voice like it before.

The rain was mizzling off now and they could see that in
its erratic way the skiff was nearing. Pulled strongly by first
one oar and then the other, but never the two at once, it
moved like a tacking sailboat. Its course was a length on the
zig and then a length on the zag. If the old man had ever
rowed a boat before it hadn't taught him much, Bo concluded. He'd have done better to paddle, for as often as the
alternating oars dug water they missed and flailed. One thing
was certain, however. Whatever his age the old man was no
weakling. He was using up a strong man's full energy.

Bo could see only the back of the man and the white hair
that drained down lankly onto his shoulders. If he had been
wearing head covering, as he must have been, it had been
lost in the collision. He was swathed in a capacious cape that
threatened with each stroke to become entangled with an
oar and drag him overboard. It gave his arms an awkward,
winglike look.

In the bow, the girl was so low in the boat Bo judged she
was sitting on luggage in the bottom. She wore a hooded
cape or a shawl with some kind of wrapping over her head
so that all he could see of her was a dark lump. She was very
busy with a small bucket, bailing out the leaking boat.

Tobe was waiting with a boat hook and when they finally

came within reach he lunged it out and caught the stern of the skiff. The old man was jolted forward almost off his seat and he swung around angrily. "You add insult to injury, my man! Angels and ministers of grace defend us against your good offices if they add indignity to our other ills."

"Grandfather," the girl chided.

"Sorry, sir," Bo said, then to Tobe, "Heave in!"

The boat was pulled smoothly alongside and Bo braced to stretch his hand to the girl. She avoided it, bending and twisting oddly away, working at something behind her. He had got only an impression of her—dark wet hair, dark young face, very pretty, lively, and entirely unafraid.

She was wrenching and tugging and Bo stared and the old man stared and then the old man threw his head back and raised a shout of laughter. "Hoist by her own petard, sir! She's caught by her dresstail!"

The girl said, "Hush," but there was only amusement in it.

"You came nigh splitting us in two," the old man said, "and Phoebe stuffed her skirt in the crack. She is in difficulty freeing herself." He stood and teetered toward the girl. He was very tall and very lean. He was also very wet. The long cape hung like a carpet around him and his face and hair dripped streams of water. As wet as he was, however, there was an air of grace and elegance about him. His face was craggy, all juts and angles, but lit with humor and tenderness as he looked at the girl. His forehead was bony and bald, marked across with dark and wildly bushy eyebrows, which were in strange contrast to the white hair, mustache and trim goatee. His head was nobly shaped.

Bo stepped down and touched the old man's arm. "Let me help you aboard, sir. Then I'll see to your . . . to your . . ."

"My granddaughter, sir. Thank you. I'm obliged."

Aboard, he wrapped his cape about him and beamed radiantly at Foss and Tobe who had helped him. He might have been a pirate, or a fallen angel, or the noblest Roman of them all.

Bo made his way around a small, humpbacked trunk and numerous cases and carpetbags to the bow of the boat. "Miss? Can I help you?"

She twisted agilely to look up at him, bone and muscle as fluid as a kitten's, and pushed a swathe of disordered hair back under her hood. She was pretty, very pretty. She was what, back home, was called dark-complected, though her skin looked more like thick cream than anything else. She had a short, fine nose and a wide mouth. Her eyes were gray, the light clean gray of new-burnt ashes. They were intelligent and alive and, at the moment, merry. She smiled and a dimple sank deeply in each cheek. "If you have a knife, sir," she said. "It's caught firm, and the stuff is too new to tear. It will have to be cut."

Bo inspected the crack and gave a tentative tug or two at the skirttail. "Be a pity to cut a nice dress, miss," he said.

He thought about it for a moment then looked up at the old man, who was watching with interest. "The skiff's not worth saving, sir," he said. "Wasn't but a hulk to begin with. If you'll give your leave I'll pry the crack open. But it'll sink her," he warned.

The old man made a wide gesture and said magniloquently, "Sink the old tub, sir, and I wish the man I bought her of might sink with her. He said she was trim and tight. She was neither and from the moment we embarked she has been a rogue. I shall be happy to see the last of her."

Bo grinned and from among the roustabouts crowded around he beckoned two. "Unload her," he said, "but be easy. She's already so full she'll overset without trying. Foss," he added, "fetch me a crowbar, will you?"

The girl was sitting on a low box, her feet in the slush, and she sat quietly as the hands shifted the little humpbacked trunk and the ruined and squashed carpetbags. She could have screamed or vapored and fainted, Bo thought. It was expected of women nowadays to faint easily and often, over the least thing. But she sat with her hands in her lap as still and composed as if she had been sitting comfortably in her own parlor. She was wet and she was surely cold and her feet were bound to be a misery to her, but she gave no sign of it. And she was caught tight if the boys overset the skiff. But she must know, Bo thought, he was standing right beside her so as to snatch her free if that happened. He knew what he would do. He'd rip her skirt loose at the waistband.

When the boys came to the battered old instrument cases the old man leaped forward and roared at them. "Handle those gently, men! My fiddle is priceless and Phoebe's guitar is very valuable. Take care! Give them over easily!"

As though they had been explosive the boys tendered them to the old man, then they hauled themselves aboard the *Rambler*. They drew away looking askance at the old man who set the instrument cases safely behind him.

Foss handed down the crowbar. Bo hefted it, then he told the girl quietly, "When I pry the crack open, your dress'll come free easy. You needn't to rush about it, or worry. There'll be time. She won't sink quick. She'll just settle down slow."

"I understand," the girl said.

Bo set the crowbar into the seam and pried. "Now," he said.

The girl tugged her dress free. Foss reached down a hand

and Bo gave her a hand up and she was quickly on the deck. "You want this box?" Bo asked.

"I doubt the flour and sugar it contains have increased in value by their soaking," the old man boomed. "Let it sink with the tub."

"There is meat," the girl told Bo, "and some real coffee that may not be too damaged."

Bo tossed the box aboard and hauled himself up. The water was bubbling and rising more rapidly than he'd told the girl to expect. The old skiff was settling quickly. All eyes watched, but without comment. The only sound was the hissing bubble of the water. Bo thought how the death of even an old rowboat was awesome to watch and how it gave you a shivery feeling of the frailty of even the solidest deck under your feet. All rivermen were always conscious of the thinness of the hull between them and the watery depths.

When the skiff disappeared, with a final suck, a large and mutual sigh was heaved by all watching, then Bo turned briskly to the old man. "My name is Bohannon Cartwright, sir, and this is my boat the *Rambler*, bound downriver. I'm sorry we ran you down but the rain was so thick I couldn't see you in time." He grinned and added, "Nothing more unlikely than a skiff out in this squall was to be expected."

The old man snorted. "Can't say we were expecting a steamboat to come bearing down on us, either."

"Well, sir, steamboats *do* run on rivers," Bo said mildly. "Would it be an impertinence to ask what you were doing rowing around in a flood and a rainstorm?"

The old man patted his goatee. "Should think it would be obvious. We were trying to escape the flood. The rainstorm was one of the improvidences of the Lord. It was even more unexpected than your boat." He drew himself up and flung his cape about him dramatically. "I am Sir Henry

Cole," he said, "the great Shakesperean actor, late of London and New York."

Bo bowed politely. He looked a little puzzled, however, and said, "The Green River country is a pretty long way from London and New York, sir."

"On a whim," the old man said, "I engaged to play in repertory. One has to keep one's finger on the pulse of the great public, you know." It was said a little grandly.

Bo stole a look at the girl. She was watching the old man affectionately but her mouth was twitching with a small smile. "Yes, sir," he said.

"Unfortunately," the old man continued, unfolding his arms and allowing his cape to fall, "the company made no money and the manager was a misbegotten ass. He closed the show three nights ago at a place called, I believe, Horse Branch. Upon my word, sir," he went on, a mischievous twinkle in his eyes, "you have a great plenty of horse towns in Kentucky! We played at Horse Cave, Horse Hill, Horse's Neck, until I began to wonder if propriety had deterred the people from conferring the opposite end of the animal upon some hapless community."

Bo laughed. "So far as I know, sir, there is no town called Horse's . . ." but he caught himself in time.

The girl's laugh rippled out then seemed to catch in her throat.

The old man continued, his voice touching lightly, almost gaily, on their misfortunes. "When the manager of the company decamped three nights ago, he left the entire company stranded, sir—without funds or means of transportation. Phoebe and I—this is my granddaughter, sir, Phoebe Cole, who travels with me and in a manner of speaking makes a home for us wherever we are—Phoebe and I made our way by one means or another to the river." The twinkle returned to the bushy-browed eyes. "I might add, also, sir, that the horses these villages so honor in these parts, are very indifferent creatures. Those which we could hire, at least, wore their honor dubiously." He waited for his laugh and got it before going on. "We meant, if possible, to take passage on a packet. But—only temporarily, you understand—we took refuge for a brief time in an abandoned house. Had it remained abandoned we should have fared very well but, alas, an unwelcome intruder paid us a visit." He waved grandly at the flooded field. "When the water had surrounded the house we were compelled to embark on this perilous journey. I bought that skiff of a farmer, and may his sons give him nothing but trouble. The man was a knave and cheated me of five dollars. She leaked almost as badly before you rammed us as afterward, sir."

"Yes, sir. Where were you headed, sir?"

The old man looked out over the water and for the first time he looked old. His face turned bleak and he shrank a little and the bombast left him. Even his voice lost its strength. "Any place. No place. To dry land. To shelter."

And for the first time Bo suspected the truth. The old man was a tent show ham, maybe a medicine show quack—with a fiddle and a guitar and a pretty granddaughter, if she really was his granddaughter, to help him with his act. Pity rose in him, and sympathy. It was a life of total uncertainty at best, and little more than that of a mendicant at worst. It was hard lines for a nice old gent, pretentions notwithstanding, to be stranded here on the river. He said firmly, "You may not have meant to shelter on a steamboat, Sir Henry, but it's where you've landed, and it's dry and you're welcome." He made a quick mental rearrangement of the cabin. There were four bunks and they were using only three. They could hang a blanket across one end for the girl. The old gentleman could have a bunk. Foss, he knew, would be scared to death to go into the cabin with a girl in it, so he would bed down in the engine room. It would serve until they could set their passengers off.

From the corner of his eye he saw the girl shiver. "Here," he said, "I'm not being very hospitable. Kept you standing while we talked. Miss Phoebe's cold and you're both wet. Tobe, bring the luggage up." He scattered the curious rousters with a word and steered Sir Henry and the girl toward the companionway. "Just up those stairs, sir, and straight ahead you'll find the cabin. Our quarters," he added, "are strictly for crew and they aren't fancy but you'll be out of the weather. Soon as Tobe brings your luggage I'll be up to make a place for Miss Phoebe so's she'll be to herself."

The old man's head bent, then lifted, and some of his pride and all of his eloquence returned. "We have fallen in good hands, Phoebe my girl. Sir, I accept your hospitality."

Bo thought, a little dryly, there wasn't much else he could do, but he gave no sign of his thinking.

Sir Henry mounted the stairs slowly, his fine old head high. Every eye watched him as he made his splendid exit. At the top of the stairs he swept his cape about him. "I would give all my fame for a pot of ale and safety. Come, Phoebe, we shall settle for safety."

The girl gave Bo a quick smile as she bent to gather up her wet skirts. Bo watched her go up lightly.

Foss nudged his elbow. "Bo—fog's rising. Gettin' thick as a featherbed. Where you thinkin' to tie up?"

Bo gave it his attention. "Little creek about a mile down —ought to do."

"Be like a blind man feelin' his way," Foss said unhappily.

"Let me do the feeling," Bo said. "You keep that piston from snapping clean off."

CHAPTER 6

THEY were tied up again.

With Foss hovering over the crippled piston, watching every stroke, yearning over it and hurting over it, as if he would empty his own body of its strength to guard it and help it, they had crept cautiously to the small creek where they were going to make their mooring. They reached it only a little before dark.

Bo, up in the pilothouse, unable to watch the machinery himself, had been, if possible, even more agonized than Foss by every slow foot of the way. The creaks, the groans, the clanks that came up from below had made him wince with real pain, for he couldn't make his jaws unclench and they got tight and achy; and he couldn't make his legs stand easy and they got bunched and knotted with charley horses. But they had to get the *Rambler* tied up in a safe place so he inched her along, asking as little as possible from the machinery.

He drew his first good deep breath when the boys finally

had the *Rambler* made fast, safely tied up. When he pulled in that first relieving breath there was real pain, for his chest felt as if it had been secured in a hawser bend.

He sagged at his chart table. He didn't know when in his life he had been so tired. Not ever, he thought. Not really ever had he felt as pulled and strung as he felt right now. He scratched a lucifer match and lit his small hanging lantern. By its light he wrote up his log. More willows, another little creek, another costly lay-up, he thought wearily, were becoming the whole log of the *Rambler*'s downbound run. He made his entry and banged the log book shut and stumbled down the companionway.

Now it was almost full dark and Tobe and a couple of the rousters were setting out the lanterns. The light wavered in shadows along the deck, only partially illuminating it. Little tongues of light licked over the mud band and the willows and made two great white sycamores look discarnate and wraithlike. Bo walked restlessly, testing the lines.

His boat was safe. That was the main thing. She was hurt, badly hurt, but she was a long way from being killed. All her hurts could be healed, given time and money. He could give her the time she needed, but he had no idea what he could substitute for money. Invention, likely. He and Foss would think of something. The *Rambler* was still all right; but it hurt him to think how his boat was hurt and his insides felt as wrenched as the machinery.

He didn't feel bitter—Sir Henry and Phoebe were not to blame—he didn't even feel uncharitable. He didn't reproach them in any way, nor did he trouble to reproach himself. You made a choice, basing it on all your wisdom accumulated from all your experience; but as a human being, if not a riverman, you always knew the unpredictable could occur. There were always some things outside your control. There could never be a real and true certainty about anything. What you did was the best you could, at the time and the place, with what you had. No use, either, looking back over your shoulder and wishing and regretting. In this time and in this place, given all the circumstances, he had taken a calculated risk which would have worked except for the unpredictable. You couldn't foresee a sudden rain squall to blind you, nor could you foresee a skiff paddling about in flood waters. What you had, then, was a good try which had ended in near disaster but not, thank God, in total disaster.

Though he was so exhausted his legs felt as if heavy weights were hung on them, he continued to walk the deck for a long time. Tomorrow he and Foss would take down the machinery, piece by piece by piece, patiently and painstakingly, and tomorrow they would see what could be done. He didn't know yet what it would be; and there was no use speculating until they knew the last inch of weakness. They would do something, however. They had to.

No one joined him as he paced. The roustabouts had settled around a lantern on the stern. It was none of their worry. Foss was drawing the fires. Bo hadn't seen Sir Henry or his granddaughter since he made them as comfortable as possible in the cabin. They were asleep, he supposed. Having innocently and blamelessly contributed to his crisis, they could still with good conscience rest and he was generous enough to hope they rested well.

There was a light in the galley. Tobe must be cooking supper, he thought, and swung toward the light, knowing suddenly precisely what he wanted and needed most. He wanted hot coffee, a big mug of it, and he wanted it scalding hot, as hot as hell and as black as night. When he had warmed his kinked insides with enough of it, he wanted to sleep. He wanted to sleep long and sound and dreamlessly, all night. He thought he would. Then tomorrow could come.

He stopped at the threshold of the galley. Phoebe Cole, not Tobe, was tending a stove full of pots and pans, bending over them, stirring and peering. The heat had flushed her face a little and brought a damp shine of perspiration to her forehead. She looked busy and competent and happy. She was humming to herself, probably not even knowing she was, Bo thought. His mother did it, when she was feeling especially contented. When he was small, sometimes he would ask her, "What are you humming, Mama?" Nine times out of ten she would answer, "Didn't know I was." If she was feeling especially cheerful she might go on to say, "Just feeling good, maybe."

The girl had changed her clothing. All the black wet shrouding and hooding and shawling which had hidden all of her but her face was gone. She had put on a dark red dress that buttoned primly up to her throat but was softened there with a small white ruffle. The narrow ruffle stood up around the base of her neck like a little frame. The sleeves of the dress were long but she had pushed them to the elbow. Over the dress she was wearing a big apron. It covered the whole front of her dress with its high bib and long skirt and it tied in the back with an audacious big bow. Once the apron had been a bright print but it was now faded until the colors had melted and flowed and softened. She had made a lot of use of it, Bo thought, for a long time.

Her hair, which had been a black wet swathe under her hood when he had last seen her, was dry, or nearly dry, now, and she had pinned it up on top her head. He was surprised that it should be so springily curly and that its color should be so much lighter. It was a pretty wren-brown, the prettiest

brown you could find, warmed by a little red to give it a sunburned look.

She settled a lid on a pot and stooped to look in the oven.
When she straightened she saw him. "I found potatoes and
meat and apples," she said. She moved one of the pots a little. "And there's a huge lot of greens that seem to have been
cooked today. There's butter and coffee and I made bread.
But I wish I had a nutmeg." She frowned slightly. "For the
apples," she explained. "Nutmeg does improve fried apples
so much."

Bo stepped over the threshold. "I don't suppose we have
any. Cooking on the *Rambler* don't run to much fanciness."

"It's no matter," she said quickly. "There is sugar for
them. And I used a smidgin of your butter."

He took down a cup from the shelf. "I'd like some coffee,
please."

"Of course." She poured it for him. His tiredness even
ran down into his hands and the cup was unsteady. She
looked up at him. "You're very tired, aren't you?"

"Some," he admitted. He took the cup to the table and
set it down carefully. He eased his body into a chair.

The galley was warm and full of good cooking smells and
somehow it looked tidier than usual. He guessed that whether
she had meant to or not, being a woman she had instinctively
set things more nearly to rights. "I want my things handy to
reach," he had heard his mother say often, "and I want them
in right order." She hadn't ever liked for someone to leave
the salt out of place, or the pepper, or the saleratus, or the
sugar. There was a place for each thing and she wanted it
kept there. There was, also, a special utensil for each purpose—big spoons and knives and certain pots and pans and
skillets. She wanted them kept where they belonged and the
wench who laid them out of pocket was in for a hard time.

Most women, he guessed, having no intimate knowledge of them except through his mother, felt the same in their kitchens and he judged if a woman didn't cook but one meal in a kitchen it would be hers for that length of time and she would order it to her own ways and it would show. He couldn't tell in what way she had neatened the galley, but it looked different and it felt different, cheerfuler and brighter and more ordered; but that, he had wit enough to know, was to some extent at least because there was a woman in it.

When he had swallowed down half the cup of scalding coffee and its good heat had begun to spread through him, he said, "You don't need to be doing this. Where's Tobe? It's his job, this run."

"Mr. Foss needed him." She peered in the oven again and swung around looking pleased. "Biscuits," she said. "They're rising just fine. I was afraid they might not." There was a little flour on one arm and she brushed at it. "I like to cook," she said. "I like to keep busy."

Bo nodded. "Hardest thing in the world to do is nothing. Even piddling made-work is better'n that. Just to sit, idle, can vex you beyond bearing."

She took the tail of her apron to wipe off the last of the flour. "It just does," she agreed, "it just tires you more than anything. I like it when we are in one place long enough for me to keep house." She laughed, smoothing the apron down again. "Grandfather calls it 'playing house,' but he likes my cooking and I don't know what he'd do if I didn't mend and wash and iron sometimes."

She was awfully pretty in the dark red dress, her face all flushed up from the heat and her hair all curled up around it. And she was such a little thing. He hadn't thought she was so little. Real little-boned, but fleshed out nice and round and plump. She wasn't any bony, chicken-picked, scrawny girl. Her arms were pretty and round and smooth and the red dress was filled out pleasingly. He never had liked a skinny girl. You never could feel like you had hold of much.

"Is your grandfather all right?" he asked.

"Still asleep," she said. "I thought I wouldn't wake him."

"No. Likely he needs sleep more than he needs food. Hope the wetting and the scare didn't hurt him."

"I wouldn't let it," she shook her head vigorously. "I know just what he needs. I made him change straight off. We had some tea in our stores," she confessed, "and I came down and made him a pot. Hot tea, dry clothing, a good bed—he went to sleep like a baby."

"Won't even have a sniffle, I'll wager."

"If he does, it'll surprise me. Your cup's empty." She poured it full again.

Bo sipped thoughtfully. "What was all that rigamarole he was spouting off in the skiff?"

Her laugh was nice. It sort of rippled out, chuckly-like. When she laughed her shoulders shook a little. It was nice seeing her laugh. She looked as if she enjoyed it.

Most of the girls he had been around acted as if they would break in two if they laughed out loud, and he had been around a plenty of them on the packets. They had been more of a plague to him than anything else for he had known it wasn't himself they had an eye for. There was just something about a river pilot that made girls look twice at him. Especially if he was young and if they learned he wasn't married.

He never had believed Foss's story that one girl had ridden the *Fanny Bullitt* every week with her father just so she could see him. There had been one who did, sure, but her father was well-off and had business in Cincinnati and Louisville both. It was a natural thing for him to bring her along if she wanted to come. Foss had it that for three months she was as moonstruck as a calf and that when he had been as polite as he knew how to be but that was all, she had finally given up. Foss swore she walked down the stage the last trip she made with tears swimming in her eyes. Even if it had been true, there was nothing he could do about it. He hadn't ever had girls much on his mind—just boats.

Phoebe was still laughing. "That was about the worst misquoted Shakespeare you'd be likely to hear, mixed in with a little bit of the Book of Common Prayer and at least one line from Milton."

Bo blinked. There was a set of Shakespeare on a shelf at home. It had been his grandfather's. His father said the old man had set great store by the books and read them a lot. Bo's father hadn't and admitted it and Bo himself had found them tedious. Milton he had never heard of and his folks, being Baptists, had no use for the Book of Common Prayer.

The old gentleman, then, was really educated. Maybe, too, he *had* played London and New York, once upon a time. Maybe, once, he had been pretty good; but one thing was sure—nobody who could get an acting job in a big city would be playing Horse Branch, Kentucky. It was strictly a tent-show town. If he had ever been any good, Sir Henry had fallen on evil times now.

The girl was reaching down a stack of ironstone plates. "How many places do I set in here?"

"Four, if your grandfather's not coming down. Foss, Luke Pierce, you and me. Tobe'll take the rousters' supper to them." He moved a little so she could lay the plates around.

Without thinking how it might sound, because she was so friendly and nice, and the galley was warm and like the kitchen at home and she was stepping around light and easy, he said, "Is he really a sir, or a lord, or whatever you call it?"

The moment it was out he thought he shouldn't have said it. It sounded pretty nosy and she might get huffy about it.

Instead she laughed again. She had the old rusted knives and forks in her hand now. "That's his stage name," she said. "In show business you have to have a stage name." She set the knives and forks precisely. "His name really *is* Henry Cole. All he did for a stage name was tack the 'Sir' onto it."

She reached across to set a fork straighter and a stir of small smells was raised—a nice, girl-body smell, cooking smells, starched-clothes smell, all of them agreeable and pleasant. She stepped back and looked in the oven again. She frowned. "Seems to me they ought to be browning by now." She tested the heat with her hand. "It's not very hot in the oven."

Bo walked over and studied the draft arrangements, turning finally a damper handle. "I think you have to shut off the draft—heat all goes up the pipe if you don't."

"Oh, pshaw!" She looked vexed with herself. "I know that. How could I have forgotten?"

"No great harm done." He took his seat again. "Your grandfather been an actor all his life?"

"All his life." In the friendliest kind of way she went on. "And so was my father. My father was Grandfather's only child. He was raised in show business and I don't suppose he could have helped being an actor. Grandfather and Grandmother were both show people."

"In New York?"

"Not very often," she confessed, but cheerfully and not sorry—not sorry for the fact or for the confession. "Tent shows, mostly, and all over." She made a wide, sweeping gesture. "Everywhere. Anywhere. Showboats, too—sometimes.

Any kind of a show, any kind of a job." Her face lit up. "It's a wonderful way to live. The nicest people in the world and the most *fun!* And always different and new and not ever dull. You move on before it gets dull."

"Like the river," he said. "Never two runs alike on the river, or any two pieces of water any two times alike. Always something different. Always moving on."

"Oh, I know, I know!" Her face was almost radiant. "When we've been on showboats . . . you know . . ." she stopped to study, one finger slipping to the corner of her mouth, ". . . you know, I like showboats best of all. It's the best kind of show business. The boat—and the big paddle wheels, and the steam calliope and the band and the parades, and just sort of sliding up and down all the rivers . . ." she made slides with her hands, ". . . and the audiences on showboats are the best kind. Sometimes you get mean ones," she confided, "with a tent show, but you hardly ever do on a showboat." She thought a moment. "Grandfather says river towns always have the nicest people. He says something about the river makes them different— easier to laugh and to get to know, friendlier, easier to please. He says people who are landlocked get things locked inside themselves. He says anybody who can look out and see a river flowing by, or the sea stretching away, can let loose of his bothers." With her hands she turned loose and let bothers go. Her whole body turned loose and let bothers go, easily, simply. "But, of course," she continued with some vehemence, "that doesn't mean the tide won't bring more! You've got to expect that. But it'll carry them right away again." She smiled sparklingly. "Isn't that a nice thing to believe?"

"The best," he said, smiling back at her, "the very best. I believe it myself."

The apples frying in the big iron skillet sizzled and Phoebe spun around, grabbing up a spoon. "Mercy! I hope they've not scorched!" She sniffed and stirred anxiously, then tested with a small sip. He saw her slight, squared shoulders relax. "No. But what a fright! They only need more water." She added it and put down the spoon.

She was the most natural girl, Bo thought, the most unaffected, in this day of so much affectation in girls, he had ever met with. Everything she did, she did perfectly naturally, as though she had never been rebuffed in her life or ever expected to be. She was all outgoing friendliness, expecting to get nothing but friendliness back; and her face and her body talked as much for her as her voice. She made them accent her words for her and illustrate what she meant. She was as refreshing as a drink of cold water on a hot day.

"Sometimes," she said, her soft, smally roughed voice becoming confidential, "I wish we could work on showboats all the time."

"Can't you?"

"No." She shook her head, making the springy, sunburned curls fling about. "Not any more. The war has made a lot of them quit running. And then Grandfather isn't well sometimes. Sometimes he forgets." She said it simply and without apology, or even, with what might have been more expected, regret. It was a fact and it was as if she had looked at it, this inevitable thing which age did to you, measured it and accepted it and come to blameless terms with it.

"Do you act, too?" Bo asked. It would explain the way she used her hands and her body and her face and voice.

"Goodness, no!" She derided the idea. "I do little bits with the guitar when Grandfather fiddles, but that's all."

"You could," Bo said. "I'm sure of it."

"No." She cleared her throat and her voice was quite firm.

She was having no part of such nonsense. "*Grandfather* is the show."

"I just thought, maybe, growing up in show business and all, you might . . ."

"But I didn't grow up in show business," she said, surprise sending her voice up a tone. "Gracious, no! I've only been with Grandfather two years. Just since my father died."

"Well—you said your father acted, too."

"So he did. But, you see, my mother wasn't show people. And she didn't like show business, so we didn't travel with my father. And then she just sort of got tired of being left behind all the time and just sort of . . ." she made a limp and waving motion, ". . . drifted away."

She let the fact hang a moment for emphasis before she stooped for a stick of wood and shoved it in the firebox. When she faced around she was smiling again. "My father put me in school, then. But when he died there wasn't any money for the school so Grandfather said we were all the family there was now and we'd just by Caesar's ghost *be* a family!" She beamed at him, commanding his admiration. "And I've been with Grandfather ever since and I never loved anything so much! I love *Grandfather* so much. He makes everything we do so *wonderful!*"

And you make everything pretty wonderful for Grandfather, too, Bo thought. She was like one of those little warmers people took to church with them, which glowed steadily and gave out warmth and pleasantness and comfort. She made him forget he was tired and made him forget for a little while his crippled machinery and tomorrow's sorry job.

She took two big pans of biscuits out of the oven and nodded at them happily. "Didn't they come out nice? You turned the damper just right. You can tell the others to come to the table now. Time they get here I'll have supper dished up."

At the door Bo turned. "Miss Phoebe, aren't you pretty young to be making a home for your grandfather?" He meant only to tease her a little because she was so obviously not too young.

She took him seriously, however. "Indeed I am not! Why, day after tomorrow I'll be sixteen!"

"My," he said, laughing, "that's getting on in years, isn't it?"

She laughed, but surprisingly sobered immediately. "For a girl, it is. It *really* is."

"Oh, come now."

"It's *almost* being an old maid."

Bo started to laugh again, thinking now she was teasing, paying him back, maybe coquetting a little the way girls did, saying how old they were, wanting you to say back they certainly didn't look it, and then say on how beautiful they were, while they fluttered their eyelashes at you and pretended they didn't believe you. He caught the laugh back in time. She wasn't teasing at all. She was perfectly in earnest. He swallowed. "How old *is* being an old maid?"

"I don't really know. But I'm almost sure it's more than sixteen."

"I'm certain of it. It's bound to be more than sixteen." He had a sort of inspiration. "A man has to be twenty-one before he's of age—legally, that is. Or can vote. Maybe that would be it for a girl?"

She puzzled over it, then her laugh rippled out again. "I won't have to worry about it for a long time, will I?"

He went away chuckling and thinking: Miss Phoebe Cole, you won't ever have to worry about it. When you're ready, when the glitter has worn off show life and your grandfather is not the only man who is wonderful, there will be a line of men you can't find your way through, just waiting for you to pick.

She was such a woman in most of her ways, so able and clever and deft, it had surprised him to see a little girl peep forth. Something had kept her awfully nice and fresh and sweet and sort of clean, like a new linen shirt all spanking white and fresh from soap and water. She made him think of soap and water and scrubbed things and young, innocent things such as puppies and kittens and colts—and good, healthy things.

He began whistling, wondering if the old man would be wanting to go all the downbound run with them, and more than a little hoping he would. Things balanced out, he thought. If he had to run down a skiff, not the least of its compensations was that it had held Miss Phoebe Cole and her grandfather.

CHAPTER 7

THE unmelodious dissonance of fifty blatting sheep, all of them hungry and petulant, wakened Bo. He groaned as he rolled over, trying to pry his eyes open. The fool beasts would waken the dead, he thought. Something had to be done about them and done right away.

He hoisted his legs onto the floor and blinked as the new position brought him into a shaft of sunlight. Normally he wakened early, all at once, eager for the day, but he still felt sore and tired this morning and his mind was slow. For a moment or two he couldn't take in the reason for the curtain around one bunk. When he remembered he jumped for his pants and hauled them up in a hurry. Luke's bunk was empty, he saw, and so was Sir Henry's. Phoebe, he guessed, because of the drawn curtain, was still sleeping. Not for long though, he thought, stuffing his shirt in, if that noise kept up below.

He charged down to the main deck instinctively noting as he pounded down that the river had fallen rapidly overnight. Three foot, he made it. It had been a good tide for the time of year, but as with most fall tides, with nothing upriver to feed on, it was quick to run off. All right—that was fine. By the time the machinery was mended the locks could operate again and they could get on downriver.

The noise on the deck was clamorous and bawling and peculiarly irritating because of its flatness. Wrinkling his nose against the rank odor of crowded sheep Bo didn't know which made the most unholy noise, a jackass braying, a cow bawling, or a sheep blatting. Right now he would have traded the sheep for a cargo of either of the others just to find out. None of them made music, that was certain; but he didn't think jacks and cows went into an epidemic of herd protest so easily.

He went in search of Luke but he found Tobe instead, with the rousters, having their breakfast. "You've stirred early," he said.

"Yassuh," Tobe said. "With the privilege of long acquaintance and easy familiarity he added, "You ain't, Capt'n."

"I know it. Overslept myself a good hour. Whyn't somebody call me?"

"Miss Phoebe, she say leave you sleep. Say you done woah yo'seff out. Say you needs yo' rest." Tobe's grin was sly.

"She up?" He was immediately suspicious. "You didn't let her cook breakfast, did you? Now, look here, Tobe, last night there was some reason for it, but today—"

Tobe butted in. "She ain't ask kin she, or hab no argifyin' wid me 'bout it. I tell her it my job dis run. Mek no diff'runce. She say git out. Say she do de cookin' long as she on dis yere boat. Say she doan want nobody messin' wid her. I ain't habbin' words wid dat young miss, Capt'n Bo. She real strong-minded. She know whut she want."

"Humph."

"No humph 'bout it, Capt'n Bo. She jus' put me outen de galley."

"And had no trouble doing it, I'll wager."

"No suh. Ain't habbin' no words wid her." Tobe's grin widened. "She sho' kin cook good, Capt'n Bo. Cook a lot better'n me."

"That's the beautiful truth," Bo said, "but I don't know . . ." He wheeled about. "Well, make the most of it while you can. Likely her grandfather'll want to be set off at Rochester. Where's Luke?"

"In de engine room. Him an' Mist' Foss commencin' tek down de rod."

"I'm going to send Luke to find a pasture for them sheep, Tobe. We're going to be laid up here a spell and they got to browse. Don't wish for 'em to go down if I can help it. When he finds a place for 'em, you help him get 'em there, hear?"

"Yassuh. Be a good thing. Been studyin' dey ain't gwine be pacified wid water much longer."

"They sure as hell aren't," Bo admitted, wincing as a new and more discordant height of protest was reached. "Wouldn't nobody on the boat be left in their right senses besides. Listening to that would drive you crazy."

He clipped on down the deck to the engine room where the noise was just as loud but different. Foss was pounding on a stubborn bolt with a hammer while Luke turned the chisel for him. Bo had to lay hands on them to get their attention. "Quit a minute," he bellowed. The silence that followed was almost as deafening as the anvil-clanking had been. "You eat yet, Luke?"

The boy's head went up and down. "Hour ago. She," pointing his nose in the general direction of the galley, "has done fed ever'body." He began laughing. "That old codger, Bo. Has he got a screw loose in his head? You know what he done all through while we was eating? Kept spouting off about the morning—about taking the wings of the morning or something, and something else about the uttermost sea, and then how the morn was in a russet mantle clad. What's a russet mantle, Bo?"

Foss spoke up sourly. "The next thing to a sucklin' pig and a Triton's minnow, that's what the russet morn is." He growled on. "He's got more'n one screw loose, you ask me —he's got a whole head full of 'em rattlin' 'round. He ain't hardly safe."

"Pay him no mind," Bo said, winking at Luke, "the old man's no more dangerous than Foss here. He's just an actor. He throws words around the way Foss throws nuts and bolts and screws. Now, you get in the way of one of Foss's nuts or bolts or screws and you'll likely get hurt, but I never heard of words breaking any bones."

Going along, Luke said, "Nor me."

Foss brought the hammer down against the stubborn bolt with a deafening clang. When the ring had died away he was still rumbling, though wordlessly now, in his throat.

Bo flicked a scale of rust off the front of his shirt. "Good paying lick there, Foss," he said. "I figure you loosened half a teaspoonful of rust. Might be," he went on, "a little edifying if you'd listen to that old man. He makes more sense than you'd think."

"When he says something edifyin'," Foss said brittlely, "I'll listen. Till then I aim to keep away from him if I can and if I can't what he says I aim to let run in one ear and out the other and just hope none of it gets clogged up between. I a little doubt I'd enjoy bein' addled by it."

Bo whooped and Luke joined in. When they had had their good laugh out Bo told the boy what he wanted him to do. "We'll pay hard money, Luke, you can say. For a good pasture. But make sure the fencing is good. Don't want them sheep scattering."

"Sure don't," Luke agreed and went off whistling.

"One thing I do like about Luke," Bo said, watching him make his way down the deck, "is that it don't matter the job, he does it cheerful."

Foss picked up the chisel and held it against the bolt. "Meanin' I don't? Well, Luke just ain't old enough yet to know better."

"That's what makes you so sour this morning? Age working on you?"

"It don't add no sweetenin'. Nor it don't help you layin' in bed half the day, nor her not lettin' you be called. Whyn't you go eat you somethin' and git back here to help me. Or is it yore intentions to let me do it by myself?"

Foss was having himself a real grouchy time this morning. He never had been one to feel easy with strangers and around women he went into hiding if he could find a hole. Sir Henry and Miss Phoebe Cole had got his hackles up considerably. They were not only strangers, they were a completely strange breed of people, an untrustworthy breed in Foss's eyes— show people. If they had come from another planet they wouldn't have been more alien to Foss. Bo pondered it and wondered if it would be any surprise to Foss to know that most dry-landers put river people in the same queer, strange category—and it made no difference what their occupation on the river—steamboatmen, pushers, shantyboat folks, lock tenders, rousters, all. River people made no sense to dry-landers—rough and shiftless they thought them, always on the move, never settling one place, never accumulating much, just drifting with the tides, sliding in and out like the rats that slid in and out around the wharfs. He wondered if Foss knew one term given to all of them was river rats. Well.

It wasn't to worry. Give Foss time and he got used to anything.

Although they had studied the cracked rod for hours the night before and had come at least tentatively to a decision about what to do, Bo examined it closely again now. The crack was crosswise, against the grain of the arm, running at an angle from the middle of the rod to its upper rim. You could lay your little finger in the split along the upper edge. "Still think putting a plate on will work?" he asked.

Foss brooded over the split and ran his tumb down it. Bo knew that feeling of that spreading crack in his beloved rod was like feeling a crack in his own skin—it was worse; he wouldn't have felt or minded a crack in his own skin half so much. "I think a plate'll hold her," he said slowly. "I think it will. Plate it, say, six inches either end the crack and bolt it on good and tight. I think it will. But," he roused himself and said with vigor, "you ain't gonna jump no more dams with it, nor you ain't gonna creen her in no more wind squalls, and you sure as hell better not run down no more skiffs with her. She'll kick the shaft clean through the hull, you do. And you better send off a telegraph soon's we git to Rochester so's we'll have a new rod done started to Evansville. I *think* a plate'll hold till we git down to Evansville, but the only way it'll hold is if you take it slow and easy."

Bo nodded. Most of Foss's grouchiness and snappishness about the old codger, he guessed, was his hurt over his machinery. He wished he could get that shining new machinery Foss wanted so bad. Wished he could get it for him today. "All right, Foss," he said. "I don't want to hurt the boat any more than you do, you know that. But I don't want to get caught upriver and have to sit this war out, either. I want us to stay running. We *got* to stay running. We got to run

on whatever piece of the river we can run on and we got to
carry freight and we got to keep the *Rambler* in our own
hands to do it. We got to stay running." He meant to keep
his voice down, meant to stay reasonable, knowing how
troubled Foss was, but he found it rising in spite of his intentions, his own urgency working on him. Foss had to understand. There was the machinery, sure, but there was the
river and the *Rambler* and the war and a mortgage and the
deep need to be free to run. So near his goal. He was so near
it. He so nearly had the *Rambler* paid off. He had hurt his
boat, sure, but he did still have her.

Toward the last, when his voice rose and there was a little
shake, Foss looked up at him and kept his eyes fixed on him
until he had finished and then kept them on him, considering
him, for a long moment when he had done. Suddenly the
whole incident seemed to put him a good humor. The ten-
sion, the almost unbearable tremor in Bo's voice, the risen
tone, reached him and brought him back where he belonged
—right alongside Bo Cartwright again. His leather-smooth
face crinkled into a grin. He clanked his hammer down
against the chisel. "Go eat you some breakfast, boy. We'll
stay runnin'. Ain't nothin' wrong with this machinery I can't
fix. We'll stay runnin'."

Bo went to eat. Phoebe Cole served him. He didn't want
any talk with her this morning. Studying the rod again, talking with Foss, had put too much on his mind. He couldn't
bring it back for woman talk and the girl didn't push him.
After a pleasant greeting, a searching look, a question about
what he'd like to eat, she held her tongue. He didn't notice
what she put in front of him. It was food and he ate it, his
mind running on down the hours immediately ahead and the
job that had to be done. Strap iron. He had to get a piece of
strap iron. They'd get it hot then and flatten it and then

they'd rivet it in place. He was seeing his problems one at a time, ticking them off, putting them in their place and he wolfed down his food and strode out of the galley as unnoticing as if Tobe had served him the meal.

The sheep were still blatting. He couldn't make a rouster hear him over their noise so he went bolting down the deck to order the small boat—a skiff like the one Sir Henry and his granddaughter had been rowing about in yesterday, although in much better condition—put out. While the hands set swiftly to work he went to tell Foss he would be away an hour or two. "Going back upriver to the village," he said. "Ought to be a blacksmith there would have some strap iron. Taking Jonah and Catfish."

Foss troubled only to nod he had heard. He had Tobe turning the chisel for him now. One stubborn bolt was out and they were working on the next one. Foss wasn't wasting time on words.

When Bo wheeled about he very nearly stepped on Miss Phoebe. He choked back an oath angrily. "Miss Phoebe, this is the engine room. You can have the run of the boat except for this place. Please stay away from here."

"I will," she nodded, "I understand." She wasn't in the least embarrassed, put out or confounded by his impatience. She pleasantly assented to his request, then asked, "May I go to the village with you, Captain?"

He made a restless movement with his shoulders, half a shrug, half a bunching of the muscles, both an irritable rejection. "No, ma'am. I'm in a hurry. I've got no time for dallying."

He walked on down the deck. Phoebe clutched her front skirts and followed, having to skip a little now and then, like a child, to keep up. "If I promise not to delay you, may I go?"

"No. I'll have to wait while you find your shawl. Then you'll have to find your reticule. And when I've finished my business in the village I'll have to send a boy to find *you*. You'll be out of pocket." He flung the words back as he strode along.

The girl said no more but she did not lag behind. When they came up to the skiff she was still beside him. He stepped into the skiff, but he could hardly avoid looking up at her then. She didn't say a word. She showed him she was fully ready to leave by drawing her shawl about her shoulders and by solemnly holding up her reticule for him to see. For a long moment their eyes held. Then she spoke. "I promise I will be waiting in the skiff when you have finished your business. You will not have to send for me."

He capitulated with a laugh. "All right, then. You're not like any other girl I ever knew—or woman, either, for that matter."

"I should hope not," she said, giving him her hand to be assisted into the skiff, "I wouldn't like to be like anyone else."

"I didn't mean to be offensive," he said, handing her down into the stern, "but I've had some experience waiting for my mother and sisters."

"Curtain time has taught me promptness, I expect," she told him amiably, settling her skirts.

She made no small talk on the journey upriver. There was an entire boat length between them, for Bo was in the bow while she sat, a straight, composed little figure, in the stern. Although the distance between them was no real deterrent she seemed entirely content to sit quietly and watch the banks glide slowly past.

Bo was grateful, this time, for her silence. It put no burden on him. Chatter right now in fact would, he felt, have driven him wild. He didn't know whether she sensed it and fitted accordingly into his need of quiet, or whether she simply had the most unusual gift in a woman of silence herself when she had nothing to say. She had been full enough of chatter last night. But today, when proper behavior for a young lady would have required her to converse pleasantly, she held her tongue. She was either old beyond her years or very wise in the ways of men. Without ever being improper, she seemed to have no concern whatever for conforming to what he had learned was expected of social young ladies.

At the village landing Bo handed her out.

"Will the skiff remain in this place?" she asked.

"Yes. For an hour. Maybe longer. May take me longer than that, but at least for an hour."

"Thank you."

With no explanation of her business in the village she trudged off up the bank. Bo couldn't help wondering what the business was. But he shrugged it off and went his own way. Some small purchase likely. Some woman's need.

She was waiting, precisely as she had promised, when he returned to the skiff at the end of an hour and a half with his piece of strap iron. One glance told him she had no bundles or parcels. Whatever she had bought was small enough to be held in her reticule. More cheerful now, in a better humor since he had found the iron for his plate, he felt apologetic for his roughness with her. His troubles weren't hers, after all. "Kept you waiting, didn't I?" he offered in peace.

"I had finished," she said. She lifted a small volume that had been hidden in her lap. "I have been improving my mind," she added, rather primly. "Grandfather says my mind is woefully uninformed. He says read when you have idle time. It's never wasted."

"I wouldn't know," Bo said lightly. "I can't remember ever having any idle time."

Her eyebrows arched. "Not even when you waited for your mother and sisters?"

He made a surrendering gesture, chuckling at how she had got home to him. "Usually paced the floor then and cussed."

He stowed the piece of iron amidships and she tucked her small book into her reticule. Jonah and Catfish took up their oars, Bo cast off, and they caught the tide downriver.

When they reached the *Rambler* and were aboard again, Phoebe looked reflectively upriver the way they had come. "There is a road to that village, isn't there?"

"There is," Bo said, pointing. "Goes up from the ferry right up there."

"I thought so," she nodded. "How far would you say it is?"

"From here to the village by road? Four or five miles." He felt like teasing her a little to pay her back. "Aiming to walk it next time?"

"Probably late this afternoon," she replied coolly. "I have arranged for Grandfather and me to do a show there tonight."

He was caught totally off guard and could only echo, "A show?"

"A show, Captain. It's our business to do shows for people."

"Is that what you went to the village for?"

"Yes, sir. I arranged to have some of our handbills put up and I found a hall. I believe it's a lodge hall but it will serve. We can't do a play, naturally—the two of us. But we can manage. Grandfather can play his fiddle and I can sing a few songs and Grandfather can do a dramatic reading or two. We can give them their money's worth." She added candidly, "And we need their money, Captain. My purse is flat."

Bo studied her. "If you aren't the beatin'est. Sir Henry know about this?"

Her eyes flashed at him. "Of course he knows. Do you think I order my grandfather about?"

"No, ma'am," he denied hastily, "no *ma'am!*" He roused himself. "But you don't have to walk to the village, Miss Phoebe. When you're ready to go tell Jonah here and he and Catfish will row you up. Then they can wait till your show's over and bring you back to the boat."

She responded warmly, without backing and filling, "How kind of you! I wasn't hinting, Captain. Really, I wasn't. We could have walked."

"You could, sure. No need of it, is all. Jonah, hear me? When Miss Phoebe and Sir Henry are ready to go, see to it they get to the landing. Wait for 'em there till their show is over. Bring 'em back."

Phoebe was eying Jonah and Catfish reflectively. Her finger went to the corner of her mouth. Suddenly she said, her warm laugh chuckling up, "Would you boys like to be in the show? You can jig, can't you? Do a hoedown? Buck and wing?"

Both Negroes showed their teeth whitely and pulled at their forelocks. "Sho' kin, miss, sho' kin," Catfish said.

"Catfish dere," Jonah said, "de best hoedownder on de river. Kin open his mouf an' sing, too."

Catfish backed and scraped with pride, but hung his head modestly. "Jonah, he play de mouf organ, miss."

"Wonderful! Wonderful. Do you mind, Captain? They'll make the show so much more colorful. They'll make it a real show."

"Help yourself," Bo said, "they just as well earn their way somehow." His mind practical, he turned to the rousters. "You boys got anything to wear?"

"Oh, that trunk of ours is full of costumes," Phoebe said quickly. "I'll rummage up something for them. Something gay and bright. I must tell Grandfather. He'll be so pleased." She wheeled about, then paused. "You know, I think we'll attempt a small minstrel show. Like Dan Emmett."

Bo had never heard of a minstrel show or of Dan Emmett but when Miss Phoebe Cole had run lightly up the companionway he hefted his piece of strap iron and headed for the engine room with the thought in his mind that whatever a minstrel show was if Miss Phoebe put it on it would be a sight to see—a real fine sight to see. He had one more thought, then, and swiveled around to shout at the black boys, "You, Jonah! Catfish! Keep it fit for a lady, hear me?"

"Yassuh, yassuh. Keep it pure as de driven snow."

"I'll skin you, you don't."

He didn't know when the skiff left in the late afternoon. He and Foss and Luke and Tobe were buried in the engine room. All day they had been intent on the job—heating and shaping the plate, putting the bolt holes in, making their screws to fit, and finally, long after dark, pinning the plate over the crack. They had eight hands that worked like one pair, Foss directing, with no lost motion or time. He knew exactly what he wanted, exactly when and where he wanted it. He yelled once or twice at Tobe who maybe let the fire go down a little, but mostly they worked without talk except the grunts and the monosyllables which served for questions and answers.

When the plate was on, they stopped and knew for the first time they were tired. And hungry. "Let's eat 'fore we set it in," Foss said. "Reckon what time it is?"

Bo pulled out his turnip watch. "Nine o'clock. We had a long day, looks like."

"And got as long a night," Foss rumbled.

Bo looked at them. Foss and Luke were nearly as black as Tobe and Luke's eyes were as red-rimmed from fatigue as from the fire. They were blinking and watering and he was swaying on his feet. Tobe's jaw hung slackly and he looked gray around the mouth. Bo knew he himself could call up the reserve that was needed to set the rod in that night, but it would be a cruelly driving thing for Luke and Tobe. If Foss was tired he didn't show it, but he never did show weariness when working on his machinery. He could hang on longer than any man Bo had ever seen, hang on and keep going when everybody else dropped out. When the job was done, then Foss was done and he dropped like a felled ox for at least eight hours, replenishing his sleep-famished body and his marrow-weary bones. He hadn't reached that place yet. His rod wasn't set in. But Bo said slowly, "We'll sleep tonight. We'll set her in first thing in the morning."

Foss batted his lids two or three times. "Ain't gonna set her in now?"

"Nope. Ain't that much hurry."

A sigh as vast and gusty as one of Foss's best ones blew out Luke's lips. "I've not ever heard no better news! Christamighty, but I'm wore out." He sat down on an upended crate suddenly. "I don't know if my feet or my back hurts worst."

Tobe, going in the night and as dark as the night, spoke floatingly, "I ain't even hongry. I gonna hit a sack ob freight dis minnit."

They laughed at him, quietly and comfortably, the good feeling of a job well done spreading warmly through them. Foss handed out rags, only a little less oily than those they'd been using all day, and they wiped up faces, hands and arms. Weariness made them slow but since they weren't going to work any more that night, were instead going to sleep, they took the slowness as luxury and lingered and smeared and wiped and stretched the kinks out of their backs and rubbed their arm muscles and yawned and flexed their hands and Foss sighed half a dozen times. It was a good-feeling time.

They heard, without mentioning it, the falling water lapping at the boat and swayed tiredly, each mind registering it as falling, as quiet and slack. They swayed easily and comfortably with the drift and swing of the boat against the lines, and they made no conversation until they had finished. Then Bo said, "We're clean as we're gonna be. Let's see what's to eat." He took up the lit lantern and led the way to the galley.

"Won't be no supper like last night," Luke mourned. "Miss Phoebe's not here to fix it."

"I've not lost my touch mixin' up a bannock," Foss said, "or for fryin' out a piece of meat. We'll eat."

In the galley, Bo swung the lantern up to the ceiling hook and adjusted the flame a little. All three men looked around, then, blinking a little. Luke whistled. "Now, ain't that somethin'? She's done left this galley as clean as a pin."

Bo strode to the table which was covered with a white cloth. A note was weighted on its edge. He read it aloud: "The table is set and the food is dished up. I am sorry it must be cold, but at least it won't be necessary for you to cook. Phoebe Cole."

Foss growled, "Well, she needn't of. I would have relished something hot right now myself."

Bo plucked the cloth aside. "Bread—fried apples—hominy—meat. Build you up a fire, Foss, and cook if you want. I'd like hot coffee myself but it's not gonna misput me one bit to eat this cold stuff done fixed. Come on, Luke, fall to." He heaped his plate and flung himself down. "I'm hungry enough to eat shoe leather and I'm real pleased she thought to leave us something."

"Well, seein' as it's here . . ." Foss filled his own plate, "and you can take your coffee cold, too, my friend. Is she aimin' to take over the galley permanent?"

"Far as they go downriver, looks like. She run Tobe out this morning."

"How far they goin'?"

"I've not asked."

"They could," Foss pointed out, "get off right now. We've done all we're called on for 'em."

"Nope. They're going downriver far as they want to go. Least I can do. They'll say when they want off, not me."

"It wouldn't bother me," Luke spoke up, "if they was to go plumb to Evansville. Way that girl can cook is a gift of God. I'd like to enjoy it long as I can."

Foss buried his nose in his plate and retreated into a silent and rapid stowing away of food.

Finished first, Bo left Foss and Luke and drifted outside and up the companionway. He did not often smoke but when he did he liked a cigar. Old pilot habit, he guessed. He had several in the cabin so he rummaged one out and lit it, went back out on the bridge, hauled up a stool and sat, his back against the rail.

The night was still except for the autumn-slowed katydids and a still chirpy cricket or two on the bank. It was a clear night and star-studded, a small soft air stirring that was warm and blandishing against the skin. His stomach full, the rich smoke in his mouth, his body now only pleasantly tired, Bo let himself down into slackness, felt comfortable and good and easy.

He listened to the river sounds—the suck of the water and the slide and the little slap it made against the boat and the little hissing riffle it made against the bank, and the splash now and then of something in the water, a clod of dirt falling, maybe—not likely a fish, though it might be, night-feeding—or a beaver, not quite slapping his tail, just fidgeting it. He listened to all the sounds, identifying them more from his long knowledge of them, his long hearing of them, than from his conscious hearing of them now. Identifying them with his river bones and blood and nerves; and they lulled him and made him sleepy. It was a good night and they had done a good job and tomorrow they would get on downriver.

Mind meandering, drawn now by the dry-land sound of a cowbell, his thoughts went away to the village and he wondered how Miss Phoebe and her grandfather were doing with their show. He blew out smoke and hoped they had a good crowd to pay them for their trouble. She was the managingest girl and the sensiblest, and the most honest. She hadn't minded in the least saying her purse was flat, nor been ashamed of it. He didn't, however, doubt whose idea it had been to put on a show to mend the matter. She wouldn't be ashamed of having no money but she wouldn't be satisfied to leave it that way.

He'd like to hear her pick her guitar and sing. He tried to imagine how her singing would sound and couldn't, but if her voice when she sang was as nice as her voice when she talked, hearing her would be a pleasure.

He hoped Jonah and Catfish were behaving themselves. Hoped, too, they had been some help to her. He wondered, a little, what a minstrel show was and thought he'd ask her when there was time. Wondered how late they would be, coming home. His lids were growing heavy when humor shook him at the thought of Sir Henry overwhelming a village audience with his dramatic readings. But maybe he knew something besides his everlasting and oracular Shakespeare. Bo hoped so. Villagers liked to laugh.

Luke came up, stumbling on the last step. "Can't even pick up my feet," he grumbled, "I'm so tired."

"Get on to bed, boy," Bo said, "you can pick 'em up tomorrow."

"Foss'll sleep down," the boy said, passing on.

"Allowed he would."

"You comin'?"

"This minute."

He stood and threw the end of his cigar away, watched it hiss into the water and drown. He twisted his back once more and raised his arms once more and yawned one more time, then he followed Luke into the dark. They undressed silently and neither knew when the other began softly to snore.

CHAPTER 8

ASLEEP though he was some part of his mind told him it wasn't true. He was having a nightmare. The *Rambler* was not caught in another wind squall no matter how the deck tilted or the beams shook and shuddered. This clear part of his mind sensed the absurdity and explained that although the physical sensations were very real, that although he was feeling the shaking and tilting and shuddering, there was a logical explanation, for he knew they were tied up and it was not really happening. He was dreaming and he knew it but he couldn't yet come up through the layers of sleep and put an end to it.

There was such urgency and concern out there, however, somewhere out there beyond the ledges of sleep, that he felt an answering urgency and concern to acknowledge it and reassure. It's not to worry, he wanted to say to whatever was pulling at him, and he thought he did and it would now leave him alone.

Impatience pricked at him when it did not but he thought

if he would lie very still and listen he could determine what it was. He felt very cunning lying so still and listening, as cunning as if he were stalking game down the hogback of the ridge at home. He listened for a footfall and for the rustle of a dry leaf and for the crack of a fallen limb. Instead he heard a faraway voice calling him, saying his name over and over and over. And he knew he must answer it, for the urgency and concern were in the voice.

He tried to struggle up out of his sleep but he felt caught in cobweb tangles which bound him and held him fast. The voice was echoing down into the well of his sleep. "Captain Cartwright!"

The bunk shook under him more violently and he came finally to the surface like a swimmer who has been under water for a long time, shaking his head, blowing and panting, trying to breathe. "All right, I'll take her," he gasped, "she's mine, Luke. What's wrong? Another squall?"

It was his shoulder that was grasped and shaken this time. "Captain? Are you awake?"

His mutterings ceased and his heavy panting eased as he tried to place the voice, which was not a voice he was accustomed to hearing on the *Rambler*. "I'm getting there," he said finally. As he spoke the remembrance of the voice came to him. "Miss Phoebe?"

"And her grandfather." Even Sir Henry's whisper was a resonant boom and room-filling. "Wake up, boy! There is news."

Still sleep-fogged but his mind clearing, Bo could see the girl and her grandfather silhouetted against the starlit window of the cabin. He sat up. "What time is it?"

"The vast dead and middle of the night, sir. Twelve o'clock and all is not well. Are you awake, boy? He that sleeps feels not the toothache but I fear your teeth must ache now. Phoebe and I have just returned from the village. We have a parlous state of affairs to report to you."

The old actor was edging toward staginess, his voice rising. "Grandfather," Phoebe warned, "keep your voice down."

Bo clutched his blanket about him. "Something happen in the village? Jonah and Catfish give you trouble? Folks didn't like the show? Run you out?"

Sir Henry loosed all bonds of caution and roared, "By my troth, Captain, those are very bitter words! I like not your popinjay stridulations!"

Phoebe grasped the old man's arm and shook it. "Grandfather! You'll have the entire boat awake! Do be quiet."

Bo swung his legs overside the bunk and hit the heels of his hands against his head to clean out the last of the cobwebs. "I'm afraid you don't make sense to me, sir. What's happened, Miss Phoebe?"

"We heard some news in the village we thought you should know," she said quietly. "You mean to run downriver tomorrow, don't you, Captain?"

"My intentions," Bo said, "but not early. We have to set the drive rod in."

"Is there a lock and dam at a place called Rochester?"

"Yes, ma'am—#3." He was wholly alert now. "What is it, miss?"

"Have the Confederates occupied a town called Bowling Green near here?"

"Occupied it yesterday morning."

"There is a Confederate general there by the name of Buckner?"

"Simon Bolivar Buckner, yes, ma'am. Green River man. Raised right down from here a piece."

"Then I suspect what we heard is true, Captain. The news in the village is that General Buckner is marching on Rochester to destroy the lock. The talk is that the Confederates have heard that Federal gunboats are on the way upriver to take Bowling Green. They mean to circumvent them by destroying the lock."

Bo shoved up off the bed. "When'd he leave Bowling Green, you hear?" He remembered he wasn't fully clothed. "Get behind your curtain, Miss Phoebe, I got to put my pants on."

"I'll turn my back. Besides, it's dark. He is supposed to have left around noon today. Marching overland."

Bo hauled up his trousers. "How'd the news get to Aberdeen? Who brought it?"

"A man—straight from Bowling Green, he said. Our show was interrupted when he rode in," she laughed, "a little like Paul Revere. The whole village was gathered in the lodge hall, of course. We had a fine crowd. It was very dramatic when he came pounding up and strode in and made his announcement, but of course it put an end to our show. The villagers were interested only in his news after they heard."

"I'd guess it." Bo stuffed his shirt in and cinched his belt. "Upset, were they?"

"Dismayed is a better way of putting it. Evidently no one wants the lock destroyed."

"No. Boats don't run, folks up and down the river'll be in a bad way. Depend on the boats for nearly everything they buy." He sat again and felt around under his bunk for his shoes. "How's he aiming to wreck the lock?"

"By dynamite, I believe. Isn't that right, Grandfather?"

"It is," Sir Henry said. "He means to blow the whole works right out of the river."

Bo found his shoes and stamped his feet into them.

"Perhaps it means something entirely different to you,"

Phoebe said, "and maybe we shouldn't have wakened you."
She hesitated. "I don't know which way your sympathies lie
. . . and you might . . ."

He finished the last latching and tied the knot. "They lie
with Kentucky and with the people living on this river and
with me and my boat. I've got no sympathies for either side
fighting this war. And it means a hell of a lot to me, Miss
Phoebe."

"Yes. Well, Grandfather and I thought you had said you
were bound for Evansville. And there were the sheep . . .
and I reasoned that if the lock at Rochester was destroyed you
couldn't get to Evansville."

"We got to get through before he blows that lock, is all."
Bo stood and combed his fingers through his hair. "You said
the time was midnight, Sir Henry?"

"Close on to it."

"Captain?" Phoebe interposed, "how far must he march
overland?"

"I've not ever covered it," Bo said, "but generally folks
call it forty miles from Bowling Green to Rochester by land."

"How far have we to go?"

"Little less. But we got a late start. You're thinking the
same as me. No, ma'am, we can't beat him there. He's
bound to get there ahead of us. Bound to. He'll march hard,
and if he left Bowling Green around noon he's just about
right now arriving at Rochester. But arriving and blowing
the dam is two different things, Miss Phoebe. It'll take him
a day or two to drill out those lock walls enough to do a good
blasting job—one that'll really do some damage." He rummaged for his jacket on the foot of the bunk and thrust his
arms through.

"What will you do?"

"I've got no idea yet. We can be ready to run by daylight,

I'd think. Near enough, least. And even allowing for stops we can get to Rochester by noon. But, God, I don't know . . . I got to think . . ."

"Come, now, Captain," Sir Henry boomed, "against ill chances men are ever merry; heaviness foreruns the good event." He forsook his quoting. "I am no machinist, boy, but I have a pair of hands and I can do as I am told. Phoebe, here, is as good as any man. Your crew has increased by two."

Bo laughed. "And I'll sign you on, sir. Will you wake Luke, please? Get him down in a hurry. Miss Phoebe, if you'll make some coffee—Rivermen live on coffee as you'd no doubt noticed already." He swung out the door. "I'll rouse Foss and we'll see if we can't outwit this Confederate general."

They worked swiftly but without skimping the job. Whatever they might have gained in time by hurrying too much they would have lost with more trouble unless the rod was properly set in and tightened. Sir Henry proved to have his wits about him when it came to handing over nuts and wrenches and Foss at least thought it a mercy he kept his mouth shut. Toward the end when the old man was obviously too weary and sleepy to stay on his feet any longer and Bo sent him to bed, Foss mentioned the silence. "Didn't figger he had that much sense."

"He's not stupid," Bo said. "For one thing he was too tired to talk and for another he knew it might be muddling to be spouting off his pieces while we's working."

"I dunno. That might be creditin' him too high."

They worked on in silence for a while and then Bo began talking, in a running, thinking-aloud, studying sort of way. "We got to get through, of course, come hell or high water but that ain't all's been on my mind. Ought to be some way of stopping him. He blows that lock it'll ruin the river. Won't be any shipping for untelling how long. State's already put out because the locks don't pay. Might not ever rebuild the lock. Ruin everybody with a boat on the river. Ruin the towns and ruin the folks depending on the boats. Just about finish Bowling Green off, being cut off from the downriver trade. Ought to be some way of stopping him—keeping him from doing it."

"How?" Foss was practical. "What he's aimin' to do is stop them gunboats. He ain't carin' 'bout the river."

"Ought to. He fixes the river so's they can't use it, he's gonna fix it so's it'll be hard for him to use it, too. Looks to me he could see that. How's he gonna get his supplies up?"

"Mebbe you ought to ask him."

"Somebody ought. Give him something to study on."

"Maybe he's aiming to haul 'em up from Tennessee," Luke put in.

Bo pondered, then said dispiritedly, "Reckon he could at that. Reckon using the river wouldn't be much of an argument. But you'd think," he went on bitterly, "an old Green River boy'd have some feeling for the folks he was raised up with. Not want to do 'em harm."

Foss snorted. "He's got a army to think about. He ain't got time for studyin' 'bout the folks he was raised up with. Them gunboats has got him spooked. You ain't thinkin' straight, Bo."

"I know it. Just as well put it out of my mind till tomorrow. Not really thinking at all. Just sort of bothered, though."

Five minutes later he was at it again, standing and absently rubbing one hand back and forth across his chin, leaving a wake of oil smears. "How many guns we got?"

Foss heaved up out of the machinery slowly. He stared at

Bo. "My God," he said, "you aimin' now to fight the whole
Confed'rit army? With three squirrel rifles? That's what
we got to shoot with on this boat—yours and mine and Luke's.
You better wait till you can mount you a cannon!"

"We got plenty of cartridges," Bo said, "I know that." He
sounded bemused to Foss.

"Tobe's got a Derringer," Luke volunteered. "Don't
know whether it'll fire or not, though. He won it in a poker
game a while back." The boy's voice grew suddenly excited,
"And that old man's got a couple of horse pistols, Bo.
Showed 'em to me yesterday. Said he sometimes had a shooting scene to play."

Bo's voice was suddenly crisp. "You collect up everything
on the boat that'll shoot, Luke. Some the other boys might
have a gun. Collect 'em all up and work 'em over good. Get
'em all ready to fire if you can. Bring 'em up to the pilothouse
when you get done."

"No you don't," Foss said, "I want mine handy. Anybody
gonna be shootin' at me I aim to be ready to shoot back in a
hurry."

"I'd like to keep mine alongside, too, Bo," Luke said.

"All right, all right. Bring the rest up, though."

"Who," Foss put in, "is gonna be shootin' them horse pistols of that old feller's? Him? You turn him loose with 'em
and he's like to kill one of *us!* Do us more harm than the
Confed'rits."

"God's britches, Foss," Bo exploded, "I'm not aiming for
anybody to shoot at anybody else! You think I'm crazy?"

"It's beginnin' to go like it," Foss drawled.

"If it comes to hand-to-hand," Luke put in, still excited,
"the boys have all got knives and razors, and the old man has
got a sword and a dagger."

Bo sucked in his breath, held it, then blew it out. "I'd just like to know what you two fools think I'm aiming to do!"

"Run the *Rambler* right smack through the middle of Buckner's army," Foss said mildly.

In the yellow soft light of the lantern Bo looked at Foss's bland, oil-smeared, innocent-looking face for a long moment. Then he laughed. "If Buckner has got possession of the lock, and he undoubtedly has, *how* am I gonna run the *Rambler* right smack through him? Tell me. I'd like to know. We got to *lock* through, recollect? We lost the tide and we can't go over the dam without a tide. We have got to sit in that crib like a settin' duck—" His voice trailed off.

"I wouldn't know *how* you're aimin' on doin' it," Foss said, "but that's exactly what you're aimin' on doin'. It's what you're studyin' on right this minnit."

"I'd be interested to know what *you'd* do."

"Whatever you're fixin' to do."

Bo glared at him. "Then what the hell is all the talk about?"

Foss hitched up his pants and drew his eyebrows down and studied first one suspender latch and then the other. He sighed, then, gently. "Blamed if I know. I hove up here to get you to hand me that big wrench. That'n right there. You done got my mind sidetracked."

Bo hefted the wrench. "Good mind to crown you with it. Ought to. *I* got you sidetracked! God's sake! You get yourself sidetracked ever' time you open your mouth. Here." He tossed the wrench quickly. Foss lunged for it but missed and it fell with a clang.

Foss gave him a mild and unangry look, but he said reprovingly, "You done that a purpose, Bo."

"Can I help it if your belly gets in the way of your reach?" Bo stepped outside.

"Where you goin'?" Foss called.

"Gonna get rid of some of that coffee I been drinking all night. Any objections? Can't hold it forever."

"Me, too," Luke said and joined him.

Comfortably and in silence they added their water to the river. Without knowing the time and with the darkness still thick on the river, Bo knew daylight was coming soon. He thought how it was the skin knew it first, for what lay heavy on it all night, all during the dark, would lessen and lighten and the skin of the hands and the arms, and the skin of the neck and the face would cool and feel thinner. His skin was knowing it now. Then, so slowly that if you never took your eyes off the treeline you still couldn't tell when it happened or how, the sky would bleach. Low above the trees at first, it would spread wider and wider like a gray stain across a black one, until the dark was covered and the first slow shoots of color would thrust up. It would be soon, now, and he knew how it would be.

Buttoning up, he cocked his head. "Listen. Ain't that them sheep blatting?"

Luke waited to listen. "Sure is. And that's a relief to me. I was commencing to worry. Figured Tobe and them ought to been back an hour ago."

A cackle of laughter rose and whooped and soared, joined at its height by Tobe's rousing bellow. Bo chuckled. "Been fooling some, I'd say. Any wenches on that farm?"

"Couldn't say. Didn't go around the house. Found the feller in the barn. Could of been, though."

"If somebody," Foss called plaintively, "will gimme a hand here I can finish this job up right now. They don't, it'll take another hour."

"I'll help him," Bo said, "you count them sheep, Luke."

The boy swung about. "Day's coming, Bo."

"Yes. We'll be running soon."

He was almost startled enough to lose his balance and go overboard when Phoebe Cole spoke out of the darkness. "Breakfast will be waiting for you, Captain, when you are ready to run."

He went hot with embarrassment and broke into a sweat that he and Luke should have been so careless, so forgetful even for a moment she might be near around, cutting loose with their duties in the way of their custom. And it took him three half-strangling tries before he could say a word. He tried to be casual. "Be half an hour I expect, Miss Phoebe."

"I'll set the bread in, then." There was a pause and he heard her sniff a little. "Isn't it nice—the morning? Doesn't it smell good?"

Bo thought she couldn't have heard him and Luke, or seen them. She couldn't have been so casual if she had. But he probed a little, cautiously. "Little chilly. You been out on the deck long, hope you threw something around you."

"Oh, I just stepped out. Just this minute. Heard you say you'd be running soon and thought you'd like to know there'd be food beforehand. I've got to get right back."

The relief was immense but he could find nothing to say but his repeated and inane remonstrance, "You needn't to bother." He already knew the galley and their meals had become her special province and her way of helping and that she considered it no bother. He added lamely, "I've got to help Foss."

"Yes, and I've smelled the daybreak long enough."

He heard her skirts swish, saw her briefly against the light of the galley door, and she was gone.

Looking at Foss and Luke as they filed into the galley half an hour later, Bo laughed. "We're a sad-looking bunch to sit at your table, Miss Phoebe."

She beamed at them warmly. "You deserve to sit at a king's table. Just sit and I'll wait on you."

Foss was for taking his plate to the engine room but Bo shoved him into a chair. "You mind your manners, hear!"

Foss glared at him and drew his mouth down disapprovingly, but it straightened cheerfully with the first taste of the smoking good food. He would never have told her, for it didn't do to blow up a woman's pride, but the girl mortally could cook good. She had a light hand with bread and her meat was fried out just dry enough and the eggs stood up round and weren't frilled and browned on the edges. It depressed him a little to think how often his bannocks were heavy and his meat soggy and his eggs hard and crimped. He brightened, however. Except he made it his work, as some men did, a man wasn't supposed to cook good. It was a woman's work and it stood to reason she could do it better. When it fell his lot he did it mostly left-handed sort of. It was comforting, also, to think Miss Phoebe Cole couldn't run machinery the way he could. Wasn't anybody couldn't do *something* better'n anybody else.

Having served them, Phoebe stood in the door fanning her face gently with her apron tail. "Captain," she said after a time, "the fog is rising."

"Yes. Does this time of year. Don't amount to much. It'll burn off soon as the sun comes up."

"It won't delay you?"

"Some," Bo admitted, "but not much." He glanced out the window. "Pretty thin stuff—mostly patchy. Won't be a real eyeblinder."

He finished his meal and joined her at the door. She was watching the river. Almost absently she reached up to reset her tuck comb, wasn't pleased with it and set it again, then patted it to make it feel firm, and said, "How much has the river fallen?"

"Almost all the rise."

Still bemused by the sliding water she yet looked pleased, a smile tucking her mouth at the corners. "I guessed it my-self."

"How?"

"The mudline on that bank. See?" She pointed. "The drift in the undergrowth shows the highest stage, but the mud has dried a little, about three feet down. That was yes-terday's fall. Bound to be or it wouldn't have dried. The dark mud, still wet, is last night's fall." She was triumphant.

Bo looked down at her and grinned. "Getting to be a right noticing person. Be a good riverman first thing you know."

"Anybody with eyes could see that," she scoffed.

"You'd be surprised how many don't."

She was wearing a lilac print dress this morning—the kind his mother and sisters called a housedress. The print wasn't new-bright and there was one darn at the shoulder. She had it well covered with the big apron just the same. He guessed she didn't have many dresses and, not knowing where the next would come from, maybe, knew to take care of those she had. The dress was crisp and starchy and it had been ironed neatly. She looked like a clean little girl in it—about, he thought, if the skirt hadn't reached to her ankles, ten years old. Just about ten. Then he remembered.

From the corner of his eye he saw Foss rising from the table. Bo touched the girl's elbow and swung her a little so he could pass. As Bo passed he said so only she could hear, "I wish it could be a happier birthday, Miss Phoebe Cole, but I wish you well of it just the same."

Her eyes widened and he saw the pupils grow and darken. The gesture he was coming to know was made. One finger went to her mouth. "You remembered? With all on your mind, you remembered." The finger was dropped immediately and she flounced her apron in the first confusion he had seen upon her. "Oh, pshaw, what's a birthday! Only children count birthdays. I," she added staunchly, "count my blessings." She counted them on her fingers. "The rod is mended and set in. Mr. Foss is ready to get up steam. The sheep have browsed and Tobe has brought them aboard. Grandfather is having a nice sleep. I had good luck with my biscuits again this morning and no trouble with the damper. We'll soon be running and if we can just get past that lock, all will be well, won't it?"

Sir Henry had forgotten, Bo judged. And brave words or not, she did still count birthdays. "Try to give you the lock for a present, Miss Phoebe," he said.

Foss, who had lingered to speak to Luke further, came up behind them, ducked his head awkwardly at Phoebe and squeezed past Bo. "Who's firin' for me?" he asked.

"Mose and Boone. Gimme steam pretty soon, Foss?"

"You'll git steam when I got it for you," Foss replied truculently and passed on.

Phoebe watched him stump away, her eyes a study. "Mr. Foss does not like me, does he?"

"No reflection on you," Bo said. "He acts the same with all women. Not that he don't like women, he just don't know what to do around 'em."

Phoebe's brow unpuckered. "I'm glad. He was making me feel bad."

"Don't let him. Foss is the best engineer on the river but all he really cares about is his machinery."

"And you." She didn't say it special at all, or even with any emphasis. She just said it plain—a fact to be noted and said plain. But it stopped Bo and he knew what she was really saying. All right. Foss didn't much like him to be taken up with her. Foss was jealous—sure. Not in any unnatural way. But what they had and how it was with Foss and him wouldn't be any good trying to say. He didn't believe women knew or ever experienced or could even understand the kind of comradeship men could have together. It was just specially for men. He'd seen no signs of it, ever, in women together. So it wasn't, really, any part of Phoebe's knowing. It was just between him and Foss and all the time on the river. And to say it, too, would be to admit he had let her be closer than she was. He didn't owe it to her. She was a pilgrim and a stranger, by chance on his boat, just wayfaring down the river. That's all he would make of her. So he said only, his eye on the sliding water, "We're going to waltz today. We're really gonna steamboat."

CHAPTER 9

THE river was a love that morning, a pure love.
She wore only her best manners and showed only her sweetest guiles. She had pushed all the heavy tan water down ahead of him and she gave Bohannon Cartwright only her prettiest face. She didn't even bother him with a wind ripple. She dimpled at him in the sun, smiled and flirted with him, and she moved like a lady between her banks, keeping her skirts full dry.

"You needn't to show off so audaciously," Bo told her chucklingly, loving this lady river to the bursting point, but not wanting her to get by with too much. "I've seen you like this before. Don't mean a thing. Sure, you're all glassy and smooth and green and deep and still today. But don't you forget I've seen you get your dander up, too. I know what you're like in a temper. You've got the bones of too many boats lying on your bottom and there's too many good men filling graves on your account for you to fool me. Oh, I like you well enough. But you don't impress me much with

your smiles this morning. I'll say thank you for minding
your manners, but I've got more than you on my mind today. I got plenty other things besides you to think about."

He looked around, feeling foolish. Foss knew he talked
to the river and he guessed in time Luke would catch him
at it. He wouldn't want more than them to know, though he
knew plenty of pilots who did the same. It did go a little
foolish, though. Grown man talking to himself.

But you got in the way of thinking the river was almost
human. Spend enough time running up and down the same
river you couldn't help it. The Green was especially easy to
feel personal to—so much like a brilliant, changeable, saucy,
beautiful woman. Next thing you knew you got into the
habit of talking to her—cussing her or scolding her or quarreling with her or laughing at her or taking her into your confidence. Some rivermen would know how it was, but no dry-
lander born but wouldn't think it foolish. Daft, they'd say.
He didn't know of any farmers who talked to their land, or
any merchants who talked to their shelves, or any lawyers
who talked to their books. But a river was alive and moving
and, he could swear sometimes, it was answering and feeling.
You were alone with the river in the pilothouse, and it got to
be, almost, as if you were both the same.

It was a relief not to hear the loud clank of the rod. There
was still a knock—you couldn't tighten it in enough to get
rid of it all—but it was nothing compared to what it had
been. Up here it was mostly a small jar and muffled thud.
Up here the machinery sounded almost the way it ought to
sound, the quiet deep smooth chug that Foss tinkered so
eternally to get, nursed to keep, and loved to hear. As much
for Foss as for himself, Bo was glad to be rid of that clank.
Foss could use some peace of mind about his machinery.

He was taking the *Rambler* down pretty fast but he wasn't

pushing her. He wasn't tilting her down. No need for it. He wasn't running any race with Buckner for Buckner had already won it. He just didn't mean to lose any time was all. He'd need all the time he could store up.

He was coming down into the piece of water that would lead into the Bend itself now, with Cromwell Island looming up. It was a long willowed bar that split the river for several miles. It took a long time to make an island as fat and long as Cromwell. You couldn't guess how old it was. He wondered if it wasn't maybe inching into the channel a little every year and where, a hundred years from now, the channel would be. Eaten out of the bank, he judged. A river got pushed one way it usually pushed for itself another. It would nibble at that good land along the bank and slowly swallow it up, making room for itself.

High View came next and they'd stop for wood. Bo flexed one arm and breathed in deeply. Without the bother of General Buckner, it was a day and a river to take delight in—air and water as soft as old silk, the sun like a flame on the land. The pilothouse was hot with it and it was fast burning up the last shreds of fog that were still wisping around in the trees. The trees weren't showing much color yet, except for a maple here and there whose top leaves, feeling the sun earliest, had touched up with the first hints of their turning. In a few weeks they'd outblaze the sun.

You wouldn't believe there was trouble on this river. Hard to make yourself believe it, for here it was as lonesome as ever, as still and as peaceful. He knew that the life that used the river, lived in it and upon its banks, was constantly embattled. Big fish ate little fish and little fish ate littler ones. Birds ate insects and worms. Small mammals ate smaller ones. It was a full time war that never ceased; but they kept a kind of balance about it and while they did harm to each other, did none to people or the river. It took people to do that. Took something that could think and reason to do great harm to themselves and to each other and to the world they lived in. He made a rough sound in his throat. Sometimes he thought the Lord ought to start over again, with something better than men.

He blew for High View and warped the *Rambler* in. Tobe shouted, "Lower away," and the stage went down. The rousters romped across and began loading the wood.

A bystander watched morosely as if they had invaded his personal world and he could easily do without them. He could not have, for it was his woodpile and if the boats quit using it he would be hard put to find so rewarding a substitute. He kept a dozen Negroes cutting wood and three teams of mules hauling it. He was making a fine living furnishing steamboats with their wood.

Bo asked for the news. "Any word of Buckner?"

The man, who was long and lean and dirty, bit off a hunk of tobacco and wallowed it around before replying. "On his way is all we've heard."

"You've not heard if he's got there?"

"Nope."

"Any news of the gunboats?"

The man emptied his mouth. "Biggest batch of rumors ever floated up the river is all. Some says they's three of 'em on the way. Some says there ain't, ain't but one. Some says they's none. Some says they're to Rumsey upbound. Some says ain't a gunboat on the river or ever gonna be. Take your pick."

This man, Border was his name, always riled Bo a little. He was full of his own spleen and spilled it over too much to suit him. Didn't hurt anybody to be pleasant, Bo thought. But you never caught Border trying it. Acted as if he had a sour taste in his mouth all the time. Bo said, "Thanks. I'll do that," and made no more conversation with him.

Luke kept the hands hustling and the woodpile went down fast. When they'd done he signaled and Tobe came romping aboard yelling, "Done loaded!"

Border rose from the log on which he had been sitting. "Be obliged if you'd pay me now—for all of September."

Bo's temper rose and he snapped back at the man, "I'll pay you the first of the month—way I always do."

Border contemplated him lengthily, his jaws moving rhythmically on his cud. "Have to git my boys to unload you then. Ain't givin' no credit now."

"When did that commence being your policy?"

"Right now. Buckner's gonna blow up the dam. Don't allow you'll be needing no more wood of me for a spell. Need my money." He eyed the stage plank where a couple of rousters stood waiting to heave. "Wouldn't try nothin' like raisin' that stage and tryin' to run yer boat off, neither, if I was you." He motioned and half a dozen blacks came out from behind the far end of the woodpile. Each of them carried a gun. "Be right unhealthy fur you if was to try such."

"For God's sake! You been doing business with me for a year, Border!"

"Oh, it ain't nothin' personal. I'd like to accommodate you, but things has changed is all, and I got myself to think of. I'd like it in hard money, too."

"You'll take it in dixies or unload me. I've not got that much hard money on board," Bo said.

The man reflected. "Well, dixies has allus been good. Reckon they still are. I'll take 'em."

"Pay him, Luke," Bo said shortly.

When the bank notes had been paid over, Bo nodded at Tobe who shouted at the rousters and the stage went up.

Bo gonged Foss with one hand and hauled down on the whistle cord with the other. He saw Border wince as the hoarse bellow blared out and grimly he held it down an uncommonly long time. Let his ears hurt. Let 'em hurt good. He'd like to bust his eardrums for him. Then abruptly he cut the whistle off. No use using up Foss's steam. Acting like a kid paying back a meanness with another meanness. Poor paying thing to do.

Back in the channel again, trotting along, he made an effort to put Border out of his mind. He had enough on it without letting Border put any extra weight on. He could ill afford paying out the money was all. He'd been counting on it to pay for the new rod. It occurred to him he probably wouldn't be able to order the new one by telegraph. Buckner, or the Yankees, would likely have cut the wires. He shoved his cap back and rumpled through his hair. Everything was getting too iffy and chancy for comfort. You couldn't put your finger on a solid fact and expect to keep it there. The whole situation was like trying to bail water with a sieve.

He gave Austin's Rocks on the right bank room as he slid the *Rambler* past. Pretty rocks—all those colored bands streaking through them. But he liked to see them showing above the water the way they were today. Gave you an unpleasant feeling for them to be lurking down below. No give in a rock. Rake your hull across one that was submerged, or get blown against one, and it'd be the hull that gave.

Six gulls flapped up frantically as the *Rambler* chugged by and squawked and circled and made a great fuss over this noisy thing swimming down the river. "Think it belongs to you, don't you?" Bo said. "Not a day goes by a boat don't pass here. You always gotta squawk at it."

He had to add to their annoyance by tooting for a rowboat. A lone man was fishing. The man pulled to the bank and waited for the *Rambler*'s swells to rock him. He raised his hand to Bo, but his face was sour. And *you* think the river belongs to you, Bo thought. You don't like having to pull over for a steamboat. Like to see me pile up on them rocks, wouldn't you? But it's a free river. You fish and I'll steamboat.

He hadn't heard her but there was a flutter of her skirt ahead of her and Miss Phoebe Cole came onto the bridge. She smiled at him and lifted her hand and said, "Is it all right if I sit up here in the sun a while?"

"Sit as long as you like," he told her. "Been asleep?"

"Not yet. I've been making some apple pies. And washing up. We've had fried apples long enough." She pulled his stool into the sun and sat and leaned against the rail. He thought she leaned tiredly, glad to be sitting.

A flicker of annoyance ran through him. Up all night, she'd been. Giving a show, then keeping coffee made and hot for them while they worked. Cooking breakfast for them and feeding them. Then she didn't have any better sense than to redd up the galley and cook some more. He spoke sharply. "Miss Phoebe, I'm not going to fuss with you about the cooking. You're going to do that to suit yourself, looks like. Have that your own way without argument. But I am going to put my foot down right now about you washing up. There's ten blacks on this boat. Pick the one you want and see he does the dishwashing and the scrubbing and cleaning for you."

"I don't mind . . ." she began.

"I do. I mind like hell, if you'll excuse me. I mind enough I'm not going to have it. It's not fit. If you want to cook, go ahead and cook, since you like to do it so well. But you let one of the boys do the heavy work."

"Yes, Captain. I'll remember." She lifted her face and closed her eyes against the sun's brightness. "It's almost hot, isn't it?"

"Hot enough to burn you if you burn easy." He still felt put out with her.

"I don't. I just get brown. At the end of the summer like this I'm as brown as an Indian."

"I thought you were naturally dark-complected."

"I am, but not *this* dark." She stirred, finding more comfort for her back, finding an easier place for her head. The breeze caused by the *Rambler*'s motion blew her hair about her forehead and she let it blow. It made her skirt ruffle about the edges. Her hands lay folded in her lap. They were bleached and crinkled from a long immersion in hot water. They were small hands, as all of her was small, and they were like a child's hands, fleshed well to hide their bones, soft, rounded and cupped. A man could fold one hand around both of them.

Uneasily Bo kept stealing glances at her until at last, thinking he saw her head nod, he warned, "Don't fall asleep there. Might fall off the stool."

She roused. "I won't. It's just so nice here I hate to go in the cabin." She leaned away from the rail and arranged her hair. "Which of the roustabouts is of the least use to you, Captain?"

"That won't go down, Miss Phoebe," he said. He thought about it. "I'll give you Catfish. He's the handiest in a galley —outside of Tobe. But I may need Tobe too bad."

She stood and yawned frankly, not troubling to hide it. "You should have seen Catfish last night," she said, then, the remembrance making her laugh. "I rigged him out in a long-tailed coat of Grandfather's, with a purple waistcoat and a tall hat. He was the proudest thing! He was a little shy at first but when the show began he took to it like a duck takes to water. Pranced around all limber-legged, sang, did a hoedown, and the way he can make a banjo ring was enough to set the whole audience to rocking! He stole the show, Captain. Just plain stole the show. He's a natural-born showman."

Bo nodded. "Most ways, they all are, I guess—rousters. Put on a right good show at every landing. Seems to come natural to 'em. I'm glad," he added, "if he was useful to you."

"Oh, he was. I wish we could afford half a dozen like him. We could have our own minstrel show." She paced slowly across the bridge. "It wouldn't take any time to teach them a walk-around, and they are natural musicians—got rhythm born in their bones, I guess. It might be more trouble to teach them lines, though—how to tell jokes and so on."

"I wouldn't want to trust 'em with jokes, Miss Phoebe," Bo grinned, "they got a way of adding to 'em isn't always what you'd expect."

She flashed him an amused look and nodded. "It happened last night. I taught him a simple come-on. He only had one line to remember. It's a joke as old as show business. Grandfather was to ask him, 'Catfish, who was that lady I saw you with last night.' Catfish was to say, of course, 'That wasn't no lady, Mister Sam, that was my wife.' You won't believe what he made of it!"

Bo groaned. "Knowing Catfish, yes I would."

Phoebe came up to the apron, her gray eyes sending out sparks of fun. "He forgot, I suppose. Got confused. He stammered and stuttered around, kept saying over and over until I thought he'd never finish with it, 'Dat warn't no lady, Mister Sam . . . dat warn't no lady, Mister Sam . . .' And then, just as I was trying to come to his rescue, he sort of gulped down his Adam's apple and blurted out, 'Dat warn't no lady, Mister Sam, dat was de madam fum de Palace ob Joy!' "

"Good God!" He was appalled.

But her laughter rang out so full and rich, so joyously appreciative, so honestly amused, that he had to join her. "It's the only kind of woman he knows," he said apologetically. "Catfish has no experience of wives."

"Oh, it was all right. The moment I heard him say 'madam' I hit a crashing chord on the guitar and broke into song. But it nearly killed Grandfather. He went into such a convulsion of wheezing and coughing and sputtering I thought he was going to choke. He couldn't say a word or do a thing. I never saw him laugh so hard. But I spieled off my little song, very hearty and very loud you may be sure, and then I had Jonah join Catfish for a buck and wing. But I can see," she nodded, "you'd have problems with real Negroes. I suppose that's one reason Dan Emmett uses white men in blackface. They can keep their wits about them. And then," she paused, thinking, "blackface is a grotesquerie, an exaggeration. People really like them better." She paused and turned to look ahead, down the long river with its sun glints and its bright reflecting water. "Isn't it strange that comedy is nearly always, if not entirely always, built on something a little cruel, maybe even tragic, and nearly always with some element of the grotesque? I've thought about it a lot. I'm not sure I like it—but laughter itself is so good." She let it go, breathed deeply and said, "What a beautiful river. And what a beautiful day."

It occurred to Bo that he had never before in his life heard a girl—a nice girl, that is, or a nice woman—speak of an area of men's lives, black or white, they were supposed to know nothing about. Nice women, though they were bound to know, couldn't help knowing, ignored it as if it didn't exist. He didn't know what they thought, but he did know they never mentioned it. And he knew no gentleman would dream of mentioning it before them. It was what, he knew, had made him so appalled and horrified—that Catfish should have blurted out such a thing, not before an audience, but before this girl.

But she had told the story as naturally as she had told him she had baked apple pies that morning and she had genuinely relished the predicament in which Catfish had found himself and his resolution of it. She had either let go or never seen the vulgarity and the embarrassment; she had kept and enjoyed the humor. She was, he thought, so much more than a nice girl. She was, in its true meaning, an innocent. There was in her no sense of guilt or sin, no guile, no acquaintance with evil. In its absolute meaning, she was pure, and because of it, she could be sensible and honest and plain-speaking and earthy and radiant and joyous.

It made him wince from what he might have to ask of her. He cleared his throat to ask it, then backed off from it. Wait till he knew. He'd just say for now, "Miss Phoebe, I might have to ask a favor of you later."

She took her eyes off the water and slowly turned to look at him. She could not see him clearly, he knew, for there was water-dazzle still. She blinked rapidly, "Yes, Captain?"

"Not now. Later. But I might have to ask you to do something for me—something a little bit dangerous perhaps."

She braced away from the front of the pilothouse. "It has to do with General Buckner and the lock?"

"Yes. But it might not be necessary. Depends on what I learn."

Her face flushed up and her eyes began to sparkle and in her excitement she began to chatter. "You just ask it, Captain Cartwright, you just ask. Do you want me to disguise myself and spy on him? Penetrate the enemy position? I can do that easily . . . and with no danger. Grandfather even has a uniform . . . !" She struck her forehead. "What am I thinking? It's a United States Cavalry uniform! But I can find something. And I can tuck myself into some small hole and listen for hours to the general and his staff. I can learn all his plans for you. And I have a wonderful memory, Captain. Even Grandfather says so. I might," she confessed, "not remember the exact words but I would never mistake the meaning. Oh, I've read about spies, Captain—and I know I could—"

"Miss Phoebe, Miss Phoebe," Bo pled, "just hold up a minute, will you? It would be nothing like that."

"No? Not spying?"

"No, ma'am," he said firmly. "Whatever spying is done, I'll do for myself. And don't you go slipping off trying any such thing, you hear?"

"Well, I wouldn't, of course . . ."

He laughed. "I'm not so sure you wouldn't. You like excitement mighty well, Miss Phoebe. If I have to ask this favor of you I promise you'll get a plenty, though. Will that do you?"

Her dimples sank. "You promise?"

"I promise. Solemn oath. Much excitement as you can take."

"Very well." But the next moment she sighed. "I do wish people wouldn't think I'm too young to be trusted—or that because I'm a woman I'm not to be trusted. I think I am very trustworthy, Captain. I can keep a secret like a clam. I have kept *dozens* of secrets." She waved a whole skyful of secrets upon him, showered him with them, her hands flinging them extravagantly.

She was so obviously disappointed, so like a good child put off and trying to be obedient, that he decided suddenly she deserved some kind of small secret. "All right," he said, "I can tell you this much, but it *is* a secret, remember."

She hesitated. "Even from Grandfather?"

"Well . . ."

He watched her struggle with her need to be honest and her great desire to know the secret. She bit her lip, puzzled her brows, slid her finger to her mouth, screwed up her eyes, divided and torn. He didn't think why he let her struggle, gave her no help. He simply waited to see what she would do. Nor did he think why he felt like applauding when honesty won and she said, "I have never had a secret from Grandfather. I should have said Grandfather and I had kept dozens of secrets."

He pretended to give it deep consideration. "You can tell your grandfather," he concluded at last, "but no one else. Understand?"

"Oh, I vow that! No one else at all! Torture couldn't drag it from me. Cross my heart!" She made the childish gesture.

"I believe it. Well, this is what I plan. I'm not going to go steamboating right into Rochester and risk having the general confiscate my boat. That's what I've been trying to do this entire run—get away from the general. So what I'm going to do is run up a little creek I know, a few miles up-river from the lock, where there's some thick willows to cover her a little and give some hiding. And then I'm going to do some scouting around."

It wasn't a big enough secret, he could tell immediately, and besides it didn't involve her. It came to him quickly how to include her. "Now, this is what I want you to do. Luke'll be having those sheep on his hands, keeping 'em quiet. They get noisy they'll give the hiding place away.

Foss don't ever think of nothing but his machinery. He'll be greasing and shining and tinkering. I want you to sit up here in the pilothouse, where you can see farther, and keep a watch. You see any soldiers at all, even one or two, either side Confederate or Yankee, you scoot down and tell Foss or Luke, quick."

She surprised him. "If I may have one of Grandfather's pistols, I won't need to."

"I don't believe . . ."

"I can shoot."

"I'm sure you can. But shooting, right then, wouldn't be any help. What Foss and Luke would need to do would be to run the *Rambler* off—head her back upriver."

She understood immediately. "Why, of course. Of course. You *have* to keep the *Rambler* safe. I'll be glad to keep the watch, Captain, and I will let Mr. Foss and Luke know immediately. Is that the favor you wanted to ask?"

"Oh, no. No. That would come later—depending on what I learn in Rochester."

"How long will it take you?"

"I don't know, Miss Phoebe. I've got no idea. We'll be in that creek before noon. I'd think to learn what I need to know by three or four o'clock. But I might not. Might take longer. Maybe till night. You might have a pretty long watch." He felt less inspired now and a little fretted at himself. He oughtn't to have set her this chore, made it up so she could feel helpful. Didn't really know why he had. The *Rambler* needed a sixteen-year-old girl on watch about as much as a hog needs a sidesaddle. Foss would be keeping up a low head of steam but he and Luke both would have their eyes peeled. "Tell you what . . ." he began.

"It doesn't matter," she interrupted, "it doesn't matter at all, Captain, how long it takes you. I only asked because I wondered if we should show lights if you weren't back before dark."

Hell, he thought irritably, now she's going to take over running the boat. "No lights," he said shortly. "But Foss will know." He continued firmly, so there would be no mistaking it, "Foss is always in charge, Miss Phoebe, when I'm not."

"Oh, I know that," she said, "but I might thoughtlessly have lit a lantern up here. Or Grandfather might, if he isn't warned, show a light in the cabin."

Wryly he acknowledged her good sense. He'd been thinking of deck lights. "I'm obliged to you for remembering," he told her and tooted for a ferry as yet unseen but which lay only a quarter of a mile around the bend they were entering. He brought the wheel down and held the *Rambler* into the bend. Coming out of it he saw that the ferry was on the right bank, a wagon piled with hay loading on. He whistled again and the ferryman signaled he'd heard. The wagon pulled up in the middle of the ferry flat and the driver turned to watch the *Rambler* plow on down. As she passed, both the ferryman and the wagon driver slowly, gravely, saluted her and Phoebe turned to watch the swells roll toward the shore and lift and rock the ferry. "What if he had already put out for the crossing?" she asked.

"You whistle in plenty of time for him to make it."

"Yes. You whistled around that bend first. Don't you ever forget a ferry or landing? With all the dozens there are up and down the river?"

It was a question he had been asked since he was a cub. Dry-landers always seemed to think it phenomenal a pilot should know his job and his river—seemed to think it miraculous he should remember all his landmarks and never get them mixed. He searched for an analogy. "You play the guitar, Miss Phoebe. You have to change your fingers all the time to make your chords different. How do you remember all the changes?"

"Oh, you don't—really. You just know, once you've learned—you just do it . . ." Her throat became full of laughter. "I see. You remember the river the same way, don't you?"

"Mostly," he said.

He didn't go into more detail. It would be too bewildering to explain that in addition to the landmarks that never changed, such as crossings and landings, bridges and ferries and bends and rocks, there were the constantly changing things to notice, to keep in mind and mark against future changes, to be added and subtracted to that charted knowledge—such things as new slides and bars and islands and snags; the differences the stages of the river made, that rain or mist or, most treacherously, wind, made; the weird effects of moonlight and shadow when you were running at night, which could make you swear if you didn't know your river the channel was plowing you straight into the shore, and which worked on you an almost irresistible compulsion to bear toward the middle, where there was a jagged bar; the difference between a wind ripple and a shoal ripple. There was no end to it, but there was nothing miraculous about it. It came with time and with unremitting attention until marking down a new knowledge you did it as naturally as you took the next breath of air. Until, as time passed and you built up a lifetime on the river, you had banked away so much knowledge there wasn't anything new to add. You'd learned all the river had to teach you and you'd put it all in the bank and it was there to draw on. He hadn't that much banked up yet but every run he made added to his fattening account.

Phoebe yawned again. "I'll sleep a while now."

"Do that."

They were closing Galloway's Bluff and a small figure at the water's edge was signaling him down. All he noted of her going, as he gave Foss the gong, was the absence of her presence, the unobstructed view of the near left bank which she had blocked.

CHAPTER 10

EXCEPT for Foss, who loafed in the doorway, they sat in the cabin to listen to what Bo had learned. Luke sat beside Bo on his bunk and Phoebe Cole and Sir Henry sat opposite. The old actor was tinkering with his fiddle, replacing some strings and trying to tighten others. He kept fussing over a broken key and muttering, "Damned spleeny E-string keeps slipping. Had a new key on that peg it'd hold."

Phoebe went, "Sh-sh-sh," and the old man subsided.

At four o'clock in the afternoon the sun had slid a long way down but it had had all day to build a fire in the cabin and it was still pouring on heat. Every face turned to Bo, including Miss Phoebe's, was glisteny with sweat. Now and then somebody raised a hand to wipe it away and Foss, one arm bracing him in the doorway, scratched occasionally at the itch on his ribs. With Sir Henry quiet there was now a hard intent upon Bo's words.

He began obliquely. "Want to thank you, Miss Phoebe, for your help this afternoon. Appreciate it."

She smiled brightly at him. "No trouble, Captain. It was as quiet as a millpond all afternoon. All I did was sit in the pilothouse and darn Grandfather's socks."

Bo's head inclined. "Yes, ma'am. A help anyway."

He looked around at each of them, seemed to need to search a moment for words, then plunged straight into the heart of the matter. "Buckner's there," he said, "and he's got his engineers already drilling." Foss grunted, Phoebe looked thoughtful, and Luke, beside him, moved restlessly. Bo resumed hastily, "Now that's no surprise to us. We reasoned he'd be there, and we've known it certain since Galloway's Landing where that old codger hailed us down had seen 'em. So it wasn't unexpected."

He didn't usually have to exercise any control to keep from being fidgety for he wasn't normally given to fidgets. Now, however, he had to struggle with an impulse to rub his thumbs, to shift his position, to keep from crossing and uncrossing his legs. Still worked up over what he'd learned and what he'd done, he guessed.

"How many men's he got with him?" Luke asked.

"Don't know exactly. Not being a military man I don't know how many's in a company or how many companies in a regiment. But he's got several."

"Do you mean several," Sir Henry asked, without raising his eyes, "in the sense I would use the term, meaning, say, half a dozen—or do you mean it in the sense I've learned Kentuckians use it—a goodly group?"

"Several hundred," Bo said, smiling. "I'd say, offhand, he's got maybe three companies with him and that's what the town folks say too. Got enough to stand off the gunboats if they come. He's got 'em positioned on the lock side of the river and they spread out considerably. Got a well-found camp, I'd say. Placed in good position to defend the lock and he's got sentries out. He's taken over the ferry and uses it to go back and forth to the town."

"The town is across the river from the lock?" Phoebe asked.

"Yes, ma'am. Both of 'em. There's two." It was a relief to use his hands to show her. "This is how they lie. Rochester is upriver from the dam a little, on the left bank. Mud River empties into the Green below the town. Comes in from the left, too. Then the Green makes a sharp right bend below the mouth of the Mud and the lock is built on the right, just in the bend, with the dam to the left of it. Right across from the lock and dam, round the bend, is Skilesville. Just a scattering of houses. Buckner's got an outpost placed there, too."

"No town on the right bank."

"No. Lock's built against the bank and then there's a flat of land that rises up to a good-sized hill. He's all over the flat, clean to the bottom of the hill."

"On either side the river lie," Sir Henry intoned, "and he hath crossed his army over."

Bo grinned. "He's crossed 'em, yes, sir."

"What about them gunboats?" Foss asked.

"Nothing sure. Most the folks in Rochester and Skilesville think it's so. They think Buckner's had the word and the boats are upbound."

"Anybody seen 'em?"

"No. Nobody's come up from downriver. The *Mary Lee* was supposed to depart Evansville day before yesterday. Regular schedule. But she never. She'd have been up by now." He swung one ankle up on the other knee and pegged his shattered cap on it. "Likely," he went on, "the Company heard the gunboat talk or heard Buckner was going to blow the lock and held her back. Didn't want her in trouble."

Luke said, "You hear whether the *Southern Belle* got through all right? She left Bowling Green half a day ahead of us—downbound."

"Don't know. Telegraph's cut to Evansville. But she likely did. If she'd met gunboats somebody would have brought the word. But that don't mean there's no gunboats on the river *now*. She could have got through yesterday and they could be in the river today."

Foss scratched, the comfort of it blissful on his face, and reflected. Then he said, "*Rambler*'s only boat on the river, looks like."

"Looks like it," Bo agreed quietly.

He studied his cap, shifting it now and then, lifting it, setting it back down. The silence remained unbroken until Phoebe asked, finally, "Is that bad? The *Rambler* being the only boat on the river?"

"In a way, Miss Phoebe. See, don't anybody know how long the Confederates are going to stay in Bowling Green, or what they're there for; what they aim to do next or when. Don't know if Buckner is going to want some boats or not. Had there been a big Company boat or two on the river the *Rambler*'d have a better chance maybe of escaping his notice. She's a little boat and can't carry much. He'd maybe pass her up if he could get his hands on a big boat. But if she's the only one handy and if he's needing her . . ."

"Yes. It does increase the danger."

"Some."

"What I really don't understand, though, is . . . if he blows up the lock how can *any* boat be useful to him?"

"Well, Miss Phoebe," Bo said, "there's eighty miles of river between here and Bowling Green. Could do a considerable amount of carrying. And if he could get his hands on a boat the other side the lock, he could shuttle."

"It's very important, then, he doesn't get the *Rambler*."

"To me it is," Bo said dryly. "I wouldn't wish my boat impounded, nor I wouldn't wish me and my crew forced to work for the Confederates."

"They couldn't do *that*, could they?"

"I don't know," Bo admitted. "I don't even know if Buckner wants to use the river. There's more I don't know about all this than I *do* know. Reason I'm not taking any chances."

"Yes," she nodded, "I can see that."

Bo shifted his look from the girl to Foss. "Something else, Foss. Folks are real upset about this. Milling around and stirring and trying to come up with some way to prevent him dynamiting the lock."

"Would be," Foss said. "Natural." He was scratching his back, now, rubbing it against the doorjamb.

"What's eating you," Bo burst out, "you broke out with the hives or something?"

"I got a itch," Foss said.

"God's sake, you gimme the fidgets."

Luke laughed. "What he's likely got is fleas. He let a mangy cur aboard this afternoon and bedded him down in the engine room. Him and Miss Phoebe—" he choked and looked guiltily at the girl.

Her eyes met Bo's and they held a glint of amusement. "We fed him," she said. "Is there a rule against dogs on a steamboat?"

"Not unless this'n bothers those sheep. No rule, no. We've just not ever had one and we need one about like a hog needs a sidesaddle."

"He ain't got fleas," Foss put in amiably, "and I've not neither. I'm sweatin' and it's runnin' down my back and my back itches and I aim to scratch it."

"You gonna keep that dog?" Luke asked, his mouth still twitched with humor.

"Mebbe. What was you sayin' about something else, Bo?"

Bo's eyes dropped to his cap and he lifted it, looked at it as if he had never seen such an article before, turned it this way and that and then clapped it back on his knee. "There's a big raft of logs tied just up from the dam. Good big poplar logs."

Foss looked at him steadily, his shoulder rubbing away at the door. His face showed no sign he was thinking. You'd swear his mind was as blank as his face. But it didn't take him long. He nodded. "It'd do it. Do it good."

Every time this happened Bo felt a special delight. It wasn't only you knew Foss could take the tag ends of your words, few or as many as you wanted to hand him, and put them together so they'd fit. It was a somehow kind of joy to watch him do it. Like they were oiled and only needed sliding into place. "That's what I told 'em," he said. "Got to talking with some of 'em. Nobody doing much except standing around and watching the engineers drill. Just standing around and looking on and wishing there was some way to stop 'em."

"Which side the lock they drilling?" Luke asked.

"River side. And, sweet mercy, but it's slow work. Them rock walls are hard. Be tomorrow, anyhow, before they can be ready to dynamite."

There was a long stillness, then Foss said softly, "Tomorrow?"

"Tomorrow."

The two men locked eyes, understood, and put it away.

"What was it you told them men?" Luke said.

"Told 'em why didn't they get up a committee, like, that'd go wait on the general and tell him if he'd break up that raft and jam the lock with them logs it'd work as good to stop the gunboats as blowing up the walls. And then he could use the river free himself. Said he was an old Green

River boy and he'd know what the river meant to folks and how much they needed it. All he wants is to stop the gunboats, oughtn't to make any difference to him how he does it."

The lids of Foss's eyes creased as the face leather cracked in a grin. "They like the idea?"

"Seemed to. All is, I'd have wished for Capt'n Wing to lead the delegation."

"He won't?"

"Can't. He's sick. They say he's dying. I've heard he was a good friend to Buckner—helped get him his appointment to West Point. Might have had more influence than anybody else."

Foss's rumble was agreement and then there was a silence. The only sound was a thin squeak-squeak-squeak as Sir Henry slowly turned the keyless peg to tighten his loose string. There was a final squeak, he picked the string and sighed with satisfaction. "Got it!" He picked once more to test the string further and there was a high quick plink as the string snapped. "Hell's pains!" the old man exploded, flinging the fiddle onto the bunk. "A pestilence upon you! Dog! Whoreson! Boar-pig!" Each epithet called for a splatting spank on the offending instrument. "Oh, that my grief were thoroughly weighed and my calamity laid in the balances together! The wild ass brays and the ox loweth!" A last splat slid the fiddle onto the floor and the old man's hands clutched his lank hair. He raised his eyes heavenward. "The arrows of the Almighty are within me, the poison whereof drinketh up my spirit! He hath vexed my soul!"

Foss turned a fearful eye on the old man and backed a little out of the door. Luke's jaw dropped and Bo looked on with astonishment himself. The girl, however, laughed, her shoulders making their small shakings of mirth, the laughter welling up in little chucklings, like a fine spring bubbling. "Grandfather, Grandfather, what a deal you make of a broken string." She recovered the fiddle and laid it on the bunk beside her. "Leave it be, dear, and I'll attend to it." She smoothed the old actor's hair. "I am pleased you didn't mention worms in your flesh and boils. This time you did leave Job some minor tribulations."

"I'd rather have boils than a cranky fiddle," the old man snapped. He poked once more at the instrument. "Almost minded to throw it in the river."

"You'd drown yourself trying to recover it. Now, don't fret. I'll manage something."

"Mind if I take a look?" Bo said, recovered.

Phoebe handed it over.

"Take care," the old man roared.

Bo gave him a flat look. "Way you been batting it around I'd say this fiddle could take a right smart punishment." He inspected the head and the broken key. "Tobe can whittle you a peg," he said, then. "Just give it to him so's he can fit it proper." He started to hand the fiddle back, then stopped, thoughtful. "I'll give it to him myself."

Phoebe said, "Don't bother, Captain. There's no hurry."

"Yes, ma'am, there is. I'll get to that in a minute, you don't mind." He deferred to Sir Henry. "You wouldn't mind for Tobe fixing it, would you?"

"No, no," the old man's hands flapped. He gave Bo a suddenly merry look. "Truth is, and I suspect you know it, the instrument is not valuable at all. Nothing but varnished pine. Cheapest fiddle I could buy. And I might add, entirely worthy of my feeble efforts on it. As a fiddler, I barely scrape through." He laughed at his own pun. "I'd be obliged if your man would whittle a new key."

"It'll be done," Bo promised. He glanced at Foss, who still

looked a little like a spooked horse and kept his distance outside the door. "Might as well light and tie, Foss," he said,
"you ain't going nowhere yet."

Foss edged in a little. "Something else on your mind?"

"Plenty. Such as getting the *Rambler* through the lock
tonight."

"I was wonderin' when you was comin' to that," Foss
sighed out. "You've showed 'em a way to save the lock if
Buckner's a mind to listen, but I ain't heard that first thing
about savin' the *Rambler*. How you're aimin' to git her
through, or what you aim to do when you meet up with them
gunboats once you git her through."

Sir Henry's wild eyebrows pulled together. "Save the *Rambler!* Save the *Rambler?* What's her danger if the lock is
spared?"

Bo went over the old ground again, told of his fear of confiscation. "Can't afford even to ask if he'll let us through,"
he finished. "We got to slip by someway." He turned back
to Foss, "And for God's sake, let's take one thing at a time.
Let's get the *Rambler* through the lock. *Then* we'll worry
about gunboats."

Foss shrugged. "Suits me. Looks like you've bit off a pretty
big chaw gettin' the *Rambler* through."

"You bite off what's to bite. We'll see how the chewing goes." He wheeled to face the others. "It'll take us all.
I rounded up a dozen men this afternoon—all of 'em got a
gun or can get one—" he grinned, "craziest bunch of guns
you ever saw collected up—squirrel rifles, carbines, shot-
guns, and one old fellow's even got a flintlock. But they'll
shoot. Luke, here, has rounded up the arms we got on the
boat. We have three squirrel rifles, two carbines, a Derringer and Sir Henry's horse pistols. Now, this is what I've got
in mind. Miss Phoebe, you and Sir Henry . . ."

He kept them for an hour detailing his plan.

CHAPTER 11

SHE was as pretty as the *Lucy Wing*, he thought. She had the grace, the look of fleetness, and a little of the sheer and swagger. She also had almost as much gingerbread on her superstructure. "Good Lord, Miss Phoebe," he laughed, "I didn't ask you to put their eyes out."

"It would help if I could, though, wouldn't it?" She had come up onto the bridge to show herself off. She whirled to make her dazzle more impressive. "This is every bead and bauble I could find in the trunk. Every bracelet, sequin, necklace, pin and brooch. And the gaudiest dress. Isn't it dreadful?"

It was, he had to admit, the brightest pink he had ever seen—the color of a slice of dead-ripe watermelon. It looked like the Sunday dress of one of the kitchen wenches back home except that it was much more elaborately constructed. It was cleverly cinched in tight at the waist and the full, flowing skirt was gathered over a set of extremely wide hoops. Every inch of the skirt was flounced and ruffled clear to the ankles, with beaded fringe dangling from the ruffles. The bodice was cut very low and a tiny shred of sleeve was worn off the shoulders.

There was, he couldn't help noticing—nobody could have helped noticing—a difference of several shades in the color of the sun-browned face and V of her throat and the pale gold honeyness of her naked shoulders. His eyes followed— where he knew any man's eyes would follow—to the deeper, paler cleft between the high small breasts pushed up and rounded into fullness. Like a pointing arrow it marked the way to the cleft and inevitably on downward and he felt a hot discomfort as his eyes traced the arrow, knowing the pale honeyness was the color and the unblemished smoothness the texture all the way. He felt a spirt of spleen at the disclosure, a resentment and pique at her willingness to show herself. Didn't she know how daring it looked? How open to misinterpretation? If she'd tried she couldn't have found a more wanton way to draw attention to her body than to bare her shoulders and leave that brown V plunging downward.

She had made good use of the beads and baubles she had collected, stitching and pinning them onto the dress so as to catch and reflect the light. She had wound necklaces about her arms and added bracelets to glitter and jingle. Earrings dangled from her ears, and in her hair, which she had pinned high on her head, was a glistening, gorgeously jeweled butterfly. It perched lightly as if it had stopped to taste a curl, to sip, maybe, something of the flower scent which blew from her.

The sun was down now and the late light shimmered through the willows that made a roof over the creek and became water-glowed and leaf-reflected. The light was luminous as if sieved through the sea into some underwater cavern, palely green and ambient. The air was still and heat still weighed it, but now and then it stirred the willow fronds into a sound of sighing like the sea.

In this drowned and luminous air Phoebe Cole paced slowly about the bridge, a glowing incandescence, a lit candle, a gaudy shimmer and shine and glitter—and Bo felt pettish that it was so. Pretty as she was, he couldn't decide whether she looked most like Catfish's madam from the Palace of Joy or a little girl dressed from an attic trunk of her mother's. Neither, he thought, disgruntled, was exactly suited to the occasion.

Her slow pacing set the exaggerated hoops to swaying. She peered down at them. "They bump against my legs," she said. "I'm sure they shouldn't do that. Perhaps I'm not managing them right. I may not," she went on confidingly, "even have them on right. I've never worn hoops before. I only wear crinolines." She hitched at them uncomfortably. "Do you suppose there could be a front and a back, or a left side and a right side?"

"I wouldn't have the vaguest notion," he said shortly.

She didn't notice. "There is a string," she worried on, "and I judged it tied in front. I can't think how you would tie it in back, without help. I wish I knew where Grandfather had got to. He could tell me." She began her slow pace again. "Do they look all right? Are there any humps or bumps where there shouldn't be?"

He watched her sway the length of the bridge. "Look all right to me. No humps or bumps. But there sure is a noble lot of hoops!"

"I know." She giggled. "And look what they do if you're not careful!" She batted them down in front, flat against her, and they hiked dangerously up behind. "I do hope I remember this is the way they behave. Wouldn't it be disgraceful if I forget?"

Bo took a firm stand. "Don't wear 'em, Miss Phoebe. Just don't wear 'em."

"I have to," she cried, "the dress is made for them."

"Can't you wear your what-you-may-call-'ems?"

"Not with this dress. The skirt is too full. Don't you see it takes these wide hoops to take up the width of the skirt? It would trail all over the floor without them."

"Then don't wear the dress."

"But I want to. I went to all sorts of trouble to make it as showy as I could." Her chin went up. "You said keep them distracted. Hold their attention. There's no better way of doing it than with this dress, Captain."

Except no dress at all, he thought to himself. Aloud all he said was, "What I had in mind was more to keep your show moving along, keep singing and making a lot of noise, keep everybody watching you and listening." Another thought struck him. "When the time comes, how're you gonna be able to move as fast as you'll have to? In those contraptions."

"I've taken care of that," she said. "I took the bodice off the skirt and put a drawstring on the skirt. See?" She hoisted the front of the bodice the least bit to show him skirt and bodice were separate. "And under these hoops is another skirt. When the time comes, I'll only have to snip the drawstring, and the hoop string, and they'll drop. I can run like a deer in the underskirt. I have even," she told him triumphantly, "made a little pocket here," and she showed him, "to hold a pair of tiny scissors."

Bo rumpled his hair. "Looks like you've thought of nearly everything, and I don't mean to be contrary, Miss Phoebe. I know you've gone to a lot of trouble. But how do you aim to handle all that skirt and those hoops in the skiff? They'll hang over and get wet—bound to, much as there is of 'em."

Her mobile face reflected several things in quick succession

—consternation first. The ash-gray eyes rounded, blinked, and one hand crept to her mouth. Then the eyes clouded and showed dismay. When her hand dropped, the mouth was turned down in woe. "I clear forgot! I never once thought about having to arrange them in the boat. They'll never fit." Suddenly she batted the hoops furiously, first on one side and then on the other. "Dad-burn it! Why must the only real show dress in the trunk be made for these plague-taked iron things! Why must the fashion demand them? Why do women want to hang them around their waists and trundle around in great wide skirts? It's a silly fashion—a stupid fashion!" Tears burned her eyes. "The dress was so perfect, Captain. It was exactly what was needed. Oh, dad-blame it, doggonit, confound it . . ."

"Try God's britches," Bo proffered, amused.

It stopped her and she glared angrily at him, her breath coming in puffs. "It isn't funny, Captain."

"I know it isn't. Why don't you cut off about three of those bottom ruffles and wear your petticoats and quit having conniption fits? Wouldn't that work?"

Like a thermometer cooled by a rain shower, her anger dropped. She hoisted the front of the immense skirt and examined it. "Now, why didn't I think of that? Why, it'll be simple." She dropped her hem and asked eagerly, "Have I time? It won't take a minute. I don't even need to take the dress off. Just snip and snip." Her hands snipped the air rapidly.

"Plenty of time. We said six-thirty. You've got at least fifteen minutes yet."

She caught up the great skirt and fled.

Bo leaned on the rail and spat into the creek. He ought to have known it'd be whole hog or none with her. That, given a role to play in the plan for the night, she would build it up into Sir Henry's dramatics. She wouldn't be satisfied with something common or ordinary. Though she didn't know it, she was too much an actress, and come by it naturally, not to know instinctively, and with great flair, precisely how to accomplish what he had wished. He couldn't fault her for that. She and Sir Henry would take care of their end of the plot, not only with zeal, but with considerable relish. He grinned, wishing he could see the show they would put on and watch its effects on Buckner's troops. He still wished, disquietedly, there didn't have to be such a display of bosom and shoulders, but she was so set on wearing the dress he didn't have the heart to complain further.

He didn't examine very far his dislike of the display of honeyed flesh. All it amounted to was an inner uneasiness, an involuntary and ingenerate reaction because, he supposed, it might make trouble. He put it away firmly. Her grandfather would be with her. Sir Henry was to seek out the general, or an aide, and ask permission to put on a show for the troops. Phoebe wouldn't be alone, not for a single second, with a soldier. She couldn't come to harm.

She came running onto the bridge, her guitar now clutched in her hand. "Goodness, how glad I am to be rid of those iron things, Captain! I feel like a bird out of a cage. I can't think why it didn't occur to me to snip off those three bottom ruffles earlier. You must know a dreadful lot about women's clothing."

Bo looked her over. The crinolines held the still full skirt out stiffly, but the width had been lessened by a good three feet. He fetched up one of Foss's sighs. "I have three sisters, Miss Phoebe, and a mother. My father had to buy a second carriage to accommodate their hoops when they go to church on Sunday morning. It was impossible to put the four of them in one carriage. You ought to see the procession my family makes when we're all at home on Sunday. My four brothers, my father and I, on horseback. My mother and one sister in the first carriage. The two older sisters in the second. We look like a parade—all because of the fashion for women today."

Phoebe laughed. "Isn't it silly? I will never wear them." She flounced the great skirt generously. "The crinolines do very well, I think. And you were absolutely right. I can move so much more freely." She settled her ruffles. "Have you seen Grandfather at all, Captain? I thought he might be in the cabin but he wasn't."

"No," Bo shook his head, "not seen hide nor hair of him. He was sitting around talking to that bunch of wharf rats I hired last I saw of him."

"I don't know where he could have got to." She bit her lip and puzzled, then brightened. "He has dressed, however. He meant to wear his minstrel costume and I laid it out for him. It's gone, so he has dressed."

"He's probably prowling around somewhere."

"How much more time is there?"

He looked at his watch. "Five minutes or so, maybe ten. You feeling nervous?"

"Oh, no. Not nervous at all. I don't want us to be late putting off is all." She arranged a ruffle, touched the gold lace edging the bodice of her dress, shifted a bangle on her arm and sat, suddenly, on the stool, out of breath. "Yes, I am. I am as nervous as a witch. I'm so afraid we may not do our part well, Captain. I'm so afraid something may go wrong. Grandfather and I owe you so much. I want so badly for us to be of help to you. But I think of a hundred things—suppose the general doesn't want his troops entertained? Suppose we can't hold their attention? What if . . ."

"Now, Miss Phoebe," Bo said, "we have gone over every bit

of that. If the general, or his aide-de-camp, turns you down, just go back to the skiff and drift on down to the lock. Sit there, in the skiff—I told you about the willows there. And if that don't work, row across the river to the town. Wait for us. Be no trouble taking you aboard."

"I know. I'm just excited."

"Whyn't you calm down a little. I tell you. Play me a tune on your guitar. Play me a tune and sing. I won't get to hear you tonight."

She picked up her guitar and plinked it to see if it was in tune. "What would you like to hear?"

"No matter. Whatever you want to sing." He draped himself over the rail. "You know 'Lorena'?"

"Who doesn't? It's come to be the love song of both armies in this war."

She fiddled with the pegs of the strings a moment, tried a chord or two, then settled back on the stool and began. She sang effortlessly and without affectation, the song pitched a little low so her low-pitched voice could manage it, the slight roughness of her speaking voice plain in her singing, too. It made a break and catch and breathiness that was nice to hear. The ballad's slow tempo was suited to the light and the hour:

> A hundred months have passed, Lorena,
> Since last I held that hand in mine,
> And felt the pulse beat fast, Lorena,
> Though mine beat faster far than thine.
> A hundred months, 'twas flowery May,
> When up the hilly slope we climbed,
> To watch the dying of the day,
> And hear the distant church bells chime.

She broke it off with a crashing discord. "I am sick of that song, Captain. It's too stupidly catter-yowling and sentimental. A hundred months! Why couldn't he have said seven or eight years?"

Bo laughed. "I doubt eight years and four months would have fitted the rhyme, Miss Phoebe."

She fetched a brisker tune out of the guitar. "Oh, I don't doubt I'll have to sing 'Lorena' tonight, and watch every soldier present wipe a tear away. What's there to weep about?"

"Absence," Bo said promptly, "and the fear it may be forever."

She sobered a moment, then brought a smile back. "For you, sir, who are not absent, here is a gayer tune." She trilled a run up the instrument and said mischievously, "I'll bet you never heard this one."

> Oh, I wish I was in de land ob cotton,
> Old times dar am not forgotten,
> Look away, look away,
> Look away, Dixie land.
> In Dixie land whar I was born in,
> Early on one frosty mornin'
> Look away, look away,
> Look away, Dixie land.
>
> Den I wish I was in Dixie,
> Hooray! Hooray!
> In Dixie land I'll take my stand
> To lib and die in Dixie,
> Away, away, away down south in Dixie.
> Away, away, away down south in Dixie.

She slowed the last phrase and held it homesickly, till you'd have sworn, Bo thought, she'd been born south in Dixie herself and was pining away to get back. "You sure ought to do that one for Buckner's boys, Miss Phoebe."

"I mean to. You know, the Confederates are beginning to use that song for a marching song."

"Hadn't heard it. Where'd you pick it up?"

"It's a song Dan Emmett wrote for a minstrel show. He was up north one winter, so they say, and it was cold and snowy and he got homesick for the South and the warmth. Got to remembering all the good times and the good weather. He was sick to death of the cold and the snow and the ice and the hard times. So one day he sat down and wrote this song. Used it for a walk-around in his show."

"It's a good tune. It'd set anybody to prancing. I'm obliged to you for singing it for me." He looked around and measured the light and confirmed it with his watch. "Time to go, Miss Phoebe. You ready?"

She stood up and, taking a good breath, braced her shoulders back. "Yes."

"You won't forget your instructions?"

Her eyes met his steadily. "Of course not. You've drilled them into my head enough. We are to drift down until we come abreast of the ferry. We are to put in to the right bank —the lock side—and tie up. Grandfather is to ask the sentry if he may see the general or one of his aides. If we are allowed, I am to go with him and Grandfather is to tell him that we are stranded actors, we'd like to put on a show for the troops and we'll do it for whatever we may be able to collect when the show is over." She went on, reciting one step after another. "We do the show and we make it a lively and noisy show—with a lot of singing and jigging and stepping about. When the confusion begins we are to act panicky. I am to cry, 'The gunboats! The Federals are coming!'" She looked pensive. "I still think you should let me faint, Captain. That's what any lady would do, frightened out of her wits."

"No," he still denied it. "It'd take too much of your time. You and Sir Henry are to make a run for it. Nobody'll notice you in the mixup. Just unfurl your heels, Miss Phoebe, and keep going. Stick to the shore. We'll haul up about three miles below the lock and wait for you. Just keep to the shore and you can't miss us. And I misdoubt you'll be stopped. We'll wait till . . ."

"Till ten o'clock. If we aren't there by then, you'll have to leave us behind. But we'll be there, Captain, I promise you. We'll be there long before ten o'clock."

"And if you miss us," Bo took up, "you're to backtrack and borrow a skiff off Will Surrey. Don't go back to the *Rambler*'s skiff. He'll be on the watch for you. We'll hole up in some creek or other farther down and wait."

"And if we have to borrow the skiff we are to drift downstream until we find you."

"Good. You've got it pat. Now, don't try anything but what's been agreed on, hear? Don't go thinking up something else. You do, and . . ."

"I know," she said, "and we won't. Everything has got to work together. We have to rendezvous with you on time. You needn't worry, Captain, I know exactly what you want us to do and we'll do it, I promise. Oh, Captain, do take care!" She suddenly reached to clutch one of his big hands to her bosom. "Don't risk your life for your boat, please!"

She was so warm with enthusiasm and excitement he felt as if his hand had been burned. Embarrassed, he didn't know what to do but struggle to free it. "Risking my boat is risking my life," he mumbled. He recovered a little of his composure by handing her her guitar. "Here. We better get down on the deck now. Boys'll have the skiff ready."

She grasped the guitar with one hand and lifted her skirt with the other. They turned toward the companionway but stopped as they heard someone coming pounding up. "Now, what . . ." Bo began.

Luke came shinnying up, skipping two steps at a time. "Bo," he panted, "something's gone wrong. The skiff's gone!"

Bo stiffened. "How in the hell can the skiff be gone? Wasn't somebody watching it? Weren't some of the boys with it?"

Luke nodded, trying to catch his breath. "Sure, but that old codger said he wanted to borrow it a minute. Said he'd set a fishing line upcreek a ways. Allowed he had time to run it 'fore leaving. Boys didn't think nothing of it. Nor would I, had I known it."

Phoebe was incredulous. "Grandfather? Grandfather did that? Is that who you're talking about?"

"Yes, ma'am. All dressed up in that blackface outfit of his'n, too. But he never went upstream. Went down, fast as he could row. Just clean lit a shuck out'n here."

Bo swore.

"Grandfather never set a fishing line in his life," Phoebe said flatly. "I don't understand . . ."

"You checked your guns?" Bo asked Luke.

"No. Never thought to."

Bo looked off downcreek, his tongue probing and swelling his cheek. "Believe you'll find his pistols are missing."

Luke looked consternated, then pulled thoughtfully at one earlobe. "I'll be damned. Who'd have thought it?"

"What?" Phoebe wanted to know. "What are you talking about?" She caught Bo's arm and shook it. "What do you mean, his pistols are gone?"

Bo looked down at her and felt the sorriest for her. She would worry now—but there was no help for it. "I'm afraid our little scheme for you and Sir Henry to put on a show

for the general's troops has got to be forgotten, Miss Phoebe,"
he said. "Looks like your grandfather has made a change
according to his own ideas. Looks like he is aiming to join
Luke and his crew."

She stood very still, taking it in. He thought she might
throw another conniption fit. Thought she might even
screech and faint. Or try to get him to stop the old gent. He
thought she might stamp around and rage and carry on. He
watched her anxiously, but she just stood there very straight
and quiet. Then her eyes filled with tears. "Wouldn't you
know that's what he'd do? Wouldn't you just know it?" Her
voice was soft with love and pride. "I should have suspected
when he was missing half an hour ago. But he needn't have
slipped away. He needn't have been afraid. I wouldn't have
tried to stop him. Not even," she whirled on Bo, "not even
for your very great kindness, Captain. Nor to assist you more.
How wonderful of him. Oh, didn't I tell you there was no
one like him? Just no one!"

"I believe it," Bo said dryly. "I just hope he remembers
enough of that part of the plan not to get in trouble."

"Do you take him for an idiot?" she said furiously. "A
man who can learn his lines for a new part in one day? Of
course he'll remember!" She brandished her guitar a little.
"And he'll probably lead your wharf rats in an even more
brilliant strategy!" She gathered her skirts to march away.

"Where you going, Miss Phoebe?" Bo called.

"I'm going to take off this silly dress, Captain. I'd feel an
utter fool trying to help you get the *Rambler* through the
lock in it."

They watched her go around the pilothouse to the cabin.
Bo fetched a deep sigh. "I dunno how she's aiming to help,
but I've not got the least doubt she will, Luke. Tobe didn't
miss the mark when he said she was strong-minded."

Luke struggled with his laughter. "Reckon he was right about having no argifying with her, too."

"You don't get far arguing with her, at that," Bo agreed.

They drifted down the companionway. A check of the *Rambler*'s arsenal showed that Sir Henry had taken both his horse pistols. He had left a short note among the guns. "Don't like the idea of play-acting when there's shooting to be done. Will find your men and play a more active role." He had added in a cramped postscript, "Besides nobody can shoot my pistols but myself. They kick like a mule."

Bo folded the note. "Old grasshopper," he said. "Hope nothing don't happen to him. It'd kill her."

"Won't nothing happen to him," Luke said, "I'll sort of look after him."

"Do that." Bo looked around. "Not long now till you boys can start."

"No. Bo, Tobe don't like his part either. Being left on the boat. Wants to go along with me. Better keep an eye on him."

"No need. I've talked to him. Told him why he'd have to stay." He looked down the deck at the riffraff he had picked up in town. They looked to be desperate characters, not much to put your dependence on. "Reckon any of 'em will panic?"

"Figure I can handle 'em," Luke said.

Foss, a murky figure in the dusk, loomed up. " 'Bout time, ain't it?"

Bo scanned the willowy tunnel overhead. "Another ten minutes, I'd say. Be lighter on the river in the open than under these willows. Don't want it too light."

Luke watched Bo lean against a hogshead as loose and casual as if he embarked a dozen men and the *Rambler* on a dangerous venture every day of his life. He had never admired him so much. Nobody but Bohannon Cartwright, he believed, would have thought of this plan to get the *Rambler* through the lock right under the noses of the Confederates. And nobody but Bohannon Cartwright could ever pull it off. Luke didn't doubt but what he would. Bold and risky as the plan was, it had a lot of sense to it. It didn't ask for trouble and wouldn't give any. But when things quietened down, later, the *Rambler* would be a safe distance yon side the lock. If it didn't work—but Luke put that thought away. Bo would make it work.

"Where'd you get them skiffs for Luke and the boys?" Foss asked.

"Will Surrey got the lend of 'em for me. Didn't ask where he found 'em."

"Wouldn't be hard," Foss said. "Everybody in Rochester has got a skiff."

There was a silence. Though he gave no evidence of anxiety, kept slack and easy in his body, Bo's thoughts went on ahead—went over again the entire plan, went over the timing, went over every possibility. If it went wrong, it would go wrong bad, and Buckner would have the *Rambler*. But he didn't think it would go wrong.

Luke asked, out of the dark, "Them not giving the show, Bo, will that throw you off any?"

"No. Not exactly. Been good if they could have given the show. Anybody watching a show is resting easy, not thinking. Off guard. But it don't make that much difference. Engineers'll be making a God's plenty of noise to cover."

There was another long pause. "What you aimin' to do if they don't quit drillin' when Luke springs his little surprise?" Foss asked, then. His voice was quiet, unworried. Just a question, almost idly asked.

"They'll quit," Bo said, just as quietly, just as unworriedly. "The scare will be too great. Drilling won't be very important when they think the Federals have come. All right, Luke, get 'em rounded up, get 'em moving."

Luke fumbled in the dark and found Bo's hand. He gripped it tight. "Sure. See you in Paradise."

They all laughed. Foss said, "Don't take no chances on makin' it nothin' but Paradise landing, Luke."

"I won't."

"Got your money to pay off them town boys?" Bo asked.

"I've got it. Safe."

"All right. Pay 'em off soon as it's over and turn 'em loose. Collect up the old codger and bring him and our boys on down. Good luck, Luke."

Luke mumbled, strangely touched, not knowing what to say, finding it best finally to repeat what Bo had said, "Good luck."

There was the sound of the boy's swift feet on the deck, a stir and commotion on the head, a rattle and subdued clinking of the guns, a murmuring of voices, then the *Rambler* rocked a little as Luke's small army jumped ashore. There was a rustling and sliding as the men made for the skiffs tied up below, then nothing but silence so quickly did the boy move the men away. A few moments later there was a scraping sound. "They're in the boats," Bo said.

Foss shifted to let the *Rambler* rock him more comfortably. "It ain't to worry, Bo. He'll do good."

"I've got no doubts of it."

The *Rambler* was steadying up. Bo listened and could hear nothing more. One good thing, wasn't anybody in any river town, idlers, loafers, riffraff though they might be in every other way, but didn't know how to handle a boat and handle it quiet as death. There'd never be a sound from the oars.

He looked up to judge the sky, forgetting for a moment the willow tunnel overhead. He waited for the breeze now springing up to push the limbs around a little, peering for a star. "No stars," he said, then. "Clouded over."

"Allowed it would," Foss said, "from the mare's tails all over this afternoon. But it don't smell like rain. Well," moving away, "say when, boy."

Bo let him go a piece. He called softly, then, "Foss? Whaddya name that hound of yours?"

Foss's unruffled reply came back. "Sir Henry. The two of 'em is about alike mangy."

Bo's laughter floated out to follow and to meet Foss's coming back, to join and meld and make one easy, companionable sound, an economy of understanding and pleasure. Bo was still taking delight in it when he went onto the bridge. When the Old Master made Foss, he broke the mold, he thought, satisfied he'd done either the best or the worst he could and willing to abide by it either way. He'd turned loose in the world a crotchety, quirky man with few passions and those the nice ones of total loyalty and willing commitment. Add a quick and saving wit and a training in thrift and a mighty good job had been done.

Bo put his hand on the wheel and rubbed its worn satin. Foss and him—they'd have a real proving tonight. But if all things else worked as well as Foss and him would work, it would prove out fine. He rubbed the spoke absently and searched out down the creek and both banks and overhead. Dark of night on them, now, and nothing to do but wait for their own time. He had an idea it was going to feel like a piece of eternity and he set himself to be as patient as he could.

CHAPTER 12

THEY were running dark.

Bo was steering by the treeline, sliding the *Rambler* slowly along in the shadows as best he could, avoiding the middle of the river except when he had to bear out for snags or slides. He was glad for the good water under him, for the depths the Green had gouged out for herself along here. They said it was near seventy feet in this piece of water and he judged they were right. Save in an extremely low stage you had no worries.

Tobe and Jonah were firing for Foss, tending fire cautiously so as to blow no sparks from the stacks. And Foss had even found a downed ash while they were tied up, to make a quick fire and no smoke.

Bo was letting the bells alone. Till they got to the lock Foss didn't need a bell. He had his steam exactly where he wanted it and Bo was letting him have the say. They had need to slip quietly. You couldn't steamboat silently, but you could prowl along at a snail's creep with a minimum amount of noise. At that speed there was a down-far breathing of the machinery, a muffled snuffling and panting, which had no pride or swagger but which also raised no disturbance to be heard a mile inland.

Moving, under way again, the die cast, Bo felt almost equally his absolute possession of himself and his boat. He was calmly certain of his control of his boat and no experience or emergency had ever found him more calm or cool-headed, more completely in control of himself. Not that he felt tranquil or serene, for he didn't. He knew he was tight and geared up, but it was the gear and tightness of readiness. Like a good general he had foreseen every contingency but the unpredictable. The scales were always weighted against you there and nothing to be done about it but trust to your own quick judgment. And like a good general, all care taken and his troops now committed, he felt keyed up but steady and unagitated, brought to the brink but undismayed by the depths. His only concession to his not quite total nervelessness was a cigar which he chewed on without lighting.

He pulled into the middle to bear past the Enola Ferry. It would be moored on the right bank for the night because the ferryman lived nearby. Watching the left treeline to gauge his distance to the middle he saw a shadow darker than the night outside his door. To keep from startling her he made his voice quiet and unstressed. "Whyn't you come in the pilothouse, Miss Phoebe? There's a bench along the back for sitting."

Her own voice was kept hushed. "I don't want to be a bother."

Until now he hadn't seen her since they had got under way. Just before casting off he had gone to the cabin looking for her. He had found the door closed and he had knocked.

She had answered instantly but her voice was so muffled he guessed she was lying down. "Yes. What is it?"

"Wanted to talk to you a minute. We're about ready to cast off." He wondered if she might have been crying a little. She was the kind who if she did have to weep would find a place to do it alone. She wouldn't want her defenses down before others. He imagined she was a little afraid, in spite of her brave words, for her grandfather. And though she hadn't said so, she was bound to be more than a little disappointed to lose her own role in the plan for tonight. Like a child promised a picnic then the promise broken.

Her voice sounded clearer when she spoke next, as though she had got up and come closer to the door. "I'm not dressed, Captain. Can you tell me through the door?"

"Sure." He told her then, quietly so as not to alarm her, that just before the *Rambler* got to the lock he wished her to go down on the deck. "I've made a kind of hidey-hole for you down there with some bales and barrels. It'll be the safest place on the boat. Up high here, in the cabin, it'll be too exposed if there's any trouble."

"I see." She sounded listless. "Thank you, Captain, I'll remember. But until we get to the lock?"

"Oh, till then, go anywhere you please. Like always."

"Yes. All right, Captain."

Now he told her, "Be no bother to me. Come in."

She came and he saw that over the dark dress she wore she was trailing a dark blanket. It was folded about her shoulders. "You cold?" he asked, wonderingly.

"No," she said, "it's to take down with me when I go below. Do I have to sit on the bench now?"

"Well, no. Thought you'd rather is all."

"I'd rather stand and watch."

"Whatever you want."

It was the first time she had been in the pilothouse. Behind him and a little to one side she was out of his range and vision. She kept so quiet he could almost have forgotten her except that she moved occasionally, he could hear her breathing deeper from time to time, and once in a while she spoke. Once she said, "Is the dark night a good thing for you?"

"No difference," he said. "It won't be dark when we get there. The camp'll likely have lights and the engineers will be drilling with flares."

A little later she wondered if the clouds weren't breaking up. "I can see better. It must be growing lighter."

"You got your full nightsight," he told her. "No night is so dark you can't see. There's no such thing as blind-dark. Except down in a cave. They say down in Mammoth Cave there's a place that is pure dark."

Normally she would have been curious. She would have questioned him eagerly, but she let the statement go without comment. It was a gauge of her disappointment, he supposed. She had been so full of the plan, so excited by her part. To have her grandfather go hightailing it off, leaving her behind, had left her downhearted and she couldn't lift herself above it yet.

"How much farther?" she asked, then.

"Not much. See that glow on the sky? That's their lights. We're gonna stop along here pretty soon and wait till time. Won't be long."

Ten minutes later he began to steer the *Rambler* close in to the right bank. "Tell you what," he said, "I don't want to gong Foss. Whyn't you run down and tell him this is where I'm aiming to wait. Tell him to give me slow and then backing, commencing right now."

She threw off the blanket and he heard her feet pad lightly.

Then she was between him and the horizon briefly before she disappeared down the companionway. When she came back he thought of another errand for her and he used her for several messages to Foss before they stopped in the deep shadows. She was back in the pilothouse. "Listen," she said, "what is that noise? I didn't hear it before."

"Machinery was making too much racket. That's the engineers' hammers. I counted on them drilling all night. We couldn't have got this close to the lock without them hearing us if they hadn't been. I figured they'd be making such a racket it'd drown us out."

"It sounds like heavy pounding."

"Don't you know how they drill in rock?"

"No."

"One man holds a steel point against the rock face and turns it between every lick of the hammer. Another man swings the hammer. Sometimes, if they're good enough, two can swing. But Buckner's not got any that good. It's gonna take 'em a time and a time to get deep enough to hold a charge of dynamite."

They waited quietly, then. The dark was not quiet, however. It was full of small sounds all around them, splashings and rustlings and night birds and katydids, the deep, slow breathing of the engine. Overlaying all of the natural and familiar sounds was the steady ring of steel on steel until even it began to be a part of the other sounds. Once Phoebe started to speak and Bo said, sharply, "No. Don't talk now."

He was listening so hard now that he felt as if his ears had to grow bigger to hear better. As the minutes passed he grew anxious and he finally risked a match to look at his watch. "Right now's the time," he muttered. "Wonder what's . . ."

As if Luke, too, had looked at his watch, there was a crackle of gunfire. Bo flung himself at the wheel. "Get below, Miss Phoebe," he yelled and forgot her.

He didn't need to ring, nor did he now need a messenger. Foss had been listening and waiting, too. The gunfire was the bell and the gong. Foss would be ready.

Still quietly the *Rambler* pulled out into the river. Over the chuff of the engine Bo could hear heavier firing now, brisk and staccato. Luke was bunching his men, keeping them firing steadily. He couldn't tell yet if Luke was also moving them about on the hill. That was the plan. The hill was the rear of the Confederate position, downriver of it. Luke's ragtag army of village loafers and the *Rambler*'s roustabouts was to create a diversion, make a lot of noise, draw the Confederates away from the river. He was to keep his men bunched so as to make the firing sound heavy, he was to keep them firing as steadily as possible, and he was to move them about from time to time to give the impression of a solid number of troops. No military man, Bo hadn't known precisely what Federal skirmishers feeling out the rear of the Confederate position would have done but as a born-and-raised Kentucky hillbilly he knew what he would do, what any cautious country boy would do. Sneak in from the back and keep moving around.

"They have quit drilling," Phoebe said from behind him.

His head jerked around. "I thought I told you to get below."

"You did, Captain, but I'm not going. I'm not going to be burrowed behind your bales and boxes like a coward. I would die of anxiety. Whatever happens, I'd rather meet it in the open. I'm going to stay right here!"

He didn't have time to argue with her or to plead and at that moment he had no inclination to do either. What he would have liked to do was shake her till the combs in her

187

hair rained down. He swore roundly, not caring that she heard, and let it go with a warning. "It's your risk. There's glass on three sides of this pilothouse. If there's any shooting at us some of that glass will likely be shattered and sent flying. If you're fool enough to stay here, take care. I'll not have time to do it for you."

"I don't expect you to," she said coolly.

"And don't get in my way," he added.

She made no reply except to sniff, but the sniff was eloquent. It said plainly, what do you take me for, and when did I ever get in your way? All the time, he felt like saying churlishly, and it seemed like years she or her grandfather had been underfoot having to be taken thought of.

They said no more.

A sound Bo had been listening for came to him now, shouts and yells from the camp. His grip on the wheel eased a little. The alarm and confusion in the camp had begun. One of the sheep in the pen below bleated suddenly and it sounded as loud as a trumpet blast. Phoebe said, "Shall I go down?"

"No need," Bo said. "That grass the boys cut this afternoon has kept 'em quiet when it was needed. They can blat their heads off now." He paused and cocked his head. "Listen. What's that?" There was a new, more booming sound, dulled by distance but still louder and more reverberant than Luke's crackling musketry. "Have they broke out the artillery? They've got two pieces."

"I think," Phoebe said, "that was one of Grandfather's pistols. They sound like cannon, Captain. There's the other one, now."

Bo listened, a little awed. "Why, he'll make Buckner think we've got cannon!"

"I expect that is Grandfather's idea."

As the dull exploding boom came again Bo broke into laughter. "The old pirate! Who'd have thought it of him? He'll make Buckner think he's being invaded."

"If you time the intervals, Captain, you'll notice they are the exact interval a good gun crew uses to load and fire a small piece of artillery. Grandfather has perfected it because he uses his pistols for artillery fire when it's needed in a show. He gets some very good effects."

"I can see he would. I suppose you knew this was what he meant to do?"

"Oh, yes, I had no doubt of it when we learned he had gone. He couldn't resist putting his pistols and his technique to work for you."

"Well, I'm obliged. He'll really bewilder 'em."

They were coming up to the bend now. The whole camp was before them, lit dimly by lanterns and a few flares, and they could see plainly the great confusion Luke's little army had caused. Like ants disturbed in their hill, men were dashing about yelling, shouting, running in and out of the tents, charging into each other, bounding away only to turn aimlessly back. Caught by surprise some of them were still struggling with articles of clothing, trying to get on shirts and pants and coats. Men were grabbing at the stacked guns, fighting over them, jerking them away from each other. It was a madhouse of disorganization, congestion, turmoil and bustle, a pandemonium and a riot, and the Tower of Babel couldn't have been noisier. It drowned out Luke's gunfire altogether now.

Bo's spirits rose to elation. He shouted to Phoebe, "It's working! It's working fine. Just like we planned. All that noise and hubbub will cover us perfect!"

"If the engineers have just been drawn away . . ." Phoebe said, a little out of breath.

"And if the locktender has had his chance . . ."

As the bend sharpened the lock began to come in sight. There was a long, eternal-feeling moment when they yet could not tell. Phoebe came up beside him and stood straining forward with him, her shoulder rubbing his. "Can you see? Can you see, Bo?"

"Not yet." Then he let out a whoop. "They've not only quit, but they've taken their flares with 'em! Look how dark it is! Oh, this is gonna be like sopping molasses! This is gonna be like cutting butter with a hot knife!"

"Oh, look, Bo, look! The gates are open! The locktender has the gates open!" Phoebe blew out a long breath. "Oh, my goodness, what a tremendous relief. It was most worrisome about *that!*"

"I knew if he had a chance—if the engineers run off—I knew Dan Fields'd do his part—if he could." His jubilation was making him talk in spurts, like stage asides. "He was the worst put-out man you ever saw—having his lock blown up. Seemed tickled to help if he could."

The white lock walls loomed near and Bo shut up to give cribbing the *Rambler* all his attention. He signaled Foss and the boat slowed to a crawl. So slowly she was like some huge inchworm, she nosed through the dark opening, slid down the length of the walls and sighed gently to a stop.

Jonah and Tobe were onto the land wall instantly, and a shadowy figure came alongside on the river wall. It stepped aboard to lean on the front sill. "Hey, Bo! God damn, man, where'd you find cannon for your boys to shoot?"

"Dan!" Bo shouted, then he lied, on the spur of the moment, but with great joy, "Stole one of Buckner's—right out from under his nose!" Just let that story float up and down the river! What a fool it would make Buckner look! How it would be rolled over tongues and savored! A steamboat-man had put it all over the general!

"I don't believe it," the locktender said, but he said it be-lievingly and delightedly.

"Make what you will of it," Bo said. "You got some boys on the job, have you?"

"Sam and Will. They're skeered but willing."

"What happened when the firing commenced?"

"All hell broke loose. Them engineers done just what you said they'd do—dropped everything and run."

"Even took their flares with 'em," Bo said.

"No, me and the boys doused 'em. They just cut and run. They had all the gates open so all we had to do was close the lower ones. You'd come any sooner, though, you'd a had to wait."

"Allowed for it. How'd the boys make out with the gen-eral?"

"Why, he said he'd take our proposition under considera-tion. Said he didn't much want to blow up the lock, but he couldn't see no other way. Several of us expounded on us-ing them logs, but I couldn't say how impressed he was. He kept his men drilling right on. The most he'd say was he'd ponder on it."

"You keep pestering him about it. Logs jammed in this crib'd stop those gunboats flat. Keep bothering him with the notion." Bo creened around. "Ain't they through winding them gates up yet?"

"Just now."

Four dark forms sped silently down the walls. Dan Fields laughed. "Them boys is so skeered they run like greased lightning. Bet if you could see their faces they'd be several shades lighter than they was a while ago."

"Don't know as I blame 'em," Bo said. "Anybody happens to spot us they're liable to get hurt first."

"Ain't nobody gonna spot you. There's too much commotion going on."

"We don't get down in this crib before that commotion begins to ease off, they will," Bo said.

"You're on your way right now," the locktender said. "Well, good luck, Bo. They got a patrol boat downriver a piece—couple of miles maybe. Keep your eyes open for it."

"How big a boat?"

"Just an old ferry flat."

"I'll look out." The locktender stepped off onto the wall as the *Rambler* began to lower. Bo called after him, "Thanks, Dan. Oh, one other thing. Any new word about the gunboats?"

"Nary a word."

Bo watched the walls rise as the *Rambler* went down rapidly. He rubbed the back of his neck and said, "I'm just as pleased to be getting out of sight of those folks ashore. Felt too much like a sitting duck up there."

"I think they must be getting organized, now," Phoebe said. "There doesn't seem to be as much confusion."

"We're not gonna make it a minute too soon," Bo admitted. "Twenty minutes is about as fast as you can lock through. I figured it ought to take them about the same time to come to their senses, but I dunno . . ."

There was a rattle of musketry very close and a sudden shouting on the bank. There was also an anguished yelp down the lock wall. Bo shoved Phoebe down as he rushed past her to the bridge. "Stay there. They've spotted the boys. They're shooting at 'em."

On the bridge he heard their bare feet slapping the wall as they came flying. The Confederate guns sounded like a bunch of enormous firecrackers set off all at once and there was the whine of bullets overhead. The two Negroes dropped to the deck. Bo yelled down at them, "Tobe? Jonah?"

"We is bofe heah, suh," Tobe answered.

"Either of you hurt?"

"No, suh. Not us. Ain't scratched."

"Dan's two boys?"

"One ob dem nicked, ah reckon. Dey done jumped in de river. Gwine swim de other bank."

"How far did you get the gates open?"

"Might' near all de way, Capt'n. Might' near. Ain't but a crack to go."

Bo clipped back to the wheel, gonged Foss for slow ahead and waited, fidgeting, until the *Rambler* began to move. He was most afraid, now, of being boarded. The *Rambler* was hidden in the lock chamber and he hoped, desperately, the troops would be slow to follow up their fire. There was a good chance it wouldn't even occur to them there was a boat in the lock. They wouldn't be expecting such a thing. Spotting the boys on the lock wall, he hoped they would believe they were Federals trying to operate the lock for the gunboats downriver. But whatever they might have believed when they opened fire, it wouldn't take long for some officer to order a closer investigation. He had to have the *Rambler* in the open before then.

He nudged her against the gates, rang for full ahead, and as Foss gave it to him plowed her through and out of the crib. He heard a guard rail crumple and splinter, like the slow toppling of a falling tree, the high scream of pain first, then the groan of rending and tearing. But the gates gave and the boat dipped out of the crib.

The moment she left the protection of the lock walls she was fully exposed to the raking fire of the troops on the bank. Bo could see the men deployed along the bank and he heard their shouting when the *Rambler* came into view. Their fire was increased, harassing the boat and thudding into her superstructure. The glass on the right side of the pilothouse suddenly shattered and Bo ducked, wincing as the shreds bit into his face and hands. But they were scooting along now, rapidly leaving the encampment behind. The soldiers on the bank were running behind them, still shooting, but in a few more seconds, just a few more, the *Rambler* would have shown them her heels.

Her nose was plowing water, her paddles were churning, and sparks flew from her stacks. She was like a duck, Bo thought, grinning at the idea, getting up on the step and all but flapping her wings to take off and fly! He held her steady down the middle and let Foss pour on steam, and Foss was pouring it on heavy. He felt a heady sense of triumph as he left the camp behind and he didn't want to stop the flight of the *Rambler*. He wanted to send her all the way down, down and on down, with this giddy sense of flying, this magnificent elation at having conquered all odds, this swelling and bursting feeling of pride and more pride in his old lady of the river, his old plain-faced lady, and Foss and Luke and Tobe—and, God, the clouds had blown away and there were ten million stars in the sky and he was right up among them and crazy enough to try to pick a bouquet of them and dizzy with joy and victory and the river was dark and the camp was only a glow behind. He pounded the wheel and shouted and kept the *Rambler* tearing on down.

The most commonplace sound on earth brought him to his senses. The sheep were about to raise the hurricane deck with their bleating. As recognition penetrated, the exaltation drained slowly away until in the shoes of a joy-mad man stood the sobered, responsible captain again. Running the lock under fire was all very well, exciting and exhilarating—but his job was carrying freight and seeing to it it was delivered in good shape. Those sheep were his most valuable cargo. He rang for half ahead, then slow, and settled his job back on himself like an old and well-worn coat.

A stir behind him reminded him of Phoebe. He was consternated to think he had forgotten her, too. "Miss Phoebe, you all right?" He tried to find her, peering about on the floor where he had shoved her and couldn't. Then he began to feel panicky. Lord above, maybe she'd been killed or struck down by a flying splinter of glass.

"Perfectly all right, Captain," she said. "I've been sitting here for quite some time. Here on the bench." There was a tinkling fall of glass and she laughed. "I'm still shaking glass off my blanket but I'm all in one piece. Thank heaven I had sense enough to cover with it when the pane shattered. My only wound," she continued cheerfully, "is a lump on my head where I fell against the wheel when you shoved me down."

"I'm sorry," he said. "Those were real bullets whizzing around."

"I gathered that. But I felt an absolute idiot lying there when I meant to be so helpful if I could."

"Most help you could have been," he assured her.

"Were you injured, Captain?"

"Some scratches, I'd guess. Not had time to think about it."

"Couldn't we have the lantern, now? I could see . . ."

"Not yet," he cut her off, "not till we pass that patrol boat. And don't get up and move around, Miss Phoebe. There's broken glass all over."

As if she sensed some beginning impatience, she gave over talking.

They had gone racing past Davenport Landing in their first wild dash and had chugged more temperately past Chiggarville. Nearing Woods, now, Bo guessed he would find the patrol boat soon. He didn't think Buckner would have had time to alert the boat, even with his fastest horse, and this far downriver no sound of the late excitement could have been heard. The racket the *Rambler* was making would probably be the boat's only alert. What the patrol's reaction would be depended on their orders. If they were set as an outpost only to keep watch for the Federal gunboats, there would be no trouble. If their orders were to stop all boats, upbound or downbound, for whatever purpose, search, confiscation or merely permission to pass, Bo meant to meet the trouble head on. It was his river, the state of Kentucky's river, the steamboat companies' river, the people's river. He needed no permission to run it and he did not propose to be stopped and searched or confiscated.

They were cruising, slow ahead, running easy and dark, feeling along pretty quietly. Even the sheep had let up on their bawling except for a few bleats now and then. He guessed Tobe had got among them and eased their fright and bother. The relief from their clamor was great.

A slow bend, little more than a pucker in the river, lay ahead. Keeping well to the middle Bo shifted the wheel the small degree it needed. The *Rambler* had barely answered when he saw the shimmer of light on the trees along the left bank. He stiffened and automatically moved his feet wider apart, feeling the deck and gripping it. Here it came, he thought, and about where he had expected it.

As he pulled the *Rambler* on around the lazy bend he saw the light itself, smack in the middle of the river. It was a lantern, waving. He reached for the whistle and held it down, sending a long hoarse blast bellowing a warning. The light didn't move except to continue its waving—a warning, in turn, to him to stop. Which, he thought grimly, he had no intention of doing.

He set himself to remember his river. They were above Woods a little piece and just beyond Woods was Hollman's Bend. There'd be an old slide on the right bank along here with some snags held fast in it. There were some low-hanging willows along the left. But the water was good there. He didn't mean to ram the ferry flat, so as between the willows and the slide he didn't have much choice. It would have to be the willows, for he couldn't afford the snags in the slide. He rang for half ahead and felt the *Rambler* plunge, and felt as he always did pure thanks for Foss as an engineer. Foss was never late for him. Foss gave him what he wanted, right on time.

He blew again and saw the light waver a little. Now if the idiots didn't decide of a sudden to veer in his path. It took a lot of nerve to hold steady in the face of a downbearing boat and he wondered if they had it. He blew once more and saw the light lower and steady. They'd set the lantern on the deck, he guessed. A flash of intuition told him then what they were doing. They had the flat anchored in the channel all right, but they had now set the lantern and abandoned it. They were at this moment pulling for shore in a skiff, or swimming for it.

The whistle must have pulled Phoebe Cole to her feet for she spoke now at his elbow. "Their camp is on the right bank, Captain," she said, "for I just saw a pinprick of light through the woods."

"That's a relief to know," Bo said, "for I've got to steer left to miss that flat. Better get back down, Miss Phoebe. There's some low trees and we may lose the roof."

He made his move well above the ferry flat, not knowing yet whether she was anchored lengthways or sideways.

Lengthways, she'd fill up most of the channel and he might have to slice her end off. But if she was an old boat she'd probably give like butter and do no great harm to the *Rambler*.

He bore into the shadows and the lower limbs of the willows began brushing the pilothouse. For a moment, just a fraction of a moment, he recalled the long dance downriver he had made once on the Barren, with its crazy wild sheering off of the willows as, out of control and without power, he had ridden his boat into the ground finally. He had power and control tonight, but he could hurt his boat just the same. He wouldn't have called what he felt a prayer—just a strong hope there would be no tough, thick upper trunks to rake him.

There was now a constant slap and drag against the sides of the pilothouse as he ran closer under the willows and there was an occasional stinging switch against his own face. He was closing up the ferry fast, though. The light rocked crazily as the first sending waves reached it. Then from the right bank a fusillade of shots broke out, scattered and not very accurate. The men had only the sound of the boat and perhaps a glint of light from the engine room as a target.

There was a rending wrench as one limb, bigger than any hit before, was torn free of its trunk, and the *Rambler* shuddered. In the pilothouse Bo ducked, wondering if the whole superstructure was going, but he hung on to the wheel and kept the nose steady. The limb tore loose with a tearing crack and blocked out all sight of the river in front of him. Held by the front of the pilothouse, torn loose by the speed of the boat, it had fallen and lodged on the bridge. Running blind now, there was nothing for it but to slow. Bo was less worried about the annoying, but essentially harmless firing from the shore than from the willow on the bridge. "Miss

Phoebe," he called, "there's a mess of willow branches up front. Reckon you could get through it and go down and tell Tobe and Jonah to come up here and get that limb off the bridge. And fast, please."

He had rung for slow, then shipping up and stopping, and the *Rambler* was easing off. He heard Phoebe scrambling around and saw the willow fronds shaking violently as she plunged through them to the companionway. Foss was loafing along so as not to wrack the machinery by his stopping and Bo began to fidget. Slow as they were moving they were closing up Hollman's Bend and he had to see.

He glanced back quickly. One good thing—the ferry was now a quarter of a mile behind them, its lantern still rocking wildly in their wake, and the boys on the bank had given up their shooting. He wondered, contemptuously, how Buckner thought they could stop a gunboat. They were a poor-paying outfit to send on patrol.

When he squared around again the limb had begun to move. Phoebe had been as fast as he'd meant her to be and Tobe and Jonah had moved fast, too. They dragged and heaved and in the light dark Bo saw that Phoebe was doing her part, dragging and heaving with them. When the *Rambler* had come to a full stop Bo called for Phoebe to come hold the wheel. "Just keep her steady where she is," he told her, "I'll help the boys."

When he lent his own great strength to the dragging and heaving they quickly got it overboard. The debris on the bridge was thick and Bo guessed the roof of the pilothouse had suffered some damage. But not to hurt, and no matter. He hadn't lost the superstructure.

He came to take the wheel again and they got under way. "I reckon," he said slowly, "that'll be the end of the excitement for a while. We got to pick up Luke and your grandpa

at Paradise, then all we got to worry about is the gunboats—
but not tonight."

"I, for one," she said firmly, "am not sorry. This night
has provided all the excitement I can use for a while."

"Been scared?" he asked.

"Yes, I've been scared. Haven't you?"

"Just once. When they spotted the boys on the lock walls.
I was scared they'd board us. I think we'll have lights now,
Miss Phoebe. The worst of it is behind us. Luke will need
to see us. You mind telling Foss?"

She disappeared and a few minutes later the glow of the
deck lights went out over the water. He guessed she was helping Tobe set them out. When she came back Foss was with
her, carrying a lantern. They picked their way through the
debris and Phoebe came into the pilothouse while Foss
fixed the lantern in the bracket atop the roof. It made a
dim light inside the pilothouse—not strong enough to ruin
Bo's nightsight, but enough light that the wheel, the chart
table, the old stove and the bench behind it, were visible. It
showed them each other, too, and glancing at Bo, Phoebe
exclaimed and advanced on him. "Your face is all over
blood! You've been cut all about! You must let me attend
to it!"

He dodged her hand. "When we tie up tonight will be
soon enough. I know it's cut. I been tasting blood. But I
know it's not cut deep. I'd know if it was. Just scratches,
is all. Now, your grandpa and Luke and the boys are gonna
need something to eat, and something hot to drink. They're
gonna be plumb wore out when we pick 'em up. Whyn't you
go down and see to it?"

Without a word she left and Foss, who was phlegmatically
kicking the trash and debris to one side, let her pass silently.
He didn't even look up as she went by him. He went on

clearing a path. It took him a good ten minutes but not until he had a walkway made did he quit and come to prop one elbow on the front sill and lean bulkily against it. He still said nothing—just leaned and sighed.

Bo looked at him and, amusement rising in him, determined to wait him out.

He had a long wait, for it wasn't until they saw the light from Luke's signal fire on the shore ahead that Foss finally spoke. He heaved away from the sill and said, then, plaintively, "I still think we ought to put a blade on the head of this boat. You and Luke both takin' up plowin' the bushes a blade before makes as much sense as a paddle behind."

He lumbered off, leaving Bo whooping with joy.

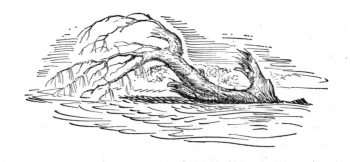

CHAPTER 13

SIR HENRY came aboard first, looking like a blackfaced wreck. His face was smeared with burnt cork and sweat and gunpowder, his eyebrows were singed and curled, and his hair had taken all leave of its senses. It literally stood on end, every hair having declared its independence.

He came aboard still drunk with the wine of battle. He set foot on deck flinging his mongrel Shakespeare about, flourishing both pistols, and with his cape blowing wildly about him. He strode magnificently about as Luke and the rousters clambered up, booming so loud it set the boat to shaking. "Now, *Esperance!* Percy! and set on! I have led my ragamuffins where they are peppered: Give me life; which if I can save, so; if not, honour comes unlooked for, and there's an end!"

When Phoebe flew to him he kissed her, hugged her fiercely and swung her off her feet, roaring at her, "Now, swear me, Kate, like a lady as thou art, a good mouth-filling oath."

"I'll do no such," she retorted. "Grandfather, what mischief you have been in!"

"Well, I'll repent," he bawled, giving her another hearty hug and kiss, then setting her back on her feet, "and that suddenly, while I am in some liking; I shall be out of heart shortly, and then I shall have no strength to repent."

She tried to calm the wild sea of his hair but he wrenched testily away from her hand. "Let be! What the strong winds of cannon and bullets have disordered, no woman's hand should arrange!"

She stood off and surveyed him before she said, composedly, "Fiddle-de-dee, Grandfather. Neither cannon nor bullets have disordered you. Scrambling through the underbrush has done it. You've torn your cloak and there's a scratch on your face, and I suspect you of having set your hair on end with your own hands!"

The old man glared at her. "Silence! Have you no respect . . ."

Before the storm could break, Bo interrupted to shake the old man's hand and to give him his thanks. "You served us a good turn tonight, sir, and we're obliged."

"Pish, tush," Sir Henry denied, his good humor restored instantly, " 'twas nothing, Captain. In peace there's nothing so becomes a man as modest stillness and humility. Good plot, good friend, and full of expectations: an excellent plot, very good friend." He dropped his fustianism and confided sweetly in a lowered voice, "I did you dirt, you know, making off with your skiff and leaving Phoebe in the lurch. But empty as my purse is, no amount of money would have tempted me to miss such an adventure. And I do believe, sir," he continued, poking Bo chummily in the ribs, "I did you a greater service thereby."

"No doubt about it," Bo agreed heartily.

Sir Henry peered at him. "But, zounds, man, what has happened to you? Your face is a bloody mess!"

"A little mixup. Nothing. I haven't had time to wash up."

"He," Phoebe put in, "is the one who has felt the wind of bullets. And I. We were fired upon in the lock. A glass in the pilothouse shattered and Captain Cartwright's face was cut in a dozen places."

Sir Henry looked daunted and crestfallen. "I'm a windy old ass," he murmured.

Bo looked at the girl uneasily. He couldn't think what had got into her to run the old man's big adventure down. It wasn't like her. Usually she bolstered his vanity loyally. She seemed put out at him about something. He guessed it still rankled with her that the old man had not taken her into his confidence—her with her love of secrets—and had left her behind with only a helpless role to play. He interposed hastily. "The main thing is nobody got hurt, the plot worked, everybody did their part and we got through the lock. Now, I'd guess you've got a pretty good appetite for some food, sir."

Falling into his role easily again the old man agreed. "I am feeling a few pangs of hunger." He roared at Phoebe, "Come girl. To the latter end of a fray and the beginning of a feast, fits a dull fighter and a keen guest."

Phoebe led him to the galley, the cloak billowing around them both, the pistols still brandishing about.

"I'd feel a heap easier," Foss muttered, "if you'd of took them things away from him, Bo. I've not got over mistrustin' him with 'em."

"They ain't loaded," Luke said. "He's just having his fun with 'em now. And don't think you can't trust him with 'em. He's forgot more about guns than you and me'll ever

know, Foss. That old man knows guns like he'd invented
'em.''

Bo moved off to go among the roustabouts. He spoke to
each one, called him by name, pulled a forelock here and
there or slapped a back, commending each man for his part.
"You boys did me a good turn tonight and I'll not forget it.
Now, Tobe's got a jug of whiskey waiting for you. Go have
yourselves all you want. Eat if you want, then turn in for
a good sleep. We're going to run downriver a piece before
we tie up, but you've earned time off and you'll get it. Git,
now."

They scattered, full of cackle and chatter and anticipation
of Tobe's jug.

"Where you aimin' to tie up?" Foss asked.

"Airdrie, I thought."

Foss nodded, picked up his lantern and plunged off to the
engine room.

Bo drew Luke up the companionway with him. "Sit," he
told the boy, "and rest till we get in the channel. You can
talk then if you're a mind to."

"Oh, I ain't all that wore out. We been sitting on that bank
waiting half an hour. Sort of got our breath back and rested
up."

The *Rambler* slid away from the shore. Bo steered her
silently into midstream. When the slow deep chug of the
engine and the steady, unhurried splash of the paddles satisfied him he hauled up his high pilot's stool and rested his
own legs. "We had a little fracas," he said then. "Delayed
us some."

"Wasn't worried none," Luke said.

"You run into any trouble?"

"None. Only time I was anxious was when we couldn't
find the old man straight off. He was scouting around on his

own and we had to kind of beat the bushes for him. But he'd done us a good turn. Said he'd explored the 'perimeter' and already spotted out the best places for us on the hill. Don't yet know why he didn't stumble into one of their outposts, though. They had 'em, clean up to the foot of the hill. But he's a real sharp old coot, Bo. They don't come much sharper. He ain't the least bit crazy like Foss thinks he is."

"I've not ever thought it," Bo said. "He did sort of startle me, though, when he commenced popping off those horse pistols of his. I never thought they'd go that loud. For a minute I figured Buckner had unlimbered his artillery at you. Give me a scare."

"He overloads 'em to make 'em sound louder. One of them guns is gonna split the barrel on him some day and he's gonna get a face full of powder." Luke laughed. "*You* was startled! You ought to seen us! I like to jumped out of my skin when that first one went off. And it set several of the boys to running. Thought we'd been jumped from behind. We got used to it, though. That's one way he's sharp, Bo. He timed them shots, just like cannon. And he kept us moving around while he stayed put. Said you wouldn't move cannon around on a damned hill. You'd emplace it and stick with it and blast away."

"Phoebe said he was timing 'em," Bo said. "I didn't notice for I was too busy, and soon we got in the midst of all the hubbub and confusion you were causing and I couldn't hear you any more." He stopped and laughed, the memory of it bringing the exhilaration back. "Luke, you never saw anything like it! It worked just like we planned it. They were sure caught by the short hairs. Most of the camp had gone to bed, I guess, for they come pouring out of them tents like ants, going in every direction all at once, all whichaway and mixed up. Took 'em a good fifteen minutes to begin to pull themselves together."

"But when they did so," Luke said, "they seen you in the lock, didn't they?"

"Saw the boys on the lock walls. Commenced firing. It wasn't to worry. All we had to do was slide out and give 'em steam. They ever charge that hill?"

"Not exactly. Not a charge, no. They sent some skirmishers up was all. We pulled back when they come on. Time they was three-quarters up the hill we'd legged out of there. Sir Henry, he was the last one to leave. Kept blasting away. He was having such a fine time I couldn't hardly get him to quit when we had to cut and run. Wanted to stand his ground and engage 'em with bayonets! Kept saying something about doomsday being near and die all and die merrily! Which I wasn't aiming to do—die all or merrily or any other way. Besides it was time for us to light a shuck out of there if we was to be where you'd told us to be." He paused, reflected, then went on. "That was the worst part of the whole thing, actually. Getting down that hill on the back side in as big a rush as we was. Two of the boys had to get holt of the old man and hang on or we'd of lost him time and again. I believe he's night-blind, Bo. He run into trees and got hisself tangled up in bushes and fell in ditches like he'd got a full load of whiskey on. I thought he'd kill hisself 'fore we got him to the river. Miss Phoebe was wrong. He never set his hair on end himself. Falling all over hisself done it."

"He may be night-blind," Bo said, "but likely he can't see too good any time."

They talked on and on, remembering, patching the details together here and there, putting them side by side until, a mosaic completed, they had a full picture and could each envision where the other had been, what he had been doing at any given time. When it had all been said, the last piece sketched in, Bo took in his breath and unconsciously quoted from Shakespeare himself. "Well, all's well that ends well, I reckon. I wouldn't want to do this every night but I can't say I didn't find it right exciting to do once. I'm just glad nobody got hurt." There was a short, easy silence. "You hungry?" he asked the boy, then.

"No, but seems like my eyes are closing in spite of me."

"Go on and turn in. You wore yourself out worse than you knew."

Luke protested. "I don't mind to wait till we tie up."

"Jonah and Tobe can do it. You sleep. You've got a good sleep coming to you."

"Well—" The boy lingered, shuffling in the door. He burst out suddenly, "I sure am glad you made it, Bo. I wasn't ever worried about us for all we had to do was what you'd told us. But I was the worst afraid for the boat. Seemed like it was taking an awful chance, and you up here in the pilothouse like a setting duck. I didn't see how they could help but see the *Rambler*—in time—and when they seen her you was bound to be the target. All I didn't like about my part was not being here. I sure am glad it turned out good."

"So am I. So am I," Bo agreed. He wasn't at all embarrassed by the boy's emotions for he didn't take it personally. On the *Rambler* they were like that, all for one and one for all. There was nothing shaming in being fearful for each other. If Luke hadn't been anxious for the *Rambler,* and for him, it would have been to wonder at. "You go on," he told the boy. "All we got to worry about now is the gunboats, *if* there are any gunboats on the river, and that sure ain't to worry tonight."

"No. Well, wake me early."

"We'll be running by daylight," Bo promised.

The boy cleared his throat, lifted his hand and made a vague motion. "Well . . . in the morning, then."

"Sure. In the morning."

Alone in the pilothouse, the river seemed still and lonesome to Bo. But it felt good to be still and lonesome. There had been too much noise and racket and too much excitement. It needed a quiet time to drain away. His nightsight was good but the illusion of narrowed water always persisted at night, and the *Rambler* seemed to be nosing down an ever-squeezing path. Ahead, where the deck lanterns flung a short stretch of light, the trees looked as if they met in a tunnel. It didn't make him uneasy. He had run at night too many times. It was an illusion. There was good water and wide enough and it lay as still as a pool. Crawling like a tortoise, it seemed, the *Rambler* chugged sweetly and peacefully on down.

A shadow loomed at the head of the stairs and Foss padded across the bridge. He leaned an arm on the sill and rested against it.

"You're not trusting Tobe with the machinery, I hope," Bo said, lightly.

"He's awake."

"Wouldn't be too sure. He can sleep standing up with his eyes open."

"He's too worked up. He's had enough of that jug to stimulate him a right smart. He's awake all right and full of his importance. To hear him tell it, you'd think he took the *Rambler* through all by hisself."

"Let him," Bo laughed. "No harm. He did his part good enough. Boys bedded down yet?"

"Most. A few has got a crap game goin'."

Silence fell between them, a tranquil, easeful silence. The engine breathed gently and the paddles churned lazily. The deck lights picked up a deer in the shallows. It froze for a moment, frightened, then thrashed madly to escape back up the bank. Both men laughed. A few minutes later a beaver slid without a ripple around a log and slid back just as easily. A raccoon flattened itself against the mud and waited for the unfamiliar noise and light to pass. Foss stirred and spoke. "You'd think there ain't a thing stirrin' on the river as quiet as it is at night. But it's when there's the most goin' on. Little wild things that hide out durin' the day come out at night, frisk around and play and eat and drink."

Out of habit, Bo nodded, though Foss couldn't see.

Foss shifted his arm. "I ain't sure but I got one of them Confedrits back there, Bo."

The shift of subject was made so suddenly and so quietly Bo thought he hadn't heard right. "You did what?"

"I took a few potshots at them soldiers back at the lock. Think I got one of 'em. Seen him fall, anyhow. But it could of been your shot. You do any shootin'?"

"Hell, no! I had my hands full. When'd you have time?"

"Well, Jesus, Bo, I'd done give you steam. Had plenty of time. They commenced it," he added defensively. "I didn't admire bein' shot at without shootin' back."

"Lord, I'm not caring," Bo said, "you didn't start no war by shooting. I'm just astonished, is all. No," he continued intensely, "I'm not caring in the least. It's their war and they can expect shooting. Whichever side."

"Well," Foss said, "you never said not to."

"Wouldn't have done any good if I had, would it?"

"Don't expect it would," Foss admitted. He waited a moment then said, thoughtfully, "First time I ever drawed a bead on a man. Always figured I never could. But him with a gun in his hand, shootin' at us, he never meant no more to me than if he'd been a fox or a coon, Bo. Only thing is, I been thinkin' since, I'd hate it if he was somebody we've knowed on the river. Reckon it could of been?"

"If it was somebody we've known on the river and he was shooting at the *Rambler*," Bo said hotly, "he was bound to know we were his own kind of folks. No way he could have believed the *Rambler* was one of those gunboats. We come from upriver and when we come out of that lock into the open anybody could see we were just a plain ordinary steamboat. You've no cause to be sorry, Foss. If he got hurt it was the risk he took when he joined up."

Foss straightened up as if a load had been lifted from his solid shoulders. He nodded his head vigorously. "No, it ain't. I see that, now. He wasn't no longer river folks. If he was with them Confedrits, he was a Confedrit."

The strangeness of Foss's bother and their conversation struck Bo then. There wasn't one chance in a thousand that Foss had wounded or killed someone who had ever been on the river. But that one little chance had been worrying him. He had been reaching for comfort and Bo had unconsciously and angrily provided it.

Bo felt a melting inside himself. Old Foss . . . old Foss. Tender as a woman inside his misshapen bulk. Worried he might have hurt somebody that belonged to their own fraternity, belonged as they did to the river. The long rope of the river bound them all so tight and close each human being that formed a strand was never unseparate, impossible to separate. The rope was woven too strongly and too tightly of habits and customs and ways and loves and hates and troubles and tides and winds and water. There was no hacking a single strand off and letting it go. The instinct was to cherish it and to hold on to it. Though it frayed, it could always be spliced and made strong again. And not even war could use it and ruin it and throw it away. The wonder of it pierced Bo and he said strongly, "He wasn't no riverman, Foss. You can put your dependence in it. He *wasn't* no riverman. No riverman would have fired on the *Rambler*."

But Foss had let it go. Sliding his bother to Bo, he was empty of it. He grunted and peered about. "A mile up from the landin', ain't we?"

"Just about."

Extraneously, no connection at all between his last word and the next, Foss said, "We'll be eatin' mutton tomorrow."

Bo gaped. "Whaddya mean?"

"They kilt two of them sheep. We just as well eat 'em."

Bo swore.

Foss said mildly, "No use cussin'. Couldn't hardly expect 'em to fire on the boat 'thout killin' something. Best be glad it wasn't none of us."

"All right." But Bo felt vexed. He'd meant to carry those sheep through whole and entire. "All right, dress 'em up. We'll eat mutton tomorrow and for the rest of the run, likely. I'll be glad when we unload them sheep. They almost been more trouble than they're worth to us."

"Not actually," Foss protested. "We been doin' real good with 'em. Just a couple got in the way of their gunfire."

Bo's temper flared. "I said all right, Foss. I said dress 'em up. All you're thinkin' of is eating 'em. You got your stomach on your mind. Now, will you git so we can make the landing?"

The mild voice, tempered by love, came back unaccusing. "Sure, Bo. Sure."

The barrel shape lumbered off, spent of words, to take over his machinery again, to give with his own hands what Bo wanted when he warped into the Airdrie landing. Watching him disappear down the companionway, Bo felt like kicking himself. He didn't know what had got into him. The disappointment, he guessed, of losing even two of the sheep —and he was feeling tired. He thought how many years Foss's hands had served him and how much he depended on them serving him. It moved him, but he caught himself up before he wallowed in sentiment. For if Foss served him well, he also served himself well. There was nothing else Foss wanted to do but run his machinery and he would never have known about steamboat machinery if Bo hadn't lifted him out of the hog trough he existed in in Cartwright's Mill.

Bo stood and kicked his high stool back out of the way. Time to begin his long crab-crawl to the landing. You could say, he thought, they had served each other well.

When the *Rambler* was moored for the night, made fast by lines fore and aft, Bo wrote up his log then took the lantern from the roof bracket and went down to the deck. Tobe was turning out the running lights, except for one lantern on the head and one other on the stern. In the dimness the light streaming from the galley looked bright. Bo turned toward it.

Halfway along the deck he met Sir Henry weaving around barrels and bales. The old man was too tired to walk straight, he thought, and avoided him. He had no enthusiasm for any more bombast and spouting tonight. Sir Henry was muttering to himself and didn't see him and Bo let him go.

He wanted, he thought, a cup of coffee and he wanted it laced good and strong with some of Tobe's jug. If there was any of it left. He waited, leaning on a hogshead until the black man came back down the deck. He called softly to him. "Tobe? Got any of that whiskey left?"

"Yassuh, dey's some. I ain't lettin dat trash hab all ob it —ain't 'bout to. Saved you an' Mistah Foss plenty."

"Where is it?"

"In de engine room."

"Bring it."

"Yassuh. Right now?"

"Right now. I'll wait."

Tobe's feet made a running patter, then he was back to hand over the jug. Not a hard-drinking man, Bo didn't know why he raised the jug at once and took six quick, deep swallows from it. He had thought only of lacing his coffee, but the impulse had been there and he had followed it, and the whiskey was strong and good. He raised the jug again and drank, then corked it and went on to the galley.

Phoebe was puttering around the stove, drawing the dampers for the night, wiping the caps with a wet rag. She turned when she heard him and smiled. "I've been waiting for you. Now, you sit down and let me bathe your face. I have plenty of hot water."

"Coffee first," he said, thudding the jug on the table. The whiskey was already flowing out into his body, warming it and easing the tiredness.

She reached down a cup and poured it for him and watched interestedly as he dumped half of it into the sink and filled the cup to the brim with whiskey, stirred it and took half the cup down in one long gulp. "Ah-h-h," he said, breathing out and savoring even the smell of his breath, "that's good."

Phoebe said, "I made Grandfather a toddy, too. But I used hot water and a little sugar. I never saw coffee and whiskey mixed before."

Bo laughed. "Was that why he was wobbling around so out on deck? I just met him and he was having to hold."

Phoebe's laugh chuckled up, too. "I don't doubt it. I made it extra strong. He never takes but one. But for some reason he insisted on having another tonight. I expect he's a little drunk."

"A little," Bo agreed, "but he'll sleep well."

"That was the general idea."

She made his next coffee and whiskey herself, measuring it exactly as he had done. She set the cup on the table. "Now, come, Captain, and sit here. You can drink while I see if there are any slivers of glass in those cuts."

"There's no hurry," he grumbled. He felt too peaceful and good to bother with his face.

She pushed him into the chair. "There is. I don't mean to go to bed until I've seen to you and I'm very tired and want very badly to go to bed. So please do as I say."

He was beginning to feel a little sleepy himself. "Sure. Sure, I wasn't thinking."

She filled a basin, tore a clean white rag in two, and approached him. He gulped another dollop of his drink, aware just then that his face felt stiff and a little sore. "Right smart of a mess, I expect," he said.

"Right smart," she agreed. "Hold still now."

The first touch of the water made his face burn as if it had been set fire to. In spite of himself, Bo drew away and yelped.

"Hold still!"

"Hold still, hell! What have you got in that water, liniment? Skinner's greased lightning? You trying to peel the hide off?"

She went on calmly bathing his face. "A tiny smidgin of carbolic acid is all. Good gracious, Captain, you aren't a child. It only burns a little."

"A little! A little! If you used pure neat's-foot oil it couldn't sting worse."

"There, now," she said, finally, "you're clean." She produced a small pair of tweezers and tilted his head so that the light shone directly on his face. "Now to see if there's any glass." She bent down very near and searched, sliding her fingertips over his skin. "Yes—there's a tiny sliver." She extracted it quickly and neatly and the fingertips resumed their searching. She found several more and removed them, then she exclaimed excitedly, "Why, your eyebrows are full of glass! Dozens of pieces! They don't show, but—wait, don't move. I need a brush. I'll get mine. I won't be a minute."

She was gone quickly. As he waited Bo sipped his drink. The fire of his face was dying and the stiffness had gone. The blood, dried, had caused the stiffening he supposed. Funny he hadn't noticed it until so late. Too busy, he reckoned. Too much else to think about. He moved his fingers about over his face and felt the scratches. There were more of them than he had guessed. He grinned. He must look like he'd tangled with a wildcat.

Phoebe came back, breathing a little fast from her hurry, flourishing a small brush with a handle. "Now," she said with satisfaction, "now, we'll get that glass out properly."

He felt like a fool when she combed his eyebrows, holding a rag to catch the slivers. ". . . curried just like a horse," he muttered.

"Be still."

"I'm being still. You got such a handholt on me I can't be nothing else."

After a little he began to enjoy it. The small, even strokes were soothing and he finally closed his eyes, let all the way down inside and gave himself over to the pleasure.

A mockingbird, very near outside, started up a song. He tried a few scales first, running them rapidly up and down, then he added a few experimental flourishes. Tuned up properly, then, he began to improvise with all sorts of trills and flutes and little ecstasies which got clear out of hand very soon and he had got involved in something so intricate and rhapsodic he had no idea how to get himself out.

He just went on spiraling up and up, making up his trills and flutes as he went along until he had run himself completely out of breath. He had to break off on a high, unfinished note. As if he had caught his breath, then, he plucked the note with no nonsense and brought it firmly back down where it belonged. Bo laughed. "Silly bird."

"Beautiful bird," Phoebe said.

Bo didn't know but what he dozed then. For he didn't really notice when Phoebe left off with his eyebrows and began on his hair. He heard her clucking and muttering and felt the soothing stroking, wondered if he was getting drunk, too, and decided he didn't care.

But he knew when she had finished with him completely, for she smoothed his hair down, sighed satisfyingly, gave it a pat, then bent and kissed his forehead as lightly and as unaffectedly as if he had been a child. Or her grandfather, he thought, grumblingly. He had an impulse, a strong wish to pull her down and make her kiss him properly—to let her know he was neither a child nor an old man, to teach her what her mouth was for with a young man. It was so strong in him that his hands moved and lifted.

"There," she said, unseeing and turning away, emptying the basin and spreading the wet clothes to dry, "you're all fixed up."

The impulse faded as quickly in him as it had risen and left no residue behind. He got to his feet. "I'm obliged. If you've finished with those things, we'll go up now." He took the lantern from its bracket.

She thrust the tweezers and small brush in her apron pocket and joined him at the door. He motioned for her to go ahead.

The deck was dim and very quiet. Everybody was bedded down and asleep. The rousters had quit their game and Foss had got his fires drawn and his machinery put to rest. Bo saw him, in his mind's eyes, a sleeping hulk on the pile of rags in the engine room, the mangy cur curled beside him or at his feet.

He followed Phoebe Cole up the companionway, the light from the lantern going ahead and the steps of the stairs breaking their shadows sharply. Silently they crossed the bridge and veered around the pilothouse, dark and deserted and only palely gleaming in its white paint.

At the door of the cabin, he doused the lantern and set it inside the opening. He felt rather than heard Phoebe's curtain drawn aside. Its small breeze fanned his face. There were little rustlings which he was barely conscious of, for he was suddenly almost overcome by weariness and sleepiness. This run down the river, he had time to think as he yanked off his shoes, had been just one long spell of tiredness. Just one long spell of being tired every day over and over again. You didn't have a chance to get rested up till something came up and you got tired all over again.

"Captain?"

"What?"

"Thank you for my birthday present."

Befuddled he wondered what she was talking about. "Birthday present?"

"You promised me the lock."

"Oh. That. You're welcome, Miss Phoebe."

He fell back onto his bunk, thought he ought to get under the blanket, lacked the energy to move, and forgot it, sinking deeply and immediately into sleep. He didn't hear Phoebe Cole say goodnight, nor hear her when she came and eased the blanket from under him and covered him over with it. He didn't know she patted his hair once again and touched, lightly as butterfly feet, the cut skin of his face. He didn't know that she stood a little longer looking down at him, or that tucking the blanket more firmly, she sighed. He felt no fan of breeze on his face when her curtain dropped into place again and he did not hear her small nestling rustlings this time.

Whiskey and weariness had felled him in his tracks.

CHAPTER 14

"WHAT day of the week is it?" Foss asked.

"Sunday," Bo said, looking at him. Foss was sitting humped over on a low stool, holding his head between his hands as if he was afraid it might fly off if he turned loose of it.

"I've sure got no Sunday feeling."

It was coming day and the engine room looked bleak and untenanted in the gray light. At best it was no beauty, except to Foss, and without its fires glowing and its machinery pulsing it was a drab and dingy place. "What you've got," Bo said unfeelingly, "is a whiskey head. Wouldn't matter what day of the week it was. What'd you do, Foss? Drink the rest of that jug? Smells like it in here and you look like it. You're plumb green around the gills."

Foss groaned and risked rolling his eyes at Bo. "Don't stand there talkin' holy. You drunk your part, too. Only thing is whiskey don't bother you. If I didn't ever have no more reminder of my drinkin'," he mourned, "than you do, I'd likely be a sot drunkard. I like drinkin' it down just fine but I sure don't admire it backin' up on me next day." He retched, turned loose of his head to grab his stomach, groaned and fluttered his hands back to his head. "Don't know which place I feel the worst."

"Pour a bucket of cold water over his head," Bo said to Tobe, who was beginning to fire up, "and pour half a gallon of black coffee down his gullet."

Foss came thrashing up off the stool as if a wasp had stung him. "You tend to your own whiskey head, Bo Cartwright, and I'll tend to mine." He swung around on Tobe, "And you try drenching me with cold water, you black jackanapes, and I'll fire up with your lard!"

Tobe cackled, unafraid. "Capt'n Bo jus' joshin', Mist' Foss. Ain't nobody gwine drench you wid cold water. You be fine you gits on yo' feet an' gits goin'."

Foss muttered and eyed Bo obliquely. "I'd like to know," he said aggrievedly, "what happens to whiskey inside you. You don't ever have a head or a queasy stummick."

Bo had had a head that morning but not much of one. He had dunked it in the river, drunk down two cups of cold coffee and that took care of it. He didn't know what happened to whiskey in his body, either, when he occasionally overindulged, but it never gave him the trouble it did other men. Foss was always sicker than a dog and he'd seen his father pale and languid after a bender, but the most he ever had was a dull headache which went easily away.

Tobe said, now, "Capt'n Bo's drinks gits 'stributed round inside, Mist' Foss. Goes all over an' gits used up good. Ain't no 'membrance."

"I could do without my remembrance," Foss said flatly. "All right, Tobe, get a move on. Don't take all day to get steam up. This lightnin' pilot we got will make us start rowin' he don't have steam when he wants it." He picked up his oil can and began poking its snout in the bowels of the machinery.

Bo grinned. Foss would be all right. As green-gilled and as queasy as he was, he'd have steam up on time. Never was so sick he couldn't function and make his machinery function too. He was never too sick to eat, either, and when he'd belted a good breakfast away what was left of his queasiness would be gone. By the time they were running, you'd never know Foss had had a drink.

Luke came in, looking a little worried. "Bo, them sheep are getting gaunted down a right smart and they're awful restless. Getting tired of the boat, I reckon."

"No tireder than I am of them," Bo said. "No help for it, Luke. Do the best you can for 'em and we'll get 'em to Evansville in as good shape as we can."

"Why didn't you sell 'em to Buckner to feed his troops?" Foss put in.

"Now, that's a good paying idea," Bo said, "but it comes a little late, like most of your other ideas."

Foss was twiddling with the pressure gauge. "Reckon you're aimin' to run like you owned the river today."

"Well, don't I? Nothing else on it except maybe those gunboats. Even if it's Sunday and folks not expecting a boat we ought to pick up a pretty good load. We'll take on all we can carry. Only thing, Luke, I don't want no passengers."

"Not even short trippers?"

"Nope. Not even short trippers. We meet up with those gunboats might be right in a stretch a short tripper was traveling. Best if we don't have anybody but ourselves on board."

"What you gonna do if we meet 'em?" the boy asked.

"Don't know yet. Depends where they are."

"Git your arsenal ready again, Luke," Foss advised.

"What arsenal?" Luke said, laughing. "It went back to town with them men last night. Well, I reckon I'll go give them sheep some more water. Wish they was camels." He went away.

Bo inspected the plated rod and satisfied himself it was holding, eyed the progress Tobe and Jonah were making on firing up, watched Foss turn screws and valves, then drifted out on deck. He heard clanking noises in the galley and stuck his head in. Catfish was stumbling around, only half awake, rattling stovelids and dampers, poking wood in the firebox and mumbling to himself about young wimmins that wanted a hot fire time the sun was up and before a body had a chance to get his eyes open. "How *you* feel this morning?" Bo asked.

Catfish jumped and slewed his eyes around warily. Seeing who it was he relaxed and flashed his teeth in a wide grin. "Feelin' peart, Capt'n Bo, feelin' real peart. Janglin' some in de haid an' a mite pucker-mouthed, but it ain't to worry. Good whiskey you gib us las' night, Capt'n. Fine whiskey. Go down easy an' set easy. Ain't no trouble."

"Go tell that to Foss," Bo said. "It didn't set too good on him."

"Mist' Foss ain't what you'd call a real drinkin' man, Capt'n. He jus' drink now an' den. Gits outta practice 'tween times."

"I wouldn't want him to practice no harder," Bo said, "I'd lose me a good engineer. Reckon when we'll eat?"

The good cheer and humor on Catfish's face faded and he said glumly, "Miss Phoebe say hab de stove red-hot 'fore sun-up. Say you wants git runnin' time de sun show an' she ain't aimin' nobody to wu'k on a empty stummick. Capt'n Bo, ah lak to go back to roustin'. I ain't no hand at dis heah galley-in'."

"Best hand we ever had," Bo said firmly, "main reason I picked you. Why, Catfish, you're living high on the hawg. Eating better'n you ever did on a boat, and doing less work. Don't have to heave no bales around or limber your legs loading wood or sweat your skin away firing for Foss. You got it the best of anybody on the boat."

Catfish brightened. "Dat's a fack, ain't it? Hadn't studied it dat way. I gits thoo helpin' Miss Phoebe, I is thoo. Lay round an' watch de others sweat."

"You're top rooster, Catfish. You have Miss Phoebe's fire hot for her now, hear?"

"Yassuh, I do dat."

Bo wandered on down the deck, his eyes automatically checking the cargo stowage. It was always good—Luke was training up into a fine mate—but long habit made the checking instinctive, if perfunctory. A good captain walked as many deck miles as a good mate to make certain cargo was well distributed. He looked this morning especially for ways of compacting the cargo so as to take on more and all he could. Sunday though it was, when boats didn't usually run, there'd be a scare about the *Southern Belle* and the *Mary Lee* and the war, and he was reasonably sure he'd be blocked off before the day was over.

He went on down to the head of the boat and draped himself along a stanchion. The Airdrie landing was under a hill and the *Rambler* lay in its dark, cool shadow, the air still soft with water heaviness. Save for the sounds on the boat a deep hush brooded over the river and a lonely silence. The dense woods along both banks were opening up from their night blackness into a widening gray and the river flowed gray between them, each time the eye following showing a longer

and longer stretch. It was as if the river itself was being made
new, coil on coil slowly emerging and stretching and flatten-
ing. The color of the sky, it merged into the sky at its farth-
est point, a soft haze obscuring the meeting.

Bo watched it and felt it and knew it, but his thoughts
were wandering. The whole crew would be jangling some
in the head this morning and more than a little pucker-
mouthed but it wasn't to worry about any of them. They
were long experienced in throbbing heads and dry mouths
and it never interfered with their work. They would load
and unload and sweat it out of their systems. And they had
earned their whiskey heads. They were good boys with him
this trip. Skirmishing around back of the Confederate line,
shooting and being shot at, wasn't what they had signed on
to do. But not a one of them had held back from it. They'd
thought it a real caper and had got a lot of fun out of it. He
wondered what kind of a coonjine they'd make of it, for as
sure as God made little apples they'd use it. Next stop, likely,
they'd be shuffling up the stageplank poking fun at the foolishness of somebody. He thought it would probably be Sir
Henry and he thought it just as well only a trained ear could
understand the words. What they would do with the old man
and his blackface get-up and his wild hair and his horse pistols
would likely be abrasive to his feelings.

Briefly he considered the possibility of meeting the gunboats this day but he didn't borrow any trouble about it.
When he knew for sure there were gunboats on the river
would be time enough to consider what to do about them.

Phoebe spoke behind him. "Good morning, Captain."

Bo swung around. She looked as bright and cheerful as
the dawning day, as fresh and new and promising. Her face
was still rosy with sleep but her eyes were lively and spar-
kling and bracing. The lilac print dress with the darn on

the shoulder was crisp and he wondered how she kept it so fresh. She looked sprightly and efficient, brisk and invigorating. "Good morning," he said, smiling, "you look to be feeling peart."

"Peart?"

"Good—fine—pert."

"Oh. I think I am. Yes. A night's good sleep, a good conscience, a good appetite. Yes, I think I'm feeling peart." She smiled, accepting the word.

"How's the lump on the head?"

She explored the bruise above her right temple delicately. "A little sore yet." She broke into laughter. "Have you looked at yourself in a mirror, Captain? You look like you'd been in a fight with a tomcat."

"Thought the same thing when I shaved this morning. But you did a fine job last night. Precious little soreness left."

"I'm glad. And as Grandfather would say, we bear our wounds nobly." She looked around curiously. "This is a pretty place. Where are we?"

"Airdrie. I like it, too. One of the nicest places on the river."

She moved to the rail to see better. There was a narrow strip of level land which had the trim and neatness of a park just beyond the landing. From it the steep hill rose sheer away and a long flight of stone steps led up it. "Where do they go?" she asked.

"Up to the town. It's on top the hill."

"How strange they'd build a town up there."

"Not very. This hill is actually a mine—a hill full of coal and iron ore. Fellow by the name of Alexander—Robert Alexander—came down here about six years ago from the bluegrass country. He was born in Kentucky himself but his folks were Scotch and they sent him back to Scotland for his education. Seems his grandfather had some ironworks over there, and plenty of money. Promised if they'd send him to Scotland for his education and to learn the iron trade he'd make him his heir."

"Did he?"

"I reckon. After he come back to this country he commenced looking around for a vein of iron ore and found it in this hill. He bought seventeen thousand acres here. He had an idea the Scotch were the best ironworkers in the world and I guess he had a right to it. They'd made the Alexanders rich enough. Anyway he went back to Scotland and brought over a lot of the workers used to work for his grandfather. Chartered a ship for 'em. Brought carpenters and engine builders and furnacemen and smelterers. Didn't hire much labor in the neighborhood. If you'll look right down there you can see the stone house and the furnace and stack." He pointed down the level strip.

Phoebe followed his finger. "It looks abandoned."

"It is. He had big ideas and he spent money like it was water. Some say he spent more than three hundred thousand dollars. Built that three-story stone house and furnace and stack—built a whole town up on the hill, stone houses for the men and their families, stores, mills, taverns. Everything the best and for the most comfort. But it didn't work out and inside of two years he'd got tired of it and closed down the works. Some say his mistake was bringing Scotch workers over to run the furnace. They were used to a different kind of ore and didn't know how to work this Kentucky ore. They say if Alexander had changed his management, he'd have succeeded."

"After he'd spent all that money?" Phoebe said amazed, "and built a whole town and brought all those people over? He just closed it down?"

"Set a day to close down and closed down right to the minute. Wouldn't hear to working another day. Quit cold and just walked off and left it. Didn't give a hoot about the money."

"But what about the people? What did they do when he left?"

"Oh, they stayed on. Some of 'em bought land of him, or nearby, and took to farming. Some mine a little coal out of the hill. They're good folks—Torrents and Kiplings and Pattersons and Muirs and Williamsons." Bo grinned. "I've had some fine times up there at A-drie—that's what generally it's called—they like to dance and they got a prime fiddler up there, fellow name of Jarret Wallace. There's a stillhouse over near Paradise that turns out the best corn juice and barley beer ever slid down your throat. You had to be pretty handy with your fists over there when those furnacemen got to drinking, though. They were champion fistmen. I've seen some fine roughhouses in that place."

Phoebe gazed up the hill speculatively. "Funny. I always thought the Scotch were so stern and religious."

Bo laughed. "They may be stern about their religion but they don't let their religion interfere with their pleasures. Presbyterian, most of 'em. Reckon they think being sanctified and among the elect they can risk more than most. Must give a man a right safe feeling to know for sure he's among the saved, been chosen and singled out."

"I don't believe that way," Phoebe said crisply, "and while I thank you for an interesting story, Captain, this isn't feeding your crew." She marched off with her shoulders squared and Bo could see her mentally tilting at the Calvinist theory or predestination and sanctification and salvation by grace. She hadn't said what way she believed but he expected Miss Phoebe Cole thought you had to earn salvation.

A hail from the stone steps swung him around. A man, halting half way down, had made a trumpet of his hands. His voice was thick with a Scotch burr but at least it had the virtue of carrying loud and clear. "Can you delay your departure? I have some fowls to ship."

Bo bellowed back at him. "Got 'em caught and penned?"

"They are in the chicken yard but the coops are ready. If you've got half an hour they can be aboard."

"Go ahead. We'll wait."

Bo shouted for Luke, then, who took it up like an echo shouting for the rousters and they began to shout at each other and to scramble up from their beds on sacks and bales and from behind hogsheads and crates. Like woolly black blooms they blossomed out of cracks and crevices, grinning, rubbing their eyes, yawning, hitching up their rags and shaking the leftover whiskey fumes from their heads, slapping their heels into a trot, yelping, "Yassuh, Mist' Luke, yassuh, yas*suh,* Mist' Luke!"

Bo followed to keep an eye on shifting the cargo to make a place for the chicken crates. The boys put their backs into it and it was well done by the time the coops began to pour down the hill.

They came so regular and fast Bo said to Luke, "He must have got every able pair of shoulders in town to help him."

"Looks like it. McDougal, ain't it?"

"Yeah."

"Hell, he must be getting shut of his whole flock. I better commence tallying."

The crates continued to flow down. They were set at the bottom of the steps where McDougal waited and where Luke joined him. Sir Henry idled out onto the deck. He eyed the tide of chicken coops engulfing the landing. "Hell-kite," he said, "more livestock. Do you run a Noah's ark, sir?"

"Oh," Bo said casually, "wait till we take on some cows and hogs. It's not Noah's ark we run—it's a floating barnyard."

"Your friend," Sir Henry said, pointing at McDougal who was marking the coops with a blue chalk, "must agree with Henry IV. You recollect that monarch's desire for his people, no doubt?"

Bo, who had never heard of Henry IV, shook his head. "Can't say I do."

"The king is quoted as saying, 'I want there to be no peasant in my kingdom so poor that he is unable to have a chicken in his pot every Sunday.' Your man's intentions must be to provide a good many pots with their Sunday chickens."

Bo laughed and said, "His intentions are to put some cash in his pockets, I'd guess."

Sir Henry paced down the stageplank and moved among the coops with his stately step, stooping occasionally to peer at the fowls.

The chickens were nervous from being crowded into the pens and from being jostled about, but by chicken standards they were relatively quiet, only gawking their necks and clucking worriedly, pecking a little at the wooden slats and scratching around in the straw McDougal had floored the coops with. But they weren't making too much fuss until Sir Henry suddenly squatted down in front of a coop. Bo was watching him but he couldn't believe what he saw. The old man reached in quickly and snatched a handful of tail feathers from a magnificent red rooster.

The startled fowl let out a squawk and went into a wild-eyed flapping frenzy which sent every hen in every coop promptly into hysterics. Chickens began to fly at the bars and at each other, to beat and flap their wings, to peck at each other and the wooden slats, to tread on each other and to spur and claw at each other. Blood began to flow and feathers began to fly until the soft downy under feathers floated out in all directions in a small blizzard. But it was the noisiest blizzard on record. The air was filled with the outraged squawks and cackles and screeches of the chickens. It spread to the sheep and as crazy scared as the fowls they began running around, butting their heads against the rails of their pen, butting each other, adding their terrified bleats to the high hysterics of the chickens.

It happened so quickly and was out of control so fast everybody was paralyzed for a moment or two. McDougal hung over a crate as if he didn't believe it. Luke gripped his tally sheet and pencil, his mouth dropped open stupidly as if he wondered what had hit him. Sir Henry, clutching his handful of bright tail feathers, stood like a statue in the midst of the cacophony, horror at what he had let loose on the peaceful Sunday morning freezing him.

Even Bo had trouble reacting. It was unbelievable. You couldn't make yourself believe a grown man, supposed to have good sense, would suddenly snatch a handful of tail feathers from a rooster like a mischievous six-year-old kid! He had seen the old man do it, but he couldn't make himself believe what his eyes had seen. He hung on his stanchion, his muscles as lax as strings.

Not until Foss came pounding down with Tobe and Jonah on his heels was Bo galvanized into action. "What in the name of God is goin' on here?" Foss yelled at him.

But Bo was already moving. "That old fool has broke all hell loose," he shouted in passing. "Take Tobe and tend to them sheep! I'll help Luke and McDougal."

Phoebe came running, too. Wide-eyed she watched the chickens battling each other, but suddenly she spotted her grandfather. She screamed at him, then realizing he couldn't hear her she gathered up her skirts and flew to his rescue. Bo already had him by the shoulders and was propelling him toward the boat. Phoebe took him over. "Get him on the boat," Bo shouted at her, "and keep him there! For God's sake don't let him get loose again!"

Phoebe glared at him indignantly, but she led the old man, still staring and frozen, still clutching his tail feathers, gently up onto the deck.

It didn't take as long as Bo had feared it would to restore what could pass for order. Everybody pitched in to help, the men from Airdrie and the rousters, and under their soothing and clucking and quieting hands and voices the chickens slowly calmed down. The casualties weren't has heavy as Bo had feared they might be, either. Out of two hundred fowls only eight had been trodden or pecked to death, and perhaps two dozen were injured to some extent. With Scotch fortitude McDougal removed them from the coops and turned them loose to find their way back to the roost. "They would not sell," he said briefly, "nor would I want them to. When McDougal sells a chicken it is a healthy chicken."

Luke kept a tally of the hurt and dead and when it was all over and the coops were loaded on the *Rambler*, Bo said his apologies. He didn't know this man well. He had not shipped with the *Rambler* but once or twice. Those times he had been a man of so little conversation as to have almost none. But today he had every right to explode all over the *Rambler*'s captain. Not knowing how it would be taken, Bo still said, "I'm right sorry about all this, Mr. McDougal. The old man is a passenger and he must be getting too old to have good sense. I don't know what to make of it except that. And it happened so quick I don't reckon anybody could have stopped him."

McDougal hauled an ancient pipe from his pocket and

filled it unhurriedly. As he applied a match he looked past Bo to the boat and shook his head wonderingly. "It was a most peculiar thing for a man to do, wasn't it? And most unexpected. It may be as you say, Captain, the old man is senile."

"But the harm was done," Bo said, "for whatever reason. What would you consider the damages, sir?"

The Scotsman pondered and puffed on his pipe. "Well, now, Captain, I don't know that you can be held responsible. The fowls were not yet on your boat. What does your river law say about it?"

"What the river law says about steamboat responsibility is one thing, Mr. McDougal," Bo said firmly, "and what I think right is another. The man is my passenger and I consider the *Rambler* responsible."

McDougal puffed a while longer then said, with a twinkle in his eye, "We will compromise, then, Captain. I will sell you the dead chickens for your galley. The chickens that were injured, I will nurse back to health. Someone in Evansville can pay for them next trip or two."

"Done," Bo said, "and gladly. You're a fair man, Mr. McDougal."

Two bits each was what the Scotsman thought a fair price for the dead fowls. Paying him, Bo began laughing. He explained. "Just before that old fool snatched those tail feathers he was standing on deck beside me. He's an actor, stranded in these parts. Always quoting from some play or other. He had just spouted off one of his quotations to me— something an old king said about wanting all his peasants to have a chicken in their pot on Sundays. I'd expected the *Rambler* to eat mutton today, but it looks like our pot will have Sunday chickens instead."

McDougal removed his pipe from his mouth to laugh. Bo shook hands with him, thanked him again for his fairness,

and marched on board. Before the *Rambler* got under way
he meant to learn why Sir Henry had done such a fool thing.

He found him in the galley with Phoebe. The tail feathers,
brilliant and iridescent, lay on the table where the old man
sat with a cup of coffee. Bo's anger had faded, but he wanted
an explanation. He took coffee from Phoebe and sat opposite Sir Henry. "Now, sir," he said, "why did you do it?"

A look of bewilderment still on his face the old man gazed
at Bo. "My word, sir, I had no idea . . . all I wanted was a
few feathers. A cap I wear in a certain play has feathers.
They've become rather bedraggled, from being packed so
often, perhaps. When I saw that rooster's beautiful tail
feathers I thought what an excellent replacement for my
cap they would make. I was hasty, impulsive, but I had no
idea . . ." He pointed to the feathers. "I only took a few."

"You only took all he had," Bo said. "Maybe you meant
to take a few but what you did was grab a handful and yank.
Didn't you know what would happen? Don't you know anything about chickens?"

Ruefully the old man shook his head. "My acquaintance
with chickens has been limited to their being served to me
on a platter, I'm afraid."

"I'm afraid so, too. Chickens don't have sense enough to
come in out of the rain, sir. They're the most witless things
the Lord ever made. And they lose what little sense they've
got when they're scared. You set off chain lightning out
there and the result is eight dead fowls and two dozen hurt.
I've settled with the owner for 'em." He looked at Phoebe
who had been standing quietly, her hands shoved in her
apron pockets, listening. "Those eight dead hens will have
to be cooked today, Miss Phoebe. They won't keep over."

"They will be," she promised. Her eyes on her grandfather were gently amused. "He meant no harm, Captain."

Bo gave up trying to be stern. As witless as the chickens, the old man had yielded to an impulse but no great harm had come of it. He gulped down the last of his coffee and stood. Picking up the feathers and studying them, he suddenly yielded to an impulse of his own. He selected a gay red feather and planted it in the wild tangle of Sir Henry's hair, at the back where it thrust up regally. Beside it he planted two green ones. Toward the front he put a speckled feather and bolstered it with a gorgeous rainbowed one. He thrust iridescent black and blue and green ones over Sir Henry's two ears at rakish slants.

He stood off to view his handiwork, then set his hand over his mouth and uttered a startling war whoop. Drawing up a knee he went into a stooped dance around the table, chanting war cries as he danced.

Sir Henry flung himself out of his chair, his eyes glittering with fun, his feathers a trembling crown, and tilted his head back and shouted his own war cry. Then he stomped into the dance and followed Bo around the table.

Phoebe watched a moment, laughing at their ridiculousness, then the craziness hit her and she couldn't resist joining in. Making the tail of the line she whooped and yipped and stomped with vigor and glee, showering hairpins and combs recklessly over the floor.

Foss, come to see what new catastrophe had hit, stood unbelievingly in the door, his eyes bulging. After a long frozen moment he went away. Luke found him sitting in the engine room staring blankly in front of him. "What's the matter with you?" he asked, "you got the pip? Why ain't we running?"

"I don't know," Foss said in a flat, dead voice, "whether we're ever gonna run again. I don't know but Bo's brains is addled."

"Aw, come off it, Foss," the boy said scoffingly, "you couldn't addle Bo Cartwright's brains if you stirred 'em with a stick. What's got into you?"

"It ain't what's got into me," Foss said, "it's what's got into him. You know what he's doin'? Him and them is in the galley doin' a war dance."

Luke rocked back and stared, then he marched off to see for himself. He came back laughing. "They've done quit. Just having fun, Foss. All out of breath and dying laughing. Bo's going up. Said he was ready."

Foss heaved himself up, sighing. "*He's* ready. Finally, he's ready. First time since I been Bo Cartwright's engineer it was ever me to wait till *he* was ready. Always on my back—git me up steam—git them boys movin'—git goin' a hacklin' and a hurryin'—you couldn't ever git ready fast enough to suit him." He shook his head grievingly. "Ain't been nothin' on this trip natural."

The gong exploded its noisy warning and Foss reached quickly to give the signal back. He waited for his bell and moved his backing lever a split second after it rang. Flawlessly and fast he gave his pilot what he asked for—backing, shipping up—slow ahead. Then he sighed again. "Been the damndest run we ever made." He looked balefully at Luke as if it had all been his fault and felt called upon to add, "And it ain't over yet."

CHAPTER 15

THE morning which had promised so fair with its great splash of color changed its mind soon. The sky had grayed over before the *Rambler* made her stop at Ceralvo. No great threat of a storm yet, but a fresh breeze spanked the water smartly and tore the smoke from the stacks into boiling plumes. There wasn't going to be anything recreational about today's run, Bo thought. He'd earn his keep if the wind held on, for wind made every landing dangerous and every bend something to negotiate with care. He thought it *would* have to blow up just as he was coming up to the great head of Kinchloe's Bluff and one of the sharpest, meanest bends on the river—Shrewsbury. On the outside knee of the bend lay South Carrollton with its great deeps and its treacherous rocks. But whatever the weather you made your stop at South Carrollton. It was a good trading town. Bo hoped if a storm was coming he could beat it to South Carrollton. He didn't hanker to slither into that wharf in the middle of a storm.

Luke came up with the slips for the cargo taken on at Ceralvo. "That was a good paying stop," he said, checking them over. "We taken on twenty cases of eggs, ten stands of lard, sixteen hogs and five head of cattle. Biggest load we ever took on there."

"Most of 'em," Bo said, "been used to shipping with the companies. Had their stuff there waiting for the *Mary Lee* or the *Southern Belle*. Got anxious, I reckon. Way I figured they would. Might not be another boat up for a month."

Luke filed the tallies in the wooden chest which was Bo's lockbox, office and filing cabinet. "Good luck for us." He fronted around.

"We get to South Carrollton," Bo said, "see if you can buy us a skiff. Don't like being without one."

"That's right, we ain't got one now, have we?"

"Not since last night," Bo said.

Luke nodded. "I'll see to it." He watched the roughened water. "She freshening up any?"

"Not much change since she begun to blow."

Luke began to whistle an aimless wandery sort of little tune. He had a pretty whistle. He could make it quaver and he could split it into two harmonies. He was shy about doing it when asked, though. Said when somebody was listening his mouth dried up on him. Going about his work, his mind on something else, unconscious of an audience, he whistled a lot. Bo liked to hear him but he'd learned never to speak of it. You asked him, even, what it was he was whistling and he'd get fussed and say he didn't know—just a tune going round in his head. Bo guessed the whistle with Luke was a lot like a mockingbird's song—a trying and a following and a climbing and spiraling. No real tune he'd ever heard. Just whistling.

Luke broke it off. "Maybe this blow'll keep them gunboats tied up."

"You got 'em on your mind this morning, Luke?"

"Ain't you?"

"Some. Be foolish not to have. But I a little doubt a breeze'll keep 'em tied up."

"You got any idea where we might meet up with 'em?"

"Not even the vaguest one. I only hope it's not in the middle of a bend. If this wind don't flatten out, them bends will give me enough to think about without adding on a couple of gunboats."

"They're like ghosts," Luke said, moving restlessly. "All you hear is talk, nothing but talk. Wish we'd pick up something certain at South Carrollton."

"We don't," Bo said philosophically, "we just keep running till we do."

"I don't see how you can be so calm about 'em," Luke burst out.

Bo gave him an amused look. "How do you know I'm all that calm?"

"You act like they wasn't no more than the *Southern Belle*—something to speak to and pass."

"They're on my mind, Luke," Bo twisted the wheel a little, "they're on my mind, but so's Kinchloe's Bluff and Shrewsbury Bend. You got a river to run, you got it to run and you got to put your mind to it. If those gunboats are downriver someplace, there they are. We'll get to 'em when we get to 'em."

The boy brooded and watched the water, then shook himself together. "I don't know as I better try to be a pilot, Bo. I get too worked up."

"You won't—after a few years." Bo glanced up overhead and burst into laughter. "If we don't look like we been to the wars! Look at the hole that limb dug out of the roof. And half the guard rail left at the lock. *Rambler* looks like a real tramp now."

"She's running, though, and running sweet. Old Foss has got that machinery purring like a kitten."

"How's he feeling?"

"If you mean has he still got his aftereffects, he's not. But he's still feeling grumpy. Allows you been addled in the head."

Bo laughed. "Grumpy is Foss's natural way of feeling. I'd be scared if a day came he wasn't grumpy. I'd think there was something bad wrong with him. And I don't recollect we ever made a run that some time or other he didn't allow I was addled in the head. If I'd been addled as many times as he's said I've been, I'd be sitting on the bank somewhere counting my fingers and toes."

Luke laughed, too, and didn't say it looked to him there was something a little different about Foss's grumpiness this morning, something sad in it, sort of grieving and forlorn, as if he'd seen something inevitable and accepted it, though not wanting to and wishing he didn't have to. Something given up, maybe, some hope run out. It wasn't a talky grumpiness Foss had this morning. Luke shrugged it off. Maybe it was mostly aftereffects. And didn't know why it followed he should say, "You like that Miss Phoebe pretty good, don't you, Bo?"

"Sure. Don't you? I mostly like her," he amended. "Sometimes she's right aggravating but she's a smart girl. Been a big help this run."

"I like the two of 'em," the boy admitted. "Kind of funny, though. Some ways it's like they belonged on the *Rambler* almost as much as us. Like they been with us a long time. I never seen two make theirselves more at home. Reckon it's because they're show people and used to making their home wherever they light."

"It could be," Bo agreed.

The bluff was looming ahead and realizing suddenly where they were, Luke went into action. "Got to get below."

Bo put his full attention to taking the *Rambler* safely in, giving the bluff all the room it needed, then he bore well into the inside of the Shrewsbury bend, glad he had the wind on his nose for warping into the South Carrollton landing. Halfway into the bend he blew for the landing and Foss began pouring black smoke out the stacks. You liked to make a smart arrival, especially at a town landing, for half the town would pour down to the wharf to watch you come in. You liked to give them their money's worth, come chuffing round the bend with the black smoke pluming out the stacks, come in smart and sharp and proud, whistle blowing, bell ringing. Some day Bo was going to have one of those wildcat whistles you could play a tune on and he was going to have a bell made with silver dollars melted in. Luke pulled a good bell. He had the knack for it, and if he had him one of those Belgian bells he could pull as sweet as any mate on the river.

The plank went down and Bo eyed the confusion of crates and barrels set aside to be loaded. It was as he'd expected. Word had preceded him that he was taking the *Rambler* down and fear that this might be the last boat for untelling how long had galvanized the shippers. Luke was going to have his hands full with all that cargo and he'd have no time for seeing about a skiff. Bo thought he'd better see to it himself.

He went ashore among the crowd and prowled around asking if anyone knew of a skiff could be bought, if anyone had one he was willing to part with. He didn't have much luck. Skiffs were plentiful enough but they were needed. People who lived in a river town made constant use of the river— for fishing or for traveling short distances up and down. They needed their small boats.

He was thinking he'd have to let it go and try at Livermore or Rumsey farther down when a farmer whose casks and crates had already been loaded spoke up thoughtfully. "Judge Hafner's got an old leaky boat he don't use any more. Might see him about it."

"Who's Judge Hafner? And where'll I find him?" Bo asked.

The farmer turned to another man. "Joe, the judge back from Frankfort yet?" He said to Bo in explanation, "He's in the state legislature. They just been meeting and he might not have got home yet."

The man called Joe said, however, "He's back. Been back three or four days." He continued, "You'll find him at the store, I reckon. He keeps a general store in town. Lives right next door, if he ain't at the store."

"Be open on Sunday?"

The man nodded. "Usually is. Opens till church time. But this not being no ordinary Sunday he might not close at all today. Been a lot of folks come into town since the word got out you'd come through Buckner. He'll likely keep open all day to accommodate 'em."

"Think he might sell his skiff?"

"I don't know," the farmer said, "but he don't make no use of it. He's getting on in years, the judge is."

"What's he a judge of?"

"Nothing. Just been in the legislature so long folks commenced calling him that. Out of respect, I reckon."

The man called Joe spoke again. "It ain't much of a boat but I reckon if it was dreened and caulked it'd float."

"That's good enough," Bo said, "and it won't hurt to ask him. Much obliged."

He went back on the *Rambler* to get some money in case he and the judge struck a trade and then it occurred to him Phoebe might like to stretch her legs. She'd be in the galley, he guessed, and he went to find her. She was rolling out dough on the tabletop and good smells were coming from half a dozen pots on the stove. Bo sniffed and said, "Smells like you're stewing McDougal's chickens."

She gave him a quick smile and a nod. "And making dumplings to go with them. They're just ready to cut and drop in."

"Let Catfish do it and walk into town with me. We'll be here an hour."

She put down the rolling pin, stripped off her big apron, rolled down her sleeves and brushed up her hair. "Let's go," she said. At the door she warned Catfish, "Be sure you put the lids on. Dumplings should steam if they're to be tender. Mind, now, Catfish. And set them off in twenty minutes. They'll be mush if they steam longer than that."

"Yessum, I mind. Twenty minutes. I tek keer, miss." He rolled his eyes helplessly at Bo, who chuckled. Didn't make much difference what Catfish had to mind on the stove, what he most minded was any part of this galleying. But they left him with it.

The wind blew Phoebe's dress and her hair but she didn't clutch or grab. She let them blow as if she enjoyed it. She climbed up the bank as easily as Bo, as surefooted, without scrambling or sliding or slipping. He hadn't thought about it but if he had he would have known she would ask for no help and need none. At the top she was no more blown than he. She had a tough, strong young body and she used it well.

She was interested in the town, looked about curiously, but this was not one of her most chattery times. She walked along beside him silently, examining the homes and the yards, the late flowers still blooming, the late gardens, the cows in the back lots, the apple trees with windfalls already littering the ground. Not until they had passed a dozen such places did she open her mouth. "I sometimes think I'd like to live in a house, with real rooms and beds and a real kitchen and a cow and an orchard. Sometimes I think it might be very nice to be so settled."

"Maybe you will be some day," Bo said, laughing, "some day when you're married. Most men expect their women-folks to be right well settled in a house."

She shook her head and laughed with him. "Then I'll just have to look for someone who doesn't, for I know better really. That's just a sometime notion of mine. I'm too used to moving about. I'd miss it too much. I'd grow to hate staying in one place and I'd be very unhappy in no time at all."

Teasing, Bo said, "What you and your grandpa ought to do is get you a shantyboat. That'd be a house you could move when you pleased."

"Don't think I wouldn't like it," she flashed, adding immediately, "when he gets too old for the stage, of course. I wouldn't mind at all. Get weary of one place, just untie and move on." Her hands fluttered a shantyboat on its way up-river, downriver. "It would be so exciting." She skipped to catch up and blew her breath out. "Where are we going?"

"To the general store. I want to see a man about buying his skiff."

"A store? Do you think they might have some vegetables? The gardens are full of corn and beans. I wish we could have some. They'd give us a change from meat and potatoes."

Like most men Bo saw nothing wrong with meat and potatoes. Garden truck he could eat but without much real liking for it. "Won't be any to buy in a store," he said. "Be no use with everybody having a garden full. We buy such stuff straight from the folks. I'll send Tobe up after we get back to the boat."

They had no difficulty finding the store for it was the largest one in the village and a big sign across the front said plainly, "Burke Hafner—General Merchandise." Bo thought the man leaning against a porch post was probably the judge but he asked courteously as they came up, "Judge Hafner?"

"Yes, sir. What can I do for you?"

He was a man beginning to show his age in gray hair, a stoop, and corded veins on his hands. He was only middling tall and as chunky as Foss. His face had some weather seams, but it was a mild, kindly face. His eyes were blue and if he could have put it in words Bo's notion of them would have been that they were wise, a little sad, and endlessly patient, as if he had seen all the cupidity of which man was capable, all his meanness and orneriness, maybe a little of his nobility, too, still liked him pretty well and expected him to be very little different. They looked as if they'd seen so much nothing was left to surprise them.

Bo told him who he was and introduced Phoebe, who had been peering through the door and whose face was suddenly eager. "They have dress materials, Captain. I think I'll just look at some."

Judge Hafner gave her a pleasant smile and bent his head. "Go in, ma'am. Mama's in the back. If there's something you want to see she'll find it for you. She commonly waits on the womenfolks."

He motioned Bo to the long bench set against the wall. "Sit down, sir." He pulled up a rocking chair for himself and set it in easy, slow motion.

Bo went straight to the point. "I was told at the wharf you had a skiff you didn't make much use of and might sell. I lost mine last night and am in need of another."

The judge shook with quiet laughter. "We heard you'd run plumb through Lock #3 last night. Plumb through all of Buckner's army. That when you lost your skiff?"

Bo smiled. "Yes. Well, didn't exactly lose it. Had an errand for some of my boys which made use of it. We had no time to recover it."

"Wouldn't think so," the judge said, wheezing through his chuckles, "sure wouldn't think so. I can probably accommodate you."

"I'd be obliged," Bo said. "News about last night has got around, has it?"

"Whole country's talking about it. Not talking about much else today. How'd you do it?"

Bo told him. "I had a lot of help," he finished. "Folks were pretty het up over Buckner aiming to blow up the lock and ruin the river. Seemed like a good many were willing to help me. Locktender and his boys, bunch of fellows that loaf around the landing and fish. And my boys . . . I've got a good bunch of boys this trip and they all pitched in. Everybody pitched in. We couldn't have done it, without."

The judge nodded. "Folks around here didn't like Buckner interfering on the river, either. Kind of took a special pleasure in learning you'd forestalled him at Rochester."

"I don't know as I did that," Bo said. "All I did was get my boat through the lock before he blew it up."

"You've not heard he decided not to dynamite it? Decided to jam it with logs? Way we heard it, you were the one thought of it."

"Well, I named it," Bo admitted, "but I couldn't wait around to see what he did about it. So he made use of that log raft, did he?"

"They say he never did set the engineers back to drilling after your little fracas last night. Called 'em off and put his men to breaking up the raft and jamming the lock. Word is they finished this morning, early. She's all full and there won't be any boats locking through #3 for a while."

Bo plucked at a rough place on the edge of the bench and

tore a splinter off. Absently he stuck it in his mouth and chewed on it. "Well," he said, "I'm glad. That's better'n having it destroyed. It'll be a right smart inconvenience for a time but when Buckner moves on, the logs can be taken out without much trouble."

The old judge's eyes squinted and he looked at Bo shrewdly. "You think Johnston and Buckner are going to move on?"

Bo hesitated. He'd been used to holding his tongue, keeping his opinions and his confusion and his fretted feelings to himself. He didn't know this man so he kept cautious now. "I don't know. I got all I can say grace over running my boat. Don't hear too much news. I got no idea what their game is."

"I do," the old judge said sharply and he rocked forward suddenly, "I know exactly what their game is. Their game is to bring the war to Kentucky. They've got a thin line thrown clear across the southern half of the state—from Cumberland Gap in the mountains to Columbus on the Mississippi. They mean to advance it if they can and push the Federals out. They mean to have Kentucky for the South."

"But Governor Magoffin issued that proclamation," Bo protested. "That's a violation . . . he said Kentucky would be neutral . . ."

The judge spat. "Not a chance. Not as much chance as snow in July for this state to be neutral. Folks began choosing sides before a gun was fired at Sumter. Think how this state lies. It's a border state, but it's southern in all its ways and institutions. It's a slave state. Half the folks in the state think it ought already to be out of the Union fighting with its sister slave states. Other half is crying Save the Union and pulling to the North. How could you have neutrality? Just words. And can't either side afford to *let* Kentucky be neutral."

"I don't see why not . . ." Bo began.

The old man interrupted him testily. "Because they're afraid. Lincoln can't afford to let it stay neutral for fear Davis'll move in and take it over. Davis can't sit by and leave it alone for fear Lincoln'll move in. Both sides been recruiting and putting up their camps and now both sides have got armies on Kentucky soil. How you going to keep 'em from it? How you going to keep 'em out? How you going to get rid of 'em, make 'em stay out?"

"The state militia . . ."

"State militia!" the judge snorted. "That was the state militia you come through at Rochester last night! They been secesh right from the start and most of 'em went with Simon Buckner when he quit as their officer and went south last month. The biggest part of your state militia is in Johnston's army right now."

Bo said bluntly, "How do you know?"

"How do I know? I'm in the legislature. What you think we been doing up at Frankfort? We been studying and pondering and struggling—about the state militia and the Home Guards and Sherman in Louisville and Johnston in Bowling Green and the governor's southern leanings and the new legislature just elected last month mostly Union men. How do I know? I've been where you've *got* to know! Man, we got a civil war right in our own state house!" The old man leaned forward and tapped Bo on the knee. "And I'll tell you another thing. We're going to have a secession in our own state. Buckner and Johnston are hoping to foster another state government—a *Confederate* state government—and they don't have to go far for help. This country all around here is a hotbed of southern sympathizers. They'll do it.

They'll pull away from Frankfort and mind what I tell you, they'll put 'em a Confederate capital at Bowling Green or Russellville, sure as shooting."

Bo felt stunned. He couldn't doubt the judge knew what he was talking about. His opportunity for knowing was too good. A man couldn't sit in the legislature up at Frankfort, hear all the talk and the arguments, listen to the problems and try to decide, *without* knowing. Bo said, "You think that's coming?"

The old man slapped at a fly that was buzzing around his head. "I sure God do think so. And not far off."

Bo felt a great heaviness settle on him. He gazed down the road where the wind was lifting and skirling the dust. He watched as it caught up a sheet of old newspaper, scuttled it around a time or two, then dropped it over a dog's head, who yipped in sudden blinded terror and began chasing his tail. A woman yelled at the dog and threw a stick at him. The wind caught her skirt and billowed it for a moment and she looked as if she would be blown like a kite into the sky. She fought her skirt down and fled into her house. No more, Bo thought dully, than that dog blinded by a newspaper suddenly dropped on him did a common, ordinary, average man know what was happening to him and maybe to all the rest of his life. The wind of war blew, without your asking or wishing, and it spun you blind, chasing your tail in terror. He shifted on the bench. "Kentucky has sure got embrangled, hasn t it?"

"In the worst way," the old man said. "Kentucky is going to have its own kind of civil war. South Kentucky will split off from North Kentucky. Families will be split and friends will be split and the state will be split. There is going to be a lot of heavy hearts and a lot of blood spilled on Kentucky soil before it's over." The old man passed a hand over his whiskers. "And right here on Green River is likely where it'll commence, too. The first battles will be fought near this river."

Stung, Bo cried, "Why? What makes you think so? Why here? Why not Louisville? That's where the Federals' headquarters are."

"But Johnston picked Bowling Green for a jumping-off place. Ain't you wondered why yet?"

"I've not had time to wonder," Bo said shortly. "I been too busy. It's happened so quick and sudden and I've had my own kind of troubles."

"Yes. Well, think how the railroads run south from Louisville. Straight through this country into Tennessee. Say you were Albert Sidney Johnston and your army was in Tennessee and you wanted to take Louisville, where would you begin?"

The railroad bridges across the Green were suddenly and sharply clear before Bo's eyes. "Bowling Green," he said slowly, "Bowling Green and then work right up the railroad lines."

"And that's just what he's going to do. That's just what he is already commencing to do."

Bo couldn't sit still any longer. He had to get up on his feet. It was worse, a thousand times worse than he had thought. And there wasn't going to be any quick end to it. This wasn't any sudden little sashay of Buckner's to jam a lock and stop a couple of Federal gunboats. This wasn't any quick jabbing raid into Kentucky and then withdrawal. This was no longer the probing and feeling and jousting. This was the closing in, the coming to grips, the siege and the battle, the stabbing guns and the death and the carnage.

As if it were slowly being unreeled in front of him, clear picture following clear picture, he saw the changes that

would come to the river country. The map of the river and
its touching lands was engraved on his mind and in his heart.
The Green wound in almost its entire length right through
the middle of this country that had been invaded and would
now be fought over. Whichever side won those battles, the
river and its people and its touching lands would be the
loser—for years and years and years to come. It was enough
to stop the heart in your chest.

The old judge had risen too. Bo heard his voice going on
and on and on. He didn't pay much heed. His mind was too
full of what he now knew. How blind, he wondered, how
blind can you be?

His attention was suddenly riveted when the old man
mentioned the gunboats. He swung about. "Those gunboats
. . . I'm sorry, sir. What were you saying about 'em?"

"Why, I was just telling that they're between Spottsville
and Rumsey. Tied up at Mason's Landing last day or two.
But they're upbound. You want to keep guard."

"You know that for a fact, sir?"

"Ought to. My nephew saw 'em."

Bo reflected. Since they had locked through #1 at Spottsville and were now upbound for #2 at Rumsey, obviously
they were small boats. No lock on Green River could accommodate a boat longer than a hundred and thirty-nine feet.
They were probably sternwheel packets, not much bigger
than the *Rambler*. He felt a little easier. What he'd been
most afraid of was ironclads at the mouth of the Green.
"How many of 'em are there, sir?"

"Two. They got the main deck sheeted up to the rails,
but no rams. Plenty of guns though, my nephew said." He
scratched his grizzled head then shook it. "We been trying
to straddle a fence here in Kentucky, but the fence has been
torn out from under us. Time appears to be here now when

every man jack of us has got to pick and choose, take a stand. We got to fish or cut bait."

"Fish or cut bait . . ." Bo repeated, then he went on so softly, so slowly, he hardly knew he spoke aloud. "All I wanted was peace. I wanted my own boat and I got it. I got it almost paid for. I didn't make this war and didn't want it. But it's come and I reckon I'll help pay for it. What I wanted wasn't much. Just to run my boat and live my life on this river."

"It's what all men want, my friend," the old man said, his voice suddenly roughened. "It's what all men want and it's what's guaranteed them under the constitution—the pursuit of happiness, in full freedom. But freedom's a hard-bought thing and it don't stay bought. You've got to keep buying it over and over again. And sometimes you get killed buying it—like that young man at the lock last night."

Bo turned around stiffly, as if his joints hurt. "Last night?" he said stupidly.

"Maybe you didn't know. Young fellow with Buckner's army was killed on the lock wall. Only casualty, they say."

Foss's popshot, Bo thought quickly, Foss's popshot!

The judge was going on. "Boy by the name of Stern. They say he was from up near Bowling Green—some place on the Barren. Thomas Stern, he was. Say his pa is dead and he lived with a brother. William Stern, I believe. Boy and his ma both lived with the brother." The old man sighed. "Be a lot of that kind of thing for folks on this river before it's over."

Bo felt as if an iron claw had got its hooks in his chest and was closing up slowly, strangling and shutting off the blood. One shot—just one shot fired from the *Rambler* and it had to kill William Stern's young brother he was worried about! And the old mother sick and looking for letters and now there'd be no more letters at all. Not ever. What she'd get would be her youngest's dead body brought home to her. And it would kill her, likely. The irony of it, the appalling irony of it turned Bo to stone. It was as if death had pointed a finger at one man, one young kid, and said devilishly, that one's mine. As if then he had guided Foss's trigger finger, sighted along his muzzle for him, and spat the bullet from his own flaming mouth along its destined track.

Foss, he thought with blind, protective instinct, Foss mustn't ever know. He'd got somehow to keep Foss from ever knowing who it was. He'd been worried enough it might have been a riverman. It would make him feel like a murderer to know it was William Stern's young brother. You've got to get back to the boat now, he told himself, and keep Luke or Tobe or some other bigmouth from blabbing where Foss could hear. That's all the good you can do about it now.

He was aware suddenly of the judge's gaze. He guessed the old man knew the shot had come from his boat, but his look was neither judging nor condemning. It was tired, sort of, and a little sad, and wise and old and accepting—accepting of the things that men do when they must. Bo shook himself back into his skin and said evenly, "I'm sorry to hear it." He had to let it go at that.

Phoebe was in the door, now, calling a goodbye back into the store. She had two brown-wrapped parcels in her arms and automatically Bo stepped forward to take them. "New dresses," she said, her eyes lit up like stars, "actually two new dresses for me! It's been so long since I had a new dress I almost went mad trying to choose from the prints. What a nice stock of goods you have, Judge Hafner."

"I'd be interested to know what you chose, ma'am," the old man said, chuckling.

She tore a bit of the paper from each parcel. "This nice black and white print, because it's so sensible. And this little red print because it's so pretty."

"I see," the judge said, twinkling at her, "one for the head, and one for the heart."

"Precisely, and how prettily you put it. How fortunate that Grandfather and I did that show in Aberdeen and I had a little money to spend in your store, sir."

"And how fortunate we still had some prints for you to choose from. I fear it won't be long until our shelves will be barer."

Phoebe's smile disappeared. She looked soberly at the old man. "You think it's going to be a long war, sir?"

"A very long war, ma'am—and it's just begun."

"Oh, I wish not!" she cried passionately, "I *wish* not! I wish there were no war at all. I hate war!"

"Your young friend here feels the same," the old man replied.

"And can't afford one for the heart," Bo said bitterly.

The judge said quietly, "I'm afraid not."

"Come on, Phoebe," Bo said roughly, "our time's about gone. Goodbye, sir, and thank you."

The judge touched his arm. "That skiff you were wanting, Captain. Look for a black man answering to the name of Cuff, down at the wharf. He will show you where it's tied. And I reckon a couple of dollars will be about right for it."

Blindly Bo felt for his money and counted out two dollars, and mumbled thanks again.

He walked so fast going back to the wharf that Phoebe had to trot to keep up but she made no complaint. He was troubled; she could see that plainly. Something in the conversation with Judge Hafner had upset him. If she said a word right now he'd probably snap her head off. But she was glad when they reached the boat. She had a stitch in her side and couldn't have kept up much longer. And he forgot all about sending Tobe for the vegetables and she was afraid to remind him.

On board she took her bundles, thanking him briefly. She had to tug at the parcels. He seemed surprised that he had them. Looked at them queerly as if he had never seen them before. She fled up the steps hoping he hadn't heard some dreadful bad news. It must be the gunboats, she thought, and that was bad enough.

When the skiff had been loaded, Bo said curtly to Luke, "Get that stage up and let's move! Now!"

But no amount of bother and no amount of troubled mind could make him forget he was a steamboatman. His mind was boiling—Thomas Stern—Thomas Stern—fish or cut bait—fish or cut bait—Thomas Stern. But he gave his signals smoothly and there was nothing sloppy about the *Rambler*'s departure. Luke pulled his good bell, Foss poured black smoke from the stacks, chuffed his machinery, backed, shipped up and went ahead with smartness. Bo blew and they gave South Carrollton a departure that had style.

CHAPTER 16

A FEW miles downriver Luke came up with his cargo slips. "We're commencing to get a little crowded, Bo," he said.

Bo nodded absently. "Stack it up. We'll take on all we can."

"Well," the boy said. "I don't know as we can take on any more livestock, though." He laughed. "Can't stack pigs and cows up very good." He went on happily, shuffling through his slips, "It sure is being one hell of a good run."

"It sure is," Bo said bitterly, "one hell of a good run!"

The boy didn't catch the bitterness. "Never seen the deck so full. Oh," he added, "about to forget. Had to turn down some passengers back there."

Bo heard him with only one part of his mind. With the other he was telling himself he had to quit this brooding on Thomas Stern. No amount of brooding would bring the kid back and no amount of brooding would undo what had been done. He had to put it behind him. He had to get over feeling so soggy and heavy about it. He still had a boat to run, he still had a cargo to deliver, he still had his own people to take care of.

It wasn't him that had brought the war to the river. He hadn't made the kid enlist. He hadn't given the orders that brought him to Rochester. He hadn't given the orders that brought him with a gun in his own hands to fire on the *Rambler*. You could twist yourself in knots, sorry and hurting, blaming yourself. You could have this odd feeling in your head that something, fate or God or something, had put you in a given place at a given time—that it wasn't accident or a coincidence, but somehow meant, and meant since time began. You could think like that until you thought yourself into a babbling state of idiocy. You could think yourself into somehow loading the blame for everything onto yourself, because you were a man and had chosen to be a steamboat-man and had got yourself a boat and used it on the river; and the river and your boat and the time and the place, and Buckner and the war, had all come together to meet in a small, fateful, focused moment.

He thrust it away irritably. One man wasn't big enough for it and it was a kind of arrogance to think it and one man didn't owe it. Take your own blame and no more. And when he looked at his own blame he thought, harshly, I'd have to do it again the same way. He had cargo to deliver and he owed it to his shippers to deliver it at Evansville. He had people on board he was responsible for. The roustabouts all were from Evansville; Phoebe and Sir Henry were headed there. He owed it to get them where they belonged.

It made an acid taste in his mouth to think that maybe a shot from the *Rambler* had caused the first casualty in Kentucky's civil war, but that was the way it was. If he had it to do over again, he'd have to do it. Nor would he, he knew, unload his guns. Foss might just as easy have been killed. He was captain of the *Rambler* and his people and his shippers and his boat had to come first.

His mind, having picked its way to the end of that hard track, went back to what Luke had said. "Who was it wanted to ride with us?"

"Fellow by the name of Steed. Him and his family. Six of 'em, him and his wife and four younguns," Luke said. "When I'd turned him down and they'd went away one of the boys at the landing said they was scared."

"Scared of what?"

"The war, I reckon. He's been working in the mines across from Livermore. Railroad goes by there and there's talk that General Sherman in Louisville has sent troops down on the cars. Steed figured there'd be a battle pretty soon. They said he was from up north some place—Pennsylvania, they said. Worked in the mines up there. Reckon he allowed he'd better get back quick while he could."

Bo digested this rumor. If it was true, it was beginning fast and there probably would be a battle somewhere along the railroad line. He wondered if Buckner was moving up the railroad now to meet the Federals. He thought of the railroad bridge across the river at Livermore.

"Well," he said slowly, "we got our own worries, Luke." He told the boy about the gunboats. "The *Rambler* is no place for passengers now."

"It sure as hell isn't," the boy agreed. He was thoughtful after that, studying the slow, deep river ahead. "Them wind ripples don't look to be quite as strong to me," he said, after a time.

"They're not," Bo said. "Wind's been easing off since we left South Carrollton, and I'm glad." He scanned the sky briefly. "Looking more like rain all the time. Rain," he said, after thinking about it a moment, "I could use. Makes a pretty good screen."

Luke's wandery little whistle began but he broke it off almost at once and laughed. "You gonna play hide-and-seek with them gunboats?"

"Maybe," Bo said. "Depends. Here," he said, standing away from the wheel, "you take her a while. Wind's on your sta'bbord but it's not too fresh. I want to talk to Foss."

The boy's eyes lit up. He had been hoping Bo would give him the wheel. He sometimes did in this pool of water. Once he'd let him take the *Rambler* from the Point Pleasant ferry clear to the lock at Rumsey. The wind hadn't been blowing that day but if Bo thought this breeze wouldn't trouble him he wouldn't be afraid of it.

Bo had shaken himself out of his fit of blame and blues enough by now that he walked down the deck automatically checking the cargo. He'd been too blind-shocked when he came aboard to give it a thought. The boy was right. They couldn't take on any more stock. They had room for a little more hard goods and that was all.

He hadn't thought about being hungry until he passed the galley and then he realized his stomach was gnawing. He'd used up his breakfast, he thought, stewing—and a poor-paying job it had been. You did what you had to do and put it behind you. He went in the galley and found it empty. Even Catfish had wandered off.

He took two plates from the shelf and heaped them with chicken and dumplings and carried them to the engine room. Foss was sitting on his stool fingering his hound dog's ears. "How'd you know my stummick was rumblin'?" he asked, looking up and grinning.

Relief was like something warm running all through Bo. He'd have known the minute he looked at Foss if he had heard about Thomas Stern. Foss had been born with a face-skin so tough it wouldn't seam or crease to give him away but he had the most giving-away eyes ever set in a man's head. You could always tell when Foss was grieving or bothered. His eyes looked as begging as a dog's. Foss's were clear and untroubled. Bo handed him a plate. "My own stomach was growling," he said.

They ate rapidly, wolfing down the steaming food, and didn't talk until they had finished it off. While Foss gave the bones to his dog, Bo told him about the gunboats. He told him about Steed, the man who had wanted passage on the *Rambler,* and the rumor that Sherman was sending troops south from Louisville by railroad. "My opinion," he concluded, "they add up. It's my opinion now that those gunboats aren't heading upriver at all. Looks to me, they're patrolling, keeping out feelers for what Johnston and Buckner are doing, making sure, of course, they don't use the river, but mostly keeping Sherman posted. The more I study it, the more it looks to me there'll be no battle at Bowling Green, now. It's gonna be somewhere along the railroad line. If Johnston's as smart as they say he is, he'll have his cavalry out and his skirmishers and they'll cut the tracks. I been worried some Buckner might be headed downriver to hunt out the gunboats, but I don't think it any more. There's bigger game to flush. So the way I see it now is we've seen the last of the Confederates this trip and all we got ahead of us is the gunboats."

Foss fed the last bone to his dog and wiped the grease off his hands on his pants' legs, but he'd been listening. "That's a plenty," he said.

"But not as bad as it could have been." Bo rubbed the dog's flank with the toe of his boot and got a growl and raised hackles for his pains. "Aw. shut up," he said, "I don't want your bone."

"You'd durn burn sure not get it if you did," Foss said.

"Wanta bet?"

Foss looked at him, blinked, then hastily said no. "I just recollected the way you used to stop a dog fight, grabbing one of 'em by the hind legs. Got 'em always to turn loose their throat hold to commence finding out what had holt of their legs. No, I reckon old Buckner here'd turn loose quick enough you done that to him."

"Buckner? Last I heard you named him Sir Henry."

"I did. But I dislike Buckner now more'n I dislike the old codger so I named him over."

"Why you want to name him after somebody you don't like?"

"Comes in handy you want to cuss him out. Get double your value. Cuss the dog and the feller you don't like at the same time. His name is General Simon Bolivar Buckner, now."

"Kind of a mouthful, ain't it?"

"When I'm rushed I call him Buck."

Bo laughed. "Foss, you're the biggest fool ever was."

Foss leaned back and belched comfortably. "I make sense to myself." The dog crept up and laid his head on the big man's knee. Foss scratched it for him obligingly. "When you gonna get to the point, Bo?"

"Right now. This is the way I been thinking. Old man Hafner said the gunboats were between Spottsville and Rumsey, upbound. Mason's Landing, precisely. Tied up. Not running at night. Suppose they're patrolling is all. They'll be coming on up to Lock #2 at Rumsey today. But they're farther from Rumsey than we are. We can get locked through before they get there."

Foss's hand had fallen away from its scratching. The dog nosed it and whined and Foss took up his rubbing again. "No doubts about that," he said, "but what then?"

"You recollect the mouth of Pond River? Where it's at?"

Foss didn't make any reply but he raised his eyes from the dog's muzzle to Bo and the skin around his eyes wrinkled as he caught Bo's intention and grinned. "That's a good idea, boy. Lay up there till they pass going up, then scoot out and head for home! It'll be easy."

"What I thought it'd be—if we're lucky."

Foss pulled the hound's long floppy ear gently through his fingers. The dog, without moving his head an inch, rolled his eyes up at this big man whose hands were so easy and so sure in knowing what a dog most liked. Foss blew on the ear and the hound shivered in ecstasy. "What if we ain't lucky?"

"We've come this far," Bo said slowly, "and we're going on."

"Like last night?"

"If we have to." He added, wryly, "No use playing favorites. We give Buckner a bad time last night. Might as well give the Federals a bad time today." He shoved up and groaned. "God, I feel like this trip had put ten years on me."

Foss gave him a flicking look. "It don't show."

It showed a little, he thought. The boy was bone-tired. He hadn't slept enough. There'd been just one thing after another to worry him and bother him since they'd left Bowling Green. You'd never doubt but that Bohannon Cartwright would meet all his worries and bothers, but they'd been piled mighty high this run. Foss hoped when they got past the gunboats it'd be an easy trick on in to Evansville. He didn't like to see the boy beginning to look like the frayed end of a piece of hemp. One thing—they would have time to rest a little when they got to the end of the run. They hadn't been able to order the new rod. They'd have to order it when they got to Evansville and it would take a little time to get there. Then they'd have to set it in. The boy could catch up on his sleeping and eating and resting while they waited.

Bo was looking at the pressure gauge. He pecked it with his finger. "We'll get through, Foss," he said, but absently as if to himself. Then, like the words had been pulled out of him, he said, "And then see what's to do."

Foss gave the hound a gentle shove and stood, too. "What's to do, I reckon," he said, "will all be on the lower river. Ain't nobody gonna be running clean up to Bowling Green for a while."

Bo scrubbed his hand down his face. "We'll see. I got to think on it some more."

He looked at the big misshapen, barrel-bellied man and a twist of pain, as if a knife had been stuck in him, hit him. Such a time they'd been together—such a long, good time. And such plans they'd had—such big, good plans. And they'd always worked them before. There'd never been anything to stop them before, and it took a war to do it now. He looked out and knew without thinking about it where they were. He knew by the trees and the look of the bank and the look of the water lapping the bank. If it had been night and only the treeline to go by, he'd have known. It was like the skin on his face and the breath in his body. This, he told himself heavily, is to worry. *This* is to worry.

Foss brought him back into himself. "It's raining," he said.

Bo went to look. It was an easy rain, a soft gray silk screen let down from a soft gray silk sky. On the river the little drops fell in small plops that splatted gently and raised only little spouts before they fell back on themselves as if too tired or too timid to make any more of a show.

The wind had gone entirely, scudded off eastward and up-river someplace. Blowing, likely, Bo thought, on the mill-pond at home now. "I hope this rain has settled in for the day," he said. The dampness crawled on his neck and raised the hairs and he shivered a little. "Well, Luke has got to eat."

At Livermore they had to turn down the first livestock. The man had more cows and hogs and sheep penned than they already had on board and seeing them penned, Bo went to deal with him personally. Luke had his hands full with the hard freight to load. Bo and the man huddled out of the rain under the projecting roof of a shed. The man did not take it kindly when Bo told him, with genuine regret, that he couldn't accommodate him. "Well," he blustered, "what am I gonna do with 'em? I been waiting here for you three days. Now you say you can't handle 'em. What am I supposed to do? Drive 'em to Evansville on foot?"

"I'm sorry," Bo said, "but you can see for yourself, sir, we can't take another head of livestock. We can't take on much more cargo of any kind. We're almost flattened out now."

The man fumed on. "I've got a trade already made for this stock at Evansville. Union army wants 'em. I stand to lose a lot of money if I don't ship right now."

"I'm losing money not being able to accommodate you," Bo told him, "and I'll lose more having to turn down freight the rest of this trip. But I can't stretch my boat any bigger."

The man blustered and grumbled and fretted on, like a misput child. He kept telling over and over how long he'd had the stock penned up and how they'd lost weight already and how he'd had to wait three days for the *Rambler*. A persistent leak was dripping down Bo's neck and his patience was rapidly going. It went completely when the man said for the tenth time that he'd been waiting three days for the *Rambler*. Bo said smoothly, "I don't recollect you ever shipping with the *Rambler* before, sir. I believe this is the first time."

"What's that got to do with it?"

"Commonly you ship with the *Southern Belle,* don't you?"

"Well—yes," he was truculent, "I've shipped with the *Belle.* But a man can change his mind, can't he?"

Bo's temper frayed out entirely. "Yes, he can," he snapped, "particularly if he's missed the *Belle* and if she's now tied up at Evansville and not likely to make another run for untelling how long! Particularly when my boat is the only boat on the river! You picked an awful good time to change your mind about who you wanted to ship with!"

"Looks to me," the man lashed back, "you'd be glad to get new business. Own your own boat, don't you?"

"Yes, I own it. And I am glad to get new business—when I can accommodate it. But I've had to take care of my own shippers and I've done as well as I could by everybody else. First come, first served, is all it is, sir. Nothing personal in it."

The man swiveled around and kicked at a stone, sent it flying into the river. "I'll not forget this, Cartwright," he said, glowering. "I'll remember you turned me down. You'll never get a chance at another pound of freight from me—nor anybody I can influence. You'll wish you hadn't turned George Washington Wheeler down before I get through." He stalked away angrily stubbing at the rubble ahead of him as he went.

Phoebe, who had been standing on the deck out of the rain, but not twenty feet away, watched the man leave. When he was out of earshot she said, "Mercy, what an angry little man. And how important he thinks he is. Wouldn't you know he'd have an impressive name? Mr. George Washington Wheeler! My goodness!"

"Small honor to his namesake," Bo snorted and lunged aboard, shaking himself like a wet dog when he'd got under cover.

"Where's your cap?" Phoebe scolded. "Out in the rain with

nothing on your head. You'll catch your death." She took her shawl to towel his hair dry, then she turned his face to inspect his cuts and scratches.

"You think I'll live?" he asked, grinning, when she had satisfied herself.

"Unfortunately," she said loftily, "yes. You won't even have any scars to make a boast of."

They both laughed. Bo put his arms on the rail and leaned on it to watch the rousters finish the loading. Imitating him, Phoebe leaned by his side. He looked down at her, amused. When it was damp, from rain or fog or even a heavy morning dew, her hair frizzed up like tight little corkscrews around her face. Looked like a curly sheepskin cap, he thought, and feeling easier with her than he'd ever expected to be, he gave it a light pat. "Keep you warm?"

She ducked and laughed. "Don't be fresh, Captain Cartwright."

"I wouldn't know how," he protested.

She made her eyes into a squint, ranging them over him. "You'd be a quick study," she said, then.

A rouster dropped a barrel and it rolled clatteringly and dangerously near the water before he could catch up with it. Bo yelled at him to take care, and both he and Phoebe, the thread of their joking broken, watched as the line of rousters resumed their work.

"I wonder," Phoebe said after a while, "why that man wouldn't be reasonable. What could he have expected you to do? Unload some of the cargo already on board? You made it quite clear why you couldn't accommodate him. And actually all he had to do was look at the deck. He could plainly see there was no room for his stock. Why did he keep going on and on about it?"

"Just misput," Bo said. "Wasn't in any humor to be reasonable. My guess is he was bothered and a little scared. I didn't put any dependence in that talk of a deal in Evansville. What I think—he's heard the talk—knows there's two armies heading for each other in this neck of the woods. He got to figuring his livestock would look mighty good to either one of those armies. I hear they've got a way of taking what they want and leaving you with a piece of paper promising to pay. I'd guess he figured to ship his stock while he could sell for dollars instead of paper."

Phoebe thought about it, then nodded. "I expect you're right. I'd feel sorrier for him though if he hadn't been so ugly. What will he do, now?"

Bo shrugged. "Drive 'em home, likely. Take his risks."

They were silent again until Phoebe said, pensively, "This war is going to hurt so many more people than are involved in the fighting. Before it's over there will be no one who isn't involved one way or another, who hasn't lost a son or a husband or a brother or father, or home or wealth or property. It's going to reach out and touch every human life in this whole country, north or south. There'll be no one whose life isn't changed by it."

Her voice went on and on as she thought and pondered and spoke her thoughts and ponderings, but Bo closed it off. His face had gone dark. He moved his shoulders the way a horse moves its skin to shudder off a biting fly. He didn't want to talk about it now, or even think about it, or even hear. He had to do his thinking about it, he knew that. But he had to do it his way and he had to do it when he had time. He had to plow through any kind of thinking pretty heavily, and especially he'd have to plow deep on this. He wanted to be let alone when he did it.

He didn't really know when she quit talking about the war, but he was aware suddenly she was on a different tack. ". . . and they haven't sung or done that queer cross-step shuffle since we left South Carrollton. Until then they raised a song and pranced up the gangplank at every landing. Now they just load, with that odd look on their faces."

"They're scared, too," Bo said slowly. "They heard what we all heard at South Carrollton. The war is right on our doorstep and they're black and they're scared. They don't know what they're supposed to do or how they're supposed to act. They don't know what may happen to 'em."

"Are they free Negroes?"

"Some of 'em. Most are hired out by their owners. Tobe is mine. But free or slave, they're all black. What would you do—how would you feel if your skin was black and folks were saying a war was being fought over you?"

"Be scared," she said promptly.

Bo laughed. "Me, too. I'm scared anyhow." He caught Luke's signal. "They're done. We'll be leaving."

Phoebe watched him push himself up from the rail and she thought, he looks taller and thinner and he looks older and he looks tireder. Only that morning there had been a skinful of boy in him, sticking those silly rooster feathers in her grandfather's hair and cavorting around in a war dance. But now it was as if he'd forgot any boy in him and grown up soberly and suddenly and wholly to be a man.

She watched him walk away and she thought, he doesn't walk as quick or stand quite as straight and his shoulders look broader and heavier. She watched him start up the companionway and she thought, it's the first time I ever saw him take those stairs one at a time. She felt sad with pity for him, under all the wearying load he was carrying, not understanding all of it but sensing some of it and being troubled for him. She would have liked to say something comforting to him, but she felt young and gauche and inept. And he had not confided in her.

She felt suddenly very lonely, and she looked about her with an odd and strange feeling of being misplaced, as if for the first time she saw the river and the *Rambler* and the boat's people whose whole way of life was so passionately river and boat, and wondered why she was here.

She touched the railing and thought, this is real; it is made of wood and it is solid. She touched a barrel and thought, this is real; it is made of wood and it is filled with flour which came from wheat grown on the land. She looked at the sheep and cows and hogs and chickens in their pens and stalls and crates and thought, they are real; they have bones and flesh and blood. She watched the roustabouts scatter over the deck and thought, they are real; they have homes to go to and people to be with. Everything else—the river, the boat, the shore, the people and the livestock, all had reality. But she was set apart and dislocated and unbelonging. She felt droopy and unwanted.

She took herself firmly and promptly in hand. Fiddle, she told herself, you've got the vapors. It's the gloomy day and the news of the war and of course he's broody and has a lot on his mind and a lot of work to do. And so have you. And the best cure in the world for the megrims is work, so just march yourself up those stairs and begin sewing on your new red print dress!

CHAPTER 17

THE ten miles between Livermore and Calhoun was as pretty a piece of water as there was on the river. You always had good water just above a lock and Lock #2 was located between the towns of Calhoun on the right bank and Rumsey on the left.

There were no landings between Livermore and Calhoun and Bo pushed the *Rambler* on down. He was glad to leave the railroad behind. The bridge could be of prime importance to either side and even if he missed being there when it was blown it would cause such a mess it would be as effective in stopping passage up and down the river as dynamiting any of the locks. He wanted out of the way if Buckner or Sherman's troops saw the advantage of destroying the railroad bridge.

As nearly blocked off as she was the *Rambler* had little glide. No swan for grace at her best, she plowed water worse now than ever, but she had plenty of deep to plow and the big waves rolled away to the shores like the long swells of the sea. She bucked a little and plunged and she threw a lot of water but she was sounding good still and the steady churn of the paddles pushed her sturdily.

It was still raining—more than a drizzle but not what you'd call a hard rain at all, not a goose-drownder. It was just a gray, drippy, steady, light fall. The kind of rain that would have to wear itself out and would take a lot of wearing. There'd be no sun today and maybe none tomorrow.

It fuzzed the shoreline and blurred the water and made steering harder but not to matter. You ran through this kind of weather with common ordinary care. It wouldn't have made Bo feel as taut as he did when he rang for slow to begin his approach to the lock, a mile upstream from it. What made him feel taut, and no need hiding it from himself, was what he might learn at the lock. Might be good—might be bad, and no way of knowing till you got there. This groping your way from one thing to another without knowing what you were getting into, having to use your wits without knowing what you might have to use them against, was wearying and no doubt about it. It really cut your strings. You had to keep hauling up on your nerves and you had to keep whetting your brain and at the same time you had to keep running your boat as if that was all you had to do.

Phoebe ducked into the pilothouse, sheltering her shoulders and a piece of her sewing under her shawl. "Do you mind if I come in? The cabin is so gloomy I can't see to sew. Besides," she flashed him a smile, "I knew we'd changed speed and thought we might be coming to the lock. I want to watch us go through."

He didn't mind and said so. He didn't say he'd even felt a spurt of pleasure to see her for he didn't recognize it as pleasure. Running as shorthanded as the *Rambler* did, double-ending as they did, he didn't often have company in the pilothouse for very long stretches of time and he only thought now that it was right nice and that he'd been lonesomer than he'd known.

She put her sewing on the bench and took off her shawl, shook the rain off, then folded it back around her shoulders and came to stand near the open front. "Last night," she said, "it was too dark to see."

"And you were a little busy ducking shots and broken glass," Bo said, grinning. He blew a long blast for the lock-master. "Well, there oughtn't to be anything uncommon about locking through #2 today. And it's broad daylight and you can see pretty good. You've not ever locked through on a boat before?"

"Oh, yes, many times. But it's always fascinating to me."

"We've got one more lock, #1 at Spottsville, before we get into the Ohio, but we'll go through that one while you're asleep tonight, likely."

"Yes." She was watching the shoreline and she pointed suddenly to the little mists rising to the treetops. "Does that mean fog?"

"No. Groundhog's making coffee is all."

She looked at him curiously and he smiled. "Old saying from up home. Means the rain's not over yet."

None of the locks crowded the *Rambler* for length since she was under a hundred feet. You never had to haul the stageplank straight up to accommodate the *Rambler*. Even the shortest of the locks accommodated her. But her beam was almost as wide as that of the bigger boats and it gave her little leeway on the sides. You had to nose in with care. Some pilots didn't mind scraping a boat a little but it was Bo's pride he never had—not since his cub days. He took a boat into a crib the same way he drew a bead on a squirrel—dead center. He considered it sloppy steamboating to disturb a lichen on the old log walls.

When he had the *Rambler* cribbed he told Phoebe, "I've

got to see the lockmaster. If it wasn't raining you could get off and walk around a little."

"I'd rather stay with the boat," she said. She confessed to a childish pleasure. "I like to ride down."

The lockmaster was as tall as a Georgia pine. Ordinarily he was a man of good humor, who liked his work, liked the steamboats and the river people, was friendly with all of them and had a huge interest in them. He had a long jaw and it was known he liked to flap it. He liked to hear gossip and pass it on.

Today he looked as raw as if he'd been tapped for turpentine, wet, gloomy, long-faced. He came to meet Bo with his hands shoved in his pockets and his shoulders hunched. He was also shaking his head. "Bo, ain't no use you locking through. Them gunboats is on the way up. Feller just rode in little while ago and said they was almost to Steamport and coming ahead. You're gonna meet 'em head on."

Bo settled his cap a little, twitching the bill. "Maybe so, Ben," he said, "but I'm caught between a rock and a hard place. I can't turn around. Buckner's behind me. Even if he wasn't I got the biggest cargo I ever hauled and I got to get it through."

The man eyed the *Rambler*'s deck. "Durned if you ain't. Nearly blocked off, ain't you?"

"We could sink the boat with freight this run. Everybody's shipping. Scared they're gonna lose their stuff. No boats but me running and I can't handle it all. I'm not going to be able to pick up but precious little more. Done turned down a fellow at Livermore. Had some livestock we couldn't take. Made him so mad he threatened to run me off the river."

The lockmaster snorted. "The war's not gonna wait for him to run nobody off. It's gonna run all the boats off soon enough." He wiped his nose with the back of his hand, reflected, and burst out angrily, "Don't know why they had to bring their plaguey armies down here. Upsetting peaceful folks. Ruining their country. It's the steamboats bring happiness to folks around here—about all the happiness they get out of life. Watching them boats go up and down the river is a real happiness and getting to ride on 'em and just shipping on 'em, seeing 'em come chuffing up to a landing, smoke a boiling, paddles churning, rousters singing and prancing. I tell you, God never give the folks up and down this river nothing better'n the boats, nor nothing prettier."

Bo was a little surprised at the depth of Ben Bledsoe's feeling. He'd known the man liked the boats and the river people but hadn't thought how deep it went.

He kept still as Bledsoe went on. "You know how it is. Everybody knows the boats, when they're due, upbound or downbound, takes a pride in 'em and kind of feels they own 'em, too. Everybody knows your old bull whistle and the *Belle*'s three-chime and the *Mary Lee*'s pretty bell. Don't even have to know what time of day it is. Hear a steamboat whistle and say, 'That's the *Rambler,* or the *Belle,* or the *Mary Lee.*' Don't even have to think is she upbound or downbound—just know, like you know when it gets dinnertime. I don't know what I'll do come every Tuesday morning and you don't blow for me upbound, and every Friday and you don't go down. And the others. I already got my days all mixed up. Ain't no feeling right about 'em. *Belle* went down and ain't come up again. *Mary Lee* didn't make her run. *Lucy Wing* didn't come up. And I don't look for you to be coming back up soon. What am I gonna do? I got me a lock, but there ain't no boats using it. I tell you, it's gonna be like the stars had quit shining for everybody on Green River!"

Bo tried to be reasonable. "Might not last very long. Few weeks, maybe, and the boats'll be running again. If I was you, Ben, I'd keep it all greased and oiled and ready. This river's not much for 'em to fool with. It means a lot to us, but it don't go nowhere but up and down Kentucky. It's not important to 'em the way the Ohio and the Mississippi are. Maybe they'll fight their battle and get it over with and move on. I wouldn't, if I was you, let the lock fall into disrepair yet."

"I'm nervous about them gunboats," the lockmaster confessed. "What if they're aiming to take over the lock? What if they're aiming to blow it up?"

"If they're after the lock they'll take it, Ben, you know that. Nothing you can do about it. Nobody was ever expecting a lockmaster to fight off gunboats, so they didn't furnish you with cannon. Let 'em have it is all you can do, like the folks at Rochester."

"They talked Buckner into jamming #3 with logs, we heard."

Bo nodded. "I heard it this morning, at South Carrollton. If the Federals want #2, maybe you can talk 'em into doing the same thing." The *Rambler* was beginning to lower and he turned to watch her sink. Phoebe was looking up at him and he smiled at her and lifted his hand. She was like a kid, he thought, taking delight in the least little joy. Her face was lit up now like a Christmas tree. He said, then, "No use borrowing trouble till it comes, Ben."

"This lock is state property," Bledsoe said, "and I was hired to keep it in operation. I got no orders about what to do with this kind of trouble, though. I don't like the notion of turning my lock over to anybody, either side. Looks like it's my duty not to—but I dunno, what else can I do?"

"With guns in your face? Nothing."

"And there's been strangers coming and going last few days."

"On the river?"

"No, just riding past. Like that feller come up from Steamport this morning. Never saw him before in my life, nor anybody else in town ever saw him. Horse cast a shoe and he had to stop at the blacksmith's."

"If you didn't know him . . ." Bo paused, then went on, "reckon how reliable he'd be about the gunboats."

The lockmaster moved his shoulders. "Couldn't say. But everybody knows they were at Mason's Landing last night. No reason they wouldn't get up to Steamport this morning."

"You say there's been several strangers around the last few days?"

"I can tell you exactly—there's been five since day before yesterday. Most don't stop. Just ride past."

"Any in uniform?"

"Two. Confederate cavalry. Just clattered on by. Never stopped."

"Well, Ben," Bo said, "them two were nosing out news of the gunboats. No mistake about them. But the others . . . where was this fellow this morning heading? He say?"

"Told Herman—that's the smith—he was going to Livermore."

"Anybody see him go?"

"Herman watched him a piece. Said he went that way. But that don't mean nothing. Think he could of been a spy, Bo?"

Bo seemed to have to think about it. He said, then, "I don't know. Might be." He ruminated further before saying, "How far downriver would you guess they know I came through #3 last night?"

"Not much farther. No boats running. Telegraph's cut."

"When did you hear it?"

"This morning. Man from over at Livermore was here. He'd got it from South Carrollton. Some of the A-drie folks had been there and told it."

Bo laughed. "It could be plumb to Spottsville the same way by now."

"Well, hell, Bo, you can't keep it a secret you're taking the *Rambler* down!"

"I know it. Don't aim to. I'd have liked to keep it a secret from those gunboats till I got past 'em is all."

The *Rambler* was almost down now and Bo moved toward it, the lockmaster drifting along with him unhappily. He allowed things had come to a pretty pass through somebody's mismanagement and that it was downright agitating to think on it.

Bo nodded. "We're down. Best be getting on." He added absently, without thinking, the old hill leave-taking, "Just go with me."

The lockmaster stared at him aggrievedly. "Now, what in tarnation makes you think I can go with you?"

Bo started down the ladder but looked up to laugh. "Forgot. You was supposed to say, 'Cain't—you better stay on.'"

"Well, you God's truth better had, boy!"

Bo waved one hand and slid on down rapidly. On the deck he made a beeline for the engine room. "Foss, I don't know as we can use the mouth of the Pond." He related Ben Bledsoe's story of the stranger this morning quickly. "Could be he was sent to spy out."

"From the gunboats?"

"If he was," Bo was saying fast, "one gunboat laid across the Pond would bottle us up."

"How would they know we was there? By guess or by God?"

"By being smart," Bo snapped. "By using their heads. Say this fellow heads back downriver, rides fast, tells 'em a steamboat is coming down. If it was me, I'd sure search up every creek and branch deep enough to take a boat."

"You've et too much mutton," Foss said, spitting. "Beginnin' to blat like a goat. Ain't nothin' to say the feller was a spy. Ain't nothin' to say the gunboats is gonna be as clever as you. Ain't no reason for not toenailin' up the Pond a piece and waitin' 'em out. You act like you seen the new moon through the trees. Act like you been spooked." He peered at his gauge, tapped it, and bellowed at Tobe to lay on more wood. "How you think I'm gonna git this goddamned boat outta the lock 'thout steam?" He turned to Bo again. "Do what you want. You will, anyhow. Just gimme time on them bells is all."

Bo swung out of the engine room smarting. He felt like he'd been spanked. Maybe he was acting like he'd been spooked. Maybe he had thought too much about this. Maybe he'd worn his sharpness down too fine and was too anxious. Then again, maybe he hadn't. Foss had to be told, led, persuaded, cussed. He hardly ever agreed right off with any notion. Well, he'd have to do what he had to do—and there'd be more of this nerve-wearing groping till he knew what it would be.

They poked out of the lock chamber and gathered a little speed, but not much. Bo was well satisfied with half ahead. He didn't want to go charging down on top the gunboats if they happened to be farther upriver than he guessed.

Phoebe watched until they had left the lock behind, then she sat on the bench and picked up her sewing. "This is a sleeve," she said. "I'm putting in the tucks."

He felt like yelping at her to keep quiet. He didn't need any bright talk about sleeves and tucks right now to distract him. "Where's your grandfather?" he said shortly. He didn't like to be short with her, but it came easier than holding his tongue.

"I don't know," she said pleasantly, not noticing his shortness. "Prowling around below, I suppose."

"Wish you'd find out," he said.

Her head came up quickly and she stared at his rigid back for a long moment. Carefully then she thrust her needle into the material and folded the sleeve over onto itself. So he would know she had gone she said quietly, "I will, Captain Cartwright."

Like a horse with the saddle off his galled back, he rolled his shoulders when she had gone. Irritably he wondered why there were times when having her near was so pleasant and nice and other times, like now, when just knowing she was sitting behind him nearly drove him crazy. She didn't have to open her mouth, actually, just sit there in back, and it was a fret to him—like trying to sleep with a mosquito buzzing around, or like walking with a pebble in your shoe, or like the little nag at the back of your mind when your boat wasn't running just right and you couldn't find out why. He hit the wheel an explosive lick. God's britches, how did a man stand being married to one of them—day in and day out, never being rid of them!

And that was the end of such foolishness. You be careful, he told himself, you just be careful. You get as nerve-raw as you are now and you'll have no judgment at all you don't watch out.

He prowled the *Rambler* carefully around the lazy bends, each time keyed for the sudden sight of gunboats, each time letting down when they didn't appear. A mile up from the mouth of the Pond he made his decision. It wasn't as good as it had appeared to be this morning . . . but it wasn't at worst more than a big chance. But come to that, either choice was a chance. Open encounter with the gunboats might be nothing more than a speaking and passing. The odds were heavier, though, it would be a strong try to stop and board, search, and maybe confiscate. And the Green was too narrow for much maneuvering. There'd be shots exchanged, bound to be, and somebody might get hurt.

If he hid in the Pond he took the risk of being bottled up, but there was nothing but suspicion to say the gunboats knew of his presence on the river; or even if they knew would think of bottling him up. He had thought of it because he was a riverman and being a riverman and knowing this river like the path to the barn at home, if he was looking out for another boat he wouldn't miss searching the smallest creek he knew had the depth for a boat to hide in. But that wasn't to say the Federals would. Unless they had Green River pilots, and he misdoubted they would have, they wouldn't know the places a shallow-draft boat could slide into. It balanced out in favor of waiting, and he gonged Foss his intention. He grinned when he got Foss's gong back promptly. He could hear Foss's outblown breath of relief, could hear him tell Tobe, well, the boy's gonna use his head.

He slid past the mouth, rang for shipping up, then backing, and he held the *Rambler* to backing for a quarter of a mile up the creek, glad for the still swollen water and glad for an easy little bend that would do for stopping around. He had the *Rambler* nosed down and he could come out fast.

Jonah, Mose, one or two of the other boys, jumped ashore and tied up. That was Foss's doing. He would have told Luke when he got his first gong what Bo's intention was and the boy had wasted no time. Bo set his wheel and went down. He suddenly felt good all over, pleased with his plan, pleased with his boat, pleased with Foss and Luke and his boys, pleased with the misty, rainy day, pleased, even, with Phoebe and Sir Henry who were waiting at the rail. He came up whistling "Chicken in the Doughtray," broke off and saluted them gaily. "I see you have lost your topknot, sir."

"I have been plucked," Sir Henry said, bowing deeply, "as bare as that rooster's behind. But my cap is adorned with my lost glory." The old man waved it under Bo's nose. Bo admired it profusely. The old man looked about curiously. "We seem here no painful inch to gain, sir, far back through creeks and inlets making . . ."

"Not very far back," Bo said. "We'll bide here a spell and see if we can give those Federal gunboats the slip."

Sir Henry's wild bushy brows went up, the old eyes became shrewd as he reflected on Bo's words. "You propose, I believe, to wait here until you have them between you and the lock we just went through." His great laugh boomed out. "Then what's become of Waring, since he gave us all the slip? A fine strategy, sir, a fine strategy. But if it fails, Captain, my guns are ready."

The idea of Sir Henry popping off his horse pistols at gunboats gave Bo a hard time holding back his own laughter but he struggled with it. He liked the old man too much to make him appear ridiculous.

Phoebe, with a wry look at Bo, came to the rescue by saying to her grandfather, "Do you know what Captain Cartwright calls those mists in the trees? Groundhogs making coffee."

"Apt," the old man agreed instantly, "very apt. The steaming pot, is that it, sir?"

"Something like that, I guess," Bo said. He saw Luke coming and waited. Best they all knew, now, what he had in mind. When the boy joined him, Bo said, "Luke, it's your job."

"Allowed it would be," Luke said, grinning, "soon as Foss told me."

"Rather do it myself," Bo said, "but I'd better stay with the *Rambler*. Something might come up unexpected."

"Just tell me what you want. I'm not minding," the boy said.

"No. Well, cut across this neck of land to the river. Find you a good place to hide out and make sure you can't be seen, Luke. Not even with glasses for they'll be sweeping both shores, looking out for the Secesh. Keep a watch till they pass upriver. Soon as they've passed, cut back here quick as you can. We'll keep steam up."

Luke nodded. "They don't pass by dark, what then?"

"You don't get back here by dark, I'll send Tobe over. Use that old hoot owl signal we use hunting at night back home to let him know where you're at. You come on back, then."

"I can stay on," Luke protested. "Ain't no need sending Tobe over. I just wanted to know you wanted to try slipping out come close dark."

"No. We're staying right here till they pass or we find out they aren't going to. No reason Tobe can't sleep some this afternoon. It'll get tiresome sitting over there in them bushes."

Sir Henry shouldered in. "I can take my turn at sentry-go. I may be old but I am . . ."

"I know, sir," Bo cut him off, "you may be old but you're lusty, but . . ." He stopped. He couldn't tell the old man, it would be too brutal to tell him, that this was a job for keen eyes and young legs. The old fellow was as likely as not to mistake a ferry flat for a gunboat with his dim old sight and his walk wobbled sometimes on even keel till you'd think he'd been tippling if you didn't know better. Lamely Bo finished, "If we need you, sir, later, I'll be certain to let you know."

Phoebe's eyes met Bo's with such understanding and

warm gratitude that he flushed up uncomfortably and wished she wouldn't. He turned to Luke. "Reckon that's all."

Phoebe said, moving quickly, "I'll wrap some food for you, Luke. You'll need it and it won't take a minute."

Luke looked at Bo to see if he should wait and Bo nodded. "She's right. You'll get hungry."

Even the roustabouts came drifting up to watch Luke leave. Nobody said much. Just, how fur he got to go? How long it tek? Things like that. Nobody laughed or make jokes as they had last night getting ready to leave on their own skirmishing jaunt against Buckner. A kind of somberness lay over everybody, as if they knew that in some way they had passed the time of joking and poking fun and playing at war. As if, in the passing of a few hours, the earth itself had turned into change and they had entered upon something too big and too sober to understand but there it was right in their faces.

They watched Luke scramble up the bank. At the top he turned his head and grinned and waved, then he parted the bushes and disappeared. The bushes shook a little longer, raining off their wetness, then they stopped moving and there was nothing but the pittering sound of the light rain on the leaves and on the water. It was a sound that barely broke the stillness but when you kept quiet and listened it grew heavier and heavier and heavier until it was as heavy as their somber knowledge that something strange and fearful and real and terrible had come upon them and that maybe nothing again would ever be the same for them.

Phoebe, standing beside Bo, shivered. Absently Bo put his arm about her and pulled her against him, absently patted her shoulder. He didn't say a word. She said nothing either. They stood close as if touching was enough, some kind of warm place they could occupy together for a little while.

A catbird meowed suddenly in the bushes, so real a roustabout jumped and looked around white-eyed. Another rouster laughed at him and the heavy, still spell was broken. A dozen laughs sounded and the black boys shuffled and moved and drifted away, talking now like parakeets, all at once, as chattery and light as they had been silent and dark before.

Only on Sir Henry, looking frail and ancient and pale as paper, did the somberness still hang. Bo heard him mutter something that sounded like Cry Havoc, and ended plainly with a mention of the dogs of war.

CHAPTER 18

THEY made out to wait as best they could, each in his own way.

Some of the roustabouts drifted together and started a poker game. Some of them loafed, dangling their feet over the side, kicking and splashing water. Some of them flopped to sleep. Bo broke them all up. He sent six to chop and haul wood, telling them, "Keep in sight of the boat and keep your eyes peeled for my signal."

He set Catfish and another to splicing rope and he kept the others with him to help caulk the leaky skiff he had bought at South Carrollton.

In the engine room, Foss oiled and wiped and oiled and wiped, tightened a few valves and screws and loosened some others and oiled and wiped some more. His big hammy hands knew the face of his machinery the way some men know their wives'. You could call what he did tinkering or puttering or passing the time or whatever you wanted to. It wouldn't have mattered to him what you called it. For Foss, it was living.

Phoebe stayed in the cabin for a while trying to sew but when she had put the left sleeve in the right armhole twice in succession she balled the whole bodice into a wad and threw it in a corner. Then she marched down to the deck and boomed in Bo's best squalling voice for Catfish. When he dropped the line of rope and came scuttling, eyes rolling, she lit into him like a spitting cat. "You lazy jackanapes, why haven't you built a fire in the galley? Don't you know these men are hungry? You think I've got all night to cook supper? Didn't you hear me say I wanted a fire early? I'm going to make chess pies for supper!"

Catfish contorted his face in an agony of remorse. Far as he knew it was the first he'd heard of an early fire and chess pies, but it wouldn't do to say so. He pulled at his scalp and scraped his feet and fled, promising a good hot fire right this minute, missy, right this here minute.

Phoebe caught Bo's eye on her and seeing his mouth stretched to the edge of a laugh but not quite breaking over into it, she stiffened her back, gave him a look of fury, and stalked after Catfish with as much dignity as she could muster, which was considerable.

Bo chuckled and guessed she was nerve-wore, too. Nothing else would have made her flare up at Catfish like that. She had to take her edginess out on something and poor old Catfish had got the brunt. He figured she was already sorry and making it up to the boy.

Sir Henry was the only one on the boat who didn't try to find something to do to occupy the time. He made no pretense of it. He paced the deck, round and round and round. Every time he went by the engine room Foss felt like spitting over his left shoulder to ward off the evil eye. "Look at him," he muttered to Tobe, "just look at that old cuss. Got that cape wrapped round him clean up to his neck, like it was

Christmas. And got that fool hat with the rooster tail cocked on his head. If he ain't a sight! Walkin' round and flingin' his arms ever whichaway and mumblin' and goin' on, talkin' to hisself. Don't tell me that old man ain't crazy in the head."

"Doan talk dat way, Mist' Foss," Tobe pled. "You mek de hairs on mah haid stan' up, lak it was voodoo, an' I ain't gots no charm 'gainst voodoo now. Capt'n Bo say warn't no sich thing."

"You better get you one. My opinion, that old man is a real voodoo on this boat."

Tobe squalled, dropped the oil can and tried to run. Foss grabbed him by the collar and hung on. "Come back here, you fool. Where you think you're goin'?"

"Tell Capt'n Bo. I gots to git me a charm." Tobe struggled and begged. "Please, Mist' Foss, please lemme go."

Foss looked at him and saw that he really was terrified. He had his eyes shut tight like he didn't want to see even the shadow of voodoo, might glimpse it if he opened them a crack, and his face had a powdery, ashy look. Foss said, "Goddle-mighty, Tobe, don't you know when a body's jokin'? Bo's right. Ain't no such thing as voodoo." He turned loose of the black man. "All is, that old man gits me riled up. But just because he ain't all there in the head don't mean he's to be scared of."

"Voodoo," Tobe mumbled, trying to pull himself together, "ain't nothin' to joke 'bout, Mist' Foss. It want you, it git you. Come thoo locked doahs an' winders an' ceilin's. Ain't nothin' kin stop voodoo . . . 'cept the right kind ob charm."

"Where'd you figger to get one?" Foss asked.

"Jonah know how. He mek me one. Mek us all one, do we need 'em."

Foss had an uneasy feeling as Sir Henry went round again

that maybe Jonah had better get busy. The old man had cocked the hat over his right eye, the tail feathers bunched freakishly at the front making it look exactly as if he had the back end of a rooster trussed to the front end of his hat. He was pacing measuredly, declaiming loudly, now, with full gestures: "Come between us, good Benvolio, my wits faint . . ."

"They sure do," Foss muttered, "they sure do faint, what there was of 'em to commence with."

The old man came to a standstill, flung up an arm and shouted: "Nay, if our wits run the wild goose chase, I am done! For thou has more of the wild goose in one of thy wits than I have in my whole five. Was I with you there for the goose?"

Tobe moaned and covered his ears. "Mist' Foss, please lemme git Jonah mek us all some charms. You doan't, gonna be de *Rambler*'s goose done cooked!"

"Oh, shut up," Foss said, "the old fool's just play-actin'. Sayin' out a speech. That's the way they do in them tent shows."

Tobe crept around back of the machinery and huddled down out of sight. "Ain't no use you tellin' me come outta heah till he go 'way, Mist' Foss. I ain't gwine to, dat's all. Ain't gwine look on him, ain't gwine heah him. You tells me when he gone."

Sir Henry tilted his head and said lightly, "I will bite thee by the ear for that jest."

A shiver began at the base of Foss's skull and took a slow rippling course down his spine, puckering the skin over every bone as it passed and leaving it puckered. He flung down his oil rag. He'd had just about enough of this kind of thing. He stuck his head out and said, not forgetting to be polite, "Sir, would you just as soon go and bite that ear someplace else?"

Sir Henry bowed charmingly. "Delighted, Mr. Foss, delighted." He went into a kind of airy dance and waltzed off
on his toes, singing:

> An old hare hoar, and an old hare hoar, is very
>   good meat in Lent,
> But hare that is hoar is too much for a score
>   When it hoars ere it be spent.

Foss watched him bug-eyed. Now, what would that old
coot know about whores? At his age! He heard Phoebe call
to the old man, "Mercutio! Come here and let me set your
cap straight."

Foss turned back into the engine room feeling shaken. It
took all kinds, he guessed . . . but that old man sure beat
'em all. Fancy dancing around like that and using such words
in front of his own granddaughter. It wasn't decent, that's
what. He said, his voice graty from his ruffled feelings, "You
can come out now, Tobe. He's went."

"Till nex' time 'round," Tobe said, emerging.

"Ain't gonna be no next time," Foss said firmly. "I'm
aimin' to tell Miss Phoebe to keep him away from the engine
room. He can do his prancin' and his dancin' and his speechi-
fyin' at yon end the deck."

He watched until he saw the old man walk on down the
deck, then he went to see to it immediately.

"Why, Mr. Foss," Phoebe said, laughing, when he had
hedged and hummed and hawed and finally got out the
request, "you mean you don't appreciate *Romeo and
Juliet?*"

"Ma'am, I wouldn't know about Romeo and Juliet. What
I would appreciate is if he'll steer clear of the engine room.
He's makin' Tobe so nervous I can't get no work out of him."

"Well, we certainly can't have that. I'll speak to him immediately."

As good as her word she struck off to follow the old man. Returning to the engine room, Foss lingered and saw them talking together, saw them even laughing together, their shoulders shaking. The girl laughed so hard she had to wipe her eyes with her apron. Foss couldn't see anything funny about it and was inclined to get in a high dudgeon, but let 'em laugh, he thought, let 'em laugh. He was quit of the old man for a while, anyway.

When the sun began its long slide down behind the tree-line, Bo called off the chores and pulled his boat together. He asked Phoebe to feed the crew but shook his head when she asked what about him. "Not hungry," he said. "Worked up a little high, I guess."

She tried to tempt him. "I've got chess pies."

"Save me a piece," was the best she could get out of him.

He propped himself against the ruined guard rail and when Foss had eaten he joined him. "Time's a passin'," Foss commented.

Bo looked at the screen of drizzle and mist and nodded. "Best time'll be just at dusky dark. Anything movin' then would fool you. But any time'll do. Just so we get 'em between us and the lock."

They didn't talk much together, just waited, and in not too much of a sweat, even though Bo had told Phoebe he was worked up a little high. He was ready, was all. Didn't want the edge cut. Foss had cut a twig toothbrush and was enjoying chewing it into softness. He belched a few times and sighed several more. Bo knew he felt good. He had his belly full and he had his machinery as near to suit him as it could be, considering its age and present state. Bo felt good himself. A full belly would have made him feel doped and drowsed. He liked a lean feeling, being able to suck in his guts and feel his backbone with 'em.

He heard Luke first and lifted his hand. "He's coming," he said softly. He looked around to judge the time and the light. "Man, it's perfect. Couldn't be no better."

Foss chucked his toothbrush overboard and said, "Time we drop down it'll be gray as Aunt Rhody's goose. Just gimme what you want, boy, and you got it."

"If we're clear," Bo said, "what I want is to slide down easy but when we come out I want full ahead. Best wait and see what Luke says, first."

Foss nodded.

Luke broke through the bushes and slid down the bank. Bo gave him a hand to the deck. He had run most of the way and they had to give him a little time to get his breath. He leaned on the rail and panted. When he could talk it was still in gasps. "They passed . . . just now . . . trouble was . . . second one was about a mile behind the first . . . looked to be having some kind of engine trouble . . . kind of crawling along."

"They both passed now?" Bo asked.

The boy dragged in a long breath and nodded. "I waited, like you said. Both of 'em has passed up. When just one come by, first I thought maybe the other'n was lingering down-river. But I hung on, just on the chance they might be strung out. And that was the way of it. Second one come on finally, kind of limping, not making much time, but keeping on."

Bo asked, to make certain, "They ironclad?"

"No. Regular packets—sternwheelers. Got some kind of plating around the main deck is all. But they got plenty of guns—look to be six-pounders. Ugly-looking with them snouts bristling all over."

"What about troops?"

"Bluecoats all over. A plenty of 'em."

"How long you wait after they'd passed?"

"Not long. But I let the second one get 'round the bend. Then I come on."

Bo nodded. "All right. Foss, you got it? Full ahead when I gong you. Don't wait for no bells. Just give me full and we'll come fogging out. I don't want no loafing." He swiveled on his heel. "Let's go."

Like a ghost they slid down the gray river, the rain drizzling down, the mist woolly in the trees, the engine breathing quietly, chuffing a little, the paddles lifting water and letting go of it gently.

Phoebe and Sir Henry had followed Bo up but they had gone into the cabin and let him alone in the pilothouse. Sir Henry was still wrapped in his cape, his rooster-tail cap still perched on his head. All he had left off was his oratory and prating. He was as silent as the river, and in the fast-fading light looked as gray. Bo warned them to show no light in the cabin and they promised. "But I'll be keeping watch," the old man said, "I'll be keeping watch."

"You do that, sir," Bo said absently. He only wanted them to get settled someplace and stay out of his way.

They slid around the easy little bend and came into the wider mouth of the Pond. Here the Pond flowed almost due south, debouching into the Green, which flowed more west than south at this point, at an angle. The angle had formed the little neck which Luke had crossed to watch for the gunboats. The channel was toward the left bank, which favored Bo, and which he meant to hug as he came out. As if set for a race he leaned over the wheel now and gonged Foss. Now— set her back on her heels, Foss, and let her rack! Show me what that machinery can do! Make this old *Rambler* really ramble!

The boat was seized with a shuddering, the paddles churned, the nose dug and plowed, then lifted, and the *Rambler* gathered speed rapidly. Bo yelled his delight as she went charging down. Speed always made him want to yell. When he was a boy he used to catch up a horse, leap onto him bareback and go racing across the pasture, yelling like a wild Indian. He'd had a harness strap laid across his behind many a time for it, his father not appreciating a boy's need to ride greased lightning once in a while. Bo yelled now, baying and yipping and shouting, dancing at the wheel, as charged with speed as the *Rambler*. Old Foss would be using every swear-word he knew, cussing Tobe and Jonah to pile on more wood, pile it on, boys, keep piling it on—how you think I'm gonna keep up steam? I'll break your backs, I'll sweat you dry, I'll oil you good—pile it on—keep that fire hot—keep that steam up—you, Tobe, you're lallygagging—you, Jonah, I'll feed you to the boiler!

Bo held the *Rambler* to the middle of the Pond until he was ready to bend her into the Green. She was plowing white water, bucking and snorting, but she was riding, when he cramped the wheel easy to port. It was an easy bend.

He saw the gunboat first as a great gray block, dead ahead in the channel. The shock of it stopped his heart for a moment—Goddlemighty! The crippled one! She'd dropped back!—stopped it dead, then lurched it into a race and pound that sent the blood pouring all over his body, breaking him into a sweat. The time he had was seconds, no time to think, just time to act. Every instinct of the riverman, all his knowledge, all his experience, was called up and answered instantly. He didn't need to think. He didn't need to decide. He let the wheel spin, caught it and pulled it hard to starboard, walked it down and held it. The *Rambler* groaned under the strain, she shivered and the starboard rail shipped water under the sharp lean.

There were shouts from the gunboat as the *Rambler* bore down on her, and a light waved frantically from the hurricane deck. Bo fought the wheel another degree over, and held it with his full weight. There wasn't time—there wasn't room—he was going to scrape her—The *Rambler* was a babel of noise, now, too—roustabouts yelling, sheep and cattle bawling, chickens cackling—every blessed thing on board that could make a noise was making it.

The stern of the *Rambler* was swinging around now, sliding like a pig on ice. Bo eased off a few degrees. He wanted to sideswipe the gunboat, not crash his own paddle wheel into her. He held on hard.

Sir Henry suddenly ran out onto the bridge, waving his horse pistols.

"God's britches!" Bo swore. "Get back, man, get back!"

The old man couldn't hear him. His rooster feathers were drooping in the rain, his cloak hung limply, but he was magnificently defiant, roaring into the rain and the teeth of the guns his personal challenge to combat. "What's brave, what's noble, let's do it after the high Roman fashion! And make death proud to take us! . . . on, on you noblest English! Whose blood is get from fathers of war-proof! . . . he who hath no stomach for this fight let him depart; What, trail'st thou the puissant pike? . . . 'Tis true we are in great danger, the greater therefore should our courage be!" He prated and pranced and flourished his horse pistols and Bo set his jaw and hung on.

The impact came in a rattle of musket fire. The *Rambler* shivered down her entire length, there was a shuddering crash, a ripping and rending, but the *Rambler*'s wheel was not fouled. She did not falter, hung up on the wreckage. She shook herself all over and slid free, scraping the gunboat all down the side. Bo let her go a split second, then swung her back to port, safe around the stern of the gunboat. He saw Sir Henry's pistols spitting fire, heard them banging away monstrously, heard the gunboat's musketry, but he was exultant. He had swung wide enough, he had scraped and sideswiped her, and he was free of her, running on down.

And then there was an explosion like lightning striking— a blinding light, the noise of ten thousand thunders, flying timber and glass and he was knocked away from the wheel and flatted against the wall. He was deafened and blinded and a little stunned. He felt a rib crack, felt it break with a snap, but there was no pain. An instant later he knew what had happened. The gunboat was using its big guns and they'd been hit. He scrambled back to the wheel not knowing where the *Rambler* had been hit, not knowing whether he had a rudder left, not knowing whether he had a paddle wheel left, not knowing even whether he had much of a boat left. They were still plowing down the river, shots following them, pushing the river up into great waterspouts where they hit. He grabbed the wheel and swung it to test it. The rudder responded. He gonged Foss and got it back and he breathed out deeply in relief. His rudder was all right and the engine room hadn't been hit. He looked back at the paddles. The light was going fast but he could see they were churning water. Then his eye caught the roof of the cabin. As best he could tell in the dim light the stern end of the cabin was a shambles. The gunboat's aim had been hasty and high. It had missed the paddle wheel but it had caught the superstructure and sheered off the cabin end. Lucky, he thought, lucky—and then he remembered Phoebe had been in the cabin and a chunk came up in his throat. And the old man—what had happened to the old man? He couldn't see him anywhere.

He couldn't do a thing but take his boat on down, out of range of the guns. They were still firing, but distance and speed were favoring him. Only a chance shot could cripple him now. It was too dark and they were firing in a general direction. He held on grimly, forcibly bringing his mind back to the river and his landmarks, forcibly putting the possibility of a killed young girl out of his mind. He would see . . . he'd see just as soon as he could, but he had other people to see to, also.

They went pounding on down and his mind began to work more coolly. Every second put the gunboat farther behind. Her fire was falling a little astern now. It was the crippled gunboat, he thought, bound to be, trying to reconstruct her reasons for being where she was. Doubtless her machinery had quit on her altogether and she had drifted downstream. Hadn't got much beyond the bend. Luke had watched her round before the machinery had just up and quit on her. She'd drifted till they could get her anchored. He should have thought of that possibility. Luke had told him she'd been in trouble. But a boat in trouble that near Rumsey would limp on in where there were boat works to make repairs. Only thing was, she couldn't make it. She'd had to lay up.

Well, she couldn't follow, then. He rang for half ahead. The gunfire had just about quit and what there was of it was so far behind you could count it done with. His chest was hurting him now and he felt like favoring it. Every time he had to turn the wheel there was a sharp stab of pain, and he kept wanting to cough.

He thought ahead to where he'd stop—not for the night, they'd keep moving on down, but long enough to see what the damage was and see about Phoebe and Sir Henry. They had to keep going, he thought. He didn't know how long they had before the first gunboat turned back. Maybe all night. Maybe it would be safe for the *Rambler* to tie up. Maybe the gunboats had signaled each other and the first one would go on to Rumsey, tie up for the night, drop back down in the morning. But maybe it wouldn't. Maybe it would stop, round to, and come back to assist the crippled boat. He couldn't risk them catching him up.

He rang for slow and they went prowling past Ray's Landing. He had decided on Steamport for his stop. An old man everybody called Doc lived on a shantyboat there. Mostly he drank whiskey and fished and maybe he'd never been anything but a cow doctor, but he'd know enough to bandage broken ribs and take care of whatever other hurts had been suffered.

Luke came up, running. "Foss said tell you they're setting out the lights and there's no great harm below. Smashed guard rail, like the other'n, braces on the stern splintered some, wheel creened a little, that's the most. Besides a bunch of shook-up rousters and livestock. She's still pushing good. Where'd we get hit?"

"Cabin," Bo said. His side hurt him so bad now he could barely push out his breath to make words. "Luke, take the wheel. Phoebe and the old man may be killed. She was in the cabin, far as I know, and he was on the bridge last I saw of him. I've not seen or heard of 'em since. I got to see about 'em."

"Bo, I ain't ever steered in the dark . . ."

"You'll just have to learn, Luke. Keep her in the middle of the river. Don't pay no attention to the shoreline except to steer by. She'll look narrow but all you got to do is head her right down the middle."

"You hurt?" the boy asked anxiously, taking hold of the wheel.

"Got some ribs busted I think."

"Sound like you can't talk too good."

"Hurts to talk." He swung the lantern down. "I'll wait and light up when I get around the deck so's not to hurt your nightsight."

Below, the boat's deck lights were blooming, like night-blooming flowers. Bo bent over to ease his side and went around to what was left of the cabin. He had to strike half a dozen lucifer matches before he got one to burn and he couldn't think why till he remembered how the sweat had poured off him just before they'd sideswiped the gunboat. He'd sweated every match in his pocket wet, he guessed.

He got the lantern to going finally and found the cabin door. The door itself had been blown off but the hole was still there, and it looked funny with the other end of the wall gone, too. He crept in and raised the lantern. God, he thought, what a holy mess! Bunks, bedding, roof, half the walls, all shredded and caved in and mixed together. The forward half of the cabin was all that was left and it was a heap of debris. There was no sign, however, of what he most feared to see—Phoebe or the old man killed, or mangled, shattered, blown to bits. He made himself look, good, all around. He was beginning to feel cold and lightheaded and the pain was getting so bad it hurt to breathe. He looked for an arm, or a leg, or her head with the hair streaming, a scrap of dress, anything to show what had happened to her. There was nothing. She must have been buried under the debris, then. He hung the lantern on the hook and began methodically moving the wreckage, lifting one piece of plank or board or bunk or bedding at a time, dreading what he might find with the next lifted piece but knowing he had to find it.

He meant to be careful, to lift easy, so as not to hurt her if she still was alive, but when he thought of her maybe broken and hurting as bad as he was hurting he knew he was scrabbling around like a dog digging for a bone. He couldn't help it or stop it. He heard his breath wheezing and when he spat once it was spumy and pink. It told him nothing. He didn't think about it, just went on scrabbling.

He didn't actually hear her at the doorway. He saw something flutter and grabbed it, knowing it was her skirt. He thought she was buried and he pulled hard on the skirt. When it resisted, he pulled harder, yanked at it, and tumbled her into the cabin and hard against him. They both went down, her on top, and he went out like a light, fainting for the first time in his life.

When he came to he was stretched out on the floor, Phoebe sitting beside him, and Sir Henry stretched out on the floor on the other side of her. Her hair was loose and streaming, her face was smudged, her dress was torn and bloody all down its front, but she was there and she was crying a little and patting his face with one hand and Sir Henry's face with the other. Not crying hard or desperately, just crying sort of soft the way women do when the worst is over and it's not been as bad as it could have been, just a tired, worn-out kind of crying.

He groaned and she said thank God, she thought he was dead, and he thought maybe he was and had gone to heaven —then he thought no, it was hell, because they wouldn't stick red-hot pokers in your chest in heaven. He closed his eyes and waited, making his head clear before he tried to think. He knew he wasn't dead. He had some broken ribs and that was why he hurt so bad. But he had to get his head to working, for Phoebe was hurt—plain to see with all that blood—and maybe Sir Henry was killed, and he had to bring the *Rambler* into Steamport Landing.

When he opened his eyes again he could make sense a little, though what he first said didn't make much. "You're not killed?"

She shook her head. "No. I'm not hurt at all."

"You're all over blood."

"That's Grandfather's. I'd gone to try to make him come back in the cabin. I thought he'd be killed on the bridge. But wasn't it lucky . . . wasn't it a miracle . . ."

"Is he bad hurt?"

"His leg is broken."

"They hit him, then."

"No. We both got knocked down. I was stunned but when I came to my senses he was still unconscious. I began to try to drag him back to the cabin—it was raining and he was so wet. His leg is all bent funny and there was so much blood . . ." she flicked her hand down her dress front, "and I kept getting weak and having to stop and rest, but he didn't come to, thank God, so he didn't ever feel all that pain of being moved."

Bo tried to think. Something about not moving people with broken bones. He mentioned it. She said, "But he was so wet. And with old people there's lung fever to consider."

"Well, maybe you did right." Bo shoved up on his elbows, caught his breath at the pain and waited for it to ride itself out. When the worst had passed he looked across at Sir Henry. There he lay, wet and bedraggled, his rooster feathers trailing across his face, his cap knocked askew but still on his head, his old wet cape streaming about him, so thin he barely made a hump on the floor, so white you'd think he was dead. There he lay, a kind of peaceful look on him yet, like he was asleep. Such a rage swarmed over Bo that it made him shake and he stormed out, "The old fool—the old idiot —the old lunatic—the old coot—what did he think he was doing? He might have been killed!"

The old man's eyelids trembled. He moved his head a little, opened his eyes, closed them again, and smiled. He was the old warrior, the old trooper, the old soldier, felled on the field of battle; he was Achilles fallen, Hector riddled, the last Spartan brought back on his shield. He sighed and murmured, "My friend, be absolute for death; either death or life shall thereby be sweeter." He was still playing his role to the hilt.

Bo's rage melted—the brave old fool, the grand old idiot, the staunch old lunatic, the hammy old coot! He brushed the rooster feathers away from the papery old face and bent toward it and said, "My friend, death has been cheated. You're not going to die. I swear it."

Sir Henry tried another line but all that came out was the tag end of it. ". . . we all owe God a death."

"Not yet we don't," Bo vowed, "not yet. We're not licked, not by a long sight. Nobody's killed. The boat's still running. We got us a river to run yet and we're by God gonna run it." He began hauling himself up.

Phoebe grabbed him. "No, you don't! You lie still and be quiet. You can't steer with broken ribs. You'll stab your lungs with them. Now, you lie down."

Bo tried to shake her off. "Tend to your grandpa. Keep him quiet and don't move him again." He wobbled up onto his feet, Phoebe still clutching him. "Turn loose! There's a doctor at Steamport and we'll get him to set his leg and tend my ribs. Now, I've got to go."

Phoebe was crying again. "Grandfather can't move. He'll be quiet. But you mustn't do this to yourself. Oh, you stubborn fool! Luke can handle the boat!"

Bo got free of her. "Luke has not ever taken a boat into a landing. He don't know the first thing about it. You see to your grandpa and I'll see to myself." He left her in a rumple of skirts and tears, collapsed beside her grandfather.

By the time he got back to the pilothouse he had to admit to himself he'd talked overly big. He couldn't steer and he knew it. Just to breathe hurt him, to talk hurt him, to move at all hurt him. If he tried to handle the wheel he'd likely black out again. Some things you were a fool to go up against and he'd be a fool to risk the boat in his shape. Luke would have to steer and he'd talk him into the landing.

That's the way they did it. At night, in the rain, with her paddle wheel canted out of true and hampering, Luke brought a boat into his first landing. And he didn't limp her in or cripple her in or shove her too fast and awkward. He kept his nerve and did what he was told. It was a help that, hearing the whistle, some men had come down with flares. In front of them, and very conscious of them, but backed up by Bo sitting on the high stool beside him and talking to him and coaching him, Luke brought the *Rambler* in pretty easy and right for the shape she was in.

When it was over he wiped the sweat off his face with his sleeve and said, "Hope I didn't shame the old lady too bad."

Bo thought with fierce joy how the sense of pride in the *Rambler* ran through them all—him and Luke and Foss and Tobe. She was almost a wreck now, with half her cabin shot off, both guard rails splintered, her paddles creened, but the boy still wanted to make a good *Rambler* arrival, worried most about shaming her. "You done good," Bo said, "you done real good. Now go find Tobe and send him for that doctor lives on the shantyboat. If he's not too drunk maybe he can patch us up."

CHAPTER 19

ONE thing was obvious when the doctor had set and splinted Sir Henry's leg and bandaged Bo's rib cage. Gunboats or no gunboats, they could run no farther that night. Bo had one rib broken and two cracked.

The doctor was not an old man, though he was always spoken of as old Doc King. He was rather a man who for some reason life had broken and appeared to lick. It had been a long time since he had practiced medicine much, he admitted. Nobody knew much about his past or where he had come from, beyond downriver. He'd appeared one day a few years before, his shantyboat shoved by a small, chartered packet. He had given no reason for stopping at Steamport. Maybe his money for the charter gave out there, maybe he liked the looks of the river at that place, maybe he just got tired. At any rate, he paid off the charter, tied up and had been sitting right there in the same place ever since, soaking up his whiskey, fishing a little but no more than he had to, going nowhere, seeing as few people as possible.

At first there had been curiosity about him and specula-
tion. Who was he? Where had he come from? Where was
he going? What was he going to do? That was inevitable at
first. But as time passed and he went nowhere and did nothing, he became, like a snag rooted in a gravel bar, one of the
landmarks of the river. He knew the schedule of every upbound or downbound boat and was always on deck to wave
as they passed. Little by little it became a tradition to toot
for the Doc.

Little by little it became known, too, that he had been a
doctor of some kind. He didn't say so. But whatever had
made him give up the practice of medicine couldn't keep him
from dispensing it in need. He wouldn't take patients regularly and nobody wanted him to—he was too often too drunk
to be responsible. But if you ailed or suffered and went to
him, and if you found him reasonably sober, he dosed you or
lanced your carbuncle or set your broken arm or went home
with you and delivered your wife of a baby. If you found him
drunk, he wouldn't touch you or budge.

It was also inevitable that it should be said he had killed
somebody, or let somebody die, tended them when drunk.
He came to be accepted as a queer old coot, generally liked,
let alone because that was the way he wanted it except when
he went prowling for company. The company he chose was
what the countryside called trash and there were those who
said he had a woman occasionally on his boat, said they had
seen women, strange ones, never the same one twice, from
time to time. It may have been. It was the kind of thing
people liked to believe, roll over their tongues and pass on,
without thinking how strange women could have come into
the country without the general knowledge of the total popu-
lation. Bo always thought they were probably local women,
but it was more romantic if they were said to be strangers.

Doc King liked to sing when drinking. You could always tell when he had begun a real bender. You could hear him a mile up or downriver shouting out his songs. They weren't anything the Steamport neighborhood had ever heard before—long and involved and in some foreign tongue. One fellow from away, hearing him, said it was opera and Italian. Most generally believed, however, it was gibberish and that the Doc made up his songs as he went along.

He was small-boned, short in height, thin, iron-grayed, and even in his cups as tidy a man as you'd ever find. No rumples, no coffee and tobacco stains, no frayed cuffs, no bleary eyes and growth of stubble. Bo sometimes had wondered about his tolerance for alcohol to be able to shave with a steady hand every morning. He usually had a whiskey breath but it was rarely offensive. He didn't go out when drunk. Left over, it was so mixed with bay rum and pipe tobacco it wasn't unpleasant.

"You ought to let those ribs heal a week at the least," he told Bo, now, "but probably you won't. I've got those sharp edges pulled together, though, and got you wrapped pretty tight. They shouldn't hurt you so bad. But if you use 'em rough they'll pull apart on you, I warn you." He had got a little in the way of talking as his neighbors did.

"I'll take care," Bo said.

The doctor stuffed things into his bag. "What about the girl and the old man? Who are they?"

Bo told him and told how they'd come to be aboard.

Doc King was tamping his pipe and he kept his eyes on the precise job his fingers were doing. But when Bo had finished he looked up, his eyes amused. "A Shakespearean actor, eh? What are you going to do with them now that the old man has broken his leg? Old bones take a long time to heal. They got any money?"

"Very little," Bo said. He hesitated. He hadn't thought what about them now. There hadn't been time. "I reckon the girl . . . they're show people, you know. She plays the guitar and sings pretty good. Reckon she can do readings like her grandpa. And she's spunky. Place as big as Evansville . . . she'll likely make out."

The doctor lit his pipe and puffed and reflected. He finally nodded. "Maybe. Maybe so. Maybe again it'd be a pretty poor making out. Like to have heard the old man do the soliloquy from *Hamlet*. Been years since I've heard it. Well, Cartwright. Take care. Move easy. Don't wrench those ribs suddenly. Ought to be knitted in a couple of weeks."

He let Bo pay him. He wasn't purse-proud and he'd done a good job on Sir Henry and Bo, knew it, and knew he deserved his fee. He pocketed it and left briskly, saying no more.

Even if he hadn't felt so crocky Bo had had second thoughts about running on that night. It was an off chance the gunboats would chase him, he now believed. The first one wouldn't want to leave the crippled one a sitting duck on the river for the Confederates to take. Saving it would be more important than chasing him. He could see that, now his excitement had left him. So he put them out of his mind for the present.

Foss and Luke and the roustabouts shoveled the debris overboard and stretched a tarpaulin to piece out the cabin roof. One bunk and a mattress was whole and while he was under chloroform Sir Henry had been shifted to it. Some of the blankets weren't too shredded to be used and Luke went among the folks on shore and bought straw mattresses and quilts, enough to make out.

It wasn't what you could call a comfortable night or a good one. When the morphine wore off and Sir Henry could feel his pain he kept up a continuous moaning. He wasn't in his right mind enough to know he was doing it but that didn't make it any easier to listen to him. Phoebe was up and down with him a lot and didn't get much rest. Bo's ribs hurt him pretty bad. He stayed with Phoebe until around midnight so he could help with the old man if he was needed, but there wasn't much to be done for him. Bo kept feeling chilly and he couldn't sleep, as much for the old man's noise as his own pain, so he decided to go down to the engine room. "He gets to flouncing around you come get me," he told Phoebe.

Sir Henry's leg was broken just below the knee. Doc King had said if he had to break it, it was as good a place for a broken bone as he knew of. Wouldn't be near as troublesome as, say, a broken hip. He might have a little limp, he wouldn't guarantee he wouldn't, but not to speak of. In her relief Phoebe had laughed and told Bo all her grandfather needed was a limp to make his entrances and exits more dramatic. "He'll use it to good advantage, you'll see."

Now she told Bo, "He can't move that leg. It's splinted too heavy. You go on and try to get some sleep."

Foss was snoring when Bo went down but he woke up and tried to make Bo take his pallet. Said he already had it warmed up. Bo said, "And fleas for company, I'll bound. No thanks. Spread mine clean over in the other corner, will you?"

The engine room wasn't entirely dark. The deck lanterns made enough light to see by and Bo watched Foss heave some junk out of the corner and fuss around for a minute or two. Then he said didn't Bo think one quilt would be a little thin. "Where's your mattress? Give it to the old man?"

"No, I didn't give it to the old man. How you think

I could lug a mattress down them steps with a broken rib?"

Foss dropped the quilt and looked at him. "Keep forgettin' you're stove up." He rubbed his chin. "First time I ever remember you bein' helpless to do for yourself. Don't go right. Goes quare. I'll get it."

Bo said never mind but Foss went anyway and when he came back he brought an extra blanket. "She sent it," he said. "Said you was feelin' the cold."

He made the bed and Bo lowered himself onto it gingerly. "Warmer in here," he said. "Feels good."

Foss dug around under the pile of ragged quilts he slept on and brought out a jug. "Here. This'll warm you up good."

Bo took it and swigged down several good slugs. It was raw and new but he was grateful for it. It went to work at once warming his stomach and working out from there. "Where'd you get it?"

"Me and that horse doctor made us a trade."

"What did you have to trade?" Bo laughed.

"A good coon hound, that's what. Said he'd been lookin' for one all over. Taken a shine to old Buck and I told him gimme two jugs of whiskey and he's yours. Blessed if he didn't do it. Went straight and fetched the jugs."

Bo hadn't missed the dog but when he looked around for him, not knowing but what Foss was joshing, he saw he was really gone. It made him feel kind of bad. He gulped down some more whiskey. "Wouldn't have thought you'd let the cur go," he said. "Thought you were too fond of him."

"Aw," Foss said, bunching up his quilts behind his back, "feller like me allus on the go don't need a dog. Dog needs to stay put."

"You don't go nowhere," Bo pointed out. "*Rambler* goes, but you stay put right here in this engine room. Dog could've stayed put with you. If it was account of me . . . if you figured I didn't want you to keep him . . ."

"Hell, no. Nothin' to do with it. I mightn't allus—hand me that jug, dammit, and mind your own business. I got my reasons for seeing to it the dog got a good home. The Doc'll hunt with him and feed him good . . ."

Bo tried to shrug, swore at the pain, and let the dog and Foss's business go as he'd been advised. The whiskey was making him a little drowsy now. He lay back and he and Foss talked on a little bit. Nothing much. They laughed over the brush with the gunboat. Bo admitted it had scared the hell out of him for a minute. "I seen I had to swing 'round her."

Foss told he hadn't seen the durn-burned thing till they cut loose firing and about that time they'd sideswiped her and he'd looked out and caught a glimpse of them cannon snouts pointing right in his face. He thought it had aged him considerably. Next he knew they'd got past her. He didn't know if they had any buckets left on the wheel or if Bo had any rudder but he just kept pouring on steam and then when that shot sheered off the cabin roof he didn't know whether they even had a pilot. "Wildest ride you ever give us, boy," he wound up. Bo could see his belly shaking as he chuckled.

"You might say," Bo said, sleepily, "this whole down-bound trip has been about as wild as it could be."

"Like nothin' we ever done before," Foss agreed. He settled himself on his pile of quilts. "Ain't been nothin' ordinary about it. I'd be just as well satisfied we don't have to do it no more. They's been times," he admitted, "when I've been right uneasy."

"I'm still uneasy," Bo said.

"Aw, them gunboats ain't gonna chase us. I ain't a bit worried."

"There's other things."

"What, for instance?"

Bo ducked the war and the state of steamboats on the river. Time enough for that later. He said, instead and a little vaguely, "Oh, Phoebe and the old man. Don't know what they'll do now, him crippled up the way he is. Gonna make it hard for 'em."

He saw Foss rear straight up and knew he should have kept his mouth shut. There would be an explosion. It came. "You can pick the damndest things to be uneasy about! It ain't none of your put-in, is it? Ain't none of your business. What they're gonna do is get off this boat soon as we get to Evansville, way they've aimed to do, and what you orta do is put 'em out of your mind. Ain't you got enough troubles 'thout burdenin' yourself worryin' over them? We got a cracked rod and don't know where to get a new one, or if we can. Got a stove-up boat, you got three stove-up ribs. We got the whole Secesh army on one side of us and the Federals on the other. Ain't got but a piece of river to run, account of the lock jammed at Rochester. And you pick a old geezer and a moony girl to put your mind on. I sometimes use up my patience with you, Bo. I sure sometimes do. And I a little doubt, sometimes, your brain is put together straight. There's times when you don't give evidence of using it." He beat up his old quilts again and flopped exasperatedly down on them. "Don't say me another word," he warned, "or you'll get me too worked up to sleep."

"Well, you shut up, then," Bo said.

He thought a little more about Phoebe and Sir Henry but it was too much work, he was too sleepy, the pain was easier and he was warm and comfortable. He wondered for a moment if he was going to have to get up and go outside, then decided it wasn't that urgent and forgot it. Next thing he knew it was morning.

CHAPTER 20

STANDING on the bank looking at the *Rambler* in broad daylight, Bo had to laugh. She sure looked battle-scarred, all right. The stubs of her guard rails were splintered and twisted, half the cabin was gone and the tarpaulin drooped over what was left, there was still a great hole in the roof of the pilothouse, and the paddle wheel canted out of true. But she could run yet, she could run. She'd taken a lot of blows, been knocked about, but she was a tough old lady—she'd just reeled, got her breath, and gone staggering on. Bo looked at her affectionately and felt like patting her.

They loaded on a little more cargo. Folks, hearing a boat was tied up at the landing and not expecting another one on the river for nobody knew how long, had brought in what they had to ship. They took what they could of it and Luke made room for most of the hard goods, but once again they had to turn down stock. This time there were no hard feelings. The farmer had eyes in his head and sense to use them.

Bo took the wheel for the departure. He was sore and stiff

but if he was careful and moved slowly he didn't hurt too bad. He felt the difference in the pushing power of the canted paddles and there wasn't much flourish to his leaving, but he did the best he could, and if there wasn't much style there wasn't much real sloppiness either.

He had told Luke to come up soon as he could and when the boy got there he gave him the wheel. "We'll not make any more stops," he told him.

"Didn't allow we would," Luke said. He added happily, "Don't believe we could cram a briar blade in now. Best load we've ever had."

Bo nodded. "I'd want you up here, anyhow. I'll take her round Mason's Bend and through the lock. I'll take her into Evansville. But you'll have to do most of the piloting today."

Luke grinned. He wasn't a bit afraid of it. Bringing the *Rambler* into Steamport last night had given him a lot of confidence in himself. Of course, Bo had coached him in. He'd only done what he was told. But he'd done it and he hadn't lost his nerve. He didn't doubt but he could take the boat through the lock. Now, Mason's Bend he wouldn't want to try yet. He guessed there wasn't a pilot on the river didn't dread that bend. He didn't think he was ready for it. But he felt like the wheel was an old friend now and he stood right up to it with confidence. "What time you think we'll get to Evansville?" he asked.

"No faster'n I want to push her," Bo said, "not much before sundown."

"End of the day—end of the run," the boy said, laughing. Glancing obliquely at Bo he saw his jaw working and guessed he was hurting again. Must have hurt himself bringing the *Rambler* into the river.

Bo stayed with him a while then said he was going back to see how the old man was.

He found Sir Henry propped up in bed. It still felt odd to come through a doorway when the entire end of the cabin was gone, and to look at mattresses on the floor instead of on bunks. It was traveling pretty light. Bo eased down on the foot of the old man's bed. "How you feel, sir?"

Sir Henry was pale and there were dark rings under his eyes to show he'd felt a lot of pain, but he still looked rakish with his wild eyebrows and his hair like a floating halo round his head, and his eyes had a twinkle and he welcomed Bo with a chuckle. "I feel," he said, "the way this boat of yours must look after our battle yesterday. I feel, in other words, like hell. I hurt, but no more than I can stand. At least I like to think so. Have you come to bury Caesar, my boy, or to praise him?"

"Oh, to praise him," Bo said airily, "to praise him. He's a long way from being dead enough to bury, looks to me."

The old man was suddenly and embarrassingly humble. "I'm an old fool," he said, "a witless old fool and now through my foolishness a burden and a trouble."

"Sir Henry," Bo said, laughing, "I thought so, too, when you come pouring out onto the bridge banging away with those pistols of yours—but don't you know it saved your life? And saved Miss Phoebe? If you had been in the cabin both of you might have been killed. Don't see how you wouldn't. Look at the damage that shell did. Say Miss Phoebe'd been sitting on her bunk at the end there. You know where her bunk is now. Blown to hell and gone. Nothing but splinters left of it. It could have been her."

The old man's eyes widened. "Why, my boy . . . why . . . why . . ." he sputtered and stuttered, then recovered. "I do believe I've been left dull-witted by that morphine." He took a long look about the shattered cabin and found his quoting tongue again. "Out of this nettle, danger, we pluck this flower, safety. A by-product of foolishness, sir, nevertheless. I am still an old ham and an old fool. All the world's a stage, you know." He went into a deep study, then shook himself out of it. "Phoebe tells me you have some broken ribs. Are you in much pain?"

"Not unless I forget and move too sudden. Most nuisance to me is Doc wrapped me so tight I can't get a good breath."

Sir Henry nodded. "Had a broken rib once myself. A fellow Thespian grew a little too enthusiastic in a scene requiring fisticuffs. Knocked me head over heels and I stove in the first vertebrochondral. I also lost two molars and suffered a severe contusion over my left eye."

Bo looked at the old man and kept his face muscles severely under control. He said, deceptively mildly, "I would say that was more than enthusiasm, sir. I would say that was anger." He paused a moment, then came out flatly with it. "What had you done to him, sir?"

Sir Henry garrumphed, had trouble clearing his throat, then roared with appreciative laughter. "I was a *young* fool in those days, sir, not the old fool I am today. I had stolen his lady. Light-of-love though she was, she was a pretty thing and cuddlesome. I couldn't resist her." He added, brows raised, "Was it my fault she preferred me to him?"

"Probably was, sir. Probably was." Bo got up. "Doc King left some laudanum if you get to hurting bad. Said it wouldn't serve any good purpose for you to lie here and suffer. Ask Miss Phoebe if you need it, hear?"

Sir Henry made a staying motion with his hand. "Bo . . ." The blanket bothered him apparently and he fussed with it, plucking at it and rearranging it. Then he made a violent movement of rejection and blurted out, "Why is it so hard to say one's thanks? Should be the simplest thing in the world. Why must a man hem and haw about saying to another, you've been kind to me and I'm grateful? I'll have no truck with hemming and hawing. I'm saying it. You have been kind to us and I am grateful."

Bo couldn't find his tongue for a moment, either. He felt himself coloring and then he laughed. "And why is it so hard to be thanked? Why can't you just say I'm glad you think so and it's good of you to say so, and be done with it? And that's what I'm saying. There'll be another day, Sir Henry. If you're in my debt now I may be in yours some day."

Sir Henry's head bobbed. "Being in debt is nothing new to me. A spendthrift poet once said, I have been in love, and in debt, and in drink, this many and many a year. Leave off the drink and it applies, and if I'd ever had a head for drink the whole would have applied. I am old," he chanted, "but I am . . ."

". . . lusty," Bo finished for him. "I've sure learned that one, sir. I got to go help Luke run this boat. He's liable to run us aground on Hovers' Bar."

As he went away he heard the old man lift his voice in a quavery song:

> Of man's first disobedience and the fruit
> > Of that forbidden tree,
> Whose mortal taste brought death
> > Into the world and all our woe
> With loss of Eden; till one greater
> > Man restore us and regain the blissful seat,
> Sing heavenly Muse that on the secret top . . .

He didn't hear him break the song off or see him ponder on the meaning of the words. Nor did he hear him yell suddenly and angrily, "Paradise lost! Paradise lost! Who cares about Eden? Give me one day of my youth again . . . one day, and I'll have paradise regained!"

The *Rambler* coasted that day. Making no stops she slid hour after hour past the landmarks—Delaware, the Double Eddy, Blackbird Bend, Hurricane Slough—one at a time she closed them, blowing for the ferries, passing the villages and landings silently so as not to disappoint the people. They gathered anyway, hearing her chuff and seeing her smoke, but they gathered to wave, knowing she wouldn't put in. "Goes like a dream," Luke said once, "so still and quiet and the sun shining so pretty and us not putting in nowhere. Seems like we're just going on and on, maybe to the end of the world. Looks like there ain't no end to the river and us running down her."

"There's an end," Bo said shortly. It was what he had been studying on all during the long tranquil hours. But no need saying more. It was for him to study.

From time to time Phoebe came in. Grandfather was sleeping—Grandfather had eaten—Grandfather was playing his fiddle. She popped in and out restlessly. Her eyes always went straight to Bo, looked intently at his face as if trying to divine what he was thinking, how he felt. She never asked. Just stuck her head in, laughed, maybe, said what Grandfather was doing, went on some place. "She's as fidgety as a grasshopper," Luke said finally. "Can't light and tie no place."

"Got plenty to fidget about," Bo said.

"I reckon she is worried about the old man," Luke said, "but I a little doubt he'll have much trouble with that broken leg. Ain't as if . . ."

"Blow for the ferry round this bend," Bo told him, cutting him off. Sometimes Luke's commonplaces got on your nerves.

They stopped once, to load on wood; they each went to eat—and when they'd got past Mason's Bend Foss came up for a few minutes. He didn't want anything. Running steady he didn't have much to do. Thought he'd come up and look at something besides machinery for a change. He took one quick look at Bo's face, saw no pain lines there, and was satisfied. Didn't stay much longer. Luke laughed when he'd gone. "Don't take him long to get enough of something besides his machinery, does it?"

When Bo didn't answer Luke sneaked a look at him. Looked as sorrowful as if he'd lost his last friend, the boy decided. There was something wrong with the day, in spite of the sun and the good water and the long, slow glide down the river and the hours. Something was against the current underneath, something he couldn't put his finger on. The girl was fidgety and Bo was broody and even Foss wasn't exactly like himself. When he came up to the bridge he came for a purpose and he never had to make reasons like he wanted to look at something different. There were undercurrents of feeling crossing back and forwards and he felt his own feelings beginning to be anxious, mostly because he couldn't think what was wrong. Everybody ought to have been in high spirits, looked to him. The *Rambler* was carrying the best load she'd ever carried; they were coming to the end of the run with no lasting hurt to the boat; of course the old man had got his leg broke, but anyway he hadn't been killed. And of course Lock #3 was jammed with logs, but likely the folks at Rochester would have them out time the *Rambler* was upbound again. There was the war, too, but it didn't have anything to do with them. He couldn't think why there wasn't rejoicing, such as he had been feeling. But you never saw such a poor-mouthed bunch of folks.

As his worry settled over him he got tired of the wheel,

got to feeling fidgety himself, couldn't keep his feet still, till Bo said, quietly, "I'll take her now. You're getting tired."

"Not tired, exactly. I dunno what it is. I can spell you when we get through the lock, Bo."

"No. I'll take her on in. You better commence making ready to unload."

Luke felt apologetic that he'd not lasted to the lock. But it wasn't far. He couldn't explain what had happened to him, but it had. Maybe Bo was right. It *was* the longest trick he'd ever stood at the wheel and maybe that was all it was, he just suddenly got tired.

They locked through #1 at Spottsville as casually as always and about as fast. Bo had a little talk with the locktender as he waited for the lower gates to be opened. He explained briefly why the *Rambler* looked the way she did.

The man said he knew them gunboats meant trouble for somebody and reckon did they mean to patrol the river from now on? In his opinion things were coming to a pretty pass when folks couldn't use their own river to suit themselves. He was lugubrious about the Ohio, too. "Guess the Federals will soon be running it all their own way, from Cincinnati to Cairo."

Bo nodded. "Stands to reason."

"Hear they're putting together a navy up at Louisville. Buying up packets and wanting steamboatmen to run 'em for 'em. They say they're gonna sheet 'em with iron and put rams on 'em and use 'em on the Mississippi." The locktender laughed. "My opinion, it'll take more'n a few ironclads to reduce Memphis and Vicksburg."

"It likely will," Bo agreed, but he thought it a shrewd move just the same. "Where'd you hear about this navy they're building?" he asked.

"Saw it in the paper."

"How big is it going to be?"

"Didn't say. They're gonna use the New Albany boat works to refit 'em, though—across from Louisville." The man swore suddenly. "Got some trouble with a winch. Have to see about it." He hurried away, still swearing.

Bo reflected on the news and on the changes overtaking all the rivers what with gunboats, ironclads, armies and navies beginning to use them. Waterways and railroads were of utmost importance to both sides and there was no use hoping some special dispensation would spare them. It was beginning to get close and tight and a man who shut his eyes to it was just ignoring the handwriting on the wall. That much was plain to him but what he ought to do was another matter.

As the *Rambler* began to lower in the crib Phoebe came into the pilothouse. Bo looked around at her and smiled. "Almost missed seeing it this time."

She pushed her hair back. "I had to give Grandfather some laudanum and wait till he dozed off."

She looked tired, he thought, and her voice lacked its richness, sounded dull. "He asleep now?" he asked.

"Yes. What a blessing that doctor had laudanum. It's saved Grandfather so much suffering."

"The worst of that will be over in a few days," Bo said.

She was watching the water flood out the gates and if she said anything he didn't hear her. He noticed she had mended her dress, though it puckered and gaped here and there. He hadn't thought of it until now but it dawned on him the gunboat shell had blown her trunks and luggage sky-high and the only clothes she had in the world were what was on her back at this moment. "Where'd you find a needle to sew up your dress?" he asked.

She confessed that she had left it in her sewing, had got angry with her stitching and wadded it up and thrown it in a corner. "It was about the only thing not blown away," she added ruefully.

He laughed. "One time it paid you to get mad, wasn't it?"

He had the silly feeling they were both just making talk and wondered why he was laboring at it. Pay him better to keep his mouth shut. He decided he would, and he was glad when it was time to move.

Phoebe watched him maneuver the *Rambler* out of the chamber. She was quiet now, too, and for a long time after they had come out into the river. She seemed to be studying the water and she kept still for so long that Bo was beginning to wish she'd say something and then thought, hell I don't know what I want today!

She moved, then, and seemed to come out of her reverie and looked about at the shorelines. "The river is very wide here, isn't it?" she said. "Much wider than above."

"Yes," he said. "Not far to the mouth, now. You might say this is Ohio water we're on."

She took her breath in sharply. "After we come to the Ohio?"

"Just a few miles downriver to Evansville. End of the run."

"Don't," she said, turning her head away. Her voice sounded choked and muffled.

"Don't what?"

"Don't say it so . . . so casual and unimportant . . . like it was the end . . ."

With what he thought was great reasonableness, he said, "Well, it is. It is the end of the run. Always has been. Where we been making for all the time."

She turned and looked at him and with consternation he saw that tears were sliding slowly down her cheeks. "What's the matter?" he said, "what's wrong?"

She shook her head, unable to speak, the tears spilling

faster. Bo knew how it was. It had been years since he had cried but when he was little and used to, for anyone to speak to him or notice him made him cry just that much harder. He thought he ought to pay no attention to her but he couldn't stand to see her bothered. "Please," he begged, "please don't cry. I know you're worried, but it'll be all right . . . don't cry, please."

It was the wrong thing to say, he knew it, for it broke her up and brought a flood and deluge and shaking shoulders and sobs and angry attempts to stop, with her hands in fists digging at her eyes and her breath choking, like she was too big to cry and knew it and was ashamed of not being able to help it, was making such an effort not to, but it was completely beyond her.

He kept his eyes on the river, set his teeth and tried to ignore her. But he felt helpless and ashamed and, he didn't know why, he felt angry. His anger rose and rose with her sobs until he exploded finally. "If you don't pick the damndest times to cry!"

He heard her catch her breath. Then she wailed, hiccupily, "I don't pick them! I can't help it!"

He could have bitten his tongue out for speaking sharply to her. He flicked a look at her. She was digging impatiently at her eyes, with the heels of her hands now, but her sobs were slowly snubbing out. She took her apron tail and mopped her face with it, drew in a good breath and had control of herself again. "I don't know what got into me," she said. She smiled shakily at him.

"That's better." He smiled back at her, and said what for him was an apology. "Don't know what got into me, either. Women have to cry, I reckon."

But her image stayed before him when his eyes went back to the river. The old patched dress, her eyelashes wet and stuck together, her hair all blowy and frizzled up, her face smeary where she had smudged it with her hands, her chin trying not to wobble, her mouth trying not to tremble. She was so darned and patched and smeared and blown, and she'd had such a damned hard time of it and had such a damned hard time of it yet ahead of her, and she was so spunky and funny and brave and cheerful. He'd have done more than cry if it had been him, he guessed. He'd have turned up his toes and howled like a hound bewildered by the moon.

He felt grumbly inside that he'd lost his temper with her and he couldn't think of any way to make it up to her until the wideness and depth of the river brought it to mind. "You ever steer a steamboat?" he said.

"No."

"Come on, then. Now's your chance."

She came toward him slowly, hesitantly. He reached out and pulled her to the wheel. "I'm afraid," she admitted.

He put her hands on the spokes. "Don't be. Just hold her there. The river's wide and deep. And I'll stand here and tell you what to do."

She flashed him a radiant smile, gripped the spokes and spread her feet the way she had seen him do. She braced her shoulders back and stood up to the wheel and turned an intense gaze on the water.

He watched her affectionately and was glad he had thought of it. There weren't many things the feel of the wheel and a good piece of water couldn't put down. They were like medicine for a sickness and balm for a soreness. He calculated ahead that he could safely let her take the *Rambler* to the log rafts that always lined the Green at its mouth.

CHAPTER 21

THE wharf at Evansville was always a busy place. It was a departure point and terminal for the Green River trade and it was an important port in the Ohio trade. Crowds always milled about but when Bo brought the *Rambler* in that afternoon the crowd was swollen beyond normal. He guessed that news of some of her troubles had preceded her and brought out the curious. He grinned, thinking they would get their money's worth. She was a sight to see, all right, with her cabin blown off, her guard rails shattered, her paddle wheel out of true. Nevertheless he brought her in as smartly as he could and the stageplank clattered against the cobblestones at ten minutes past five.

The first thing he did, before a pound of freight was unloaded, was to have Sir Henry and Phoebe moved to a boardinghouse. "It's a place I've stayed at myself," he explained to Phoebe. "I know Mrs. Jane and I know she's clean. She cooks good and hearty, too." He hesitated, then plunged ahead. "It's a place where river folks stay. Not every place will take rivermen. They've got a name for being a little rough sometimes, but Mrs. Jane is river herself. She keeps 'em in hand. You won't be bothered and she'll make you comfortable."

"Only river people stay there?" Phoebe asked.

"Yes." He apologized. "I don't know of any other place to send you. River folks don't tend to mingle much with dry-landers."

"I wouldn't want to mingle," she said proudly.

"No need you shouldn't."

Phoebe's chin went up. "I wouldn't give dry-landers the time of day!"

Bo laughed joyously. "Made a real river rat out of you, haven't we?"

"I should hope so!" Her hand caressed the spokes of the wheel. "I feel as though the *Rambler* had become a part of me." She took her hand away and straightened her shoulders. "But we've reached the end of the run, haven't we?" She looked at him quickly, and away. "You'll come to see us at Mrs. Jane's?"

He smiled at her. In spite of the straight shoulders she was a little afraid he was dumping them at the boarding-house to forget them. "Soon as we finish unloading, or if it's too late, first thing tomorrow," he promised. "I'll probably be taking all my meals at Mrs. Jane's. *Rambler's* got to have a lot of repairs and we'll be here a week or two."

The apprehension cleared from her eyes and she smiled back and said frankly, "I'm glad." She plucked at her ragged dress and poked a finger through one gaping hole, saying ruefully, "I ran out of thread. I wish Mrs. Jane could have a better impression of me. What will she think? This old ragged dress."

"She'll think you're fine. She'll be telling everybody

here's the girl had the roof blown off her head and kept her nerve and her courage. She'll be making a hero out of you." Bo patted her shoulder. "Here come the boys. Go along, now. I'll see you soon as I can."

Four roustabouts lifted Sir Henry's bunk and carried him easily and without jolt the short two blocks to Mrs. Jane's boardinghouse. Phoebe marched along beside them. Bo watched a moment, then he turned to the job of unloading.

There was a little trouble.

The wharfmaster came aboard and said hesitantly and worriedly that he guessed by rights he oughtn't to let the *Rambler* unload.

"Try and stop me," Bo snapped at him.

"Well, you ain't got a permit, have you?"

"Whaddya mean 'permit'? I've been unloading at this wharf for a year. Never heard of needing a permit before. Anybody that owns a boat and has got his papers can use this wharf."

"Not any more," the man said, shaking his head. "Reckon you've not heard. There's a new Federal general in charge at Louisville. Fellow name of Buell. He has issued an order that boats got to have permits now."

"When did he issue that order?" Bo said.

"Well . . . coupla days ago."

"Then how in the hell would I know it? I was upriver. Looks to me you'd have to give a man time."

The wharfmaster cogitated and came to the conclusion there was reason in Bo's argument. From the jut of Bo's jaw and the look in his eyes he figured he'd better listen to him. Bohannon Cartwright and his crew were capable of wrecking the wharf if they so minded and he allowed this would be one of the times they minded. "Well," he said, "the order didn't say nothing about time, but if you was upriver stands to reason you wouldn't know nothing about the order. But this'll have to be the last time, Bo. You got to go up to Louisville and get you a permit. And you got to get yourself a list of the ports you can put in at. There's only a few he's aiming to let steamboats use. Thank God Evansville's on the list. All passengers got to have passes signed by him from now on, too."

"That don't worry me," Bo said, "I don't carry passengers. All I want to do is unload this cargo right now. I'll take care of permits later. I got the biggest haul of livestock and freight the *Rambler*'s ever carried and I'm aiming to unload it—starting right now."

The wharfmaster gave token permission. "Well, go ahead. But mind you . . ."

Bo shouldered away impatiently and the rousters got to work.

They were at home now and unafraid, the strange, unusual, frightening downriver run behind them. They swung into the rhythm of their work with joy. They made a coonjine of the fracas at the lock, and they made another coonjine of the gunboat affair. But the best coonjine they made was about Tobe hiding in the engine room when Sir Henry spouted off his Mercutio piece. They laid it on thick about his begging for a charm and Bo reckoned Tobe wouldn't hear the last of it for months.

At exactly midnight the unloading was finished and an hour later Bo sat in the pilothouse, his bookkeeping completed. He hunched over the tallies for another hour, fingering them, thinking, pondering, reflecting, deciding. It was the time he had known was coming, that he had put off as long as he could, that he had flinched from. But it was here, now, the time to fish or cut bait, and he had to look it smack in the eyes. No ducking or dodging any longer.

This run had put him ahead, very little but ahead. He had enough on hand to pay off the mortgage on the *Rambler*, buy a new rod for Foss, make all the necessary repairs. He had already paid off his crew. And there'd be a little left over. A few more runs and he'd be way ahead. He could do it, he knew. Maybe for six months, even if he could only run between Evansville and Rochester. He fingered the tallies and thought, but all through his thinking and all through his temptation there was running that phrase the old judge had said—freedom is a hard-bought thing and it don't stay bought—you have to keep on buying it over and over again. And he wasn't really tempted and he really knew there was only one thing for him to do. There was only one thing he could do and live with himself. He swept the tallies into the lockbox. It was too late to go to Mrs. Jane's, so he went to bed. And he slept well, his heart lighter than it had been for days.

Next morning he told Foss they would move the *Rambler* to the boatworks for the repairs. They wouldn't, this time, he said, make them themselves. Foss was headachy and gloomy. He didn't see why they didn't do their own work. He a little doubted the boatworks would have the new rod, or could get one, and if they did they wouldn't know how to set it in. "Likely," he went on mournfully, "we'll have to wait a time and a time. Be several boats ahead of us."

"No more likely than usual," Bo said cheerfully. "Don't spill your beer on me, Foss. We got plenty of time anyhow."

"That's the beautiful truth," Foss said, "seein' the state of things on the river nowadays. One good thing," he went on, "is if we got to stay here a while them gunboats can get back onto the Ohio where they belong."

At the boatworks Bo had a long conference with the super-intendent and went away pretty well pleased. The super-intendent had a rod. It wasn't new but at least it wasn't cracked. He had plenty of paint. He was a little short of hardwood with which to build a new cabin and guard rails but he thought he could lay hands on enough. "Good thing you don't need much iron, though," he said. "They've just about cleaned us out for them boats they're plating over with iron at New Albany."

"That's where they're refitting?" Bo asked.

"So the talk goes. Fellow by the name of Ellet got the idea of using ironclads on the Mississippi, seems like. War Department has give him leave to go ahead. He's been buying steamboats at Pittsburgh and Cincinnati but he's bringing 'em down to the works at New Albany. Hear he's gonna have six or seven in his fleet."

Bo seemed to be studying the *Rambler,* laying up alongside, waiting. "Reckon you've got no idea how long you'll have to take?" he asked, picking up his cap, making ready to leave.

"Why, I'm some shorthanded, but I'd say two weeks. That suit you?"

"Be fine," Bo told him, "and I'm obliged."

He went into town, then, and looked up Mr. Finley and paid off the *Rambler's* mortgage.

"Must have been doing pretty good lately," the old man said. "I'm not pushing you for this, Captain. You need it, you've got time."

"No, sir, that's what I've not got," Bo said. "I could use it and I'll make no bones about it, but I got to have my boat clear."

Old Mr. Finley wore steel-rimmed spectacles which were always at half-mast on his nose. He usually left them there and peered over them. Made you wonder what he wore them for since he rarely looked through them. "Well," he said, "you'll be wanting that note back, I guess. Now, what did I do with it . . . ?" He began digging around in the drawers of his desk, fumbling through masses of papers. "I put it somewhere here, I'm certain."

"The bottom drawer, sir," Bo said. "I recollect seeing you put it there."

"Yes, I remember now." He upturned a few more things and came across it, wrote "canceled" over its face and handed it over. "Ever get in difficulty again, Captain," he said, "be glad to accommodate you."

Bo folded the note and put it away, feeling clean and relieved and almost light-headed that there was nothing against the *Rambler* now. "Thank you, sir," he said. "It may be a time—the war is making a difference—but if I have need to borrow again I'll know where to come."

"Yes. You've been unusually prompt paying off your debt. A pleasure to deal with you, Captain."

When he left Mr. Finley's office Bo went to see Phoebe and Sir Henry. He had taken adjoining rooms for them but he found Phoebe in Sir Henry's room reading a newspaper to him. He looked washed and combed and his bed was tidy and straight. "Are you comfortable, sir?" Bo asked.

"I am being coddled and cosseted and babied and pampered within an inch of my life," the old actor said. "Mrs. Jane intends to put fat on my bones and Phoebe means to scrub it away. She has inspected me for fleas, lice, bedbugs, and she declares me free of all vermin and fit to lie in a princely state again."

"Grandfather, that isn't funny," Phoebe scolded. "The *Rambler* doesn't have vermin on it!"

"Did I say it did? But some of the beds we have occupied in those infernal tent shows may well have had. To put it briefly, my boy, I am being well cared for. I live in the lap of luxury. I am fed on strawberries and cream. But I leave it to Phoebe," he added hastily, "to sew a fine seam. She's begun it already. Show him your new dress, girl."

Obediently Phoebe held up some new material. "Until I finish it," she said, "Mrs. Jane has loaned a dress of her daughter's." She made a little face at its drab mustard color, then smoothed its front down, laughing, "For which I'm very grateful."

Bo pulled up a chair. "I want to talk to you both."

It took him an hour. Sir Henry argued and Phoebe argued, but eventually he brought them both around. "It's what I want," he said over and over again to their protests.

"How can it be what you want?" Phoebe said, tears spilling over.

"It's my time to fish or cut bait."

"Whatever that may mean," the old man said.

"It means what I want it to mean, sir. You'll do me the favor?"

Phoebe wiped her eyes. "Your ribs aren't healed."

"They will be by then."

The old actor looked at his granddaughter, then he garrumphed and said, "Whatever you say, my boy. And we'll be everlastingly indebted."

"Fine," Bo said, rising. "She'll be tied up in the boatworks two weeks. Rest, sir, and let that leg heal. We'll move you back to the *Rambler* with no trouble then."

Phoebe's voice was still uncertain. It faltered a little as she asked, "Why do you do this for strangers?"

Bo moved restlessly. "You feel a stranger to the *Rambler*?"

"No, but . . . it's less than a week . . ."

"What's time, when there's a war?"

He left abruptly, feeling embarrassed, having no words left. He was at a loss in such a situation. The best he could do was go, quickly.

Back on the *Rambler* he called Foss and Luke up to the pilothouse. "This is the way it is," he said, when Luke had taken a seat on the bench and Foss had draped himself over the front sill. "We can run another six months or so on the Green. Only between Evansville and Rochester. But we'd make money and I won't deny it. We'd likely make enough money to buy a new boat."

Foss had a chew of tobacco in his cheek. He worked it around and spat. "Why don't we?"

Bo waited a moment to think out his words. "Foss," he said finally, "since we left Bowling Green a lot of things have happened."

"They sure God have," the engineer said.

"I don't mean we have run through Buckner's army at Rochester, or we've had a fight with Federal gunboats. I mean . . . a whole war has been fought."

"You don't make sense," Foss said, moving his shoulders. "I ain't seen no war fought."

"There has been for me. I've had to decide whether to keep on running the *Rambler* or get into the war and fight."

Foss straightened up and his face went very rigid and tense. "You ain't that foolish, I hope."

"Maybe I am. Say I am. Say I've decided since Rochester it's what I've got to do."

Foss fleered a look at him. "I dunno what you mean," he growled.

"I think you do. I think you've known it since then, too."

Luke's face had gone white and his eyes flickered from one man to the other, but he didn't say anything.

Foss chewed down hard on his cud. "You lost your mind?"

Bo squared around on his pilot's stool. He rested an elbow on the wheel spoke nearest him. It felt good under the bones of his arm. He wanted to turn around and take hold of the spokes. He wanted to take the *Rambler* out of the boatworks this minute . . . take her upriver again . . . feel the wheel under his hands . . . turn his eyes onto the water . . . remember the landmarks . . . sheer in against the bend at Mason's . . . come into the clear above . . . keep her in the channel . . . warp her into the landings . . . blow her coarse, unchimed whistle . . . ring her old cracked bell. More than anything in the world he wanted to take his steamboat out of this place, steer her upriver, pick up his freight, go his own way, live his own life. It was a wanting so strong that it hurt inside him. He beat it down. "This is what I'm gonna do."

"Don't tell me," Foss said.

"I got to."

There was silence. The little shore waves lapped against the hull and rocked the *Rambler*. All of them remembered every time they'd ever tied up and shore waves had lapped at the hull and rocked them to sleep. It hurt to remember, like acid poured over a wound. They had so many memories. There had been so many times when they'd dared and risked for the *Rambler*. Foss made a motion. Go ahead, it said, go on, say the death words.

Bo said them. "What I aim to do is this. I aim to take the *Rambler* upriver again . . . to Steamport. I aim to let Sir Henry and Miss Phoebe live on her till the war is over. I thought to tie up there where the Doc can help 'em out. He can take care of Sir Henry's leg. They can fish. They can move about some, but they'll have a good place to tie up at Steamport." He paused, looked out at the river, then he went on. "What I mean to do myself is go up to Louisville and volunteer to serve in that fleet of ironclads the Federals are refitting."

Foss cleared his throat, but Bo held up his hand. "You needn't either one of you be obligated. I'm gonna pay you off. You can sign on another boat tomorrow if you want."

His voice broke a little. "I thought, though, maybe you'd help me get the *Rambler* back up to Steamport. Thought, maybe, Tobe'd stay with Miss Phoebe and the old man. Help 'em out. When the war's over, I dunno. We'll get us another boat. No doubts about that. Or fix up the *Rambler* . . ." He was rambling and he knew it. He brought himself up short. "I got to do what I think's right. No matter how good a man has got it or how comfortable off he is or how much he likes what he's got and wants to keep it, comes a time he's got to stand up on his feet and do what he knows is right. I know I can't stand off and watch this war no longer."

"What made you pick them Federal ironclads?" Foss growled. "You're fixin' to get us all killed."

A flood of relief surged through Bo. He should have known. He should have known. Him and Foss. Always him and Foss. He threw back his head and laughed. "Hell, man, I'm web-footed! I can't go in no army. I got to run me a river!"

Luke flung himself up from the bench. "Can I go, Bo? Can I go with you?"

"You ain't but eighteen, Luke."

Luke bridled. "What's the difference. I'm a good riverman. You know I am!"

"Don't get your dander up," Bo said, "I never said you wasn't. We'll see. If they'll take you, you can go."

The boy shouted and fled, to tell—Tobe, Bo guessed, or one of the workmen, or anybody who would listen. In his excitement he had to tell somebody or bust.

Foss had drawn his mouth down again. "I reckon you know, don't you, you've fell in love with that girl. I seen it comin' from the first. That's why you're givin' her the *Rambler* while we're gone. When we get back from the wars you'll marry up with her, see if you don't."

Bo thought about it. "Maybe. Maybe you're right. I've

not give it that much thought. But maybe when the war's over I will ask her to marry me. I don't know. She's in a hard place and I can help her a little. What's ahead, I don't know yet. It'll have to wait till the war's over."

Foss snorted. "Not for me, it won't. I can see it comin'. You'll marry up with her and her and that old man will always be on the *Rambler* with us."

"You got any objections?"

Foss belched. "Not any it would do any good to mention."

"Then shut up your mug."

On the fourth of October they took the *Rambler* out of the boatworks. She was spotless and fresh and saucy-looking in her clean white paint. She had a new texas, she had new guard rails, her paddles were true. She had steam up. At the wheel, Bo felt the deck with his feet, squared up and gave Foss three crisp gongs. He got three gongs back. He rang for backing. Foss backed smartly. Bo rang for shipping up. Foss shipped up. He rang for slow ahead. He got slow ahead. And the *Rambler* was running again. Upriver. Favoring the left bank for a few miles then crossing the channel to the right bank, ready to bend into the Green.

Phoebe sat on the bench in the pilothouse. Sir Henry was abed in the new cabin. Bo pulled his whistle. It blared in all its unchimed hoarseness over the countryside. Luke pulled his bell. It rang, not true and perfect because of the crack, but Luke pulled a doggoned good cracked bell.

This was a pool of good water, from the mouth of the Green to Lock #1 at Spottsville. It was deep and wide, and you might say, Ohio water. The other side of the lock there was Bluff City, Mason's Bend, Delaware and Steamport landing. From there, nobody knew. When the war was over Bo and Foss and Luke would come back . . . if they were

lucky. Phoebe and Sir Henry and Tobe would keep the
Rambler on the Green. They would fish and they might do
some shows up and down, if they could find a crew. Nobody
knew how it would be after they tied up at Steamport.

Right now, nobody thought about it. They were taking the
Rambler on her upbound run, running her on her own river.

For now, it was enough.